MISS DAUNTLESS

MISCHIEF IN MAYFAIR—BOOK FIVE

GRACE BURROWES

Miss Dauntless

DEDICATION

To all the dauntless ladies
and the dauntless fellows who love them

CHAPTER ONE

"That is an earl, Thomas," Matilda Merridew said quietly. She'd crouched down to admonish her son at eye level. "The Earl of Tremont is a peer of the realm, an important man, *a lord*."

Also a bit stuffy, based on what little Matilda knew of him. He was dark-haired, lean, tall, and turned out in exquisitely understated good taste. His reputation among the former soldiers who'd served with him was one for rules, policies, and proper decorum.

If any force on earth was *not* inclined in those boring directions, it was Matilda's five-year-old son.

"I am an important boy," Tommie replied, grinning. "My mama loves me best in the whole world!"

He'd nearly yelled that proclamation, his voice carrying to every corner of the church hall. Vicar Delancey sent her a pained smile, Mrs. Oldbach flinched but otherwise ignored Tommie's outburst, and Mr. Prebish—current *dominus factotum* of the pastoral committee—glowered at Tommie, then at Matilda.

The earl, fortunately, remained in conversation with the vicar's son-in-law, one Major Alasdhair MacKay.

"I do love you best in the whole world," Matilda said, putting a hand on Tommie's bony little shoulder lest he hare off to make a cave out of the cloaks hanging in the corridor. "I also want to be proud of you, and if I'm to take the minutes for this meeting, then you must stay out of trouble."

"I'm always in trouble," Tommie said, puffing out his chest. "Mrs. Oldbach says I'm a proper limb."

A limb of Satan, did Tommie but know it. "You are not always in trouble. You are simply lively." *Exhausting* was a more accurate term. "For the next hour, you will please look at your picture book, practice writing your name, and *be quiet*."

Tommie would try, he truly would. He'd turn a few pages of his picture book. He'd even pick up the pencil and wave it about or make a few scratches on the paper Matilda had fetched from Vicar's office, but Tommie had a constitutional aversion to extended periods of quiet while awake.

Mrs. Oldbach clapped her hands. "*Tempus fugit,* my friends. Lord Tremont is a busy man, and it's time we brought our meeting to order."

Mrs. O was a fixture at St. Mildred's. White-haired, imperious, and well-to-do. She exuded a perfect balance of Christian good cheer and elderly ruthlessness. Matilda kept Tommie as far from Mrs. O as possible.

"Please be good," Matilda said, kissing Tommie's crown and moving to the table in the center of the hall. She took up her post as scribe at the right hand of the chairman's seat and angled her chair to give her a clear view of Tommie's corner. He'd plopped himself on the floor and dutifully opened a picture book, but his gaze was leaping all over the hall.

Matilda had packed not one but all three of his picture books, the old stuffed horse that he now sought only at bedtime, two pencils—Tommie invariably broke his pencil points—and some string. The church cat could be counted on to entertain Tommie for two minutes at a time if that good beast was in residence.

Tommie cupped his hands to his mouth and bellowed, "I'll be good, Mama!"

More winces and scowls greeted that announcement. The earl glanced over at Tommie as if noticing the boy for the first time. Matilda mentally prepared for lordly disdain—children did not belong at business meetings, not even church business meetings.

Tommie waved wildly. "Good day, Mr. Earl! Do you want to see my picture book?"

Merciful angels, deliver me now. St. Mildred's was a prosperous congregation, though a far cry from St. George's in Hanover Square. Peers did not frequent St. Mildred's, and the earl was very much a visiting dignitary.

The whole room went quiet, with gazes ricocheting between the boy and his lordship. Mr. Prebish looked positively eager to hear Tommie on the receiving end of a tongue-lashing.

Another tongue-lashing.

The earl excused himself from his conversation with Major MacKay and walked over to where Tommie sat on the floor.

Matilda did not care that Tremont was a peer, a wealthy man, a noted philanthropist, and a former officer. She marched over to Tommie's corner, prepared to inform his lordship that nobody scolded her only begotten son for merely being friendly.

Tremont extended a hand in Tommie's direction. "Tremont, at your service, Master...?"

Tommie scrambled to his feet and wrung the earl's hand. "I'm Tommie. Tommie Merridew. This is my mama."

Tremont extricated his lordly paw from Tommie's grasp and bowed to Matilda. "Madam, you have me at a disadvantage."

She bobbed a hasty curtsey. "Matilda Merridew, my lord."

"My amanuensis on this august occasion, I believe. Tommie, a pleasure to have made your acquaintance. I was told St. Mildred's is a congenial house of worship. Your mama and I must tend to business for the nonce. You will keep that storybook in good repair until I can make proper inspection of it. Mrs. Merridew."

The earl gestured in the direction of the table. Tommie, for once, was silent, so Matilda preceded his lordship to the table and managed not to faint from shock when he held her chair.

The earl called the meeting to order, and a discussion began of hiring former soldiers to look after St. Mildred's grounds. His lordship's charitable endeavors included housing a dozen such worthies. Setting them up in some sort of business was his present aim.

The sexton had vociferous objections to anybody tending to the churchyard but himself, until Lord Tremont suggested that any lot of former soldiers managed better when somebody was appointed to supervise their efforts. Moreover, gravedigging was a skill known to all former soldiers, alas, and one suited to younger men who benefited from regular vigorous exertion.

Matilda bent over her notes while keeping one eye on Tommie, who was imitating Tremont's hand gestures. The earl's hands were graceful, his manner dignified, but more than anything, his voice held Matilda's attention.

Tremont moved the discussion forward with polite dispatch. Whether he agreed with the committee member who held the floor or not, he thanked every participant for sharing their thoughts. He *listened*. He asked sensible questions and again *listened* to the answers.

Nobody dared interrupt or talk over anybody else. Nobody dared make a ribald aside. The meeting was the most civilized and productive exchange of ideas Matilda had observed. That Tommie was a witness to this gathering gave her all manner of maternal ammunition for good examples.

The orderliness of the proceedings aside, Lord Tremont had the makings of an orator. Before he spoke, he took a moment as if to gather his thoughts, and when he replied, his words were chosen for precision and economy. All that was lovely—the fellow made sense even as he flattered his listener—but what upended Matilda's usual indifference to all things masculine was the beauty of Tremont's voice.

He created a flowing stream of golden elocution in a well-modu-
lated baritone. His words resonated with courtesy, reason, benevolence, respect for his audience... all the gentlemanly virtues made
audible.

If he ever set out to be charming instead of polite, he'd be dangerous. Matilda mentally shook herself for even speculating on such a
topic and pretended to add something to her notes.

Has beautiful voice.

She was erasing that nonsense when Tommie began to sing.
Being Tommie, he did not sing a venerable old hymn or a sweet little
nursery rhyme. He burst forth with Burns's "Green Grow the
Rushes, O," an earthy tribute from a man to the charms of the ladies.

While Matilda scrambled about for a means of discreetly
silencing her son, Tommie caroled on. *The sweetest hours that e'er I
spend/Are spent among the lasses, O...*

Had the Earl of Tremont not been present, Mr. Prebish would
have been leading a charge to silence Tommie's warblings and assign
him a penance. Instead, the committee of the whole waited to see
how a peer of the realm dealt with a Proper Limb.

*But gie me a cannie hour at e'en/My arms about my dearie, O!/An'
warl'y cares an' warl'ly men/*

May a' gae tapsalteerie, O!

"Master Merridew." Lord Tremont's voice carried without
having been raised, and yet, Tommie paid him no heed.

*For you sae douce, ye sneer at this/Ye're nought but senseless
ASSES, O! The wisest man the warl' e'er saw/He dearly lov'd the
lasses, O.*

The vicar looked as if a post in Cathay had developed compelling
appeal. Mrs. Oldbach's lips were pressed together very firmly, and
Major MacKay was grinning.

Worse than that, much worse, was MacKay joining in for the next
verse. *Auld Nature swears, the lovely dears/Her noblest work she
classes, O!/Her 'prentice han' she try'd on man/An' then she made the
lasses, O!*

"Master Merridew." Tremont sounded quite stern, and Tommie was not accustomed to proper address. The boy fell silent at long last.

"While we appreciate your impromptu serenade," the earl said, "there is yet work to be done. Come here, if you please."

To Matilda's astonishment, Tommie did not order the earl to instead come to him. Tommie viewed matters logically, which often made him sound impertinent. Superior height, for example, did not make adults superior in any other way. Otherwise, according to Tommie's reasoning, the tallest man would be king and the shortest a beggar, but there were tall beggars and short kings.

And yet, Tommie scampered over to stand by the earl's chair. "Mama taught me that song, but she has a much prettier voice than I do."

"Very gallant of you to compliment your mother," Tremont said, hoisting Tommie onto his lap. "Pay attention, young sir. This is a gavel."

He held up the chairman's gavel, but did not let Tommie grab it.

"It's a hammer, Mr. Earl."

"Not a hammer, a gavel. When the chairman applies his gavel thus to the tabletop, silence reigns. Give it a bang if you don't believe me."

Tommie walloped the table with the gavel, and the whispering among the committee members stopped.

"There, you see, lad? Not a hammer, a gavel with all the special powers attendant thereto. As the vice chairman of this meeting, you will bang that gavel when I tell you to, as many times as I tell you to. You will not permit anybody else, not even your dear mama, to touch the gavel during the progress of the meeting. Three whacks now, for practice."

Tommie thumped the old table three times.

"Very good. When you are not required to man the gavel, you may draw toads, if your mother would oblige you with some paper and a pencil. All gentlemen acquire basic artistic skills, and the sooner you start, the sooner you will master the challenge. If you are already proficient at rendering toads, you may attempt a dragon or the very difficult unicorn. You will please recall the meeting to order."

Tommie twisted about to send Matilda a questioning glance.

"Two raps," she said. "One right after the other. And then you say, 'This meeting will now come to order.'"

Tommie vigorously executed the duties of his office. For the next forty-five minutes, he seemed quite content to occupy the earl's lap and draw all manner of mythical beasts while quietly humming Burns's ode to the ladies.

In the opinion of Marcus, Earl of Tremont, churches had more in common with the military than either organization liked to admit. Both were devoted to strict hierarchy, strange rituals, peculiar uniforms, and formidable edifices. Both were much concerned with cadging a substantial share of the common weal and doing with it nobody was entirely sure what, but the work was held to be very important nonetheless.

A useless observation, but then, a man of a philosophical bent was prone to such musings. Tremont concluded the meeting when he'd secured an offer from the parish committee to hire the men on a trial basis.

"No scurrilous behavior," Mrs. Oldbach had said, with a fraught glower in the direction of the boy on Tremont's lap. "More specific than that, I cannot be in present company."

If only Wellington had commanded an army of church ladies. They would have ordered Bonaparte into exile as effectively as...

More useless thoughts.

"Master Merridew," Tremont said, setting the boy on his feet. "If you would return the gavel to the vicar's office, I would appreciate it. No making free with it on any handy wall, floor, or parishioner, if you please. Gavels are not hammers."

Tommie ran a small finger along the smooth, glossy handle. "I'll put it on Vicar's desk, Mr. Earl."

Tremont risked leaning within gavel-smiting range. "We need not be so formal. You may address me as Tremont or my lord."

"Mama has no use for idle lords."

Mrs. Merridew bent closer to her notes, though the side of her neck, then her cheek and her ear turned a delicate pink. Tremont had been aware of her throughout the meeting. Aware of a light, rosy scent, the graceful curve of her jaw, thick brown hair in a severe bun, and serious gray-blue eyes that had remained fixed on the page before her.

"I have no use for idle lords either," Tremont replied. "Might I call you Thomas?"

"Mama calls me Thomas when I'm naughty."

"Tommie, then. Away with you. That gavel cannot levitate."

"Fly," Mrs. Merridew said. "Levitate means fly."

Tommie silently mouthed *levitate*, twice. "I wish I could levitate!" And then he was off at a gallop, the gavel clutched in his little fist.

"A lively boy," Tremont remarked. "You must adore him."

He'd apparently surprised Mrs. Merridew, who turned slowly—warily?—from her notes. "I do. He's a wonderful child, but too smart for his own good, and he has no siblings to play with."

Perhaps that's what Tremont had seen in the child—loneliness. Adults were often lonely by choice, but not so a small boy.

"He has you," Tremont said. "You were prepared to deal with me severely if I thought to castigate your son. A mother's devotion is no small blessing."

An odd look flickered through her eyes—consternation or longing. Tremont was a poor hand at socializing with the ladies, or with much of anybody in polite circles. If he'd ever had the ability to make pointless small talk, he'd left it on myriad Continental battlefields.

"I do love my son," Mrs. Merridew said, making her words a confession of some sort. "He is doubtless snooping in the vicar's office, though, so I ought to collect him and get him home before we're in full darkness."

Well, yes. Small boys were a curious lot. So were earls. "I'll fetch him. Do you need a moment to finish copying your minutes?"

"I do not. I make two copies as the committee members exchange their comments. They do tend to discuss every point thoroughly, and if the minutes are finished as the meeting concludes, they owe me for only a single hour's work."

That slight flush of color came again.

"I am remiss," Tremont said. "A vale for the scribe is the normal course, isn't it? Very bad of me." He passed her one of the coins he always had in his pocket for the occasional urchin, crossing sweeper, or beggar. "You would have let me prance off without tending to my obligations. Not well done of you, Mrs. Merridew."

Before she could protest, he made his exit and followed in Tommie's wake down the corridor. What was wrong with St. Mildred's that they begrudged a congregant a few coins for an extra hour's work?

Though that question was just another version of Tremont's favorite question, upon which he could dwell for eternities: What was wrong with the world?

He found Tommie inspecting Vicar's desk drawers, though the child did not appear bent on larceny.

"Find anything interesting?" Tremont asked.

"Spectacles. Vicar forgets where he puts them, and he hasn't a mama to remind him, so he has extra spectacles. Miss Dorcas used to remind him, but she married Major MacKay. I like Major MacKay. He says God made small boys lively, so it's not my fault that I climbed on the roof of the lych-gate. Did you ever climb on the roof of a lych-gate?"

"I did not. Earls are forbidden from doing that sort of thing. My father permitted me to climb my share of trees, though, where I went for a sail among the fjords of the Viking north, then returned to my homeland in my longship. My brothers-in-arms and

I made many a victorious raid upon the wealthy castles of Normandy."

Tremont had forgotten his outings in the boughs of the surveying oak. They had come to an abrupt end when Papa had died.

"I'm a Viking, too, sometimes." Tommie closed the drawer he'd been rifling. "I'm quite tall when I'm a Viking, and I wear fur robes. Mama was wroth with me for the fur robes."

"You used her best cloak."

"Her night-robe. It's warm and soft and smells like Mama."

Another memory assailed Tremont, of being a small boy, newly saddled with a title, and hiding—from whom or what he could not recall—among his mother's morning dresses. His older sister, Lydia, had found him and given him one of Mama's shawls to sleep with. Not the first or last time Lydia had found him.

"Let's return you to your mother's side, my young friend."

"I was a good vice chairman, wasn't I?" Tommie marched down the corridor ahead of Tremont, but for all the confidence in the boy's step, his question held uncertainty.

"The best I've ever had. You do a recognizable rendering of a toad, too, which is more than I could manage at your age." Tremont's road to a gentlemanly command of the arts had been long, wearying, and pointless in the end.

"Toads are easy. They're toad-shaped with big toad eyes. Mr. Prebish looks like a toad when he's yelling about the lilies of the field and giving glory to God. He means he wants the church to buy his flowers. Mama says we shouldn't yell in church, but when I asked where should we yell, she said we should yell when small boys vex us past all bearing."

"And you said, 'What if that happens in church?'"

Tommie stopped at his mother's elbow and looked abruptly bashful. "I ask Mama a lot of questions."

Mrs. Merridew tousled the lad's hair. "You make me think, Tommie. You make me use my brain, and that is a good thing. Let's get you into your coat and be on our way." She passed her son a coat that was a bit too short in the sleeves for his arms.

She was avoiding Tremont's gaze, which might have been embarrassment about the boy or about the coin. Other congregants milling about had doubtless seen Tremont pass her that coin and seen her accept it.

"Allow me," Tremont said, taking her cloak from her and holding it out. She submitted to the courtesy without comment and then bent to rebutton the buttons Tommie had done crookedly.

Probably on purpose, the little blighter. Tremont was abruptly tempted to button his own cloak crookedly. Instead, he draped that article about his shoulders and did something he rarely allowed himself to do—he yielded to an impulse.

"Might I walk you home, Mrs. Merridew?"

She straightened. "I beg your pardon, my lord?"

Women had the ability to make two words—my lord—convey a wealth of meaning. Those two words could communicate a willingness to become Tremont's countess, his mistress, or his intended. They could also convey caution, though they never had before.

"We're losing the light," he said, "you have a small child to keep track of, and I don't see anybody else on hand to provide you an escort. I'm offering my services, as any gentleman ought to. The linkboys won't be at their posts yet, and you likely wouldn't bother with them when traversing familiar ground in a decent neighborhood anyway."

Major MacKay chose then to intrude on the discussion. "You're seeing Mrs. Merridew home? Then I will be on my way. Dorcas will want a full accounting of the meeting, and she will be most pleased to know the committee acquired a vice chair." He squeezed Tommie's shoulder, bowed to Mrs. Merridew, and bustled off, humming Burns's ditty about men being the practice version of the species and ladies being nature's finer article.

Mrs. Merridew watched MacKay go, her expression caught between bemusement and vexation. "I must yield to your good manners," she said, settling a plain straw bonnet on her head. "Tommie, you will mind the earl's example. He will walk us home and provide you with a demonstration of how a gentleman escorts a lady."

True to her word, Mrs. Merridew delivered the boy a homily about an escort's duty. Tremont matched his steps to the lady's, lest he jostle her arm or hurry her. He walked on the outside, the better to shield the lady from splashing or mud from passing vehicles.

She forgot the part about the gentleman offering his left arm indoors, the better to keep his sword hand free, or perhaps she did not want to bring up swords around the boy.

Tommie, capering about on the walkway, had a thousand questions. Why not hold hands, which would make it easier to prevent a lady from falling on her face if she stumbled? Why was getting mud on a lady's skirts worse than getting mud on a gent's trousers? The laundress had to deal with either mess. Why didn't the lady just tell the gent not to walk so quickly if his legs were longer, or why didn't the person with shorter legs set the pace because Mama was much taller than Tommie, and she *always* waited for him even though she was a lady?

Tommie chattered all the way to the steps before a modest town house. No light shone through the foyer windows, and nobody had yet lit the mandatory streetlamp either. When Tremont expected Tommie to charge up the stairs, the boy instead disappeared into the gloom leading down to the half basement.

"Thank you for your company, my lord," Mrs. Merridew said, "and for your kindness to Tommie. Most people consider him a trial to the nerves."

His mother did not, though Tremont suspected that Tommie challenged his mama's patience frequently.

"You will be astonished to learn that I was a small boy once, Mrs. Merridew. Widowhood quite undid my mother, and my only sibling was a sister several years my senior. When my father died, I became a trial to the nerves too."

Mrs. Merridew regarded him in the gathering shadows while the sound of a door scraping open came from beneath the porch.

"What changed?" she asked. "You are the furthest thing from a trial to the nerves now."

"I grew up. I went to war. I realized I could never be my father, and life goes on."

"That, it does. Thank you again, my lord, and good luck with your men. I surmise they can be a trial to the nerves as well." She curtseyed and followed her son down into the darkness of the half basement.

Tremont waited on the walkway until a dim light appeared in the narrow window beside the basement door, then he set a brisk pace for his own dwelling. Walking calmed his mind and allowed his thoughts to form into tidy squares. His imagination, however, was making that exercise impossible.

A whisper of an idea wedged its way into the swirling currents of Tremont's cogitations. Mrs. Merridew might be the answer to a prayer. She was pretty, though she tried to hide it. Pretty wasn't necessary, but it did help, and she was patient. A wealth of patience was mandatory.

Mrs. Merridew was the soul of patience. She was accustomed to unruly males who needed a firm, kind hand. She was in straitened circumstances. The child's too-short coat, her widow's weeds going worn about the seams, and her willingness to accept a spare coin at the expense of her pride all confirmed as much.

Tremont marched along, the idea growing and twining like ivy around other ideas and between yet still others. By the time he reached home, he was humming "Green Grow the Rashes, O" and wondering if he'd parted with what little remained of his reasoning powers.

CHAPTER TWO

The day was sunny for a change, which made the mending less of a chore. The seat by the parlor window was nonetheless frigid, and Matilda again considered smashing some of the furniture from the floors above to burn for warmth.

But no. Winter had yet to truly arrive, and the day would soon be less chilly. She wasn't desperate—yet. Somebody would rent the upstairs soon, and until then, she had scribing for the church meetings, mending, watching Major MacKay's son on the governess's half day, and other odd jobs.

Charity jobs, and Matilda was grateful for them.

"I'm hungry," Tommie said, shuffling a deck of cards with more dexterity than was proper for a boy of his age. "Can we go to the bakery?"

"We will go to the bakery tomorrow afternoon." Tomorrow, the baker put the fancy products for the week on display, and thus the selection of day-olds was larger. "You had your porridge, my boy. Build me a castle of cards."

"I want to go to the bakery now. The bakery is warm, and Mrs. Spicer sometimes gives me a biscuit."

One of the stale biscuits, of course. "If you are cold, then put on your scarf."

"I *want* to go to the *bakery*, and I want a *biscuit*, and *I do not want to put on my scarf*—"

A knock at the front door interrupted the gathering tempest of Tommie's frustration. Not the coalman—he still did Matilda the courtesy of coming down the back steps to dun her for his payment—but who else could it be?

"We have company!" Tommie was off his chair and out of the parlor, cards forgotten.

"Thomas, you do not pelt up to the door like the first footman trying to impress his employer. I will answer the door."

Tommie slowed, his eagerness yielding to annoyance. "Why can't I have any fun, Mama? I'm the man of the house. I should answer the door."

The man of the house was still small enough to be snatched by an ambitious chimney sweep, though that would change in a year or two. Then the mines and the merchant ships would become the greater threats, to say nothing of the abbesses.

Matilda stopped by the speckled mirror in the foyer. Her reflection was pale, tired, and going gaunt. Harry would not have been best pleased to see his wife in such a condition.

Which was just too blessed bad. Matilda opened the door, prepared to see Mrs. Oldbach or possibly Dorcas MacKay.

The Earl of Tremont, in all his lordly splendor, stood before her. "Mrs. Merridew, good day." He tipped his hat and bowed. "Master Merridew." To Tommie, he offered a gloved hand. "I hope I'm not calling at a bad time?"

"Mama was mending," Tommie said. "She mends *all the time*. I want to go to the bakery because it's warm, and it smells like heaven, but I'm building a card castle. You could help me."

A riot of emotions buffeted Matilda.

Grudging respect for the earl's courtesy to a small boy.

Resignation, because a peer calling on an impoverished widow did not bode well for the propriety of Matilda's household, though in fairness, Tremont would not be the first man to proposition her.

Grim humor, because her father had predicted she'd end her days in disgrace, though Papa hadn't quite got the timing right.

And shame. Always the shame.

"You must not tarry in the cold," Matilda said, though she was loath to allow anybody to see her home. The place was spotless, also pathetically shabby. "Do come in."

Tremont had to duck to pass through the doorway. He took off his hat, but did not pass it over.

"I was wondering if you and Tommie might join me for a walk in the park? This is one of those days where it feels colder inside than out, and I am consumed with the need for a constitutional. We could pass by the bakery on our way home if a certain party manages not to fall into the Serpentine or frighten anybody's horses."

"He means me," Tommie said, slipping his hand into Matilda's. "Say yes, Mama. Please."

Tommie's fingers were like ice, while the earl was politely not glancing about at Matilda's bare floor and curtainless windows. He did not wrinkle his lordly beak at the stink of tallow and coal pervading the air, nor did he press Matilda for an answer.

"The days are getting shorter," she said, feeling Tommie's cold fingers right down to her soul, "and the mending will keep. A brief outing to enjoy the sunshine will be good for our spirits."

Tommie wrapped his arms around her waist and squeezed hard. "Thank you, Mama. I will get my coat, and Mr.... Tremont will hold your cloak for you. When I am taller, I will hold your cloak for you too."

The boy rocketed back to the parlor—he and Matilda wore their outer garments indoors on the coldest days—and the earl took Matilda's cloak from its hook beside the mirror.

"You have made two fellows exceedingly happy with your decision. When winter arrives in earnest, we'll consider a day such as this balmy."

He settled Matilda's cloak around her shoulders and no doubt noticed the careful stitching that attempted to hide the wear at the collar. The cloak was one of the last fine articles Harry had bought for her, because never let it be said that Harry Merridew's missus went without.

"I won't keep you for long," Tremont said, "and I meant what I said about stopping at the bakery. The boy will hold me to it, and I do fancy a rum bun on such a day."

"You did not stop by to talk of rum buns, my lord." Hunger was making Matilda snappish, or perhaps earls paying casual calls did that.

He passed her the gloves sitting on the rickety sideboard. "You are right, and I am an utter failure at small talk, but I cannot appear on your doorstep without making some attempt at polite conversation, can I?"

Tommie thundered back to the door. "I buttoned my coat right this time!"

Tremont tousled his hair. "Because you are desperate to get into the fresh air, but please recall that the bakery will not grace our itinerary unless your behavior is exemplary."

"Be good," Matilda said, wrapping a scarf about the boy's ears, "or no biscuit."

"I will be a saint, Mama. An angel. I will be perfect, and you will be so proud of me!"

He bolted out the door and up the steps, and true to his stated intentions, he for once stood at the top of the steps and waited for the adults to join him.

Tremont offered his arm, and Matilda had no choice but to take it. At the crossings, Tommie dutifully took her free hand, which was their rule more honored in the breach. When they reached the park, Tremont suggested that if Tommie ran to the large oak fifty yards off, Tremont would time him.

The earl produced a pocket watch, and Tommie scampered across the grass.

"Is that a trick your sister pulled on you?" Matilda asked.

"My father. I was his only son, a long-awaited miracle, or maybe he understood that he and I might not have long together. The distances gradually got longer, and I picked up speed. Papa made room in his schedule for me, and I adored him. He showed me all the best Viking sailing trees and told me Norse legends when I had nightmares. I understand why my mother so desperately grieved his passing. I suppose you miss your late husband?"

A complicated question. "I've been widowed longer than I was married, and yet, sometimes it feels as if I'll come around a corner, and there Harry will be, grinning at me as if the past few years were just some sort of joke. He had a perverse sense of humor."

"Any sense of humor must be a boon to those who have one," Tremont said as Tommie tagged the tree and started back at a trot rather than a sprint. "I could tell you that I was just passing by your door and taken with a sudden notion for some company in the park, but I'd be prevaricating if I did."

Matilda endured the same sinking dread she'd suffered when she'd realized her courses were late. Tremont was about to proposition her, and he was doing so *honestly*.

Damn him for that. "I much prefer plain speaking, my lord."

Tommie stopped several yards away and flopped dramatically onto a bench.

"I note that your home is not well heated," Tremont said quietly. "That the boy needs a new coat, that you accepted a coin from me that you'd rather have graciously refused. You are taking in mending, which is surely the hallmark of a lady fallen upon difficult times."

"I am a lady." In only the most attenuated sense, because Papa had been a vicar.

"One deduced as much, and thus I put a topic to you that might offend. I mean you no insult, but I have few other options, and my situation grows vexatious."

How prettily he referred to the inconvenience he suffered for want of a handy mistress. Harry had been similarly convinced that a man must not be without regular pleasure, lest civilization topple. Widows, by contrast, were expected to devote themselves to pious good works and other people's mending, because civilization would be equally imperiled if widows comported themselves as gentlemen so freely did.

Not that Matilda missed Harry, ever.

"Was I fast, Tremont?" Tommie called.

"A flat streak across the horizon. Twelve seconds to the tree. We will have to change your name to Lightning Merridew."

"I'm Lightning Merridew! Mama, let's throw pebbles into the water!" Tommie hopped off the bench and jogged toward the pool of water reflecting the bright sunshine of midday.

"He's not skipping rocks yet?" Tremont asked, following Tommie at a purposeful march. "I am convinced that the objective of skipping rocks is to keep a child who is intent on leaping into the water otherwise occupied on the bank. My sister is a prodigiously talented skipper, and for a time, my sole aim in life was to best her. Petty of me."

Raising offensive topics in the park was petty, also shrewd, because Matilda would not make a scene here and flounce off in high dudgeon.

"I don't know how to skip rocks," Matilda said, "else I would teach him. The child wants constant diversion and constant activity."

"Not diversion," Tremont said as they gained the grassy bank of the Serpentine. "Recreation. Or occupation, in the child's sense of the word. The boy has a lively mind, and that mind wants obstacles to climb, much as he'd delight in climbing a tree." Tremont picked up a round, smooth stone and idly flicked it into the water.

The rock bounced four times, and Tommie was instantly fascinated. The next five minutes were spent explaining and demonstrating the manly art of skipping rocks, while Matilda silently argued with herself.

Town had emptied for the winter. The probability of renting out the rest of the house was not great, and spring was far away. Tommie did need a new coat. The mending was ruining Matilda's eyes to the point that she could barely see to read Tommie his stories by the end of the day. She could move in with Aunt Portia—the last, dreaded alternative to destitution—but Portia was barely managing.

She was also unrelentingly serious.

Tremont was comely, clean about his person, and he'd be willing to bind himself to terms under a written contract. Matilda's duties under that contract would be merely... to welcome him and him alone into her bed for coin.

For coin. For the ten thousandth time, the admission trudged through her mind: *Papa was right about me.*

And behind that thought, a more insidious, seductive thought: *At least I would be paid. At least Tommie would be warm. If I'm to be ashamed of myself, might I please suffer that indignity with an occasionally full belly?*

Tommie managed to make a rock bounce once, and he was in alt. Passersby smiled at the man patiently correcting the child's form and finding him another good skipper. Tommie was soon busy amassing a collection of smooth, flat, round stones, while the entire armada of waterfowl—swans, ducks, and geese—paddled madly for distant shores.

"Shall we sit?" Tremont said, gesturing to a bench. "The bank will be denuded of rocks, or Tommie's arm will fall off before his interest flags. I'm not sure even that eventuality would dissuade him from his purpose."

The bench was warm, despite the chill in the air. Tremont took a seat a proper foot away from Matilda while Tommie scoured the bank.

"About your offensive topic, my lord."

"The topic that I hoped would not offend, but that has grown rather pressing."

"I must refuse your proposition," Matilda said, the words leaving her more sad than angry. "I refuse not because I judge women for doing what they must—or what they claim to enjoy—to survive, but because I hold to the quaint notion that some activities should be undertaken only out of mutual affection and esteem."

She expected a polite, gentlemanly rejoinder about this most impolite topic. An insistence that she hear his terms, a little touch to her sleeve, and an allusion to wild sexual pleasure. The oldest Prebish boy had referred to paradise and raptures and heavenly transports— oddly theological terms for a lot of heaving and panting.

"You haven't heard my proposition." The earl sounded a trifle confused, but then, he was probably a stranger to refusals.

"I've heard enough others like it, and while I should doubtless be flattered that a peer would notice me in any capacity... I am not flattered. Silly of me. No offense intended, my lord."

Silence greeted this declaration.

"We can skip the bakery," Matilda said, swiping at the corner of her eye with her glove. "Tommie must not become accustomed to luxuries. That way lies nothing but misery."

Tommie's rock bounced three times, and Matilda dutifully clapped and cheered, while Tremont declared the job well done.

"Let's go." Matilda rose with as much dignity as she yet possessed. "I believe we've said all that needs saying."

Tremont rose, as a gentleman must. He peered at her as if she'd suggested they attend a flying-pig race.

"I am cudgeling my brain for what the philosophers, etiquette books, or even newspaper advice columnists would suggest in such a situation, and my mind is a mortified blank."

"Most women would find you to be in every way a desirable specimen, my lord, but I'm not... That is... Please just take me home. If our paths should cross again, we will pretend we did not have this conversation."

"But we did," Tremont said, "and though you are mistaken about my intentions, this discussion convinces me more than ever that you are the perfect candidate for the position I have in mind. You have fortitude and integrity, and you are tolerant."

Matilda was prepared to push his lordship into the water if he made a pestilence of himself, but Tremont remained at a proper distance, and his expression held only faint puzzlement. No sneering, no leering.

"You aren't considering me for the post of mistress?"

"I am not." He looked as if he might say more, but he remained silent, and his gaze went to Tommie, still whipping rocks into the water.

Matilda sank back onto the bench. "I have just made a first-class cake of myself, haven't I? Put my foot in my mouth and covered myself with mortification. I apologize, my lord."

He came down beside her. "I apologize on behalf of my gender, because apparently, others have been less than respectful toward you. The fact is, I need your help, Mrs. Merridew. I honestly, sincerely need your help, and I am happy to pay you for it."

Tommie was picking through his pile of pebbles and choosing several to stash in his pockets. What sort of boy hoarded rocks? A very poor boy.

"I'm listening, my lord. I am a hard worker, and I set my pride aside the day I realized I was to become a mother."

"No, you did not, which I understand more than you might think. Let's take this discussion to a tea shop, shall we? Major MacKay has acquainted me with several in the area, and I believe Tommie will fall in with the suggestion readily enough."

Tremont rose and offered Matilda his hand. His gloves were spotless and likely lined with fur. Matilda allowed him to assist her and took his proffered arm, all the while trying to keep her teeth from chattering.

~

So that's how a man propositions a woman.

Tremont could not express that thought, but it circled in his brainbox on wings of consternation.

The boy Tommie babbled away, about skipping stones across the

Channel, someday owning a kite big enough to take a boy into the sky, porridge being much better with butter and honey, and at Christmas last year he'd had his oats with cinnamon.

Tremont, meanwhile, wondered who had presumed on Mrs. Merridew's good name.

"You must forgive me, my lord," Mrs. Merridew said quietly. "I leap into situations, make unsupported assumptions, and build castles in Spain. My father said imagination was my besetting sin and that I would pay for it."

"I am the opposite." Tremont tipped his hat to some dowager swaddled up to the eyes in furs. "My sister says I am a careful thinker, but the more accurate term is that I am a plodder. It's within the realm of honesty to say I am simply dull-witted."

"You are not dull-witted." Mrs. Merridew took the boy by the hand as they approached a crossing. "You were three steps ahead of St. Mildred's wiliest committee members and got exactly what you wanted from them. They consider themselves the souls of benevolence for taking a chance on your soldiers, when, in fact, they've spent two years tiptoeing around how to retire the sexton."

"He is not a young man," Tremont said. "I look for churches with aging sextons, if you want to know the truth, but Tommie won the day for me."

A fancy coach rattled past. The Dorning crest registered vaguely in Tremont's awareness. Recognizing crests had become a sort of game for him when he'd been living in the stews. Avoiding the enemy and passing the time.

"How did Tommie win the day?" Mrs. Merridew asked, setting a course across the intersection.

"He is charming, in his innocence and candor. He charmed them, and I slipped in behind his advance guard. The tea shop is up on the left."

"Tommie is as charming as a rat terrier with a loud bark. My husband had real charm." This was said with an interesting hint of wrath.

"Whereas I lack charm," Tremont replied. "I have manners, though. My mama and sister saw to that. Then I grew all impressed with my own consequence—a young peer is susceptible to such nonsense—and went off to war. Combat was a humbling experience."

He held the door for her and wondered if Tommie's voluble nature was contagious. Spain was better left in the past, and Waterloo should be consigned to complete oblivion.

"Most men find war glorious," Mrs. Merridew said.

"Then most men are either cursed with a faulty memory or they are liars. The table at the back is quiet. MacKay prefers it."

Mrs. Merridew paused inside the doorway and inhaled through her nose. The little shop smelled of baking bread and sweet spices, and Tommie had gone quiet.

"The hot chocolate they serve here is not to be missed," Tremont said. "One of few consolations for the colder weather."

They got through the business of cloaks and bonnets, and Tommie took the seat facing the window, leaving Tremont to face the lady.

"How do you know Major MacKay?" she asked when Tremont had placed their orders.

"His cousin is married to my sister. I am thus a cousin by marriage to him, and he is cousins with a host of other luminaries, all of whom are panting for the chance to find me a countess. I did not directly rejoin my family after Waterloo, and in recent years, I have been occupied with some business matters here in London. This, they claim, is very remiss of me."

That recitation put a pretty bow on years of wandering the stews and more recent efforts to collect fellow former soldiers who were also prone to wandering the stews.

Mrs. Merridew produced pencil and paper from her reticule and passed both to the boy. "Toads were too easy for you. Draw me a dragon, please."

Tommie set to work with a focus that was doubtless characteristic of his mother.

"You are not capable of finding your own countess?" she asked.

"I have tried telling my matchmaking relations that I am better suited to that task than they are, but I haven't taken the time to tend to it. They are right to feel a sense of urgency. The heir in line for the Tremont title is a rascal kicking his heels in America. The notion that my cousin might become the earl is insupportable, and thus I must stop lollygagging and find a wife. That's where you come in."

Mrs. Merridew sat up straight. "I am not in the business of finding wives for peers, my lord."

"Alas for me, though you are in the business of making unruly males behave with a modicum of civility. I house a dozen former soldiers at lodgings not far from here. They are good fellows, but rough, and if they are to set up as groundkeepers and gardeners for hire, they must learn some... some decorum. Everything from basic table manners to that business of how to escort a lady. For good and sufficient reasons, they don't listen to me—not about that. But they will listen to you."

The food arrived—bowls of steaming pepper pot soup and a tray stacked with half sandwiches—and Tommie sent his mother a questioning glance.

"His lordship will say the grace," Mrs. Merridew announced, "bearing in mind that the Almighty appreciates brevity."

As did little boys and hungry earls. "We thank Thee for this food," Tremont recited in his best earlish drone, "and for the delightful company, and also for dragons. Amen."

The sketch disappeared into Mrs. Merridew's reticule, and Tommie's table napkin went onto his lap. The boy's manners were exemplary for his age, though when the hot chocolate arrived, he did get whipped cream on his nose. Mrs. Merridew addressed that situation with brisk measures, though the moment sent Tremont's thoughts careening in odd directions.

"You seek a deportment instructor for your men?" Mrs. Merridew said.

"Something like that, but more as well. You would live on the premises. We have a cook, housekeeper, and some other domestics. The laundresses come around on Mondays, and the men take care of the heavier work themselves. They need somebody to preside over meals, hold parade inspections, schedule chores, rebuke excessive profanity, that sort of thing."

"A headmistress, then."

"I had a mother and a sister to guide me onto the path of gentlemanly manners, and for a time, a father. Even my rapscallion cousin was some help when it came to tying cravats or lighting cheroots. These men have nobody, and they are willing to learn. They simply know more of marching and fighting than of holding doors or doffing their caps."

"You should help them, Mama," Tommie said. "I'm not grown up yet, but I know all about escorting a lady now. Nobody likes to feel stupid."

Mrs. Merridew considered the boy for a long, quiet moment. Out of the mouths of babes...

"Let us proceed," she said, "on a trial basis. I will do what I can with your recruits for, say, thirty days, and then we will reevaluate. If I am effective, they might not need me for much longer than that."

She truly had no sense of her own appeal. If she was *effective*, the men would devise strategies for keeping her on the premises until they were all proficient in French, drawing, pianoforte, and the quadrille.

"I cannot express clearly enough how relieved I am to have your assistance," Tremont said. "Will fifty pounds do?"

She studied her tea cup. "Per annum?"

Did she rate herself on a par with tippling bachelor curates relegated to obscure rural pulpits? "I had that amount in mind for the first month. Don't say it's too much until you've met the men."

"Very well, I won't. I will also reserve judgment until you and I have agreed upon a curriculum of sorts. Are these men literate?"

"Some of them."

"I can write my name," Tommie said, looking up from his cup of chocolate. "Mama makes me practice, and the letter T is my favorite. I write the T and the M grown up. The other letters are small."

"Capital," Mrs. Merridew said. "The big letters are capital, majuscule, or uppercase. The others are small, minuscule, or lowercase."

"Why does one letter have three names?" Tommie asked. "Why not just big and little, like people?"

Tremont wanted to put a hand over the boy's mouth, because Mrs. Merridew had not agreed to any stated compensation, and that term mattered. A contract was not binding unless consideration—such as a promise of payment—was offered and accepted.

"People have several names too," Mrs. Merridew pointed out. "I am Matilda, Mrs. Merridew, and Mama, depending on who addresses me. You'd best finish that chocolate before somebody comes around to clear the dishes."

Tommie drained his cup to the dregs, and his mother passed him her unfinished serving.

"Please say you will take the fifty pounds," Tremont said. "We can discuss the rest of it later, when you have had a chance to consider what subjects might benefit the men most, and I have given the same topic some thought. If you get the men to 'please pass the salt' and using 'dratted' instead of the less genteel options, I will be most appreciative."

"Then you set the standard too low," Mrs. Merridew replied. "These fellows bested the shrewdest military leader the world has seen in many a century. They were born the sons of shopkeepers and yeomen and became an army of unprecedented ferocity. They can master table manners."

"Mama sets great store by table manners."

"Manners maketh the man," Tremont said. "At least in the opinion of some old Etonian. Will you please help me, Mrs. Merridew?"

Mention of the money made her uncomfortable. Tremont should have seen that sooner.

She watched the boy delicately spooning whipped cream into his mouth. "I will help you."

"Thank the Merciful Creator. How soon can you change your residence?"

Mrs. Merridew fixed her gaze on a plate of tea cakes, each one decorated with a tiny icing flower, and remained silent. She was not glib. When she spoke, she spoke confidently, but she wasn't above pausing to reflect.

"No time like the present," she said, taking one tiny tea cake. "If you will send along some of your men, I can have the necessities packed in a few hours."

To pack up a life should take longer than that.

"We mustn't forget Copenhagen," Tommie said. "Cope is my horse. He's stuffed, but I've had him since I was little. Papa gave him to me."

"By all means, bring your horse," Tremont said, thinking of a stuffed dog named Charles. "I will come by your new abode tomorrow morning to see that you're settled in."

He expected second thoughts and last-minute renegotiations. Instead, Mrs. Tremont allowed Tommie one tea cake, and both mother and child were quiet on the walk back to their dwelling.

"You were wrong about something," Mrs. Merridew said as Tommie scampered down the steps and let himself into the house.

"I am frequently in error and even more frequently in doubt," Tremont replied. "Don't you lock your door?"

"Tommie knows to find the key beneath the boot scrape. You said you have no charm."

"Nor do I any longer aspire to acquire any." Forlorn hopes were notoriously bad odds.

"You do have charm, my lord. Whoever told you otherwise wasn't paying attention."

She disappeared down the steps, and Tremont set a measured course in the direction of the men's house. The encounter had gone splendidly, in that Mrs. Merridew had agreed to take a lot of unruly former soldiers in hand.

And yet... That misunderstanding in the park had been awkward indeed, also intriguing.

"Nobody observing me for five minutes would accuse me of having charm," Tremont muttered. He flipped a coin to the crossing sweeper, who touched a finger to his cap in response. "That wretched crossing sweeper has charm—and cheek."

By the time Tremont reached the men's residence, his mind had turned to another topic altogether. Mrs. Merridew had said that most women would find him "in every way" to be a desirable specimen. Of course they would—he was titled, in good health, and wealthy, though none of that was a result of his own exertions.

What qualities did *Matilda Merridew* consider desirable in a man? The question intrigued him more than it ought to.

CHAPTER THREE

"That was genius, sending for the boy," Mrs. Annette Winklebleck said, pouring Matilda a cup of tea. "Settled the men right down to put a youngster amongst 'em at table."

Mrs. Winklebleck had invited Matilda to the housekeeper's parlor for a *wee chat*. The little room would have been of a piece with the vicarage where Matilda had been raised. Clean but worn carpet, a parlor stove wedged into the hearth, a mended porcelain angel on the mantel, and framed needlepoint roses on the walls. The reading chairs were comfortable, and the slightly faded chintz curtains were patterned with more roses.

A peaceful, cozy retreat, very much in contrast with the earlier scene at breakfast.

"Tommie was rather subdued as well," Matilda said. He'd sat at Matilda's left hand at the head of the breakfast table, silently spooning porridge into his maw and goggling at the other diners. Mrs. Winklebleck had taken the chair to Matilda's right, while a half-dozen former soldiers had lined each side of the table.

Their profanity had been prodigious and their manners nonexistent. Mrs. Winklebleck had made a general announcement rather than attempt specific introductions.

"This be Mrs. Merridew. Lord Tremont sent her here to civilize you lot, may God have mercy on her soul. Treat her right or learn to go without your meals, your laundry, and your mendin'."

Matilda had offered a polite "good morning," taken her seat, and asked Mrs. Winklebleck to please pass the porridge. After a beat of silence, a roar had ensued, involving the damned salt, the perishin' butter, the bleedin' honey ye damned stinkin' sot, and worse.

Matilda had sent for Tommie in hopes that his example might do for the men what Matilda's had not, which wasn't quite what had transpired. The men had fallen all but silent as a staggering amount of food had disappeared.

"Where did they get off to?" Matilda asked.

"Biggs and Bentley go for a ramble. We don't ask them what they get up to, but the law hasn't snabbled 'em, so maybe they're looking for work. Dantry and Davis report to Major MacKay for stable help and other odd jobs. Most of the rest spend the day at dice, cards, or whorin', unless we've a churchyard to spruce up. I do fancy me this tea. His lordship don't skimp on the larders."

"You have eight men sitting idle underfoot all day?"

"The whole dozen if it's a rainy afternoon. Winter is hard on 'em, and none too easy on me nerves either. They're a good lot, though. Better than most. Watch out for that Amos Tucker. He's a pincher."

"A... pincher?"

"Yer bum. He's quick too. Wants a good clout to the ear, and from me, he usually gets it." Mrs. Winklebleck tucked a strand of blond hair behind her ear, the gesture oddly girlish.

As housekeepers went, Mrs. Winklebleck was young and robust in every dimension, rather than fat. She wore a spotless mobcap and clean apron, but something about her seemed familiar.

"You are Big Nan," Matilda said. "You and your... friends once shared a fellowship meal at St. Mildred's." At least two years ago, maybe more.

She set down her tea cup, her gaze wary. "And what if we did?"

"The congregation could talk of little else for weeks. Major MacKay's ladies, they called you. Miss Dorcas—Mrs. MacKay, rather —holds you all in sincere affection, as does the major." A lot of street-walkers, side by side with the likes of Mrs. Oldbach. The occasion had been memorable, to say the least.

"Life on the stroll is hard," Mrs. Winklebleck said. "'On the stroll' sounds so merry and fine, My Lady La-Di-Da. Half the time, you starve. The other half... It's hard. I tried my hand at drawing carica-tures in the pubs—I got a good eye for a likeness—but that don't hardly pay. Major MacKay said his lordship were looking for a house-keeper, and I kept house for me brother until he died, so here I am. Jessup and Jensen came with me."

Two sturdy, smiling maids.

Former streetwalkers. Harry would laugh himself to tears at the thought, and from his celestial perch, Papa was doubtless unsurprised to know the company his Jezebel of a daughter was keeping.

"People can change, missus," Mrs. Winklebleck said. "Major MacKay forgot how to smile, but since he married Miss Dorcas, he's all sunshine. The boy John has the major's sunny nature. You were married, now you are a widow. I was a light-skirts, now I'm a house-keeper. Only the Quality get so bound up in everybody knowin' their place. For the Quality, their place is usually proper wonderful."

The next question had to be asked, because the answer would decide whether Matilda stayed on or gathered Tommie up and returned to her frigid basement.

"You don't... That is... Your former livelihood doesn't overlap with your current duties?"

Mrs. Winklebleck laughed heartily, the sound filling her little parlor. "How fancy you talk. I'm done with all that. Whorin' is a young woman's game. A few years of that here in the capital, and a girl can take her coin and go back to the village. She'll lie about being in service or working in a shop, but nobody will mind, and some lad will be glad to find a wife with even a small dowry."

Harry had posited the same theory many times: A man or woman of enterprise could simply hop on the next coach, travel fifty miles, and take up life in any market town with nobody the wiser about his previous affairs. Too late, Matilda had realized that Harry had spoken from repeated experience.

"And the maids, Jessup and Jensen? They aren't expected to... extend favors to the men?"

"They are not. I suspect Jensen is sweet on Amos Tucker, but Tuck hasn't even regular wages, so how could he take on a wife? They might rub along well enough on Jensen's wages for a time, but then the children arrive, and somebody has to pay for the coal."

Matilda sipped her tea rather than comment on that observation. "What, in your opinion, would the men most like to learn if they're to better their prospects?"

"You'll have to ask 'em. They like good food and plenty of it. They'll tidy up a churchyard or some fancy toff's garden, if his lordship says they ought. For Major MacKay, they'll muck out a stable. For Captain Powell, they will try to spin straw into gold, though I haven't met the man myself. I'm too busy beatin' the rugs and makin' the beds to bother about what else the lads might be fit for."

That wasn't exactly what Matilda had asked about. "Who is Captain Powell?"

"Major MacKay's cousin, married to Lord Tremont's sister, Lady Lydia. Get his lordship to draw you a family map. More tea?"

"No, thank you. I left Tommie building a card castle in our sitting room, but he cannot remain unsupervised for long. If you are free this afternoon, might you tour the premises with me?"

"I do love how you talk, missus. Once we get the nooning behind us, thee and me'll make a thorough inspection. The house is in good repair, thanks be. I cannot abide the rising damp. Wrecks a place from inside the very walls, like giving a dwelling the French pox."

Matilda was torn between bewilderment and the urge to laugh. The analogy was effective, but...

But a lady did not expect to hear such a comparison, ever, and in some small, quiet corner of her heart, Matilda still wished she had made a lady's choices.

"Your wee lad can tag after Jensen and Jessup if he's bored," Mrs. Winklebleck said. "They'll find chores for 'im. He has a quick look to him, and he might even be some help. When he's a mite older, he can help in the scullery or wash out water buckets in the stable."

Honest work, but not exactly what Matilda aspired to for her son. The whole business of what to do with Tommie posed a puzzle, one Matilda would take up with Lord Tremont. Little boys left to their own devices invariably got up to mischief, and Matilda had no intention of allowing a lot of foul-mouthed soldiers to become a bad influence on her son.

She began mentally fashioning a means of explaining to Tommie that *he* would have to be a *good* influence upon the men, but she never got very far with that exercise. By the time Lord Tremont had arrived, Tommie had been missing for an hour, and Matilda was as close to hysterics as she'd ever come.

"If you'd *axed* me," Amos Tucker thundered from Tremont's left, "I'da told ye I already searched the attic!"

"If you'da *told* me,"—Benjamin Bentley returned fire from Tremont's right—"I'da not wasted me time and sneezed meself half to smithereens a-lookin' fer the boy up there!"

Jessup and Jensen joined the crowd in the library, their mobcaps less than pristine. "We've searched the attics, my lord. No sign of the boy."

A beat of silence went by, and then the arguments resumed, redoubled, and became a roar of orders, insults, and profanity. By the window, Mrs. Merridew stood with her back to the assembled household, her posture redolent of nerves on a very strained leash.

"Atten-SHUN!" Tremont snapped out the order in the tradition of infantry sergeants the world over. Chairs scraped back, chests and chins were thrust out, and silence rang though the library.

"Thank you," Tremont said. "While your efforts thus far are much appreciated, we have yet to find the boy. Some organization will doubtless yield more satisfying results. The attics having been thoroughly searched, I want Jessup and Jensen to take the pantries, kitchen, and larder. Mrs. Winklebleck, will you search your own quarters and the servants' hall? Biggs and Bentley take the first-floor bedrooms. Dantry and Davis, you will take the second. Mind the closets and wardrobes, look under every bed. MacIvey and MacPherson, the garden and alley, and don't forget to look up. Small boys can get stuck in trees, as I have reason to know from personal experience."

Tremont went on handing out assignments so that the child would be found and so that every member of the household could feel that they contributed to that happy outcome—or had done what they could to avoid a tragedy.

"And for the sake of all that is holy," he went on, "look into any space that closes or locks. Trunks, cupboards, wardrobes, crawl-spaces, every nook and cranny, every crevice and drain. Look for our Tommie as if he were your three-months-overdue pay packet. Tanner and Tucker, you are not to tarry at the tea shop. Ask after the lad, have a look around. Make a search of Mrs. Merridew's former residence, including the adjacent alley, and then report back. No appointing yourself to scouting duty at the pub. Mrs. Merridew and I will expect reports from all points in one hour. Dismissed—and keep a sharp eye."

Several of the men saluted, though most had shed that habit. They shuffled out the door, muttering and cursing, but following orders, as Tremont had known they would.

Mrs. Merridew had at some point turned from the window, though she kept her arms crossed over her middle.

"Thank you," she said. "I have never heard so many raised voices at once. All I could think was, 'The sweeps will get him.' Whatever shall I do if the sweeps steal my boy?"

She was pale and still, though Tremont could feel the panic trying to shake her. He knew that battle for self-control, as did every soldier to take up arms.

"Has Tommie gone missing before?"

"Never. I barely let him out of my sight, but he seemed so happy here. He slid down the banister at least a dozen times, and I hadn't the heart to scold him. If I'd been less permissive... less indulgent..." Her breath hitched, and Tremont steeled himself to endure the tears of a woman who'd probably given up crying the day she'd entered second mourning.

"We will find him," Tremont said. "Little boys love to explore. They do not love to miss meals or worry their mamas. Tommie wants to be found."

"He was so good at breakfast. No rude questions, no arguments. He ate every bite of his porridge."

"Then we know he's not hungry."

Mrs. Merridew blinked and nodded while Tremont wished she would cry, wished she could collapse upon him in a heap of female misery so he could offer her the simple comfort of an embrace.

That was apparently not what she needed. "What is Tommie's favorite thing?" Tremont asked. "His greatest joy?"

Mrs. Merridew worried a nail. "He was very impressed with that cup of hot chocolate at the tea shop."

Were you impressed? Tremont kicked himself mentally. "Tommie is a canny lad. He'd know he couldn't purchase another serving without coin. When does he lose himself in enjoyment? When is he most deaf to your maternal instructions?"

"That boy can focus keenly on a task," she said. "My husband had the same capacity for single-mindedness. If Harry Merridew fixed on an objective, he let nothing and no one stand in his way."

Tremont crossed the room, took Mrs. Merridew by the wrist, and drew her closer to the fire.

"Think of a time when you spoke directly to your son, and he did not even notice. What was he doing?"

Mrs. Merridew's brows drew down, and she looked in that moment like the boy when he'd decided to master skipping stones—wholly concentrated on the challenge.

"The cat at St. Mildred's," she said. "Give Tommie a piece of string, and he will play with that cat until the last trumpet shall sound."

"Mrs. Winklebleck is not fond of cats," Tremont replied, "but a few have privileges in the stable. Come along. If Tommie went out to use the jakes, and a cat strutted past, he probably followed his quarry without a thought to asking your permission."

"But if the cat ran off..." Mrs. Merridew caught herself. "Right. Tommie would try to make friends with the cat. A good thought. I'll fetch my cloak and have a look in the stable."

Two men had been dispatched to search the back garden and alley, but not the stable itself. Nobody was due to report for at least forty-five minutes, and some fresh air and activity would doubtless do the lady good.

Tremont accompanied Mrs. Merridew across the garden and into the alley. MacIvey was halfway up a sturdy maple, having a look around from the higher vantage point, while MacPherson admonished him not to fall on his fool head and expect anybody to pay for his burial.

"Tommie is in awe of horses," Mrs. Merridew said. "He loves Copenhagen the way I used to love Christmas pudding."

What had happened that Mrs. Merridew no longer cared for Christmas pudding? "MacIvey and MacPherson would have come this way when they finished reconnoitering from the upper boughs. I should have ordered them to climb the tree. With the leaves gone, MacIvey can doubtless see into every backyard on this side of the street."

A fat marmalade tom scampered across the alley. His head was nearly as wide as his body, and many a mouse had doubtless added to his girth.

"He's a regular," Tremont said. "I think the lads call him George, owing to his size and propensity for self-indulgence."

"Is he tame?"

"Tucker leaves milk out for the cats..."

Mrs. Merridew knelt and wiggled her fingers. The cat took notice, sat upon his haunches, and sent Tremont a look that conveyed that earls, being useless, were excused for the nonce. Lydia could achieve the same look, though she never aimed it at her dear Captain Powell.

"Here, kitty, kitty, kitty." Mrs. Merridew opened her hand, and the cat deigned to stroll in her direction. A moment later, the beast was snuggled in her arms and rumbling like a feline artillery volley. "Where is my Tommie, Your Majesty? I've lost my boy, and my heart will break beyond all repair if we do not find him."

The cat stropped his fat head against the lady's chin.

"Tommie!" Tremont called, earning a scowl from the cat. "My lad, show yourself. There's a fellow here who'd like to make your acquaintance."

Nothing.

Mrs. Merridew, cat cradled against her shoulder, peered into the stable. "You have a cart pony."

"Mrs. Winklebleck and Cook's, though Mrs. Winklebleck isn't keen on equines. She doesn't know how to drive, so Cook or one of the men must drive her if she's inclined to run errands."

"Tommie!" Mrs. Merridew called, her voice conveying only brisk good cheer. "I have come across the most splendid orange cat, but the fellow needs a name, and I daresay you excel at naming. I think I would call this fellow Marigold, or Melon, or Honey, or..."

She went on in that fashion, suggesting ridiculously frivolous names for a grand tom cat.

Tremont inspected the stable as he'd been taught to do when on reconnaissance. Make a mental grid of squares and scan each quadrant, slowly, as if taking in a piece of art. Don't forget to look behind, down at your own feet, *and up...*

A tousled dark head appeared in the gloom of the hayloft. Tremont touched Mrs. Merridew's arm and pointed.

"Tommie," she said. "There you are. Have you met Carrot?" Her voice was light, but not quite steady. The cat had ceased purring and was glowering at the boy.

"I hadn't any string," Tommie said. "I thought there might be string or twine in the stable, and I climbed up the ladder, but then the ladder went sideways, and I... It's too far to jump."

A ladder did, indeed, lie on its side along the empty stalls beneath the loft. The shaggy bay pony munched his hay and watched the boy with no more interest than if Tommie had been a barn swallow.

"The situation is easily remedied," Tremont said, righting the ladder and putting a boot on the lowest rung. "Down you go."

Tommie abruptly resembled a recruit who'd seen his first glimpse of an advancing French army. His breakfast might soon make a reappearance.

"Better yet, stay where you are," Tremont said. "I'll fetch you down. If you slipped on the ladder, your mama would not forgive me, so please don't fuss." He was up the ladder and into the hay mow before Tommie could muster the pride to object.

Tremont crouched down when he'd stepped free of the ladder. "On my back, and latch on like an organ grinder's monkey. If we bungle this, your mother will never let us live it down."

"You won't tell Mama I'm afraid? I went up all right, but when I looked down, my insides felt all funny, and the ladder made such an awful racket."

"The ladder is none the worse for its ordeal, and neither shall you be. Grab hold of me, and we'll be on the ground in no time."

The boy held tightly, and the ladder took their weight. Tremont had barely divested himself of the child before Mrs. Merridew thrust two stone of feline malevolence at him. He grabbed at the cat, who managed to dig twenty saber-sharp claws into his chest at once. Tremont then suffered one fabulously rotten feline breath full in the face and a near swipe to his chin, before the beast leaped free and disappeared up the ladder into the hayloft.

"I wasn't lost, Mama," Tommie said as Mrs. Merridew knelt to hug him. "The sweeps didn't get me. I was looking for a string, and I got stuck."

"You were smart not to jump," Mrs. Merridew said, brushing the hair from Tommie's eyes. "You could have broken a leg if you'd attempted to make that leap. I am very proud of your common sense, Thomas Merridew, but in the future, if you're inclined to go on a treasure hunt, you must tell me first, please."

Tremont could read Tommie's thoughts from the boy's expression. *I was only in the stable. I would have yelled for help soon. I'm fine, Mama.* Tremont caught Tommie's eye and arched one eyebrow in a fashion that Lydia claimed made him look like his father.

"Yes, Mama," Tommie muttered, "but you cannot name that cat anything silly. He won't like it."

"What about Lancelot?" Tremont said, assisting Mrs. Merridew to rise. "That's a fine name for a fellow who's a favorite with the ladies."

"Was Lancelot fierce?" Tommie asked.

"Yes, in a manner of speaking. Not always as chivalrous as he should have been, but brave and shrewd."

"What's shrivelrous?" Tommie asked.

"Honorable," his mother said, brushing at his bangs again. "Gentlemanly. Lancelot sometimes broke the rules, and he wasn't the most loyal friend to Arthur."

"Not Lancelot," Tommie said. "Arthur. The cat is Arthur, like the magical king."

"Or the king with the magical sword," Tremont muttered. "Into the house with you, Thomas. You will be surprised to learn that half the regiment was searching for you, and the ladies as well. You gave your mother quite a turn."

This gentle scold produced a look of perplexity from the boy.

"No matter," Mrs. Merridew said. "Into the house, and wash your hands and face. A stable is a dusty place, and the men will want to see for themselves that you are safe."

Tommie grinned and scampered off. "I'll go straight to the house, Mama. And I will wash both hands, and I will use soap, not just get my paws wet."

"And your face," Mrs. Merridew said with credible sternness.

Off he went as his mother watched his progress across the alley and into the garden. MacIvey and MacPherson sent up a shout, and somebody was soon banging the triangle that signaled mess call.

Mrs. Merridew remained standing in the door of the stable, while Tremont scrambled mentally for something cheerful and pithy to say. As usual, nothing came to mind, but what did *that* matter when Mrs. Merridew threw herself against his chest and commenced silently weeping?

Harry Merridew had been one man out of many, not a representative sample of the whole gender. Papa had been one man out of many. Aunt Portia had offered those observations a hundred times, and still, Matilda expected that every man would either judge her or... worse.

She wept on Lord Tremont's shoulder, with relief, with exhaustion, with gratitude.

"You called him 'our Tommie,'" she said, trying for some semblance of composure. "You barely know that child..."

Lord Tremont had the gift of calm. He made no move to set Matilda from him, didn't pat her shoulder nervously, or let his hands hang uselessly at his sides.

He held her easily, as if they frequently came together for a little hug at odd moments of the day. Like a friend, or... Matilda had so little experience with undemanding embraces from grown men that analogies failed her.

"I know that boy," Tremont replied. "He's everything good and dear and terrifying about childhood. Were it not for the vigilance of my older sister, my mother would have disowned me before my eighth birthday in sheer defense of her wits."

He had such a beautiful voice, soothing and substantial. Matilda allowed herself one last shuddery breath in his arms before she stepped back.

"And then you went for a soldier," she said. "Every mother's worst nightmare."

Tremont passed her a plain linen handkerchief and took to politely studying the market pony, munching hay in its stall.

"The chimney sweeps must be a worse fear for you," he said, "or the street gangs and abbesses. By the time a fellow takes the king's shilling, he has some sense. At Tommie's age, a boy is a bundle of curiosity and invincibility."

The words confirmed that Matilda's fear for her son was reasonable rather than hysterical. Why had nobody else—ever—given her those words?

"Tommie is smart, but you are right—he hasn't any sense of how wicked the world can be, and he is all..." *All I have in the world.* Matilda blotted her eyes and fumbled for a more dignified turn of phrase.

"All you have of your husband?" Tremont asked, opening the door to the pony's stall and retrieving the water bucket. He took a brush down from a hook on the stall door, gave the bucket a thorough scrubbing, and tossed the water onto the cobbles.

"I wasn't about to say that Tommie is all I have of Harry."

Tremont set the bucket beneath a pump in the stable yard and worked the pump handle. "I was all my mother had of my father, or so she claimed. I did wonder if Lydia was a gift from the fairies, and I cannot imagine what my sister felt to be so overlooked. She's married to Captain Dylan Powell now, and I daresay the boot is rather on the other foot. If I lined up a hundred comely, accomplished, fascinating women, Powell would have eyes only for Lydia, and conversely."

Tremont returned the bucket to the pony's stall, gave the beast a scratch beneath his hairy chin, and closed the stall door.

"Lady Lydia's marriage is happy," Matilda said. "A blessing, that. We should go back to the house, but I will not leave this stable without thanking you for finding my son."

"Now, Mrs. Merridew, I distinctly heard the boy say he wasn't lost." Tremont offered his arm. Despite the gravity of that gesture, something in his gaze suggested he was twitting Matilda.

"Tommie was lost *to me*," Matilda said, wrapping her hand into the crook of the earl's elbow. "And that is more than sufficient to justify my thanks. I must thank the men as well. How does one make such a gesture to a lot of fellows who pride themselves on their toughness?"

"They rather do, don't they?" Tremont held the garden gate for her. "And yet, the men enjoy a joke probably more than most and were forever pranking one another in camp."

"Did they prank you?" Even as she asked the question, Matilda realized that Tremont had gently led the conversation away from missing little boys and onto safer footing.

"After a few initial gestures of welcome, they did not. I was considered a very slow top as an officer. I am younger than most of them, and I had no experience on campaign whatsoever. We had an absolute snake for a commanding officer. Dunacre was all smiles and protocol when the generals came around, but delighted in ordering the men flogged or sent on forced marches in blistering heat. I suppose the rank and file pitied me because I was Dunacre's preferred verbal whipping boy, though he could not order me beaten, in fact."

"That's awful, to have to fight the war on two fronts like that. Major MacKay said Napoleon was defeated in part because fighting in both Spain and to the east spread Napoleon's forces too thin."

"Those of us under Dunacre did fight a war on two fronts," Tremont said, holding the door to the back hall for Matilda. "You are right about that, but the enemy was defeated, and now we face different challenges."

"What happened to him?" Matilda asked, pausing on the threshold to study Tremont's face. He exuded an air of amiable rectitude generally, but she had heard him in the library, doing more to organize the search in five minutes than the whole household had done in an hour of shouting and stumbling about.

Tremont could think quickly and strategically, despite his claim to be a plodder.

He'd divined *how* to find Tommie and thus *where* to find Tommie, suggesting a canniness that was kept well hidden, perhaps even from the man himself.

"Dunacre fell at Waterloo," Tremont said. "Friendly fire, snipers —the stories vary. He was given a hero's burial."

Matilda thought back to Vicar Delancey's eulogy for Harry. "More than he deserved. I'm glad he's dead."

The look Tremont gave her was hard to parse. Wistful, perhaps? "You are very fierce, Mrs. Merridew."

She patted his chest. "So are you. That shall be our secret, though I suspect the men are on to you."

She made her way to the library, where some of the searching party had reassembled. Tommie sat on Amos Tucker's lap, holding forth about how dark the hay mow was and the great clatter the ladder had made when it plummeted to the ground.

"Let him have his moment," Tremont said quietly, coming up on Matilda's side. "He was brave. He kept his head. He meant no harm. You can scold him later for being a dunderhead too."

And there it was again, proof that Tremont was not the dullard he portrayed himself to be. As Matilda watched a lot of former soldiers make much of a small boy, she wanted to cry. She instead squeezed Tremont's hand, whispered a suggestion to him, and slipped from the room.

She heard Tremont announce that supper would be a roast of beef and that Tommie would choose a dessert from the selections available at the bakery. The safe return of any prodigal deserved a feast, news which was greeted with a great cheer from the men.

By the time Matilda reached the bottom of the steps, she was once again crying into his lordship's plain linen handkerchief. Some prodigals who found their way home were given a feast in welcome.

Others were not.

CHAPTER FOUR

How does a woman learn to cry without making a sound?

Two days after Tommie's great adventure, Tremont was still pondering that question. Mrs. Merridew prattled on about literacy being more important than table manners while Tremont nodded politely and pondered further. In the stable, the lady had been as upset as a woman could be, short of grieving for a deceased loved one, and yet, her tears had been soundless.

Tremont had held her, thus he'd felt the tremors pass through her, felt the heat radiate from her, heard the slightest catch in her breathing. He'd seen female tears of all stripes—years of Mama's polite sniffles, the great histrionic displays of the camp followers, and everything in between. He'd never seen a woman so parsimonious about expressing justified upset, and he disliked what that much self-restraint implied.

"You are suggesting that we start with teaching the men their letters?" Tremont said.

Mrs. Merridew poured him a second cup of tea. She made a graceful picture, two fingers holding the lid of the teapot, her body canted slightly along the same curve as the porcelain spout. She added the merest drop of honey and passed him the cup and saucer.

In the few days she'd been in Tremont's employ, she'd subtly transformed the guest parlor. The rugs were brighter, the windows cleaner, the brass candlesticks gleaming, and the hearth swept. More than that, the room bore the light scent of lemon oil, and the chimney no longer smoked.

A bouquet of dried hydrangeas picked up the blue hues in the carpet and curtains, and the candles in their holders for once all stood perfectly straight.

Had she done the work herself? Supervised the maids? Asked the men to lend a hand? Tremont followed Napoleon's example and did not ask for details when a general was getting impressive results.

"If a man can read," Mrs. Merridew said, "he can peruse the etiquette manuals, should he wish to learn how to properly hand a lady into a coach. He can read the little pamphlets about tying a fancy knot in his cravat. He can memorize Proverbs to give himself enough pithy aphorisms to sound wise on any occasions. If he has no letters, he must beg another for all that information."

"That was me in the military," Tremont said. "Poring over the manuals—and the army has a deuced lot of manuals—but still needing somebody to show me the obvious. I was a laughingstock for a time, then I realized that the regiment functioned better when I remained in that role."

She put a tea cake on his plate. "When did you realize that?"

"When my superior officer was preparing to hang a man for horse thievery, and I could instead claim that the beast had got away from me while I was trying to saddle him myself."

"That superior officer would be Dunacre?" She made his name sound like a foul disease.

"The very one. My groom had merely taken my gelding to the far side of the river for some decent grazing. He had not first gained my permission, though, so when Dunacre asked where my horse was, some confusion resulted. I was a peer, Dunacre's social superior despite his father being a marquess, and he delighted in making me look like an ass."

"So you obliged him, and nobody was murdered in the name of military protocol."

"Not that time." Tremont took a sip of his tea and cast about for any means of changing the subject. "For the men who are not literate, I agree that learning their letters is appropriate, but some of the fellows can read, and MacIvey can read in both English and Gaelic. MacPherson was sent to convalesce under the quartermaster's watchful eye, so he's a fair hand at ciphering."

Mrs. Merridew cocked her head, and only then did Tremont catch the faint echo of a child's voice coming from the library. A man's quieter rumble replied.

"Who keeps the books for this establishment?" she asked, as if there had been no interruption.

"I do. Captain Powell reviews them for me when he's in Town, but the ledgers are simple. I was hoping you might take them on."

"And leave you more time to hunt for a countess?"

Oh, that. "One cannot produce a legitimate heir unless one is married, so yes." Lydia and Mama were growing positively agitated on the topic of the next Countess of Tremont, and Powell—damn his smirking silences—was no sort of ally to a fellow beset by female schemes.

"Please do explain the ledgers to me," Mrs. Merridew said, "though I would prefer that we entrust them eventually to MacPherson."

"What task will you give MacIvey?"

"If he can read, he might do well in the kitchen."

"As a cook's apprentice?" An interesting suggestion.

"Cook needs the help, and MacIvey knows how to charm her. She's from Aberdeenshire, and he can understand her Doric."

Tremont hadn't known where Cook hailed from, only that her accent was nigh unintelligible, while her soups were ambrosial.

"What have you found for Tommie to do?"

"He is assigned to the maids, who are dusting in the library this morning. I believe Tucker is on hand to assist, or to keep Tommie from climbing the bookcases."

"I used to do that, and it's much harder to climb down a bookcase than to climb up one. You will make me a list of proposed activities for the men?"

"Give me a week," Mrs. Merridew said, setting down her tea cup. "The trick for me has been to find each man alone or in the company of only one or two trusted familiars. I cannot suit a fellow to a task if I have no sense of the man."

And she, being observant and astute, could gain that sense over the course of only a few discussions.

"You will work wonders, I am sure. Shall we confer again in a week's time?"

"Of course, my lord. I'll look for you Tuesday next." She rose, and Tremont was obliged by manners to get to his feet as well. Why was adult life an unrelenting exercise in doing things a fellow did not want to do?

"Shall I look in on the boy?" he asked. "One has wondered how Tommie is faring."

Mrs. Merridew's smile shifted from polite to bewildered. "He speaks to me of nothing but skipping rocks, and hot chocolate, and making another trip to the bakery to choose our Sunday dessert. You have made quite an impression, my lord."

And that, apparently, was not a cheering development. What boy would not want an earl among those taking an interest in his welfare? As Mrs. Merridew escorted Tremont to the library, it occurred to him that the problem was not the boy, the problem was the mother.

She was ambivalent about Tremont's notice of her son. "Was your marriage happy, Mrs. Merridew?"

She halted six paces from the library door. "I beg your pardon?"

"Your marriage, was it happy? The question is doubtless impertinent—I do apologize—but you did remark about my sister's union with Powell, and you seem inordinately wary of allowing me to form a connection with your son. Tommie is a delightful child, and I mean him no harm."

Mrs. Merridew ran her hand over a deal table and rubbed her thumb and forefinger together. The table wanted dusting. By the time Tremont paid his call next week, the whole house would have the sort of contented shine he'd seen in the guest parlor.

But would Mrs. Merridew be any easier in Tremont's presence— would *she* have a contented shine?—and why did he want that for her?

"I am supposed to tell you," she said, "that Harry Merridew had many fine qualities. A wonderful sense of humor, charm, industry, ingenuity, determination... And I would not be lying."

"But you would be prevaricating." Tremont hated Harry Merridew in that moment, though if Harry had been a paragon, would Tremont have hated him more? "The late Mr. Merridew disappointed you."

"When I got word of his death, I wept, my lord, with relief rather than grief. This doubtless makes me monstrous in your eyes—my father certainly regarded me as such—but if I'm to be a monster, at least I can be an honest monster."

"Matilda Merridew, you are not now, nor have you ever been, a monster. Shame upon him who said you were, and shame upon him who disappointed you." Tremont included both her father and her late husband among that number.

She smiled at him, a slow sunrise of warmth, pleasure, and feminine approval. The whole woman changed, becoming mysterious and lovely. Tremont did not know how to return such a smile, how to reflect her joy and magnificence back at her, but, oh, he wanted to.

"Do you have a list, my lord?"

Her question made no sense. "A list?"

"For your countess. The lady you will be seeking throughout the Little Season and beyond if necessary."

Had Tremont's horse been shot out from under him, he could not have been more disconcerted, but he rallied.

"I do, as it happens. One wants to go about the business with some sort of plan, and I did make a list."

Mrs. Merridew made a *say on* gesture with her hand.

Such disclosures only ended in disaster, but Tremont would not argue with this lady. "She must be of sound mind, gracious, and well organized. Content with rural society, but capable of comporting herself well in Town. Prudent, but not miserly. Take care with her appearance without being vain. Well-read, but not a literary snob. Intelligent, not arrogant. Of good character and of good humor as well. Need I go on?"

Something loud thumped on the carpet in the library—a small boy leaping from a bookcase, perhaps.

"You describe yourself in a ball gown, my lord, and you leave out the most important factor."

"I don't much care about a dowry. We're getting Tremont back on its feet, and rural Shropshire—"

Mrs. Merridew put her hand over his mouth, the scent a peculiar blend of dust and roses and her palm not exactly petal-smooth.

"*She must love you,*" Mrs. Merridew said. "She must love the man you are and hold you in honest, sincere esteem." She dropped her hand, squared her shoulders, and faced the library door. "Settle for nothing less. Not for her charm, her gracious wit, or her pretty smile, much less her perishing dowry. Demand her love and give her yours in return. Good day, my lord, and good hunting."

Tremont had promised to drive Miss Caroline Pringle in the park that afternoon, a task which had shifted in the last two minutes from pointless to vexing. He had no intention of marrying Miss Pringle. She gossiped, she clung to his arm in public, and her father had made all manner of vulgar allusions to generous settlements.

Her mother was a chattering phenomenon designed to strike terror into the hearts of young bachelors, and Miss Pringle was said to have a brother on remittance in Rome. Tremont had offered to take her driving out of something akin to pity or duty or a confused mixture of the two, so tour the park with her he would—all the while praying for rain.

The more pressing task, though, was to find out everything known about the late Harry Merridew. A fellow did not entirely lose his native complement of curiosity simply because he grew up, went to war, or became a peer of the realm.

"I tell you, 'Arry, she's not there."

A man as smart as Harry Merriman, formerly Harry Merridew, Harmon Merryfield, Hal Marigold, et cetera, needed about three days to change his name. It felt good to be Harry again, like coming home.

Harry had found that the most important part of the transformation was to address *himself* as the new person. To mutter that name under his breath, to declaim it in conversation, and converse with his new self in the mirror.

Harry Merriman, I says to myself, what could possibly be going on?

The rest—changing the mannerisms, the speech, the signature, the clothing, the family tree, the childhood stories, the preferred haunts—all followed from changing the name. This little pub, for example, was snuggled between the shops and bachelor apartments of Knightsbridge, not a venue the happily married Harry Merri*dew* had had occasion to frequent.

He was Harry Merri*man* now, had been since he'd first set foot on English soil after three years in Dublin's fair city, traveling under various pseudonyms.

"What do you mean?" Harry asked, nudging the opposite chair a few inches away from the table with his boot. "Matilda has to be there. That house is the only property she owns, and she'd sell it before she and the boy took charity." Matilda was a proud sort, determined to maintain the properties, poor dear. Much like her father, did she but know it.

"Windows are boarded over," Spartacus Lykens replied, running a hand through red hair fading to blond at the temples. "Steps ain't been scrubbed for days, according to the neighbors. No coal going down the chute. The lady and her boy lived belowstairs, but the boy ain't been seen neither, and nobody's lived in the upper part of the 'ouse proper for weeks."

Matilda would never be parted from that child. Harry was counting on her maternal devotion, in fact.

"This, my dear Sparky, is what you call your interesting development." London required being more conscientious about diction, a return to the speech of Harry Merridew, who had been ever so eloquent when courting his bride.

"She's piked off on ya," Sparky replied, tossing himself into the chair Harry had offered. "Your missus was too pretty not to remarry. Some other fellow come along and crooked his finger at her. We'd best get back to Dublin."

Sparky was very attached to his Dublin landlady. Harry doubted that good woman's affection had been exclusively reserved for dear Sparky, though she'd been fond of him.

A female had to be practical. Maybe Matilda had turned up practical?

"She attended at St. Mildred's," Harry said. "Time you reacquainted yourself with divine services, Sparky. Sunday finest, end of the back pew for you. A few quiet inquiries. You knew the lady's late husband and promised him you'd look her up if you were ever in London. He did dote on his missus, did old Harry."

"Which 'Arry was you then?" Sparky asked, signaling the girl at the bar. "Merrifield, Merribrook? Merrimount? I get them all confused."

"Merri*dew*, as in 'I do.' Don't bungle that, my friend."

The tankard arrived, and Sparky blew the foam onto the plank floor with practiced dispatch. "Merry Hell, you ought to call yourself.

Why can't you leave the lady in peace, 'Arry? She done nothin' to you."

"She married me, and that means I cannot marry elsewhere, not without risking the noose, so she owes me."

Sparky downed a quarter of his pint and wiped his mouth on his sleeve. "You married her, too, if I recall the particulars. Good ale. London ain't all bad."

"London as winter approaches is a trial. I wouldn't be here unless I'd studied long and hard on the matter." Then too, Dublin was a close-knit town, and Harry's welcome had grown perilously tarnished there. "If I'm alive, Matilda doesn't yet own that house."

Sparky heaved up a resigned sigh. "You said the prop'ty came to her from an auntie. Aunties is always conferrin' with solicitors, and solicitors is always creatin' problems. Maybe your missus don't own that 'ouse, but you don't neither. I thought you swore off sellin' 'ouses you don't own."

"I am the trustee. Matilda's papa had taken her into disfavor by the time I married her, and there wasn't anybody else who could serve. The lawyers didn't like it, and they set it up so that the boy got the house if both parents died during his minority. Thought they were being clever, but Matilda cannot sell that house if I'm alive— only I can do that."

Sparky took another pull on his pint and aimed a baleful expression at Harry. "You wasn't that hard up in Dublin, mate. You coulda laid low, nipped up to Derry, but instead, you'll swindle yer own widda outta her last mite."

"I'll do no such thing. I will split the proceeds with Matilda, assuming she isn't some lord's fancy piece or engaged to a prosperous cit by now." St. Mildred's wasn't the sort of congregation to have fancy lords stacked three deep in the loft, but a retired sea captain or gentry scion would have been within Tilly's reach there.

She'd gone *somewhere* with the boy, after all. Tilly was an attractive woman, when she wasn't all pinched up and broody. She'd been sweet once, too, and appallingly trusting.

Though the boy would give any man pause. Taking on another's fellow's get wasn't for the faint of heart or short of coin. A fancy lord might take Matilda on as his commodity, but he'd not marry a woman hauling a brat around behind her.

Harry had trouble picturing Matilda as a siren. Not a role she'd try on out of anything other than necessity.

"I despair of you, 'Arry." Sparky addressed his observation to the depths of his mug. "You were no sort of 'usband, you frittered away her money, and now you won't stay dead."

"Bad form, I know, but needs must. Last I heard, she hasn't remarried. She either misses me or has learned her lesson, and if she's not inclined to remarry, and she is finding consolation in the arms of a willing fellow, that creates another potentially interesting situation."

Oh, the possibilities when a fancy lord took up with another man's wife. Harry should have seen those possibilities much sooner.

"I miss Dublin," Sparky muttered. "One of yer 'ouse-sellin' rigs will keep a man in style for ages—or it should. Blackmail lacks fynesse."

"I have a gentleman's tastes, Sparky. What can I say?" And Sparky disliked blackmail precisely because it did take a delicate and patient touch, albeit such schemes lacked originality.

"Why don't you just sell her 'ouse like you done them others? Pretend you own it, which you almost do, and then let it go at a fair price to another half-pay officer with six brats."

"He had only five brats, and his brother bought the house for him rather than have the brats invade the family seat. The brother didn't need the money, and I did."

Sparky finished his drink. "And the brats needed that 'ouse, but now there's no money and no 'ouse, thanks to you. You used to limit your marks to grown men who oughta know better."

Sparky's reproach stung a little, because it was true. A confidence man was allowed to lie to anybody but himself. "The officer was a grown man, and his brother should have known better."

"End of the month," Sparky said, rising, "I'm fer Dublin. Told

Mary I'd tarry in London but a few weeks, catch up with old friends and look in on me sister. I'll stop around St. Mildred's and see what I can learn, but you'd be better off approaching yer missus quietlike and throwin' yourself on her mercy. She's not using the 'ouse, so maybe she don't need the money. She for damned sure don't need you."

Sparky had a sister. That dubious blessing could skew a fellow's perspective in sentimental directions.

"Matilda did need me," Harry said, "and I came to her rescue, and then there's the boy."

"You think you are so clever." Sparky patted a battered top hat onto his head. "But if your widda has got her 'ooks into a real gentleman, you may get the worse of the whole scheme, 'Arry Misery-Do. London ain't your turf no more, you don't got but a bit of coin, and the Quality stick together. You also ain't 'alf so 'andsome and dashing as you was in your misspent youth. Best tread lightly and move along soon as may be."

"Easy for you to say." Harry stood as well, because the bench was hard, and the discussion had been oddly unsettling. "You can scarper back to Ireland and spend the rest of your days cuddling up to your darling Mary. I can't go back to Dublin, and I've also worn out my welcome in Liverpool and Manchester. I don't speak Frog, and I've no taste for Scottish winters."

"Ain't it a shame how nobody has any use for Old 'Arry?" Sparky smiled at his own joke, Old Harry being one of the devil's many monikers. Sparky touched a finger to his hat brim, put a coin on the table, and nodded to the barmaid.

Some youthful brawl gone awry had left Sparky limping, though he quit the premises with an odd sort of dignity. Harry took a moment to gather up his walking stick, hat, and gloves. He was too old to play a university graduate trying to acquire Town bronze, so he was a prosperous squire in London on business. True, he wasn't as dashing as he'd once been, but he could now project an air of substance that a younger man only dreamed of.

He consulted his squire's pocket watch, which hadn't kept accurate time since Hambletonian had won the match race against Diamond, though the timepiece was a convincing prop. For one instant, staring at the unmoving hands of the little clock face, Harry considered doing as Sparky had suggested—throwing himself on Matilda's mercy, asking for her forgiveness, taking what funds she'd spare him, and leaving her in peace.

Tilly would like that—being asked for forgiveness.

But would she like it enough? Once upon a time, Harry had known what Matilda was thinking simply by watching her eyes. She'd learned to don disguises of her own in the course of the marriage, a useful skill for any woman, and one that meant Harry could not stake his future on what he'd known of her years ago.

The barmaid called a greeting to a patron sauntering through the door, a young gent, clearly from means. He tipped his hat to her and blew her a kiss. The barmaid brought him his drink before he'd taken off his gloves.

What if Matilda *had* taken up with a lord or finagled an engagement to a retired sea captain? That would change the game considerably, and not in her favor. Harry left the pub with the brisk gait of a man who was punctual for all of his appointments and entirely at home navigating the vast labyrinth of London's streets.

"Harry Merriman," he muttered to himself, "the opportunities for an enterprising man are endless."

"What do you know of the late Harry Merridew?" Tremont asked, trying to make the question sound casual.

Alasdhair MacKay lifted the eagle-shaped stopper of a crystal decanter. "A wee nip to ward off the chill, my lord?"

Tremont gave his mental backside another stout kick. Small talk. A gentleman made small talk when calling on his acquaintances.

MacKay, fortunately, appeared more amused than offended at Tremont's lapse.

"A wee nip of your whisky will knock me upon my lordly fundament."

"Half a nip, then, with a few drops of water, because you would otherwise force me to drink alone. I haven't had my tot for the day, and the temperature is dropping."

"Snow on the way," Tremont said, going to the window. The parlor was cozy, made especially so by the green and white tartan blanket folded over the back of the sofa, and the green, white, and purple thistle motif embroidered into both pillows and draperies. The sky, by contrast, was a sullen gray.

"Early for snow," MacKay said, "but the sinking feeling in my Highland bones agrees with you. Now that we've discussed the weather, why do you want to know about Harry Merridew?"

It became necessary to study the overcast. "Did she love him?" Tremont had considered and pondered and thought on the matter at some length. Harry Merridew had been a disappointment to his wife, but a lady could only be disappointed in a man she esteemed.

Ergo, Matilda had loved her husband, despite his shortcomings. Did she still pine for him, or would she be amenable to reentering the state of holy matrimony with a suitable party?

A theoretical question—mostly.

"My Dorcas was right, then."

Dorcas was Mrs. Major Alasdhair MacKay, also the daughter of the current vicar at St. Mildred's. A brisk, practical sort of woman, who put Tremont in mind of his sister.

"Your Dorcas suggested I find a widow to manage my soldiers' home, and she was right about that. A discerning woman, despite her choice of spouse."

MacKay laughed and poured a few drops of water into a scant portion of whisky. "We can say that about many ladies. Perhaps your Mrs. Merridew was one of them." He passed over the glass and poured a more substantial portion for himself. "*Slàinte!*"

"*Slàinte mhath.*"

MacKay's dark brows rose. "Do you speak the Erse, Tremont?"

"I picked up a bit in camp. You know how it was. Boredom upon boredom punctuated by the occasional attempt at mutual slaughter. If my sergeant took a bullet in the heat of battle, there I'd be, unable to tell the men to retreat or charge or form up... Another bullet to the bugler, and the day would have been lost. Bonaparte should have concentrated on neutralizing those two classes of soldier rather than on playing capture the flag. For our part, all field officers should have been made to learn all the commands in English, Gaelic, and German. To write them and speak them. That would have saved far more lives than stuffing our heads with Latin year after year at public school."

MacKay gave Tremont the same look Dylan Powell occasionally aimed his way. As if some denizen of the hog wallow had become airborne.

"To answer your question," MacKay said, gesturing to a wing chair before the blazing hearth, "Mrs. Merridew was already widowed by the time I set foot at St. Mildred's. She was newly graduated from first mourning. I have the sense nobody raises the topic of her late husband out of consideration for her. He didn't leave her much, I can tell you that."

Tremont took the second chair. "One noticed the obvious, MacKay."

"Obvious to you, perhaps. Dorcas had to speak very candidly to her father before he realized that Matilda Merridew was hanging on by her fingernails. The church began using her as a scribe. The bachelors and widowers send her their mending. She takes over in the nursery here one afternoon a week."

"Thursdays," Tremont said. "She insisted her half day be Thursday, and she plans to spend it watching your hooligan of a son." Not MacKay's son in a biological sense, though nobody could love a child more fiercely than the MacKays did that little boy.

"What else would you have us do, Tremont? Mrs. Merridew is

proud, she's proud, and she can't exactly..." MacKay's drink stopped halfway to his lips. "If you ruin her, Dorcas will geld you. She has a pathological loathing for those who take advantage of women. Mrs. Merridew is a lady, for all she's not wealthy. And if Dorcas disdains to deal with you, I will do so instead. You proposition Matilda Merridew at your peril."

"I am far from perfect, MacKay, but exploiting a lady fallen on hard times is not in my nature. I am simply curious, my besetting sin. The welfare of a dozen men and a half-dozen staff rests in her hands. I hired her without investigating her circumstances as thoroughly as I should have."

A prevarication, that, so Tremont added the honest bit. "I am also impressed with her personally, but I would not bother her with expressions of my esteem if she's still pining for her late husband."

"You aren't impressed, you are smitten, you poor devil."

"Smitten?"

"You dwell on her in your mind," MacKay said, sounding oddly wistful. "The thought of her replaces all your worries and idle imaginings. Her smile becomes your Holy Grail and her form the standard by which you measure all other females."

"You forgot the part about no old master ever penned an air to compare with the melody of her voice and her laughter... I haven't heard her laugh, MacKay. I must hear her joyous outpourings, or I shall perish... and so forth. I have no idea how this has happened, and I've hoped that the malady would fade as swiftly as it befell me, but she lectures me, MacKay."

"About?"

"My perfect countess, how to go on with the men, and then she looks at that child... She is fierce and brave and shrewd, and all the while, she has the world thinking she's just another genteel lady living a quietly penurious life on a quiet street and in a quiet neighborhood."

"You seek to rescue her?"

"The boot rather goes on the other foot, Major. You should see what she's done with the soldiers' home in just a few days. The lady was born to command."

"An odd thing to say about a woman, Tremont."

"My father died when I was a boy. My uncle soon began pillaging the estate as my trustee, and thwarting him was left to my mother and sister, the housekeeper and staff. They hid what jewels my mother didn't pawn. My sister kept household books for Uncle that bore no resemblance to reality. She and Mama and the tenants held the estate together while I was off playing soldier. For a woman to command takes all the same skills a man has, plus a complement of determination, thespian skill, and deviousness men never develop. Ask your Dorcas who ran St. Mildred's when she was at the vicarage."

"I take your point." MacKay finished his drink and set the glass aside. "She's still doing half her father's job. Dorcas says you notice more than you let on. You should ask her about Harry Merridew, or better still, ask Vicar Delancey. He notices more than he lets on too."

"I will do just that, though I must take my leave of you if I'm not to be late for tea with Mrs. Merridew."

"You should move along, then," MacKay said, rising. "That sky means business, and a fellow doesn't make the best impression when he's sopping wet and shivering."

Tremont rose, though the cozy chair by the fire tempted him to linger. He'd accomplished his purpose—to learn what MacKay knew of Harry Merridew, though that amounted to precisely nothing useful.

"Who are Mrs. Merridew's friends?" Tremont asked. "With whose children does Tommie play on fine days? With whom does she walk to services or linger in the churchyard?"

MacKay took the glasses to the sideboard. "There you go, noticing again. As best I can recall, Matilda Merridew arrives at services escorted by only Tommie, and she doesn't linger in the churchyard. Now that you ask about it, she strikes me as a rather solitary woman."

"For a widow with a small boy, that is unfortunate, MacKay. A woman needs friends." Did an earl need friends?

"She does, which gives you something to ponder, doesn't it?"

"Something more. Thank you for the libation and the conversation. Please do drop around on the odd afternoon if you're so inclined. I am home most days."

Tremont's host had escorted him to the front door, where no butler or footman stood on duty. An informal household, and it had the same sense of cozy repose that Mrs. Merridew had imparted to her guest parlor.

"I heard you were courting the Pringle girl," MacKay said. "Any truth to that rumor?"

MacKay had certainly kept his powder dry. "None, and if you would do your bit to ensure talk to the contrary is scotched, I would appreciate it. She's a delightful young lady..."

"But her smile does not signify."

"Her smile is for my title and standing, and because her mama insists that I be smiled at. The young lady deserves better." *As do I.* At least in the opinion of Matilda Merridew.

"Good heavens," said a female voice. "We're having a regular open house today. Major, you did not tell me you have a guest too."

Dorcas MacKay stood on the landing six steps above the foyer. She was smiling in a wifely sort of way, and beside her stood Matilda Merridew.

Who was also smiling.

At Tremont.

"This is fortuitous," MacKay said, a bit too heartily. "Tremont can escort Mrs. Merridew home, and they'd best hurry if they're to avoid nasty weather."

"A happy coincidence," Mrs. MacKay added, coming down the rest of the steps with her guest. "And the major is correct that you will want to be on your way with all possible haste. The days grow so short this time of year."

Tremont allowed himself to be hustled out the door with Mrs.

Merridew on his arm, though they hadn't gone three steps along the walkway before the lady made an odd sound, then she put her gloved hand over her mouth, and it dawned on Tremont that she was laughing—or trying not to.

Tremont tried for manly composure, but the sheer determination in the MacKays' matchmaking had exceeded all bounds. Thus did Marcus, Earl of Tremont, stand on the walkway, laughing with Mrs. Matilda Merridew, and as the first bitter flurries wafted from the sky, the sun burst forth in his heart.

And, he hoped, in hers too.

CHAPTER FIVE

Lord Tremont had a surprisingly jolly laugh, all good nature and merriment. He apparently took no offense at the MacKays' machinations, while Matilda... She had hoped her inquiries of Mrs. MacKay hadn't been too obvious, and then, there stood the earl, gazing up at her from the foyer as if she'd conjured him from her abundant imaginings.

Fate playing a little joke on her, or a wish coming true?

"I have never seen Major MacKay looking so devilish," she said as she trundled along arm in arm with the earl. "When I first met him, he struck me as the quintessential dour Scot. Dorcas Delancey was the equally circumspect daughter of the vicarage, but they appear to have brought out the mischief in each other."

"Is a little mischief a bad thing, Mrs. Merridew?"

Matilda considered the question while they waited at an intersection. The snow was rapidly thickening, and street traffic was hustling along. The crossing sweeper marched out into the middle of the passing vehicles and brandished his broom in both directions. The boy's trousers were raggedly hemmed a good six inches above his skinny ankles, and the lumbering coaches dwarfed him.

"It's hard to imagine that one is entitled to any mischief," she said, "when a child must face this weather. That could be Tommie—shivering, underfed, a hairsbreadth away from tragedy if some drunken lordling goes racing by in his phaeton. I was raised in a vicarage—I have that in common with Mrs. MacKay—and such an upbringing takes a jaundiced view of mischief."

"Perhaps 'mischief' is the wrong word," Tremont said, guiding Matilda across the slick cobbles. "Maybe the term I want is 'joy.' Glee, high spirits." He tossed the boy a coin, and the lad caught it in a bare, dirty paw. "In a world where children must fend for themselves from too young an age and generals send young men to their deaths by the thousands, joy can be an act of courage."

Matilda had felt a spike of joy simply to behold Tremont, and he was right—that had been an act of courage, or folly. Maybe both?

They reached the opposite side of the street, and when Tremont ought to have escorted Matilda down the walkway, he instead considered the crossing sweeper.

"The lad's name is Charles," he said. "He refuses to answer to Charlie. I've tried giving him more substantial coin, but he spends it all on his auntie, who is a sot. I doubt Charles is home much, if a home he even has."

A closed, crested carriage careened by, nearly knocking Charles off his feet.

"Tremont... He can't be nine years old."

His lordship appeared to be mentally puzzling out a geometric proof, while Matilda wanted to snatch the child off the street, sit him before a roaring fire, and acquaint him with a full plate of beef and potatoes.

"You said Cook needs more hands in the kitchen," Tremont observed, "and we've already added one boy to the household. Shall we offer the post of potboy to yonder fellow, Mrs. Merridew?"

Potboy, a job at the elbow of the cook, who would prepare six meals a day if left to her own devices. Charles would be warm and well fed and might eventually apprentice to his supervisor.

"He could also see to the men's boots on Saturday nights," Matilda said. "Shine them up for services on Sunday."

"Until he pikes off in the spring," Tremont replied. "We can but try. Charles!" He motioned the boy over to the walkway, and a parley ensued. Matilda eventually divined that Charles was reluctant to become a member of any household composed primarily of men.

A reluctance she well understood. "You will work for Cook," Matilda said, "but you will also report to me."

Charles was trying heroically to stop his teeth from chattering. "You bide there too, missus?"

"With my son, Tommie. He's a few years younger than you and will make a complete pest of himself if you allow that. The men are former soldiers, Charles. If they in any way treat you ill, they will have me to answer to."

"And me," Tremont said. "To say nothing of what our housekeeper, Mrs. Winklebleck, would do to them."

Charles's grimy countenance brightened. "Big Nan is your housekeeper?"

"She is Mrs. Winklebleck now," Matilda said, "and a more cheerful housekeeper you never did meet. Please say you will assist us, Charles, or least give it a try."

"I'll lose me patch," the boy said. "If I'm gone three days, some other lad'll take me patch. That's the rule. A fellow can miss on Sundays, and he can take ill for a day or two while the other boys keep his corner tidy, but three days straight means he's given up his patch."

Harry had known such rules, and he'd also made up his share. "If you come work with us," Matilda said, "I will teach you to read and write. I will show you how to drive the pony cart. You will have more than coin to show for your labors, Charles. You will have skills."

"My ma could write," Charles said, sniffing as snowflakes dusted his dark hair. "Some."

"Why don't you look the place over?" Tremont said. "You know where it is?"

"Aye."

"Reconnaissance is a vital part of any successful mission," the earl went on, "and you shouldn't accept the job without some idea of what you're getting into. Tell Cook we're taking you on, have her show you where you'd sleep and what your duties would be. Make up your own mind. Nobody will steal your patch if you take a day or two to do that, and this weather will soon have the streets cleared in any case."

Another man would have been arguing with the child, or worse, ordering him to give up his trade for what might be a terrible position. As a crossing sweeper, Charles set his own hours, kept all of his pay, worked no harder than he pleased, and was never beaten for a job poorly done.

None of which mattered with a winter storm bearing down. Matilda was about to shove Charles off in the direction of the house when he held out his hand to Tremont.

"I'll give it a looking over, milord, like you said, but I can come back to me patch if I'd rather."

Tremont shook. "You scout the terrain for yourself, and Mrs. Merridew and I will await your decision. If you cut through that alley there, you'll save yourself some time."

Charles gathered up his barrow, broom, and shovel and trotted off into the thickening snow.

"Perhaps we should take the alley," Matilda said. "This is turning into quite a squall."

"I have another idea," Tremont replied as they resumed walking. "We can seek shelter along the way, and twenty minutes from now, the snow will have stopped."

"You suggest we tarry at the tea shop?" A delightful notion, particularly given that Tommie was not underfoot.

"The tea shop is one street over in the wrong direction, but my town house is right around the corner."

Matilda nearly lost her footing. The Earl of Tremont was inviting her *into his home*. True, the hour was technically appropriate for paying calls, and she was a widow and thus needed no chaperone, but still...

"Maybe this is how Charles felt when confronted with a suspiciously tempting offer," Matilda said.

"We were to discuss how you're settling in and what plans you have for the men," Tremont replied. "Why not do so in comfort while Charles makes his inspection tour of the soldiers' home?"

Reason. Tremont was the very devil for applying sweet reason. "That place needs a different name," Matilda said. "'Soldiers' home' brings to mind grizzled, arthritic men rendered deaf by artillery rounds fired decades in the past. Our lot is hale and relatively young."

"I had not thought of naming the house, but that makes sense, and now, with you newly appointed to your post, is a perfect time to do it."

The wind gusted, nearly knocking Matilda off her feet. She took a snug hold of Tremont's arm. "Get me out of this weather, my lord, and we can name the house anything you please."

Matilda capitulated to the earl's offer with equal parts misgiving and anticipation. She'd wondered if his domicile would be as neat and understated as he was, or would the mental absorption of the philosopher mean boots were left in the library, and a half-full brandy glass had been abandoned in a linen closet?

He'd called himself curious, while Matilda thought of herself as cautious. Curiosity and caution were not mutually exclusive, apparently.

A dozen doors on, Tremont led her up a set of steps to a modest, tidy house. Somebody had already swept the walkway free of snow once, and the brass fixtures around the door lamps gleamed despite the day's gloom.

"Before we go in," he said, pausing inside the recessed doorway, "you should know something."

The lamps had not yet been lit, and the alcove was out of the wind, giving it a confessional air. "Say on, my lord." If he was leaving for Shropshire, that might be for the best, though Tommie would be disappointed.

"I had a definite purpose for calling upon MacKay, and not an entirely noble purpose." His tone was serious, his expression unreadable. "I wanted..." Tremont turned Matilda so the wind was to her back, and the meager light fell across the earl's face. "I inquired of the major regarding your late husband."

And here Matilda had hoped Tremont had inquired regarding *her*. "What possible interest could Harry Merridew hold for you?" Unless Harry's lingering and larcenous shadow was about to cost Matilda her post.

Tremont studied her, then seemed to come to a decision. "What was your reason for calling on Mrs. MacKay?"

Once upon a time, Matilda had been curious and forthright. Her father had called her ungovernable and bold, but such were the labels applied to women who failed to simper and scrape. Matilda would never entirely escape the damage marriage to Harry had done, but with Tremont, she could be a little less cautious and a little more honest.

"I inquired regarding you, my lord."

"Because I hired you to manage the men?"

Dignity whispered to Matilda to retire behind that proffered fig leaf. Courage demanded that, with Tremont, she put such cowering aside.

"I did not ask my questions of Mrs. MacKay because you hired me to manage the men, not entirely."

Tremont stared past her shoulder. "I see." He lifted the latch and bowed Matilda into the foyer.

I see? What did *I see* mean? Matilda had developed the ability to read Harry as closely as she'd ever attended to Scripture. She'd learned to parse his silences, to listen for the schemes brewing beneath his jests and cryptic asides. By the time he'd died, Harry had been an open book to her, one she had studied out of dread necessity.

Tremont appeared preoccupied as he set her bonnet on a hook, took her scarf and gloves, and then her cloak. Matilda slid his cloak from his shoulders, and when he turned to her, he still had the look of trying to solve a puzzle in his head.

"Let's find a roaring fire," he said, "and ring for tea. I am at your disposal to answer any and all questions you might have regarding my humble person, and perhaps you might answer a few questions for me as well?"

Tremont didn't smile, but Matilda suspected he was happy. So, oddly enough, was she.

"Ask me anything," she said.

When the various wraps and accessories had been stored, Tremont did not offer his arm. He, the soul of gentlemanly decorum, took Matilda by the hand, and she, the soul of genteel propriety, linked her fingers with his... and rejoiced.

As Tremont led his guest to the formal parlor, he began a mental exegesis on the topic of wooing a lady. A gentleman seeking to earn a woman's favor must be charming, witty, gracious, and... something else. Not alluring—that was for courtesans. Not wealthy, else fellows of modest means would never wed.

Further analysis of the subject eluded him because he was simply too absorbed with the pleasure of having Matilda's hand in his. Her fingers were cold, which made him want to place them directly on his person. He'd put her palms flat on his chest, inside his shirt, and cover them with his own, and feel her touch with each inhalation and exhalation...

Steady on, soldier.

"The formal parlor," he said, stopping outside a carved oak door. "Not because I am a formal sort of host, but because I know it won't be strewn with newspapers, my favorite pair of slippers, and three different books that I am reading at different times of the day."

"You enjoy reading?"

How to answer that? "I immersed myself in the philosophers as a youth and grew quite convinced of the wisdom of the Stoics. Then I went to war, and came home, and... It's complicated. I started off reading as a way to replace the wisdom of an absent parent, but now I read as some people enjoy meals. Sustenance for the mind."

Matilda went directly to the fire and splayed her hands before its warmth. Tremont tugged the bell-pull three times—tray with all the trimmings—and took a moment to behold his guest.

How could the bachelors and widowers of London not see Matilda Merridew's loveliness? She might hide her physical beauty behind drab colors, dull bonnets, and a quiet manner, but the lady had self-possession, common sense, a kind heart... and those treasures were in plain sight.

"Please do have a seat," Tremont said, patting the back of a wing chair. "Why don't you embark on your interrogation of me while we wait for our tea?"

She settled onto the cushions and motioned for him to take the other wing chair. "You want to know about my late husband."

A question in the form of a statement. Mama and Lydia excelled at that rhetorical device.

"No, actually," Tremont replied. "I want to know about the state of your affections. Are they available to be claimed by a worthy party, or did your late spouse end once and for all your willingness to look with favor on a fellow?"

"Because," Matilda replied, gaze on the fire, "if my answer is no, and my affections are not claimable, then you will make no further inquiries. Are you always this logical?"

"'Fraid so, or I aspire to be. I've landed in a deal of hot water and created misery for those dear to me by yielding to impulse."

"As have I," she said, "and yet, I am not as rational as you seem to be. My father frequently castigated me for impulsiveness."

"Was Mr. Merridew one of those impulses?"

She smiled at her hands, and Tremont had never seen more sadness in a woman's eyes.

"Harry was one of my regrettable impulses, not the first, alas. By the time he came along, my father was washing his hands of me, and my aunt was still married to a Puritanical old article. Uncle might have taken me in, but my life would have been difficult."

The first footman chose then to appear with a lavish tray heaped with comestibles.

"Thank you, Putnam," Tremont said. "That will be all. Mrs. Merridew, will you pour?"

"Of course."

Before Putnam blew retreat, he gratuitously poked up the roaring fire, lit two sconces in addition to the two already burning, and tidied decanters on the sideboard that needed no tidying.

"The garrison is on high alert," Tremont said when Putnam finally quit the parlor. "They spy for my mother and sister, but one cannot resent the family's concern. Have you no other relatives besides this auntie?"

"None," Mrs. Merridew replied. "I assume Harry had some family somewhere, but I'd have no idea how to find them, and I am entirely sure I don't care to. I want to gobble every item on this tray, not only because the food looks delicious, but also because Tommie isn't on hand to monitor my behavior."

The tray was the same as a thousand others—sandwiches, cakes, tarts, tea. Tremont put two sandwiches on a plate and passed it over. "Gobble away, and I shall do likewise. Your husband disappointed you."

Mrs. Merridew poured the tea, added honey and cream to both cups, passed Tremont his serving, and stirred her own.

Delaying tactics by any other name.

"Every spouse is probably a disappointment to their partner before the honeymoon ends," she said. "We build up our intended to impossible heights, or I did, and then reality intrudes. I disappointed Harry too."

More delaying, and had the bounder *told* her she was a disappointment?

"When I mustered out," Tremont said, "I could not bring myself to return to Shropshire. My mother and sister needed me, as did my tenants and my staff, but I was too muddled to face them. My sister had to eventually fetch me home, and she managed that only because Captain Powell abetted her efforts. My mother and sister have forgiven me my foolishness. I fear Merridew did something beyond forgiveness."

She sipped her tea, took a bite of sandwich, and took another sip of tea. "Why did you not return home, my lord?"

He deserved that, for bringing up his past. "I told myself that I wasn't fit company for my family, that I needed time to adjust to civilian life, but, in fact, I was hiding. I had made decisions—those impulsive decisions you allude to—and they haunted me. You might have noticed that I have a talent for rumination. I ruminated myself into a morass of misery from which I could not extricate myself."

Mrs. Merridew studied him as if he were one of those medieval paintings of fantastical beasts and strange flowers. What *could* one say about such a piece?

"Did you impulsively choose to marry a complete bounder thinking he was the answer to all your prayers?"

How fortunate for Harry Merridew that he was dead. "I shot my superior officer at point-blank range in front of dozens of witnesses."

Tremont did not speak of his gross breach of military protocol, civil law, and God's commandments, and neither did the men who'd seen him fire his pistol.

Mrs. Merridew set down her cup and saucer carefully, and Tremont braced himself to be told that she'd see herself out. That must be some kind of record to put a lady off before she'd finished even a single cup of tea.

"I'm not sorry I told you," Tremont said. "But you seem to think that marrying Merridew was an unforgivable offense on your part. That is simply not the case. We do the best we can, Mrs. Merridew, and one cannot control the results."

Her expression remained unreadable, so Tremont blundered on. "My superior officer was ordering us into certain, stupid death on a battlefield where every able-bodied soldier had a contribution to make. He ignored the very clear direction we'd had from headquarters and was willing to sacrifice his men on the altar of military vanity. What I did was wrong, a violation of military decorum, a crime, et cetera and so forth, and yet, I would do it again."

That speech settled something for Tremont. He'd pondered and considered and ruminated on the events at Waterloo until he was sick of the memory, but he'd never quite admitted to himself that he'd made the only possible choice.

"Your superior officer," Mrs. Merridew said, "was begging for a bullet, and you are right: From a certain perspective, I needed marrying. There is that."

A log fell on the andirons, sending a shower of sparks up the flue. In the ensuing quiet, Tremont reviewed Matilda's words in his head to make sure he had the sense of them.

"I cannot argue with you about Dunacre," he said slowly, "and the men have kept my confidence as well. Powell knows, as do my mother and sister. The memory troubles me far less than it used to." And making this confession to Matilda had shoved the whole business even further from the central location in Tremont's awareness that it had once occupied. "Would you marry the scoundrel again?"

Matilda took her time answering. "Yes, but I would have guarded my heart. I saw Harry as my savior, plucking me from the misery of the vicarage, preventing me from ruining my own good name by escorting me into the ever-respectable bounds of holy matrimony."

"Harry was escorting himself into possession of your settlement portion."

She nodded. "He could not get the house—that is my dower

house, essentially—but before he died, he was beginning to drop hints that the time had come to sell it. Harry spent every groat he could get his hands on, and the house was the last asset I had left to bequeath to my son."

Tremont added some jam tarts to the plate that held her sandwiches. "Battle lines were being drawn?"

"Hard for a woman to draw battle lines, my lord, when she has no money of her own, her husband stands nigh half a foot taller than she, and he is willing to use a mere infant as a bargaining chip. Harry used to call me Miss Dauntless, but the name came to feel more like a taunt rather than a fond nickname."

Tremont made himself ask the next question. He would rather remain in ignorance of the answer, but he did not want Matilda to be alone with the truth.

"Did he beat you?"

"He did not need to."

While she munched on a sandwich, Tremont silently counted backward from ten in Latin. "Because of the boy."

"For all your fine manners, you are a discerning man, my lord. I considered taking Tommie and running to my aunt many times after my uncle died, but the authorities would have forced Aunt to hand me and Tommie right back over to Harry."

If a deserter turned himself in, his punishment was usually to be shipped to the thick of the fighting, or worse, to the tropics, where disease would kill him as surely as any French bayonet could. If he did not turn himself in, he faced death upon capture. Parallels between enlisted military service and marriage began to insinuate themselves into Tremont's thoughts.

"We get into situations," he said, "where our choices are among bad and worse options. Did you kill your husband?" Did he hope she had?

"I did not. The notion appealed in the same way that being Queen of England appeals. I had sense enough by then to see that impulsive behavior had landed me in nothing but trouble. I had also begun to develop some weapons of my own. Harry sought desperately to be regarded as respectable, and thus I attended services. The self-same Church of England that had been such a source of frustration in my youth became a means of checking Harry's worst notions."

"If you were to pay calls, then your domicile had to have sufficient furnishings that you could receive calls, and so forth. You needed food in the larder, an acceptable wardrobe."

"Precisely. Harry had pawned every pearl brooch or nacre button I owned by then. If that man had worked half as hard at legitimate ventures as he worked at confidence games and swindles... but he did not, and most of his games came to naught. Everything about him was false, and as his lies piled atop one another, he needed to range farther afield. He was off to Oxford when he died, hatching some scheme to bilk university boys of their allowances."

Matilda started on the second sandwich. For a woman who longed to gobble, her manners were exquisite.

"Harry was not in London when he died?"

"On the Oxford Road. Food poisoning, if I'm to believe what I was told. A jealous husband is another possibility. The innkeeper made the final arrangements and sent Harry home to me in a plain coffin. I still have the letter condoling me on my loss and requesting payment for expenses incurred. Early in my widowhood, I read that letter several times a day."

"To make certain that you hadn't imagined his passing."

"I dwelled in that peculiar land between a nightmare and waking, the place where you reassure yourself that 'it was only a dream,' but your heart is pounding, and you cannot make your mouth form coherent words. Fortunately, I had Tommie, and that child demands constant supervision and regular meals."

"He's a wonderful boy. You must be very proud of him. Are you even a little bit proud of yourself? You should be."

Matilda set aside the empty sandwich plate and took to blinking at the fire. "Damn you."

Damn you. The only other person in the room was Tremont, and thus she cursed at him. A tear slipped down the curve of her cheek. Making a lady cry had to be at the top of the list of things a fellow did *not* do when trying to win her favor.

"Mrs. Merridew?" Tremont produced a handkerchief and dangled it before her. "Matilda?"

"I don't speak of my marriage," she said, snatching the linen and blotting her eyes. "I don't mention my late husband. I don't bring him up... He's dead, and buried, and gone... and..."

"And he haunts you. Dunacre haunts me." Tremont rose and went to the sideboard, rummaging about madly for what else he could say. He poured two small portions of brandy and brought a serving to his guest.

"To ward off the chill, and don't tell me ladies never partake of strong spirits. If you'd ever sipped my mother's Christmas punch, you'd know that is utter rot."

Matilda tasted her brandy. "Thank you."

Tremont resumed his seat and sampled his drink. "For making you cry?"

"For making me talk. About Harry. He was awful. One lives with disappointment, and when Harry strayed—which he regularly did—I was relieved. I wanted no children with that man, but I was his wife, and he treated me like a second pair of boots. Too useful to pawn, but hardly something to show off. He bought me a fine cloak so nobody would know the rest of my wardrobe was falling to pieces."

"He betrayed his vows, and he betrayed *you*. I'm sorry. You did not deserve the fate Merridew visited upon you, no matter how high your youthful spirits, no matter how much of a hoyden you might have been. The institution of marriage should have been a refuge and became instead a prison and your husband its warden. That is worth crying over."

Matilda nosed her brandy, which had to be among the loveliest sights Tremont had ever beheld. She hadn't let herself indulge in a good fit of the weeps, but her eyes were luminous and her color a bit high.

"You are right, my lord. Harry Merridew was the husband from hell. Everything about him, from his smiles, to his poetry, to his promises of marital bliss, was a lie. My aunt agrees with my assessment of him, but to hear a man pronounce sentence on Harry is a comfort I had not thought to have."

Why not? "I cannot vouch for my entire gender, but I'm sure Major MacKay and Captain Powell would agree with me. Have you met their cousins? Mrs. Sycamore Dorning and Colonel Sir Orion Goddard are brother and sister, and when MacKay is in town, he and his missus socialize with both."

"I've met the colonel. Wears an eye patch? I know of the Dornings."

"Half of London does. Lord Casriel and I occasionally collaborate on bills in the Lords. Managing eight siblings must be far more complicated for his lordship than dithering about with Parliament. More tea?"

The snow had settled into steady, businesslike precipitation, while conversation wandered from other mutual acquaintances to matters at the House Without a Name. By the time Tremont was escorting his guest from the parlor, she was again her usual composed self, and he was...

Engaged in another mental flight on the topic of how to woo a lady. Revisiting her worst nightmares was surely not a recommended course, and yet... that trait Tremont had been struggling to recall, that snippet of wisdom he'd picked up somewhere over a campfire or in an officer's mess, came back to him.

When wooing a lady, a fellow ought to put his best foot forward, of course, but he also ought to remain true to himself. He must never do as Harry Merridew had done and inveigle a woman into falling in love with a lie.

As Tremont saw Mrs. Merridew home and bowed over her hand on her doorstep, he felt a lightness of heart, despite the thickening gloom. Brilliance was beyond him, his wit was ponderous at best, and his gracious hospitality was undoubtedly the work of a conscientious staff.

But Marcus, Earl of Tremont, could be himself. He could most certainly be himself and hope that, for Matilda Merridew, the genuine man was enough.

CHAPTER SIX

Matilda had learned to despise the giddy raptures she'd fallen prey to as a younger woman. Harry Merridew had been *so* handsome, *so* gallant, *so very* understanding, and marriage to him would be *so* perfect!

Gradually, she'd come to see that a girl raised in ignorance of the world's realities had been easy pickings for such as Harry, and she'd forgiven herself—a little—for her gullibility. A mistake of the same magnitude, though, was unthinkable now that Tommie was on hand, and thus Matilda had mended her ways. No more giddy raptures, unless they were reserved for a fine buttery tea cake or a cup of steaming hot chocolate.

The Earl of Tremont bowed over her gloved hand. "I will bid you good day and thank you for a very enjoyable conversation."

He'd positioned himself to take the brunt of the frigid wind, and Matilda would have bet her last groat he'd done so without any thought or calculation.

"Was it enjoyable?" she asked. "I try to keep my troubles to myself and even more so my errors." And yet, to tell share truth—part of the truth, anyway—with somebody who had demons of his own, had been a relief. "You trust me, and..."

"Your confidences will go with me to the grave," Tremont said, crossing his heart with a gloved finger.

"Likewise." Matilda trusted Tremont to keep his word. That in itself was some sort of miracle. She liked some men—Vicar Delancey was a good sort, his son, Michael, was honorable if a bit too serious, and Alasdhair MacKay was a gentleman to his bones.

But she trusted Tremont, *and* she liked him.

A sleigh went by, harness bells jingling until they faded into the wintry quiet.

"I ought to be going." And yet, Matilda remained on the stoop, her hand in Tremont's. She wasn't giddy or rapturous, but she was... interested? Pleased? Something. "I have become so careful, so cautious and circumspect."

"Hence," Tremont replied, "the question becomes, do you trust yourself? When I came home from the Continent, I fell into an agony of self-doubt. I had crossed a line at Waterloo, and I did not trust that I could uncross it. I had never thought of myself as a rule breaker or a man who subverted authority, except that I was."

His lordship would wait for her to retreat into the house until the moon rose, and Matilda did not want to discommode him. She considered their joined hands, and she turned his words over in her mind.

"What you say is true. I was overly trusting of the world and other people, and now I am under-ly trusting of myself. What sort of fool gets herself into a situation where marrying a confidence trickster looks like the answer to her prayers? I want to blame my folly entirely on Harry, but I can't."

"He's dead," Tremont said, smiling slightly in the gloom. "Blaming him works marvelously because he's not here to defend himself. Given my sentiments toward the man, that is rather a good thing. I don't approve of violence in the normal course, and I grow positively pedantic about the stupidity of dueling—from wretched experience, let it be said. For Harry Merridew, I might once again prove that I am capable of breaking my own rules."

"I'm about to break one of my rules, my lord."

Despite that warning, Tremont remained calmly gazing down at her as the snowflakes danced onto his shoulders and the wind soughed around the corner of the house.

Matilda braced herself with a hand on Tremont's shoulder and kissed his cheek. She lingered near for a moment, catching a whiff of jasmine and green grass—a delicate fragrance for such a substantial man.

In Matilda's lexicon of broken rules, that kiss should barely qualify. Tremont's cheek was cool and a little rough, and he remained unbending in response.

"That kiss was not for my rapier wit or devilish charm, was it?" he asked.

"Nor for your sparkling repartee, my lord, and while I find you more than passingly handsome, I did not kiss you because I was overcome with animal spirits." That Tremont had inspired Matilda to even acknowledge animal spirits aloud was another marvel.

He took off his hat and ran his hand through his hair. "Please do tell me what inspired your display so I might earn a similar reward under circumstances where I'm in a better position to reciprocate."

Matilda took courage from that speech. Tremont resorted to rhetoric when emotion threatened his reserve.

"You listen to me," she said. "You talk *with* me, not *at* me. When you invite me in for tea and conversation, that is precisely what you have in mind. Discussion with you does not mean gossip about others or platitudes about the weather. You are the opposite of a confidence trickster."

Tremont put his hat back on, and Matilda resettled it on his head at a slight angle.

"Into the house with you," he said. "Much more of your flattery, and my hat will no longer fit."

And yet, he had once again taken her hand.

Between one chilly sweep of the wind and the next, Matilda realized that his lordship was asking her a question. He was skilled with high-flown discourse, and he also knew how to use a silence.

"Yes, my lord," she said. "If you were to kiss me back, I would be pleased. Disconcerted, bewildered, and a bit unnerved, but pleased."

"Then I must choose my moment carefully, such that the pleasure is sufficient to overcome your misgivings. Parting on a frigid stoop is not, alas for me, such a moment. You have set me a challenge, Mrs. Merridew, and I relish a challenge."

"Matilda."

His smile was sweet and a little devilish. "Marcus."

They goggled at each other for a moment—not quite fatuously—before Tremont unlatched the door. Matilda slipped into the house and watched his lordship march off into the shadows.

The house smelled good, of conscientious cleaning and a roast in the oven. The foyer wasn't warm, but it was a welcome respite from the elements. From the library came the strains of a fiddle lilting along in triple meter.

Home, at least for now. Matilda took off her cloak, scarf, and bonnet and reviewed the afternoon's events. She looked for the trap, for the clue that Lord Tremont wasn't who and what he appeared to be, and she found no such indications.

She looked for the mistake—kissing Tremont had been the next thing to an impulse—and impulses led to painful consequences. What she'd gained had been a sweet moment and a promise of more sweet moments.

Matilda was listening to Tommie's voluble description of Jensen's offer to take him to the lending library when she finally found a label for what was so attractive about Marcus, Earl of Tremont.

He was simply *honorable*. A younger Matilda would have found him unremarkable—once she'd stopped admiring his fine tailoring, broad shoulders, and exquisite manners—but the older and wiser lady knew him to be a rare gem.

He was kind and honest, and he was planning to kiss her at some opportune moment, and that made Matilda more happy than worried. Perhaps she was truly accepting the reality of Harry's death after all this time, and that was a very, very good thing.

Tremont lasted exactly one week before he was back at the soldiers' home, though seven days and nights of pondering and cogitating and wondering had brought him no closer to understanding how he ought to next approach Matilda.

So here he sat in the kitchen, without a plan or a clue, and without catching sight of his quarry either.

"Mrs. Merridew knows things, my lord," Mrs. Winklebleck said, taking a loud slurp of her tea. "Magic potions to stop a stain from setting, boot polish that don't stink of lard. She says I can learn all that from books, but I've already learned a power of tricks from her, and she's been here only a fortnight."

Tremont had come in the back hallway door, as was his wont when he'd cut through the garden. Mrs. Winklebleck and Cook were enjoying a cup of tea at the kitchen worktable—as seemed to be their wont at any given hour—and Mrs. Winklebleck had poured him a cup before Tremont had stomped the snow from his boots.

Mrs. Merridew did, indeed, know things, such as how to muddle a man for days on end with a simple gesture of affection.

"Missus can cook too," Cook said in her thick burr. "Has ideas, about spices and sauces. Wants the table set just so, but she's no' fussy."

"Puttin' the manners on the lads, she is," Mrs. Winklebleck said. "They'll never be choirboys, but they are tryin'."

"Choirboys in my experience are a rowdy lot." While earls, with proper provocation, could apparently be a randy lot. Tremont had largely ignored his animal spirits in Spain, there having been a war on and few opportunities for frolicking—not that he was the frolicking sort. When he'd returned to England, keeping body and soul together had left nothing in reserve for masculine mischief, but now...

Matilda had kissed him, and his imagination had gone rampaging off in all manner of earthy directions.

Cook gave Tremont a sidewise appraisal. "You'd know more about being a choirboy than we would, milord."

Her reproof was mostly for form's sake. Earls did not take tea with the staff belowstairs, but Mrs. Winklebleck had poured him a cup, and the rudeness of a refusal was beyond him. He'd known her when she was Big Nan, a pillar of the streetwalking community.

And yes, much to his fascination, there was such a thing as the streetwalking community, and it did have impressive pillars. So, too, did the newsboy community, the housebreakers' community, and the crossing sweepers' community boast of pillars—real pillars, of moral and physical invincibility, not mere snobs claiming a fine ear for gossip while sparing the poor box mere pennies for show.

More to the point, Nan had known Tremont when he'd been eking out a living as a scribe and reader in the pubs of St. Giles. He'd been no sort of pillar at all, but he'd learned a thing or two.

"Have we thought of a name for this place?" he asked. And where was the wonderful Mrs. Merridew at that moment?

Nan took another slurp of her tea. "Missus says the lads have to decide because it's their 'ouse. House, rather. We'll be living at My Weary Arse if that lot gets their way."

"The Home for Useless Reprobates," Cook muttered. "They do appreciate a good meal, though."

The ultimate test of discernment in Cook's eyes. "How's MacIvey working out?"

A look passed between Nan and Cook.

"He'll do," Cook said. "Hard worker, that 'un."

"MacPherson's jealous," Nan said. "Missus wants to show him how to keep the books, but she hasn't got 'round to it, what with the shoveling and all."

Tremont set down his teacup. "If Mrs. Merridew is having to wield a snow shovel when this house is full of able-bodied men—"

"Listen to ye," Cook said. "Cluckin' like the king of the coop. She sent the men 'round to shovel snow for some old Puritan from the kirk, and the Puritan paid the lads and sent them on to her Puritan friends, and you never seen such a lot of grown men assuring each other that more snow was on the way. The lad Charles says they all shoulda been crossing sweepers, so skilled are they with their shovels."

"So Mrs. Merridew has the men shoveling snow for hire. Enterprising of her." What else had she found to do in the past week? Tremont had accomplished appallingly little, all because of a certain kiss from a certain lady on a certain chilly front porch.

He should have kissed her back then and there.

He should have brought her flowers the next day.

He should have sent her flowers along with a witty note, but how did wit apply to the sweetest, most luscious, unexpected...?

Or perhaps the correct course was to invite her over for more tea and conversation, because she seemed to think that had gone well.

He should have sent her a smarmy poem copied in his own hand.

But no. Those were the hackneyed maneuvers of a fatuous swain, and Matilda deserved a more impressive response to her kiss.

"He used to do this," Nan was saying, "in St. Giles. Stare off into space as if the fairies stole his wits. War can leave a man dicked in the nob."

"War did not impair my hearing, madam. I am preoccupied is all. Mrs. Merridew can leave us at the end of the month if she pleases to. I am here to ensure she's not of that mind."

Nan gave him a pitying look. "You're smitten. No shame in it, milord. Missus don't flaunt her wares, but she does make an impression."

"Was married once meself," Cook said. "Settled me doon, ye might say. The handsome laddies aren't so charmin' when they wake up with a sore head on Sunday. Missus knows about more than just how to make boot black or cook up a bully-base."

"That's French," Nan said, shifting her bulk on her chair. "Fish stew with spices and whatnot."

Where had Matilda Merridew learned to make bouillabaisse? Where *was* Matilda, for that matter?

"What else does Missus know about?" Tremont asked.

"Men with sore heads, would be my guess," Cook said. "She don't suffer fools, that one, and the lads know it. Dantry tried to give her some sass, and she just give him the 'you-should-be-ashamed-a-yersel' eye. Davis kicked him under the table, and that be that."

"A woman learns the hard way that she can't bluff," Nan said, pouring herself another cup. "Missus would have drummed Dantry out o' the regiment if he'd kept it up. Coulda heard a snowflake hit the winda, got so quiet."

Dantry was one to test authority. Tremont should have expected that. "I'll have a word with Dantry," he said, rising. "Insubordination and disrespect—"

Matilda marched into the kitchen, her plain beige dress covered by a spotless full-length apron. "You will do no such thing, my lord. Mr. Dantry and I understand each other quite well, and if you take him to task, he will sulk. Good day." She bounced a curtsey at Tremont. "Ladies, I must steal his lordship from you, though I'm sure you are anxious to get back to your duties."

Nan finished her whole cup of tea at once. "That, I am. The rugs don't beat themselves, I always say."

"Nor does the goose pluck itsel'," Cook said, pushing to her feet and following Nan to the back hallway. "No rest for the wicked."

They bustled out the back door like a pair of naughty schoolgirls, leaving Tremont to face a woman who was apparently not at all glad to see him.

∽

"Is something amiss?" Lord Tremont asked, his tone perfectly polite.

"You must not abet them," Matilda said, trying without success to undo the bow at the back of her apron. "Cook likes to cook, but there's much more to running a kitchen than preparing the food. One must tidy up—regularly and well. The larders must be inventoried, lest half the day be spent in last-minute trips to market. The regular marketing must be undertaken early in the day before the best produce has been picked over. One must find new recipes, or the menus never change. Silver wants polishing... Drat this apron!"

Tremont circled behind her. "Allow me."

Matilda stood still while his lordship plucked at the ties of her apron. She flinched when he gave the bow a hard tug, and then he was facing her again.

"Shall I cut the blasted thing off you?"

"Please do not. This is my only good apron. I was in a hurry this morning, and I tied it too tightly."

Tremont regarded her. "And why were you in a hurry?"

"Because Jessup and Jensen were squabbling outside my apartment door, and Nan's reaction was to offer to hold the men's bets. That provoked the combatants to greater flights of vituperation, and then MacIvey and MacPherson came along, and MacIvey put Tommie on his shoulders so Tommie had a better view of the argument as the inevitable crowd formed. I did not know whether to chastise Nan, the maids, MacIvey, or the lot of them at once. That altercation began the day on the wrong foot. Then I find Nan and Cook enjoying one of their eight daily pots of tea, *again,* when the washing has long since been dry on the lines and is just begging to be rained upon."

A beat of silence followed that tirade, then Tremont circled around behind her again. "The new officer is always subjected to a few tests of authority. Hold still."

For Matilda to merely wait while a man, unseen, fussed with her clothing was unaccountably unnerving. A few more tugs and a good hard pull, and the knot was undone.

"How did you resolve the altercation?" Tremont asked as Matilda extricated herself from her apron.

"I sent Jessup and Jensen to neutral corners—one to inventory the linen, the other to canvass the attics. You have furniture up there, furniture the men might refurbish and sell. Amos Tucker apparently knows how that's done. He apprenticed to a cabinetmaker before the war. Why are you looking at me like that?"

Tremont's perusal had taken on a considering look, as if he might be doubting the wisdom of hiring a widow to manage a lot of hooligans and streetwalkers.

"We were to review the books today," he said. "I suggest we undertake that task at my house. You could do with some fresh air and a ramble, while I... I think better when I walk, and the situation here wants some thought. I didn't know Tucker was a cabinetmaker."

"He's not. He was recruited just six months shy of finishing his articles. His old master died while Tucker was off soldiering, and Tucker isn't about to start the whole seven years over in another shop, assuming one would take him on."

"If you come home with me, I will order us a three-bell tea tray, and you can gobble up tarts to your heart's content. Where's Tommie?"

The notion of sitting down before a full tray, enjoying a cup of hot tea, and getting away from the house was all too appealing.

"Tommie is in the attic, chaperoning Jensen while she and Tucker argue over furniture."

"He's making a fort with Holland covers, old barrels, and discarded rugs and having the time of his life. Come have tea with me, and we can spat and scrap over the ledgers, shall we?"

"I don't *want* to spat and scrap," Matilda began, and Tremont smiled at her. Not the smug, self-satisfied smiles Harry used to toss her way when he'd argued her into a corner, but a purely understanding, good-humored smile of commiseration.

"What do you want?" he asked.

What Matilda wanted astonished her. A hug—from Tremont.

A little embrace in the middle of the day to fortify her against petty vexations. Some affection to remind her that life was full of small pleasures and that a moment could turn sweet without warning.

She'd learned with Harry not to initiate such moments, lest they turn unsweet—for her.

"I want to gobble your tea cakes, my lord. Let me fetch my ledgers, and I'll meet you by the front door."

"I will retrieve the ledgers from the library. You might want to look in on Tommie and tell him you're going out. Remind him that spies like to come and go through the postern gate."

"How do you do that?" Matilda asked, starting for the stairs to the first floor. "You are the epitome of organization and self-possession, but then you offer proof that your imagination is capable of flights, even as you look all dapper and adult."

Tremont followed her up the steps, as a gentleman was supposed to. "I am sadly lacking in imagination, or happily unbothered by fancies, but I do recall my childhood. Like Tommie, I had few play-mates, and like Tommie, I dwelled in a sizable domicile full of people larger than I. A boy finds ways to pass the time."

His lordship had conceived of this house, of the landscaping venture, of a means of earning a living in the slums, and yet, he considered himself lacking in imagination.

Matilda paused at the top of the steps. "What spies came in through your postern gate, my lord?"

He gave the same smile—all sweet reason—but a little sadder. "Responsibility, duty, familial obligations, patriotism, and myriad dull pursuits attendant to adulthood. To the parapets with you, Mrs. Merridew, and I will meet you by the front door."

Tommie informed Matilda from beneath a construction of blankets that pirates were swarming up the beach, and she'd best get to safety as soon as she could. As she came back down the steps, she realized that even a short exchange with Tremont had improved her spirits.

That he would drape her cloak about her shoulders, hand her her gloves, and hold the door for her made the day inexplicably better.

That he'd *listen* while she ranted about domestic annoyances, not argue with her, offer remedies for a moment long past, or chide her for being annoyed made the afternoon nearly lovely.

"You were right," she said as Tremont offered his arm at the foot of the terrace steps.

"About?"

"I am the new officer, and my authority will be tested. Squabbling maids, wagering men, and lazy senior staff aren't the end of the world. They are normal signs of a household adjusting to change, even change for the better."

"And yet, those small tests are exasperating," he said. "One wants to simply get on with the job, not waste time and effort insisting on the obvious. The tests will become less frequent, though they never entirely stop. The military appeals to those who take a certain comfort from arbitrary order and pointless routine. Those same individuals apparently feel compelled to ensure that the order and routine will survive minor insurrections. The whole business is set up to function in combat, but so little time is actually spent in combat that the reasons and the realities can drift out of sight from one another."

They approached the intersection that had belonged to Charles, and of course, another grubby, skinny boy was at the ready with his shovel and barrow.

"Your name, lad," Tremont asked, tossing the boy a coin.

"Patrick. You're Tremont. Charles said you're a good 'un."

"I am pleased to have his endorsement. If you're ever in the mood to pay him a call and pass the time, he's at the big house with all the soldiers down the street and 'round the corner. The door will always be open to you, and I trust you'll keep watch on the surrounds for us."

Patrick saluted with his broom. "Aye, milord. I allus keep a sharp eye. Missus." Patrick offered Matilda a jaunty bow and then trotted off toward a steaming pile of horse droppings.

"I meant to inquire after Charles," Tremont said. "I suppose he would have decamped for his home shires by now if he meant to."

"He's a hard worker, and his greatest worry is that his auntie will come along and snatch him away from us. His second-greatest worry is that she will forget about him entirely."

"For the boy's sake, perhaps that would be best. May I ask you a question?"

The day was brisk enough that nobody was tarrying on the walks, and yet, the sun was out, and Matilda was very much enjoying the fresh air.

"Ask, my lord."

"You did not care to have me standing behind you when I was unknotting your apron. I didn't imagine that, did I?"

With Harry, Matilda had learned to lie of necessity, though she used that option sparingly and only when she knew she could carry off the deception. With Tremont, lies simply would not do.

"I learned to keep Harry in sight at all times."

"The better to guard against presumptions upon your person?"

Tremont posed his question dispassionately, which made answering him easier. "Not particularly that. I learned that if I simply acquiesced to Harry's overtures, he soon lost interest. He married me for my money and my respectability. Part of him enjoyed exercising his marital rights with me—he liked the idea of a vicar's daughter disporting with a rascal—but another part of him could not handle being passively tolerated as a lover. Toward the end, he left me alone."

Tremont's town house came into sight, though Matilda could have done with more walking and more talking. The past was easier to discuss when she and Tremont weren't facing each other over a teapot.

"Did you miss Merridew's attentions when he withheld them?"

That question, too, was posed without any particular weight. "No. Not in the least. On my worst, most bleak and hungry days, I am still glad to no longer be married to that man."

"I'm sorry."

"What have you to be sorry for?"

"I'm sorry, Matilda, that even in the most basic comforts the married state is intended to confer, your husband failed you. That doesn't explain why you had to keep him in sight at all times."

No, it didn't. Matilda gave the matter some thought. "He didn't strike me."

"We have established that he did not need to strike you when he could instead threaten to send your child to a baby farm or foundling home."

And that observation was offered with exquisite dispassion.

Matilda resigned herself to sharing another sordid truth about her past. "Harry stole things. From me, from Tommie. Aunt Portia somehow put together the coin to gift Tommie with a silver rattle. He loved it. He shook that thing by the hour, fascinated with the sound, with how sunlight gleamed on the surface. Harry pawned it or sold it. He pawned my best boots to buy me a fancy cloak, as if people wouldn't notice my worn boots because fancy hems were draped over my frigid toes. My little trousseau—a tea service, some linen, bride clothes, and so forth—didn't last a year."

"And let me guess," Tremont said, escorting Matilda up the steps to his town house. "When you asked your husband if he'd seen the rattle, he turned an innocent expression on you, or—if he was vexed by some detail of the day that had nothing to do with you—he'd chide you for not taking better care of your son's toys. Merridew would ask you where your good boots were and then mutter that clearly you could not be trusted with any item of value. For a long, desperate moment, you'd wonder if he was right and if you were losing your wits."

Tremont held the door for her, and Matilda passed into the quiet and warmth of his home. "That's it exactly. I began to doubt the evidence of my own eyes, and keeping a vigilant watch over Harry became necessary, though by then, I had nothing left to steal. He had shaken me from my passive tolerance, though, and that was likely his objective."

Tremont set aside the ledger he'd carried and unwrapped the scarf Matilda wore instead of a bonnet.

"And still," he said, undoing her frogs, "you watched Merridew, because by the smallest shifts of expression, by the look in his eyes and the tilt of his head, you learned to know the sewer that passed for his mind. It's a blessing all around that your husband no longer draws breath. Were I to meet him, I might have a relapse of violent impulses, and I am a dead shot."

"You aren't boasting." Did Tremont ever boast? Matilda turned so his lordship could lift her cloak from her shoulders.

"I was told my father was a dead shot, and I felt it incumbent upon me to uphold his tradition. I later learned that he was only a *good* shot, and only with long guns, but because he'd been the earl, and he'd gone to his reward, his skills were embellished by fond remembrance. Others idealized him in memory, just as I did. Papa couldn't manage a pistol to save himself, but my own skills extend to every sort of firearm."

"Because when you set your mind to a thing, you never give up."

"Because," Tremont said, passing her his hat, "when practice is all that stands between me and an objective, even I can generally achieve the possible. Brilliance has been denied me, but persistence is my consolation."

He spoke as if reviewing lecture notes. Tremont wasn't lamenting a lack of mental agility, nor was he insulting himself. He merely reported what he believed to be true.

"Have you made a study of kissing, my lord?"

He paused in the act of hanging up his own cloak. "I beg your pardon?"

"Kissing." Matilda audibly kissed the air. "Because if you bring to that endeavor the same focus you turned on your marksmanship, I must ask that we postpone our examination of the ledgers."

The words surprised her. That was the old Matilda talking, the

Matilda who'd disgraced herself and her father, who'd seen Harry Merridew's glib charm as a suit of shining armor. The Matilda who'd yielded to impulse at the expense of common sense and decorum.

The Matilda who had caused so much trouble was stirring back to life, and she had apparently caught Tremont's attention. He was smiling again, and this smile would have done justice to the most buccaneering pirate ever to storm a seaside castle.

CHAPTER SEVEN

The idea that Matilda had been so distrustful of her husband that she'd had to watch the blighter at all times made Tremont furious. How dare that varlet steal from his own wife, much less from a helpless baby? How dare he subject Matilda to freezing toes for the sake of his vanity?

Tremont's usual means of corralling rage—a handy quote from the Stoics, a pithy Shakespearean observation, a determined examination of any unexpected good that had flowed from harm—were unavailing.

And in the midst of Tremont's mental tirades at Harry Merridew, Matilda had flourished her question about kissing and marksmanship.

"You befuddle me on purpose," Tremont said, managing to get his cloak onto the nearest brass hook. "You know that I am vexed past all bearing by the behaviors of your late spouse, so you distract me with an outlandish question."

"My question is serious," she replied with perfect equanimity. "You undertake everything you turn your hand to with singular thoroughness. I wonder if you are similarly thorough in pursuit of your pleasures."

Where was the butler when a fellow needed time to concoct a witty retort? "I can see where Tommie gets his relentless logic from—and his curiosity. Let's find a roaring fire, shall we?"

He led Matilda to the family parlor this time. Tremont allowed himself to enjoy the look of her among gleaming brass fixtures, embroidered pillows, and velvet curtains. He liked that she would turn her hand to hard work, and he liked even more that she wasn't put off by his Town residence.

He gave the bell-pull the requisite three tugs and realized he'd left the ledger in the foyer.

"Shall I retrieve the account book?" he asked.

"Let's do justice to the tray first. Is this your mother?" Matilda moved behind the desk to peer up at the portrait of Mama and her only begotten son. "You were a solemn little fellow, if that's you."

"I had been breeched shortly before we sat for this painting. Papa made a great to-do out of the occasion. His valet assisted me to don my manly attire as if I were being presented at a royal levee. I wish Papa had joined us for the portrait, but we have several good likenesses of him at Tremont."

"I am trying to find the words to tell you something," Matilda said, still studying the portrait. "Something that does not flatter me."

"I do not care one flying pig if you pinched your husband's watch to sell for sustenance, Matilda."

She shook her head. "I sold myself in a sense."

She had commenced blinking. Tremont produced his handkerchief and led her to the sofa. "If you sold yourself, you had no other options. I have learned not to judge women for wanting to survive. When a soldier fights to survive, he's a hero, and he's paid for his efforts. Fed, clothed, housed, and paid. We drink to his health immediately after we toast the health of the sovereign. Soldiers kill people to survive, and we sing jolly songs about them."

He fell silent and folded Matilda's hand between his. *He* had killed his commanding officer to survive, and Matilda hadn't judged him for it.

"Soldiers," she said, "can cause trouble even when they aren't fighting."

"They can be the very devil." Rioting for days, plundering civilian homes, and worse. "Did you fall in love with a devil?"

Matilda took his handkerchief and clutched it in her fist. "Not a devil, a high-spirited young man. He was the second son of the wealthiest squire in the parish. His mother would not allow him to buy his colors, so he joined the local militia. Papa was pleased when young Joseph Yoe began walking me home from services, and I was... I was besotted. Vicars' daughters are easily besotted."

The tray arrived. Tremont poured out and passed Matilda a cup.

"You know how I like my tea," she said, taking a sip. "If Harry were alive today, if Joseph were alive, neither one of them could fix me a cup of tea as I like it."

What was so complicated about a dash of cream and a dollop of honey? "What happened to young Joseph?" What had happened to young Matilda was of far more interest, and clearly the two tales were intertwined.

"Joseph and I became close. We had an understanding, and I was in transports. I was to marry into a good family, get away from the vicarage, and finally make my father proud of me. Joseph could make me laugh—I was starved for laughter—and when he touched me, I was starved for that too. He was affectionate and passionate, and I was an idiot."

"You were young and in love. Early in life, emotions can play havoc with our common sense." Later in life, too, sometimes.

"I was desperate to be free of my father, desperate to be away from his constant judgment. I wanted to laugh and have a second glass of wine and wear pretty clothes. I had less common sense than a pullet in spring."

And now, Matilda was all common sense, all the time—almost all the time. What could effect such a radical change?

Tremont considered that question while Matilda sipped her tea, considered the hell that had been Matilda's marriage and the other hell that had been her life at the vicarage. The squire's dashing son had showered Matilda with attention, and... the pieces of the puzzle formed a whole.

Matilda had never once referred to Tommie as Harry's son. The boy was never *our* son. He was always *my* son.

"Joseph Yoe is Tommie's father," Tremont said. "Then something happened, such that you turned to Merridew to give the boy legitimacy."

Matilda stared at her teacup, then finished her serving. "You do not sound appalled."

"Oh, I am thoroughly appalled. When Yoe became aware that you carried his child, he should have had the banns read, taken up his responsibilities, and kept you laughing for the rest of his natural days." Tremont poured Matilda another cup of tea, though he'd yet to touch his own.

"Squire Yoe happened, or so I suspect. I was as ignorant as a girl can be, which is very ignorant in a country parsonage with no mother to educate me. Joseph told me I could not conceive unless he and I were married. I knew of no unmarried women with babies, so Joseph's perversion of the facts was credible. I happened to mention to him as summer drew to a close that I'd missed my courses."

"That was unusual?"

"Unheard of. I enjoy very good health, as a rule. We were walking home from services, and that was the last time I saw him. He didn't show up for our usual picnic on market day. He did not appear at services the next week. After the service, Squire Yoe was very proud to announce that his son had transferred to an active-duty unit. An uncle had bought him a captaincy. Joseph never set foot in Spain. He died of some stupid accident—stepping barefoot on a rusty nail— and I had only one letter from him. I was to remember him fondly and go on about my life. He hoped I knew that he'd bought his colors the better to make me proud of him."

Tremont rose, because movement had become imperative. "How did you not dig him up and kill him all over again? To blame *you* for *his* desertion, to imply that pleasing you motivated him, when he'd, in fact, left you to face ruin and worse... He'd run from the most basic responsibility that honor requires... And then along came Harry Merridew, handsome and understanding, and what choice did you have? I'm of a mind to ruin the good Squire Yoe and... Matilda, don't cry, please don't..."

She was crying and she was smiling. "You are magnificent, my lord. You are utterly magnificent, and Squire Yoe is on the verge of bankruptcy. Our old housekeeper at the vicarage writes to me occasionally. She eventually explained to me that Yoe was deeply in debt despite all his lovely acres, and Joseph's duty was to marry money. I did not signify in that regard, not compared to the squire's debts, and the squire had saved his son from my dubious clutches. I am not certain Yoe Senior even knew there was a child on the way—I did not know myself until the housekeeper explained it to me."

"Yoe knew. The recruiting sergeants put it thus: Why allow a scheming wench to weigh you down with her brats in some dreary, backward village when you can instead take the king's shilling, be a hero, and see the great, wide world? That speech works all too often." Another chorus in the endless procession of jolly marching songs luring young men to a battlefield death.

"And," Tremont went on, "despite the squire being in hock up to his hunter's withers, he doubtless paid his tithes. Your father chose the parish coffers over his daughter's wellbeing. You've been surrounded by strutting, lying cowards. No wonder Merridew hoodwinked you so easily."

Matilda dabbed at her eyes and turned on Tremont the same focused study she'd aimed at his juvenile portrait.

"I've told myself that Papa never guessed quite how involved I'd become with Joseph. Papa never inquired into Tommie's exact date of birth. He only railed against me for taking up with Harry when I might have waited for Joseph to return. You think Papa knew exactly what was afoot?"

"I am sure of it. He encouraged you to involve yourself with Yoe, then blamed you when the whole business went awry. Harry Merridew was the answer to your father's selfish prayers, even if Merridew wasn't a wealthy squire's son. What would the bishop think, what would the congregation think, of a pastor who could not shepherd his own daughter away from harm?"

Matilda folded Tremont's handkerchief into eighths and tucked it into a pocket. When she rose, her gaze was clouded with uncertainty. "Papa railed against me for accepting Harry's proposal. He threatened to refuse to call the banns, said I'd end up disgracing the family name, and I wasn't to come crawling back to him when my husband threw me out."

"He was manipulating your pride, making sure you would never turn to him when Merridew revealed his true colors. What a wretched old hypocrite."

Matilda frowned at the portrait of mother and son. "Papa was many things, but he was not a hypocrite. He believed all that fire and brimstone business and held himself to the highest standards of probity."

Tremont wanted nothing so much as to take Matilda in his arms and simply hold her. While she cried, while she laughed, while she came to terms with new insights about her own upbringing. He settled for holding out a hand and drawing her nearer to the fire's warmth.

"What an awful purgatory that vicarage must have been for a lonely, curious young lady. It's a wonder you didn't run away to join a band of traveling minstrels."

Matilda stepped closer and then closer still, until she was leaning against Tremont's side, her head on his shoulder. "I cannot believe that Papa knew my circumstances. He hated Harry, and that just made Harry all the more attractive to me. Harry understood me, you see, and Harry was so forgiving of my *understandable lapses*."

"Who was Harry to judge you?"

Matilda shifted so she stood in the circle of Tremont's arms. "I will say this for Harry, he never once threw my past in my face. He married me, and that was that. I was his wife."

"And Tommie?"

"He used Tommie to keep me subdued, but he was never overtly unkind to him. I think he saw in Tommie a bit of his old self, a lad born without advantages or allies. Papa, by contrast, wrote to me only to condemn my choice of husband, to wash his hands of me, to remind me that poverty was part of a holy calling, and I would get nothing from him when he died."

"And yet," Tremont said, "I doubt you were one-and-twenty when you married this blight upon the human escutcheon."

Matilda snuggled closer, bringing Tremont the scent of roses. "What has *that* to do with anything? Papa reminded me frequently that I was old enough to know better, though how is one to know better when one is kept in purposeful ignorance by one's own parent and a village that won't cross him?"

Forming words had become a challenge, while exploring the soft skin at Matilda's nape and reveling in the feel of her body pressed close consumed Tremont's awareness. He nonetheless answered her question, because only a cad and a bounder would allow her to remain convinced of a lie.

"If you had yet to obtain your majority, then your father could have stopped the wedding simply by withholding his consent. Weddings are rife with legalities—a peer hounded by the match-makers has reason to acquaint himself with the details. In the absence of parental consent, Merridew's only recourse would have been a long and expensive trip across the Scottish border. Would your dowry have inspired him to go to such lengths?"

"The cash portion of my dowry would have been barely sufficient to finance such a journey, though we could have sold the silver."

"Then your father intended for you to marry Merridew. Merridew was a solution for the pious vicar who could not raise a perfect daughter. My guess is, your father sweetened the pot when Merridew came down with a calculated case of cold feet."

Matilda was still in Tremont's arms, but he could feel her mentally rearranging furniture that had cluttered up her mental attic for years.

"My own father..." she murmured. "What a small, dishonest... He's the one I should exhume and take to task, except it's not worth the bother to dig him up. I am gainfully employed, in good health, and my son is thriving. That is as much rebuttal to Papa's sermons as I could possibly make." She stepped back and fluffed Tremont's cravat. "I am angry, but also relieved. I wasn't the only sinner at the vicarage."

"You were no sort of sinner at all. You were simply mistaken about a young man's character and then mistaken about your father's motivations. I went haring off to Spain because of a similar misunderstanding. Matters were not half so dire as I'd been led to believe, but my error took years to come to light."

Matilda wandered to the sofa, sat, and began assembling a plate of sandwiches and tarts. "Have you forgiven yourself for being deceived?"

"Yes." Tremont debated, then took the place beside her on the sofa. "That took more years, but when you've committed the next thing to murder, youthful bungling fades by comparison. You have nothing to forgive yourself for, Matilda."

"Your youthful bungling did not result in the conception of a child."

"Do you regret becoming a mother?"

She studied the plate she'd assembled, a tempting array of pretty tarts, delicious sandwiches, and two delectable tea cakes.

"No," she said, sounding a little surprised. "I regret marrying Harry. I regret trusting Joseph Yoe. I regret not standing up to my father sooner and more loudly, but if I had not had Tommie, I would still be at the vicarage, probably keeping house for the next pious hypocrite. Worse yet, I might have married one in the desperate hope that he would not be as bad as Papa. I do not for a moment regret being Tommie's mother."

She smiled at her plate, apparently having settled something in her own mind, then bit into a jam tart. "These are scrumptious. Do you suppose I might have the recipe for Cook?"

Scrumptious sat before Tremont in all her fierce, honest glory. "I can give you the recipe, but I'd rather give you my name."

Matilda paused in mid-reach toward the epergne on the tea tray, then assembled a second plate of delicacies and passed it over to Tremont.

He stuffed a tart into his mouth lest he commence a diatribe on the benefits to Matilda of becoming his countess. He was prepared for her to laugh, to refuse, to make a jest of his offer, or to leave the house in fear for her safety.

Only a fool or a madman proposed to a woman as Tremont had just proposed, and yet, he'd meant those words more sincerely than he'd ever meant anything in his life.

CHAPTER EIGHT

"The 'ouse is neat as a pin from what I can see," Sparky said, settling into the second wing chair before Harry's meager fire. "Somebody 'as tidied up the back, swept the cobbles, pointed up the masonry. Windows are spotless and all the boards taken down."

Harry passed over his flask, though so far, Sparky was repeating old news. "What do the good Puritans of St. Mildred's have to say?"

"I couldn't ask 'em. This isn't your usual tipple."

"Winter ale, winter tipple." The cheap stuff warmed a fellow as well as the other kind. "If you aren't any more effective on reconnaissance, we might be here until spring."

"I done told ye. I'm fer Dublin at the end of the month. Your missus was at services. Had the boy with her. He's growed like a weed."

Thoughts of Tommie were complicated. He'd been a lovely, happy baby, but he hadn't been Harry's baby. That had made married life much easier when Tilly had got various bees under her bonnet, but still... The lad was sweet and lovable, and Harry hadn't known much of sweetness or lovableness.

Probably for the best the lad wasn't truly his.

"If the boy has grown, then Matilda has landed on her feet. Any daughter of Rev. Quartus Samuels had to learn self-reliance." What Matilda had lacked was guile and the sense to trust her own instincts. Harry had lived in dread of the day she acquired those skills.

"Missus is looking well," Sparky said, taking another sip from the flask. "A bit trim-ish, but she seemed to know everybody. A couple fellows were with her. I thought I recognized one of them."

"That's the problem with London," Harry said. "You stand on a street corner here long enough, and somebody who knew you when you were in short coats will eventually walk by. Give me a backward English village any day over the blandishments of the capital."

Sparky corked the flask and returned it to Harry. "And then when you ran your rigs in the shires, you got chased outta one village after another. You came to London, and you could still run those rigs, but you could stay put because you didna shit where you et."

Harry thought about draining the flask, but instead put it away. Even these modest bachelor quarters cost handsomely in the Old Smoke—another reason not to bide here overlong.

"I stuck to Town because Matilda was easier to manage if she stayed here with the boy, and I tended to business elsewhere."

"What did you used to say? A swindler can lie to everybody but hisself. I wish I could place that fellow at the kirk. Had a mean look, but he was good with the boy."

"Matilda is allowing another man to look after Tommie?"

"Why shouldn't she? Her 'usband is dead and buried. She's still wearing Sunday 'alf mourning, but women do that because they can't afford new clothes."

"Matilda owns a house, free and clear. If she wants new frocks badly enough, she can sell that house. Maybe that's why she's had it all spruced up. A pretty property will fetch a better price." Except that Matilda would starve before she sold what she thought of as Tommie's birthright. Lucky boy.

"She's probably looking to rent it out. Proper 'ouses in London is ever so dear come spring."

"Spring is months away. Maybe I should let her sell the house, then explain to her that half the money is mine."

Sparky dumped a whole scoop of coal on the desultory fire. "Not if she's a widda, it ain't. Somebody should sweep these stones."

"The landlord's wife will tidy up on Thursday." Matilda had kept a spotless house. More than once, Harry had found himself in some blighted village pub, working a thimble rig and wishing he were home instead, being fussed at by his wife.

She'd tried to make him soft, Matilda had. She'd had the knack of angling a chair just so, the hassock at the exact right distance, the candles positioned precisely where they should be so a fellow could read the paper without squinting.

"Tell me more about the mean-looking men doting on my son."

Sparky let the lie pass. Harry had been knocking around with Sparky in Bristol nine and a half months prior to Tommie's birth, revisiting the home port, so to speak. Sparky had likely come to his own conclusions regarding Tommie's paternity.

"Former military," Sparky said. "I know the look, and I trailed the lady 'ome after services. If the word of a London crossing sweeper is good, then she's bidin' with a lot of former soldiers as their governess or landlady. Something like that."

"If you can't trust a London crossing sweeper, the End Times approach. Was one myself, once."

Hard, thankless, dangerous, smelly work, even for a large, healthy adolescent. Then Harry had figured out that wrangling street dung wasn't half the job. Spying, running errands, starting rumors, and spreading a juicy lie all paid much better than manual labor.

"You do have a way with horseshite, 'Arry Merchant."

Harry cuffed him on the side of the head. "Never use that name. Not ever. Not when you're drunk, not when you're at your last prayers. You use that name, and I could end up dead for real."

"Remind me to send your wife flowers, but mebbe not. You ain't worth the price of posies, and she's apparently got over her loss the once-t already."

"Hilarious."

Sparky rose. "I'll keep a watch on the 'ouse and the soldiers' 'ome, but you'd best tread lightly, 'Arry. Those men are careful with yer widda. They hold doors for 'er, escort 'er like they was promenading through the park with their best girl. You threaten the missus or the boy, and them won't take it kindly."

"They are a lot of drunks who knew which way to march only when somebody shouted orders at them. I won't threaten my wife. I'll present her with opportunities."

Sparky tapped his hat onto his head. "I might be just another drunk out of uniform, but I known you a long while, 'Arry. Good times and bad."

Not this again. "If I'd wanted to hear a sermon, I'd have gone to services." Though Sparky *had* known Harry forever, and that made all the talk of deserting for Dublin more bothersome than it should have been.

"She's too good for ye. Ye never shoulda married 'er, and ye ought not to steal from 'er and the boy now. That crosses a line, my friend, even for the likes o' ye."

Harry rose, abruptly out of patience. "She is my lawfully wedded spouse. I can black both her eyes, and Scripture will applaud my willingness to use husbandly discipline on a wayward wife."

The look Sparky sent him was infuriating for its pity. "Ye could, and it would be the last stupid thing ye do, 'Arry Whoever the 'Ell You Are This Week. I won't have to kill you. That lot of drunks out of uniform will see to the job for me, and nobody will have to give 'em the order. You been beggin' for a bad end since we left Bristol the first time. Watch your step is all I'm sayin'."

He gave a mocking salute and limped out the door.

Harry produced his current deck of cards—marked, of course— and began beating himself at solitaire just for practice. The hardest part of any rig was patience, and thanks to Matilda, Harry had oceans of it. She would have left him if he'd treated her roughly, and the shame of her potential abandonment—no matter that the law would have marched her straight home—had stayed Harry's hand many a time.

Matilda had taught him that he had more patience than he'd known, and more cunning. The way to get to Matilda was through the boy, and that had not changed.

Fortunately for Harry Merriman.

"Not well done of me," Tremont said, setting his plate aside. "One doesn't raise the topic of holy matrimony between 'have another crumpet' and pouring the second cup, but please hear me out."

Matilda had also apparently lost interest in her food, which was encouraging. Tremont had her attention, and that was a place to start.

"I believe I just heard a proposal of marriage from you, my lord." Her tone was carefully neutral, probably offering him the opportunity to turn the moment to levity—at which he would fail, of course.

"Marcus. My name is Marcus, and you are doubtless thinking that I'm headlong and precipitous and so forth, but that's not true. I am the least rash man you will ever meet."

This earned him a frowning perusal. "You don't hotspur about, yielding to every whim. I like that about you."

"The historical Hotspur came to a bad end, if I recall correctly." Drawn, quartered, and named a traitor, though the ancient past was of no moment when a man was offering his heart to the woman he most greatly esteemed.

"You do recall correctly," Matilda said. "You have a good memory, and you are honest, but what on earth makes you think I'm suited to be your countess?"

Not a no. Every particle of Marcus's being demanded that he get up and pace, the better to reason Matilda's replies closer to a yes. Instead, he took her hand.

"I think," Tremont said. "It's what I do. I ponder, I cogitate, I ruminate. Other men write poetry or give great speeches in the

Lords. They are clever with money or charming in any company. They have cachet. I have a compulsion to contemplate."

"And you have been contemplating marriage, but the notion of searching out a wife holds no interest for you. Here I am, theoretically a lady, and your pondering has led to the conclusion that I'll do?"

She was clearly trying for lightness, trying not to be insulted —again.

"You and I have a talent for communicating at cross purposes, but allow me to explain. Sometimes, I know what I'm thinking about. I will set myself a topic: What's to be done with Amos Tucker, who is discontent in his present circumstances? I will gather up all that I know of him. Hard worker, sweet on one of the maids, family emigrated while he was in Spain. Not yet thirty, but his right shoulder pains him. That sort of thing. I stir it all about in my mind and look for connections or pieces that don't fit. I'm thinking about Amos Tucker."

Matilda's expression had become vaguely puzzled. "Do go on."

"Other times, I will focus on Amos Tucker, for example, but that's not really where my mind is. In some silent, busy way, I'm thinking about a home for crossing sweepers, like a guild hall, but more of a residence. They tend to be children, often orphaned, and they are unsafe, though the city would be unlivable without their labor. But those thoughts are trotting along in parallel to my Amos Tucker thoughts, like a drover's road parallels the carriageways, just out of sight over the ridge. Without warning, my thought paths converge. Amos Tucker and his lady love could run a boardinghouse for crossing sweepers."

"Tremont," Matilda said gently, "Marcus, what are you going on about?"

He secured her hand in both of his. "With you, the paths have converged in a spectacular way. I noticed you at the church, and I thought, 'That woman has a great deal of patience, and she's very protective of the boy. Good qualities.' I was also noticing that you've learned to keep your thoughts from showing in your eyes, and what lovely eyes they are too. I noticed that you are tired, but you keep going. You were not cowed by my title, nor did you sneer at it. Your dignity did not desert you on the first, spectacular occasion of miscommunication between us. All of my thoughts, of every description, focused on you."

"I'm a novelty in your experience, a lady fallen on hard times."

"You are very much a novelty in my experience," Tremont said. "I'm in possession of more acres and farms and tenancies than you can imagine. Ladies fallen on hard times besiege me in Shropshire. Ladies trying not to fall on hard times—or trying to fall out of them—besiege me in Mayfair's ballrooms. You take a general's view of hard times. Even unforgiving terrain has advantages, and you have survived many a battle."

She withdrew her hand. "Now I'm a warhorse?"

"In a sense, which, coming from a soldier, is high praise." *Will I look more or less ridiculous if I go down on one knee while I compare my beloved to livestock?* "You are also a devoted mother, a pragmatic widow, a woman who can laugh at herself, independent, and nobody's fool. I could go on and on, because I delight in the mere contemplation of you."

Matilda rose and paced to the fireplace, which she studied as if the flames held the secret to eternal spring and spotless carpets.

"I've told you my worst mistakes, my lord, my most shameful missteps, and you offer me marriage. I am confused. Flattered, but confused."

The lady was wary, another quality Tremont liked about her, and she was on her feet, so he could also abandon the dratted sofa.

"You've been proposed to before," he said, joining her before the hearth, "and that did not end well. I'm asking for permission to court you. I considered going through an intermediary—Major MacKay, Vicar Delancey—but you would rather be approached directly, so here I am."

Here he was, blathering on about drover's roads and warhorses.

Ye gods and little fishes, she would think him daft, and maybe that's what all those clever poetical fellows meant when they referred to love as a form of madness.

"You are here," she said, "explaining to me how your extraordinary mind works, though I hardly grasp the explanation, and finding virtue in me where others have seen only bumbling and pigheadedness. I will not, on my most biddable day, be a restful or biddable wife."

"We all bumble, Matilda. I certainly have, spectacularly. What you call pigheadedness, I call determination, and I love you for it."

"Oh, you..." She turned away and pretended to resume studying Mama's portrait. "I might look to you as if I'm quite in possession of myself, but this morning, I was polishing silver, and now you expect me to consider... A countess must be presented at court, for pity's sake. You cannot just *say* you love me, Tremont. I am a difficult woman, and proud of it."

"I haven't said those words to anybody else. I love you, I am smitten, I am besotted and knocked top over tail. You are not difficult. You make perfect sense to me, though your life has been difficult. So, in its way, has mine, and I think we would rub along together quite well."

She whirled to face him again. "That was Harry's reasoning. He wanted my respectability and my dowry. I wanted marriage. We were to *rub along*, and we did, and it wasn't all awful, but much of it was nightmarish. I'm through with rubbing along, Marcus. You will have to do better."

Marcus. Though still not a yes. Tremont considered the lady before him, considered what she was leaving unsaid.

"I am happy to do the whole courting quadrille. I will enjoy it, in fact, though driving out in an open vehicle this time of year takes fortitude and warm clothing. If there's a winter assembly at St. Mildred's, I will attentively escort you. I will walk with you to and from services and call upon you at the proper hour." He was running out of ideas, because Matilda was not the blushing heiress an earl was supposed to pursue.

"That isn't the sort of doing better I had in mind, sir."

Where was even a scintilla of insight when a fellow's dignity was going begging? "Pretty words?" he said. "I can memorize poetry as easily as I have military regulations, Shakespeare, and Bible passages. Original compositions are beyond me, but I'm well versed in Latin, and perhaps a translation or two would suit?"

That offer was met with silence. Matilda took his hand and peered up at him as if trying to see into the labyrinth of his mind.

"The problem," she said, "is that I do trust you. I never thought to trust a man again, ever."

"You are unnerved?" He understood that all too well.

She stepped closer and regarded their joined hands, which meant Tremont could not see her eyes. "I do not trust myself," she said. "I've wrecked my life, twice, because I did not exercise caution where men are concerned. Then you come along... You have all the manly virtues, you are good with Tommie, kind, honorable, you say the words I've longed to hear..."

Her litany implied that something was lacking, despite those glowing attributes. What else could she possibly...?

The winding paths in Tremont's thoughts all joined up in the most glorious of possibilities. "Shall I kiss you, Matilda?"

Still, she would not meet his gaze, though she nodded. She did nod.

A gentleman never argued with a lady, much less with his intended when she had—without a word—made a brilliant suggestion.

Matilda had been intimate with two men, one of them very young, the other very experienced. Given a chance to reflect on the matter, she hadn't been much impressed by the passion of the first or by the supposed expertise of the second. Intimacies with Joseph had been furtive, inept, and quick.

Intimacies with Harry had been equally quick, because Harry had known precisely what he wanted and how to get it for himself in the least amount of time.

Was that not also a form of ineptitude?

Matilda had become widowed without *at all* mourning the absence of a lover in her life. Intimacy with men had proved to be an awkward business, undignified, and drudgery more than half the time. She had usually pretended that her husband had acquitted himself well, though she'd wondered the whole time what *acquitting himself well* would even mean.

She'd longed to ask Harry for some affection, a hug, an arm around her waist, a friendly buss, all the while knowing exactly where that would lead. She'd longed to linger in a sleepy embrace, but had made no protest when Harry had rolled over, muttered, "G'night, Tilly," and promptly begun snoring.

Tilly. Matilda hated that nickname and had told Harry so, which meant he had addressed her by it almost exclusively. His other nickname for her had been Miss Dauntless, even after she'd become Mrs. Harry Merridew.

Tremont would never display a man's authority over his wife simply because he could. Never twist her honesty into a weapon he'd wield against her.

He might also never get around to kissing her, so gravely was his lordship considering her.

"Tremont?"

"I'm thinking."

"Thinking is not kissing."

His smile was sweet and devilish. "This is kissing." He pressed his lips to her cheek, then lingered near so that Matilda caught the scent of his shaving soap. A hint of jasmine wafting over grassy summer meadows. A joyful, light scent in contrast to his prodigious capacity for rumination.

His kisses started out in the same sunny, pleasant manner,

lingering at her brow, her other cheek, and finally settling lightly on her mouth.

This was... Matilda searched for words, for labels with which to sort and catalog her first courting kisses from Marcus, Lord Tremont.

Sweet, mannerly, and... She was about to add uninspiring when Tremont slipped a hand to her nape and brushed his thumb over the base of her neck. He was, in the subtlest possible way, urging her closer. He did it again, and Matilda's sorting and cataloging drifted into silence.

She wrapped an arm around Tremont's waist, closed her eyes, and sank against him. He was lean, muscular, and warm. The soft texture of his wool coat contrasted with the unyielding plane of his chest, just as the easy tempo of his kisses contrasted with Matilda's rising awareness that Tremont would be neither hurried nor selfish in his loving.

He rested his cheek against her temple and kept up that slow, gentle caress to her nape.

This, oh, ye heavenly choruses, she had longed for *this*. To be held and cherished while desire stirred from long-dead embers. A worry Matilda hadn't dared acknowledge finally found some ease.

"I fretted," she said over the soft roar of the fire. "Was I to know only fumbling, to be one man's youthful rebellion and another's quick marital reward at the end of the day? Pleasure for them and a lifetime of motherhood and its worries and burdens for me? I told myself I was relieved to be done with it."

"You weren't relieved. You were furious."

Tremont kissed her lips before she could reply to that startlingly accurate observation. He neither thrust his tongue into her mouth, nor grabbed her hair, nor mashed his breeding organs against her, but instead pressed a progression of soft, exploring touches to her mouth.

He was apparently making a study of kissing her. Fair play demanded that Matilda reciprocate.

She traced his brows with her fingertips, brushed her thumb over his ear. He made a sound halfway between a sigh and a groan, so she did it again. His jaw was not quite smooth, and he needed a trim where his hair curled over the back of his collar.

Soft hair, thick, springy, clean. Harry had been going thin on top, and Joseph had used pomade.

Somewhere between caressing Tremont's chest and kissing him back, Matilda stopped comparing him to that pair of dolts and began to savor Tremont's version of intimacies. He was thorough and relaxed. Knew what he was about, did Lord Tremont, and while Matilda sensed confidence in him, she would not have said he was controlling the encounter.

She hauled him nearer and took a taste of him. He waited, lip to lip, and she repeated the invitation. Only then did the kiss deepen. Only then did Tremont gather her close enough that the fit of their bodies revealed the effect their kisses had on him.

We could lock the door. Matilda wasn't willing to give up the luscious kissing to say the words aloud. Tremont in the midst of his amatory investigations was a prodigiously compelling experience. He caressed her back, slow sweeps of his hand touching all the places Matilda could not touch herself. He held her with a combination of security and caring that filled a well of unacknowledged need in Matilda's heart.

He joined his mouth to hers, at times playfully, at times boldly, but all the while somehow respectfully. Matilda could pull him down atop her on the couch, but she would not be tossed there without warning and told to hike up her skirts for a bit of frolic while the baby fussed in the next room.

Not ever again, because *Harry was dead.* Matilda felt a new sense of relief, as if Tremont's proposal, his desire for her, and hers for him, somehow put Harry's ghost to rest once and for all.

"I want more." She whispered the words against Tremont's mouth. "I want more from you." And from life, apparently.

Tremont collected her in his arms and cradled her head against his chest. "I rejoice to hear it."

He wasn't rushing to lock the door or pull the curtains, but his heart wasn't exactly napping either. Matilda reveled in his embrace, in the warmth and scent of him, and in the certain knowledge the Tremont had more to say.

"Shall I court you, Matilda?"

Had he not kissed her, she might have refused his request. She might have mistaken restraint and respect for a lack or absence of passion. She might have disdained his suit, attributing to him a certain laziness when it came to finding a bride. She knew better. Tremont was constitutionally incapable of laziness in any matter of import.

She grasped—now—that a man who made intimacies a mutual exploration was a better bet than one who spouted passionate declarations while fumbling beneath her skirts, or thought himself manly for rutting on his exhausted wife.

His lordship would not be content until Matilda had experienced how a man acquitted himself *very well indeed* in bed with his lover.

"I want you," she said. "I'd never thought to desire a man again, but I desire you."

"I am not a box of French chocolates, Matilda," he murmured near her ear. "I am a fellow with many faults, a few dreams, and a vast regard for you."

"I want to know those dreams."

He stroked her hair, the loveliest caress imaginable. "I want to share my dreams with you, and join my dreams to yours, and hatch up new ones together. I want to lie beside you on a summer day and watch the clouds form into dragons and roses over our heads. I want to see you dream by moonlight and waken to the joy of your embrace on a chilly winter morning."

Oh, ye flights of angels. Those were the words a very young Matilda had needed to hear from her fumbling soldier boy. The words she'd hoped to have from her husband.

Standing in the circle of Tremont's arms, Matilda felt a tide of compassion for her younger self. That lonely, frustrated girl at the vicarage had been desperate for the attentions of any man who looked at her twice, who saw her as a person in her own right. To be *seen* mattered—the girl in the vicarage hadn't been entirely wrong— but she should have been watching for the man who had a good opinion of himself, too, not the blustering poseurs and confidence tricksters.

And yet, in that small village, in her father's household, she would have waited a lifetime for any man who could come close to Tremont's self-possession and perspicacity. Her father would have seen to that, and Matilda would have been none the wiser.

We do the best we can, Mrs. Merridew, and one cannot control the results. Tremont had said that, and he'd been right.

"You shall court me," Matilda said, "and be discreet about it."

Tremont's hand on her hair paused, then resumed its caresses. "I won't say anything to Tommie or the men, if that's what you mean. I will meet with my solicitors, though."

"You can think of solicitors at a time like this?" Matilda's awareness was focused on how well their bodies fit together, how lovely the warmth of the fire was, and how wrong she'd been about so many things.

To be wrong was sometimes the greatest relief in the world.

"Certain dreams," Tremont said, "only come true if all the documents are in order. Your settlements will include a provision for Tommie, of course, and if there's anybody else who needs looking after—your father's housekeeper, your widowed auntie?—then you must let me know."

Tremont was a peer of the realm, a man born to wealth and privilege, the very sort of person whom the satirists loved to lampoon. He was also a greater repository of decency and kindness than Matilda's ordained father had ever been.

"I can trust you," Matilda said slowly. "I truly can trust you."

"If you can't, then you are to give me my congé on the instant, madam."

She peered up at him. "Is that an order?"

"An emphatic suggestion. Without trust, what is a marriage? What is a friendship, for that matter?"

To him, those were not philosophical abstractions, while to Matilda, this embrace was not simply a passing hug. She stepped back nonetheless, because the notion of locking the door and proceeding with a particular aspect of the courtship would not leave her imagination.

"Whom do you trust?" Matilda asked, resuming her seat on the sofa.

"Most everybody to a certain extent, until they prove my trust is misplaced." He remained by the fire, a handsome fellow in a room suited to his consequence. He was also a good man who wanted to share his future with her.

"I will need time," she said, "to become comfortable with your trusting nature. My own nature is not trusting. Please do sit with me. Kissing you seems to have worked up an appetite." Several appetites. For him, for a future with him, and yes, for some of this good food too.

"Help yourself. I'll sit in a moment."

Whyever... *oh.* He needed to compose himself. What a jolly thought. Matilda retrieved her plate of sustenance from the low table and fell to, while Tremont stood before the fire and looked thoughtful.

Matilda made a graceful picture on the sofa, all tidy and self-possessed, while Tremont's world—and his body—were in riot.

Kissing Matilda had been a shocking, delightful revelation.

One could not spend time in the army without gaining a thorough education in the mechanics of copulation. Even the officers had been prone to discussing such matters with a frankness that ricocheted between clinical and coarse. The occasional brave soul had waxed sentimental about his amours, and the even rarer, usually semi-drunken fellow had wistfully yearned for his dearest lady.

None of it had made any sense to Tremont. He'd indulged in a few careful encounters, and then a few more, and finally decided that he was not temperamentally suited to frolicking.

"What on earth are you musing on now?" Matilda asked, munching on a tea cake.

"I thought I lacked some fundamental masculine quality."

She demolished the cake and dusted her hands. "I beg your pardon?"

Tremont longed to take her in his arms again, and he longed to close his eyes and let his thoughts wander where they would, down one splendid path after another.

"I have had liaisons," he said, watching how the flames danced on the silver epergne. "Encounters, trysts. Whatever you want to call the passing interludes men alternately obsess over and belittle. I did not see the point. A tremendous lot of bother for a few minutes of pleasure that any schoolboy can bring himself. I assumed that my flaws included both an excessive capacity for cogitation and a deficiency in my manly humors."

Matilda rose and prowled toward him. "Your manly humors are abundantly sufficient, Tremont." She took his hand and led him to the sofa. "You had me thinking of locking the door."

"You too?"

Her smile was dazzling. "Naughty of me, but there you have it."

That smile, and the bashful tipping down of Matilda's chin, explained to Tremont why otherwise sensible fellows turned into strutting peacocks and wrote bad poetry. He longed to open the window and shout to the world, *She wanted to lock herself in with me!*

"We are not naughty, we are courting. Will you and Tommie join me for a walk in the park on the next fine day?"

She passed him his untouched plate. In Tremont's mind, that food had been assembled in a different era, in a different land. Everything had changed in the past few minutes, and changed for the better. He bit into a sandwich, and even the mundane combination of bread, ham, cheese, and mustard was a more ambrosial offering than it would have been *before*.

"You don't have to do that," Matilda said. "Tommie is my son, and I appreciate that you are kind to him, but you need not do more than that."

"I realized he is not Merridew's offspring, because you never referred to him as such. You also said you never wanted to have children with Merridew, which raised the question regarding Tommie's paternity. The boy has been twice-orphaned of a father, Matilda. Losing my father just the once nearly did me in. You cannot think my regard for Tommie is merely kindness."

This rather unromantic recitation had Matilda blinking at her empty plate. "You suspected he wasn't Harry's?"

"You said as much, but one doesn't pry into painful personal matters."

She sniffed and set her plate aside. "And yet, knowing I was indiscreet, you still contemplated courting me?"

What was she going on about? "Knowing I am capable of murder, you still consider marrying me?"

"Not murder, Marcus. Defense of loved ones. Those men could not stand up against their senior officer, and he was commanding them to their deaths—not for the defense of the realm, but for his own glory, in defiance of more sensible orders. You did what was needful and risked your own death and disgrace in the process."

Matilda's words had a strange effect. Tremont's heart—so recently thumping with glee—began a measured tattoo in his chest. A slow, hard rhythm that gradually faded, like hoofbeats disappearing into the night. He felt light-headed for a moment, then a curious warmth.

"You are very fierce, Matilda Merridew. I noticed that as soon as I laid eyes on you."

"I am also very hungry. If you don't finish what's on your plate, I will be happy to assist."

She was shy of compliments and more tenderhearted than she

wanted the world to know. The warmth Tremont experienced spread from his body to his mind, to his memories, and to his hopes for the future.

He would court this magnificent, dear lady, and he would marry her, and they would all the joys and pleasures and dreams prove. For the first time in his life, Marcus, Earl of Tremont, felt he did not lack a mysterious collection of attributes so many others took for granted, but was instead a man blessed beyond imaginings and lacking for nothing whatsoever.

CHAPTER NINE

"I feel as if," Matilda said, arranging loops of yarn over her hands, "the closer I come to happiness, the more Harry's ghost haunts me."

Dorcas MacKay made a face at that disclosure—a considering face, not a shocked face. "For anybody raised in a vicarage, happiness itself is problematic. Papa was never a dragon of doom, as some who take holy orders are, but neither was he ebullient. When I was ebullient, his reaction was a sort of saintly tolerance that in itself chided me."

Dorcas began winding the yarn into a ball. The blue color suggested the project would be for young John, Matilda's weekly charge in the nursery, rather than for Major MacKay, who did love his plaids.

"You mostly knew your father as a widower," Matilda said. "Perhaps as a younger man, he was more outgoing." Though considering Vicar Delancey in later life, that theory was unconvincing.

"Michael used to be ebullient," Dorcas said. "My older brother was a jolly lad. After he was ordained, it was as if he forgot that happy boyhood altogether. Working for the archbishop has knocked whatever joy he still claimed right out of him."

Matilda did not know Michael Delancey well. He'd occasionally been paired with her at vicarage suppers. For all he was a gorgeous-looking fellow, his conversation was bland, and his company... uninspiring. He would probably take up his father's post when the present Vicar Delancey retired.

Over the next thirty years, the ladies of the congregation would distinguish between Old Vicar Delancey and Young Vicar Delancey. For the men, it would be Vicar Tom and Vicar Michael. Both pleasant fellows, in their way, though *pleasant* was damning with faint praise.

But then, compared to Tremont, any man's company would be dull.

"How long has your Harry been gone?" Dorcas asked.

He was never my Harry. "Three years." Or was it closer to four? *More* than four? Good heavens. "Long enough that he should be done haunting me."

"Your marriage was not a love match," Dorcas said, not unkindly. "I suspect our mistakes are meant to haunt us so that we don't repeat them, or don't repeat them as egregiously." She sounded as if she spoke from experience.

"Major MacKay could not possibly be a mistake. He suits you in every particular."

Dorcas's winding slowed. "Oh, he does, Matilda. He most devilishly, definitely does."

They shared a smile, and that, too, was a bit devilish on Dorcas's part. She was a woman made lovely by emotion and easily overlooked by those noting only superficialities. Dark hair, trim figure, a bustling air, and a profound devotion to the major and the boy John.

"Alasdhair claims the men are whistling again," she said, resuming her winding. "A whistling soldier is a happy fellow."

"The men needed a bit more order and activity. Tremont knew that, but he also knew he wasn't the best party to bring those changes about. The men are protective of him and he of them, but they are *men.*"

"And Tremont is an earl and their former officer."

He's also my intended. On the one hand, Matilda was tempted to look over her shoulder twenty times a day to make sure Harry's ghost wasn't lounging in a doorway, mocking her for ignoring his cardinal command: *If something seems too good to be true, it is too good to be true.*

The first corollary to Harry's Dictum was: *But most people nevertheless long to believe in fairy tales, and Harry Merridew is here to collect on their folly.*

On the other hand, Matilda was suffused with elation. Marcus understood her, understood the choices she'd made, accepted them, and even admired her for them. He believed her when she said Harry had been a charming scoundrel, and he understood that if Matilda's child was unhappy, she felt that in her heart.

More amazing still, Tremont was honest with her about his own misgivings and blunders. To step into Tremont's embrace was to come home to a place she'd never been before, but had longed for all her life.

"Lord Tremont," Matilda said, "is in every way an estimable fellow. His example alone inspires the men to try harder."

"Ah, but will his example be on hand much longer?" Dorcas finished her winding and retrieved a second hank of blue yarn from her workbasket. "Alasdhair's Welsh cousin, Sir Dylan, is married to Tremont's sister, Lydia. She and Tremont's mama have been campaigning for his lordship to take a bride, and his lordship is nothing if not dutiful toward his responsibilities."

Tremont was much more than that. He was intellectually rigorous beyond anything Matilda had encountered in scholarly churchmen. He was perceptive, grasping aspects of Tommie's situation Matilda herself had missed. He was tender and sweet and...

"The look on your face..." Dorcas said. "Alasdhair ran into Tremont and Tommie at Tatts. Tremont had the boy on his shoulders."

"Tommie has been cantering everywhere ever since." And yelling and imitating his elders and generally acting like a happy little boy. "There's something you should know."

Dorcas passed over the second hank of yarn. "You don't owe me any explanations, Matilda. If you and Tremont are fond of one another, that is your business, but please do be careful."

Matilda arranged the yarn around her hands and braced her elbows on the arms of the chair. The sitting room was cozy, boasting touches of green and white plaid, and the tea-and-talk was always a pleasant way to end Matilda's half day in the nursery.

"Careful?"

Dorcas picked up the trailing end of the yarn and started the next ball. "I don't take Tremont for a man who would be comfortable with a discreet arrangement involving a woman in his employ, so that means he's courting you, isn't he?"

How could she possibly...? But she was married to the major, and he was the original canny fellow, and he and Tremont socialized in various male venues.

"I am honored to admit that his lordship and I are courting, though we are doing so as discreetly as possible. You might well need to find somebody else to look after John on half days."

"Alasdhair concluded as much. He claimed Tremont would keep you too busy at the soldiers' home, and he said it with a particularly smug air that implies he knows more than he's saying. Does that place have a name yet?"

"The men enjoy debating various choices. Victory House, The Garrison, Form Squares... They trot out the topic on Sundays, when Tremont joins us for supper. He asks questions. 'Victory over what?' 'A garrison defending territory from whom?' But he never expresses an opinion. Instead of bickering, the men discuss, almost despite themselves. The whole business fascinates Tommie, who thinks we should name the place The Castle."

"Why?"

"Because an Englishman's home is his castle." While for an Englishwoman, that castle could become a prison.

"You worry for Tommie over this courtship with Tremont," Dorcas said. "I would be deranged if anything happened to John. In his way, the major would be, too, but how could acquiring a doting step-papa be any risk to Tommie?"

The major was apparently not the only canny MacKay. "Tremont is constitutionally incapable of hurting a child, but I do worry. When my marriage to Harry was at its worst, and I contemplated dire options, the thought of leaving Tommie without my protection stopped me. I brought that child into the world, and he is entitled to all I have to give him until he can manage on his own. Tremont is good and dear and wonderful, but a part of my heart will always choose Tommie over any adult male."

"It won't come to that," Dorcas said. "If Tremont is the right man, it won't come to that."

"Tremont can be the best man in the world, and life can still conspire to disoblige my dreams."

"Harry Merridew must have been a proper limb, to use Mrs. Oldbach's term, and not in its humorous sense. Is something else bothering you besides courtship jitters?"

Dorcas calmly wound her yarn, and Matilda realized that Tremont's trusting nature—or his optimistic nature, giving people the benefit of the doubt until proven wrong—was contagious.

"The men might be whistling," Matilda said, "but they are also keeping secrets. They stop talking when I walk into a room, they are more watchful, and I suspect all that whistling is intended to distract me from the fact that they are up to something, and I won't like what it is."

"Shall I alert the major?"

"I'm being silly." Though the memory of Biggs, usually so voluble, falling oddly silent—twice—would not leave Matilda's mind.

Dorcas's winding never changed tempo, but her gaze acquired a ferocity that suggested hurling thunderbolts occupied her free time.

"The worst part," Dorcas said, "of being at the mercy of a small, mean man is that he can make you doubt yourself. You cannot trust your own senses. The bonnet you thought fetching is dowdy if he says it is. The song you worked so hard to learn at the pianoforte is sentimental drivel when he declares it such. When a decent fellow finally comes along, you cannot believe in his virtue, or in his regard for you. If Harry Merridew inflicted those wounds on your soul, I am glad he's dead. You see the men hiding their conversations from you, peering out of windows more often, and otherwise behaving out of character, and that is real, Matilda. You are not silly."

"Thank you."

"You'll tell Tremont?"

"Yes. I know the look of a man keeping secrets. I can nearly smell it on him, and fellows are keeping secrets. Tremont must be told."

"Your aunt Portia is not as I had imagined her," Tremont said, guiding the gig around a beer wagon half loaded with barrels. "I expected a fluttery little dumpling aging into vagueness."

Matilda sat agreeably close to him on the bench, which suggested to Tremont that cold weather had advantages when it came to courting. Why did polite society go about the troth-plighting in spring, after all? But then, spring meant fewer heavy clothes...

And courtship was making Tremont daft.

"Aunt has learned to be both formidable and invisible. If she ever confronted Uncle Porter, it was behind a closed door with the curtains drawn. He was twenty years her senior, and she humored his moods."

"Is Portia's endless forbearance the ideal to which your father tried to conform you?"

"Unsuccessfully," Matilda replied as they passed a tavern from which emerged the strains of a filthy drinking song. "Papa's intentions were probably good. Aunt's life has been devoid of gaiety, but she has never feared for her next meal or a safe place to sleep."

Matilda's aunt—who appeared to be barely ten years Matilda's senior—had been reserved, polite, and skeptical of Tremont's intentions. She had produced a modest tea tray that was of a piece with her tidy Chelsea cottage, and yet, she had quoted dear old Aurelius, Shakespeare, and Proverbs with equal facility.

When Tremont had given her more of the same in return, she had thawed—a little.

"Should we have taken Tommie with us?" Tremont asked, because something about the visit had not agreed with Matilda. She was quieter than usual and had declined an offer to stop at a fancy tea shop in Knightsbridge.

"Perhaps next time. Tommie would rather tag around after Jensen and Tuck, and honestly, they need his civilizing influence if the household isn't to find itself in the midst of a contretemps."

"One does not like to see true love thwarted." Nor would it be for long if Tuck became intent on his goal.

Matilda was frowning at a flower seller shivering on the corner. "Tremont..."

"Of course, my dear." He halted the horse, passed Matilda the reins, and hopped down. He bought the whole inventory, added a few coins to what was due, and chose a posy of violets for his love.

"Thank you," Matilda said, cradling the flowers between gloved hands. "Violets symbolize modesty. I was allowed to decorate the vicarage with them, to a point."

The past was much on her mind today, perhaps as a result of visiting her auntie. Portia struck Tremont as haunted by regrets. Her present protectiveness toward Matilda had been balanced by a tacit admission that she had been unequal to the challenge of keeping Matilda safe when it had mattered. Without a word, Portia had conveyed a warning to Tremont that he must not fail Matilda as Portia had failed her.

Matilda glanced over her shoulder at the flower seller, who had collected her signs and was already pushing her barrow in the direction of the pub.

"Harry would have told me to distract the girl by examining her wares so he could pinch three bouquets from her, which he'd either sell to the next flower girl he came across, or use to flatter ladies from whom he wanted something."

Harry again—Harry and his rotten schemes. "Are you having second thoughts about this courtship, Matilda?"

She sat up straighter on the bench. "Not in the least."

Her assurances sounded genuine. Matilda was clever, independent of spirit, and kind, and she was not a dissembler. Tremont guided the horse into Hyde Park, intent on cutting across Kensington Gardens on less crowded thoroughfares. The park was quieter and, given the weather, all but deserted of wheeled traffic.

"Are you having second thoughts?" Matilda asked.

"My thoughts..." Tremont drew the horse up onto the verge and tried to gather up the flock of mental doves that passed for his thoughts these days. "I have never been in such a muddle. You debate the Apostle Paul's attitude toward women as enthusiastically as you argue the merits of donkeys over mules. You have a recipe for removing wine stains from linen, good little churchwoman that you are, but you kiss like... Your kisses have been much on my mind, Matilda."

"As yours have been on mine." She offered that rejoinder as politely as if she were remarking on the nippy weather.

"I doubt that. We are to inspect the ledgers now that we've called upon your auntie. I have been hoping—desperately—that you'd use the afternoon to instead make a thorough inspection of me. Of my person." His physical, male, desperately preoccupied person.

A snowflake drifted by while Tremont marveled at the complete abandonment of verbal restraint that had recently befallen him. One did not proposition his intended in the frigid confines of the park in the middle of a weekday after taking tea with the lady's dragon auntie.

"You... you want me to inspect your person?" Matilda was beaming—beaming—at her violets.

Or perhaps one did precisely that. "Every inch of me, preferably on a fluffy bed behind a locked door, where we shall all the pleasures prove, with apologies to old Mr. Marlowe."

The silence that ensued was comfortable. Matilda had a vigorous mind, and her thoughts required sorting and framing every bit as much as Tremont's usually did. He awaited her reply, confident that she would match him honesty for honesty.

"The men are hiding something from us," she said. "Whispering in corners, singing too loudly, and very much on their manners at meals. I wanted you to know that, and we must discuss it, but we can discuss it *later*."

The men were always up to mischief. Betting on illegal prize-fights, falling in love, taking in stray dogs, and so forth.

"We will, of course, discuss any matter that concerns the men when you find it convenient to do so." Tremont took up the reins, wishing the men would all immigrate to Nova Scotia. "About the other?"

Matilda sniffed her violets, which one did only the once. Their scent was most apparent on the first whiff, for some reason.

"Drive on, my lord. The sky is threatening nasty weather, and I do fancy Mr. Marlowe's poetry."

Tremont gave the horse leave to move off at a very smart trot.

Aunt Portia was clearly worried about Matilda's dealings with Tremont, but then, Aunt had been reared to worry. To fret over the men in her orbit, the coming winter, the price of bread, and the health of the king. Where occasional bouts of joy and hope should have been, Aunt Portia found troublesome matters to dwell on that reinforced the Church's admonition to cling to Scripture—and to fear.

Had Aunt Portia been sitting beside Tremont in the gig, her gaze would have been on the threatening sky beyond the lattice of dark, bare branches overhead. Matilda had been astonished to realize that

Aunt was not yet forty. Not yet *five-and-thirty*, for heaven's sake, and yet, Aunt and the fussy Mrs. Oldbach were of a piece.

And I was becoming very like them. As Tremont guided the horse along a path strewn with dead leaves, and a few snowflakes drifted on the breeze, Matilda felt as if she'd had a narrow escape. Living with Harry, worry had become her shadow. *Where is Harry? What if he's run one rig too many? Has he been taken up by the law? May he please return home safe and sound, but not just yet?*

Raising Tommie had become more of the same. *Is he a bit warm? Not warm enough? Can I afford an orange to go with his Sunday breakfast? He needs a new coat...* By degrees, worry had taken over a mother's joy in her son's good health and high spirits, until love and anxiety had become next of kin.

Tremont, by contrast, was the soul of calm. His outlook was optimistic, and he regarded life as a worthy challenge rather than an inescapable purgatory.

And he had invited Matilda to closely inspect his person, behind a locked door, on a fluffy bed.

"I ought to decline this inspection tour you've proposed," she said as a bitter gust sent the dead leaves dancing. "I should wait until we are properly engaged, rather than only courting."

The horse shied at all the skittering leaves. "Settle, my good fellow. We'll soon be home, and there'll be a pile of hay for your labors. Fix your little horsy mind on that happy thought."

The beast calmed, and the wind died as suddenly as it had arisen.

"You would decline," Tremont said, "because conception might result, and then you'd be forced to marry me?"

"I would decline, among other reasons, because I expected to review ledgers with you today, and instead, you propose a bacchanal. I dislike surprises generally, but in this case, I am willing to make an exception."

"Delighted to hear it." Humor lurked beneath his dry tone, and something else. Affection? Relief?

"I still fear that I will wake up and find that I'm back in my basement apartment, shivering beneath the covers, the stink of tallow and coal in my hair, and my only thought whether I have enough oats on hand to make Tommie a proper bowl of porridge."

An imposing pair of wrought-iron gates came into view, and despite the destination Matilda had in mind, she was reluctant to rejoin the traffic thronging the thoroughfares beyond the park.

"Scents take me back," Tremont said. "Unpleasant scents, usually. Back to Spain or Waterloo. Back to St. Giles. The heat in Spain is different from anything we have here. The cold in St. Giles is different from the cold in Mayfair. The nightmares aren't as frequent now, but you should know I have them."

Matilda leaned against his arm. "I do too." Though how casually Tremont admitted to a circumstance another man might try to hide.

"Then we shall waken in the night and offer one another comfort. If you'd truly rather look over ledgers, Matilda, then we will look over ledgers. Your company is delightful to me regardless of how we fill the time."

He meant that, and because he meant that, Matilda knew her decision—to blazes with the ledgers—was the right one. With Tremont, Matilda's worry was still present, but hope was possible too. Optimism was reasonable. Joy was within reach.

He did that for her, simply by being the sensible, steady fellow he was.

"Harry was never very impressed with my amatory skills," she said. "Joseph only needed me to hold my skirts up, spread my legs, and keep quiet."

The horse slowed as Tremont turned the gig onto the busy street. "Good heavens, what a bore. Why not focus instead on what you'd like me to do?"

A blush heated Matilda's face, despite the cold. "What I would like you to do is get us to your town house with all possible dispatch."

He clucked to the horse, and a quarter hour later, Matilda was standing beside her intended and beholding the largest bed she'd ever seen. The bedroom itself was unremarkable, given that its usual occupant was a peer.

Green silk hung on the walls above oak wainscoting. French doors led to a small balcony beyond lace curtains. The reading chair before the fire was well cushioned, the hassock slightly worn. A summery landscape of a sizable manor with imposing front steps and a cobbled courtyard hung above the mantel. That house put Matilda in mind of Tremont—stately, handsome, dignified, but nonetheless designed to weather sieges and tempests with equal fortitude.

"Shall I see to your hooks?" Tremont asked, poking up a fire that was already blazing. "Leave you some privacy? Both of the ewers are full, and you should make free with them if you wish."

What Matilda wanted was to make free with Tremont, but how did one...? "I am all at sea."

His bedroom was larger than Matilda's whole basement apartment had been, the ceilings twice as high, the bed roughly as large as her parlor. And yet, he filled the space with his sheer, masculine presence.

Tremont straightened and returned the poker to the hearth set. "I'm at sea as well, Matilda. I'm not without experience, but those other encounters were in the nature of investigations. This is... This matters. You matter. I very much want to make a good first impression. Perhaps you should hold me, lest my doubts get the better of me."

"Hold *you*? Are you teasing me?"

He slipped his arms around her. "I want you to think I am, and I'm also desperate to be near you."

Tremont's embrace was lovely, as always. Secure, warm, not grabby or pushy. A haven and a temptation.

"This will be a rehearsal," Matilda said. "A practice run. Nobody need be impressive."

"My life's ambition has become to make you see how impressive you are when you merely stand still and breathe."

Matilda tucked close, resting her cheek against Tremont's chest.

She loved the feel of his heart beating so steadily, loved his scent and blunt speech. "You aren't in any hurry. I treasure that about you."

"I am in a tearing, desperate hurry," he murmured near her ear. "I am also suffused with contentment merely to be in your embrace."

She could feel both in him—the rising desire, the endless patience. What would he be like when she joined him in that gargantuan bed?

"My hooks, please." She thought he'd step away and move behind her. Instead, he kept his arms around her as he worked his way along the fastenings that ran down the middle of her back. He paused at the halfway mark and kissed her.

"Peppermints," Matilda said. "I will always have happy associations with peppermints."

She said nothing more as Tremont alternately unfastened hooks and kissed her. As he loosened her clothing, her worries eased their grip on her as well. The idea that she might conceive was a remote concern. The more immediate anxiety—that she'd fail to impress her intended—also faded as Tremont knelt to undo her boots and garters.

"You need new boots," he said, easing off a very humble example of winter footwear.

"I need a new wardrobe," she replied. "No more pastels and lavender, all in sturdy fabrics. I want flowered borders, Tremont, bright colors, and soft textures." When he rose, Matilda felt shorter than ever next to him.

"You shall have them, madam. I want out of this coat."

She assisted and then took his sleeve buttons and cravat pin in a sequence that was at once familiar and strange. Harry's worn, wrinkled attire bore no resemblance to the Bond Street finery Tremont wore, and Tremont was a very different specimen from Harry or the youthful Joseph.

Tremont's broad shoulders were real, not the result of padding. That flat belly rippled with muscle, and his back could have been the model for one of Canova's sculpted gods.

None of that mattered, Matilda told herself as she stepped out of her dress. Tremont could be the most humble specimen, thin on top, thick in the middle, and his honor, his kindness, and his decency would attract Matilda just as powerfully.

Not, of course, that she was complaining about thigh muscles that gave her the flutters, or... Matilda fixed her gaze on the painting hanging over the fireplace.

"I'll warm the sheets," Tremont said. "You get first crack behind the privacy screen. Help yourself to a dressing gown."

He wore only his breeches, and Matilda was in her shift. She should have been chilly, but she wasn't, and Tremont's smile said he wasn't either. Perhaps army life had knocked any modesty out of him, or perhaps he was allowing Matilda to look her fill.

That exercise would take the rest of her life. She scurried behind the privacy screen, made use of his lordship's toothpowder, and began taking down her hair.

CHAPTER TEN

As Tremont ran the warmer over the sheets, he heard the little sounds of a woman at her toilette—a flannel cloth sopped in a basin, the rap of a toothbrush against porcelain. Fabric rustling... He wanted to peek and knew he must not.

Matilda was shy, and her previous experiences had been disappointing. What happened in the next hour could determine the fate of Tremont's suit, and thus the matter required thought.

"I excel at thinking," he muttered, giving the pillows a sound thwack. He'd been pondering this interlude—the advisability of it, how to suggest it to Matilda, how to proceed with it—since Matilda had granted him permission to court her.

And yet, rational processes yielded nothing in the way of inspiration. Tremont was fairly confident he could give Matilda pleasure— one had read about such matters, listened to fellow officers boasting, and tested theories with willing partners. When Tremont had come home from Spain, the ladies of St. Giles had also been mercilessly articulate about the particulars of their trade.

But what he wanted to give Matilda was more than pleasure, more than a sweet memory of an afternoon anticipating marriage vows they might never take. What did she need from him? What did she crave badly while refusing to acknowledge the longing even to herself?

What do I crave?

Not the obvious, or not only the obvious. Tremont was still pondering that odd question when Matilda emerged from behind the privacy screen. She wore his brown velvet dressing gown, and the sight of her— her hair in a thick braid over her shoulder, her bare feet on the carpet...

I am smitten. The literal sense of the word, to be smacked hard, physically applied, but so did the symbolic. Matilda in dishabille delivered a blow to Tremont's heart.

"The dressing gown bears your scent," she said, nuzzling the lapel, then rolling back a sleeve. "I like that. Please don't stare at me."

"My dressing gown has never been as happy as it is at this moment. That is a good color for you."

"Brown?"

"Chocolate, mink, like your hair." He rose and held out a hand when he wanted to snatch her up and toss her onto the bed.

Matilda took his hand and kept coming until she was wrapped around him. "I've said we needn't impress each other, but I want this to go well."

"You impress me, Matilda. With your courage, your tenacity, your determination. You impress me with your love for your son, with your ability to keep a household of louts and ne'er-do-wells in some sort of order. You impress me."

Tremont's intended bore up under that fusillade and returned fire with a smile.

"You impress me too, my lord. You are unfailingly considerate, thoughtful, and tolerant. Your humor is subtle and never unkind, and you do look a treat without your shirt."

He had to kiss her for that, a long, slow tasting that ended with Matilda's arms twined around his neck and her breath fanning across his chest.

She kissed his sternum. "You kiss differently when your shirt is off."

"I kiss differently when your dress is off," he replied, stroking a hand over her hip. "Into bed with you."

She lingered a moment in his arms, then stepped away and turned back the sheets. "Tend to your ablutions before the water cools, my lord."

"Yes, ma'am." Soon, he'd be addressing Matilda as *my lady*, though she already was his lady. She was about to become Tremont's lover, too, and thus he was both quick and thorough with the soap and flannel.

He emerged from behind the privacy screen without benefit of clothing and made a production out of lighting the pair of candles on the mantel.

"Are your strutting, Tremont?"

"The invitation was to inspect my person. I am presenting myself for your delectation."

"Present yourself in this bed, please."

He tossed the lit taper into the flames, replaced the hearth screen, and steeled himself to be inspected.

As Tremont climbed into the bed, Matilda lay on her side, looking both decadent and entirely too serious. He took up the facing posture, though that was not precisely where he longed to be.

"I know why you invited me here," she said.

To fulfill her wildest fantasies? He couldn't say that, nor could he confidently promise that. "One hopes you are acquainted with the generalities, or Tommie's existence approaches the miraculous."

Oh, that was loverlike. Tremont flopped to his back on the pillows and prayed for brilliance. Well, maybe not brilliance. A good showing, manly competence, something. He prayed he would not disappoint a woman upon whom life—and men—had visited too much disappointment.

"Tommie's existence is miraculous," Matilda said. "I was in danger of forgetting that, but his conception was entirely unremarkable. You are wooing my trust with this interlude."

"When marriage involves certain intimacies, no sensible lady would eschew a reconnaissance mission over the relevant terrain. You are very sensible."

Matilda peered at him from two feet away. "You propound courtship theories when naked in bed with me." She stroked a finger down his profile, and Tremont's cock leaped. "I am easy to impress, Tremont."

"Then your standards want raising."

She sighed and rolled to her back. "My confidence wants raising, you gudgeon. Shall I take off this chemise?"

For a moment, Tremont experienced the situation from a spot above the bed. He saw two healthy people, both a bit shy, both somewhat uncertain of strategy, but intent on a shared objective. From some vestigial well of common sense, he realized that Matilda, *of all women*, would not be in the bed with him if she did not want to be.

"You will not remove your chemise. I will relieve you of it in due course, when you give me permission to do so. My present wishes—if you were to inquire regarding them—would be to kiss you madly, to explore your person in intimate detail by touch and taste, and to stir you to a frenzy of desire."

Matilda smiled at him. "Let's start with the kissing, shall we?"

He smiled back and remained right where he was. "At once would suit."

She traced his nose again, thoughtfully. "I am to initiate this frenzy?"

"You already did that when you glowered at me in St. Mildred's hall and made it plain I had best tread lightly. You further advanced upon the field when you allowed me to escort you home and when you kissed me. I am delighted to find myself in bed with a woman who knows what she wants from life."

"I know more precisely what I do not want."

He caught her hand and kissed her fingers, lest she caress him witless. "What do you *want*, Matilda? What do *you* want?"

She shifted her grip so their fingers were laced and rose over him, pressing his hand to the pillow. "You. I want you, and all the pleasures, and I want them now." She straddled him and hesitated, her lips an inch from his. "I want you, Marcus, and that terrifies me."

He understood what she wasn't saying. She hadn't desired those other two louts. She had accommodated them for reasons—the youth because he'd piqued her curiosity and promised her marriage, the scoundrel because he'd promised her a sort of security.

"I am your first lover, then," he said, "and that terrifies me—and delights me."

By slow, lovely degrees, lips came closer to lips and breath to breath. The moment etched itself in Tremont's memory as full of fierce satisfaction and fiercer longing. His body yearned, his soul was enchanted, and all—everything past, present, and future—came right when Matilda kissed him.

She took her time learning his features—a caress here, a stroke of her fingertips there. She explored—with her tongue, with her lips, with her hands—and she considered. When she drew back, Tremont waited, then grasped that he was being invited to reciprocate, and so it went.

A thorough, mutual investigation was punctuated by sighs and smiles, and from Matilda, even a groan or two. For Tremont, sweet sensations gradually subdued the roaring river of his thoughts, and in that magical peace, he, too, surrendered to his first real experience of lovemaking.

The soft weight of Matilda's breasts against his chest.

The feel of worn linen in his hands at Matilda's muttered, "I want... The chemise, Marcus. Now. *Please*."

The absolute rightness of her beneath him when they rolled and rollicked on the great bed.

The glorious heat of her flesh pressed to his and the sharp intake of her breath when his cock brushed her sex.

"Slowly," Matilda said. "As slowly as you can."

The fog of pleasure lifted enough for Tremont to hear a note of reluctance in Matilda's voice. He mentally spared a curse for the pair of louts and schooled himself to self-restraint. *More* self-restraint. As much self-restraint as he was capable of, which would be, he vowed, enough to acquaint Matilda with the nearer reaches of frenzy.

She began to move beneath him, to undulate into the slow slide of his hard flesh against her damp sex. She tucked her forehead against his shoulder, locked her ankles at the small of his back, and clutched his bum with delicious firmness.

"Marcus..."

That note of command in her voice could inspire him to keep up the temptation all day, all winter. Over and over again, he flirted with penetration, paused, resumed, and flirted again. He palmed her breast, experimented with caresses and would have indulged in further explorations of precisely how Matilda liked her kisses, except that she yanked the hell out of his hair.

"Marcus. Now."

"Now?"

Another yank. "On the instant."

"Hmm."

As he'd hoped she would, Matilda took the matter—and her lover —in hand. She put him where she wanted him, gloved him with a slow, voluptuous slide of her hips, and appeared intent of galloping off with his much-vaunted self-restraint.

"Matilda, a moment, please."

She moderated her enthusiasms, but did not stop. "For?"

Words... He needed words. Short words. "I'll spend." And that would serve him right for assuming his control was equal to her inspiration, but he owed her restraint.

She brushed his hair back in a caress that was not particularly erotic, and yet, it was loving. "Isn't that the point?"

Vaguely, Tremont perceived that her words revealed a gap in her marital education, a lack of meaningful experience, but parsing the particulars was beyond him at that moment.

"No, that is not the point. My eventual satisfaction is *a* point, one of several, but by no means the most important. Kiss me, or I will commence babbling."

She obliged him, and that, oddly enough, helped Tremont reestablish his balance. He was reluctantly relieved when Matilda gave up her hold on his backside to clutch at his wrists as he braced himself above her.

Note for the record: I adore having her hands on my backside.

Matilda was strong, and moment by moment, her grip on his wrists grew tighter. Her undulations became determined, then demanding, then desperate, while Tremont moved in her with a relentlessly unperturbed rhythm.

Matilda was the sea, Tremont was a three-hundred-foot cliff face of male consideration against which she could surge and sigh her way to satisfaction. He had resolved that it should be so, though the precipice was perilously close to crumbling into the waves when Matilda bowed up and seized him in a tight, panting embrace.

The tremors passed through her, and still Tremont held himself in check, even when she shuddered her way to a second taste of satisfaction. She eased back to the pillows in a panting heap and at last went still.

"What is the name for that?" she said, brushing at Tremont's hair again. "There has to be a word for it. Don't you dare move."

"Pleasure," Tremont replied, his voice slightly raspy. "The word for it is pleasure."

"What just occurred is to pleasure as warm is to the center of the sun and chilly is to the polar extremes, Marcus."

He throbbed and ached to follow her into the center of the sun, but that rapture would have to wait. Tremont withdrew, rolled to his back, and, with a few brisk strokes, brought himself to completion.

"Handkerchief," he said. "In the drawer."

Matilda took pity on him and passed him the requested linen. "You did not want to risk conception, and yet, you need heirs."

"I need to hold you." He tossed the cloth in the direction of the privacy screen and wrapped an arm beneath Matilda's neck. "I need desperately to hold you."

He expected an argument, a discussion of vocabulary, a display of feminine independence for form's sake, but Matilda—blessed among women—came into his embrace and tucked herself against his side.

"Do you know, Marcus, that I desperately need to be held? The lovemaking was astonishing and lovely, and I am going all to pieces, and... Please hold me and hold me, and never let me go."

He drew the covers up over her shoulders and wrapped her in his arms.

~

Matilda gained some insight into what it was like for Marcus to go through life with six competing choruses at full voice in his head at all times.

Amazement thrummed through her, echoing the bodily pleasure she'd found with her intended.

Fury added to her mental cacophony, at Harry and Joseph, a pair of amatory bumblers who had the same equipment adorning every other adult male, but who hadn't bothered to learn its proper use with a lover.

Lassitude, because Marcus's hand stroking slowly over her bare back was indescribably soothing.

And gratitude, to Marcus and to life, for affirming her hope that intimacy with a man should be more than a bothersome interlude before a lady availed herself of a decent night's sleep.

What Matilda felt *for* Marcus defied words. She recognized

protectiveness in the mix, affection, enormous respect, physical attraction, and more, but the passion of those emotions lifted and blended them into a new experience, just as the lovemaking had been a new experience.

I have fallen in love. When all hope of romance had passed, when she'd disdained her younger self for longing for such sweeping emotions, the tenderest of sentiments engulfed her. She cast around for something sweet and memorable to say, something that would stay with a man who could quote Shakespeare, the Stoics, and the Bible with casual ease.

"I never want to leave this bed."

Marcus's chest—over which she was draped—bounced a little, and he patted her bottom. "We'd grow hungry, my dearest, and we must not neglect our responsibilities."

He was teasing her, mostly. Matilda kissed his nose for that. "You have it backward. My father had it backward too. We must not neglect our pleasures, or those responsibilities will choke us to death as surely as a lung fever can."

"The Stoics would despair of you, but I eventually learned that they were not the elixir of profound contentment I'd hoped them to be."

"A boy without a father finds guidance where he can. The Stoics were by no means a bad choice."

A beat of quiet went by, the only sound the crackling fire, then Marcus gathered her in a fierce embrace. "If you refuse to marry me, I will go on somehow, but you have ruined me for any other woman. Do you want that on your conscience?"

"The ruination is mutual, I'm sure."

His hold eased. "We are to be married?"

How carefully he posed the question. Matilda liked—very much —that her answer alone decided the matter. She could demand a longer courtship or refuse altogether, and Marcus would adjust his expectations and behaviors to her reply, without tantrums, sulks, or pouting asides.

"We are to be married," she said, tucking herself along his side. "I need time to explain the situation to Tommie. We must find somebody to manage our soldiers, and I refuse to wear half mourning as a new bride."

Tremont wrapped an arm around her shoulders and drew the covers up. "Might we speak to Tommie together?"

That small question presaged a monumental shift in how Tommie was parented. "What will we say?"

"I will tell him that I esteem you above all other ladies, but whether the three of us become a family in truth depends to some extent on if and when Tommie wants that to happen. He cannot be made to feel that he's losing you to me."

"Ah." The fatherless boy yet had wisdom to offer the man. "He might. And he's already growing attached to the maids and soldiers. We will think on this." The temptation to kiss more than Marcus's nose grew overwhelming, and that would not do. "Tell me about your home in Shropshire."

Marcus described a country house fashioned from the remains of a medieval castle. The dwelling itself was too large and perennially in need of repairs, though he spoke of it with affection.

"The older retainers are native Welsh speakers, and I can manage in that language, while my French has grown rusty. You will love my mother. Everybody loves Mama, and since Lydia's marriage to Sir Dylan, Mama has resumed management of the family seat."

"I have never managed anything more impressive than a rural vicarage."

Marcus kissed her fingers. "You will manage *me*, and the rest can sort itself out. Are you hungry yet?"

"Yes, though I still don't want to leave this bed."

He fished beneath the covers and passed her the chemise. "Pretend we reviewed the ledgers, Matilda. Nobody need know otherwise, and if they suspect anything, I will clothe myself in such stately consequence that they give up those untoward speculations after one glance at me. Do you object to a special license?"

Matilda sat up and shook out a wrinkled wad of linen. "I do not. My legal name is Matilda Susannah Samuels Merridew. St. Mildred's is my home parish now, and the ledgers can go to blazes. We reviewed them last week."

Marcus took the chemise from her, sorted top from bottom, and assisted her into it. "We might have to review them again later this week. I'm very conscientious about such duties."

She smacked him, and they fell to kissing and wrestling and kissing some more, and only by exercising self-discipline nearly equal to Marcus's did Matilda eventually leave the bed and finish dressing. Marcus assisted with her hair—more kissing—and she helped him into his clothes.

Which involved yet more kissing and a few protracted embraces.

By the time Marcus was escorting Matilda along a chilly walkway, afternoon shadows were lengthening into evening gloom, and yet, she was reluctant to return to the bustle and noise of the soldiers' home.

"May I show you my house?" she said as Marcus flipped a coin to the crossing sweeper.

"I was hoping you would. The men have been keeping an eye on the place at my request, but I will admit to some curiosity."

"The basement is humble—servants' quarters and a kitchen—but the upper floors are commodious enough. My last tenants were rather disrespectful of the premises. I will not rent to bachelors again if I can help it."

"We can help it." Marcus offered that comment mildly, but Matilda experienced a vast sense of relief. No more dealing with the sly courtesy of the rental agent who foisted freeloading bores on her. No more lectures from the solicitors about the need for economies and the rental contract being "all in order." No more gratuitous lectures from the Mrs. Oldbachs of the congregation about curbing the high spirits of a fatherless boy.

Lord Tremont's countess would be spared all of that.

She and Marcus turned the corner onto the humbler, narrower

lane where she'd dwelled since coming to London with Harry. In the waning winter light, the house looked tired rather than cozy, the dark windows bleak.

"I'd like to have a look around," Marcus said. "One can't see much at this hour, but one wants an idea of the place."

"I can start a fire easily enough, or get a light from next door. Bright sunlight won't flatter the furnishings in any case."

Marcus led the way down the area steps.

"The key is beneath the boot scrape," Matilda said, "though there's nothing inside worth stealing."

Marcus knelt. "Are you sure of the whereabouts of the key?" He flipped up the doormat and shook it. "Nothing here either."

A shivery, sick feeling out of proportion to the moment washed over Matilda. "Try the door. Maybe I'm housing vagrants. I never put the key anywhere but beneath the boot scrape." Harry had always said that people looked beneath the mat for the key and never thought to look in the next obvious place—beneath the boot scrape.

But then, Harry had been spectacularly wrong on many occasions.

"The door is locked, so the key must be here..." Marcus felt along the lintel. "Here it is. One of the men might have moved it for safety, though as to that, the lintel is hardly a clever hiding place."

He fitted the key to the lock, and Matilda accompanied him into the chilly, shadowed confines of a dwelling that, despite the absence of tallow candles or coal fires, still managed to stink of both. The unease Matilda had felt outside followed her into the house, and she was abruptly sorry she'd come.

"Matilda, is something amiss?"

"Bad memories," she said. "Hard memories." Sad, frightened, exhausted, hungry memories. "Harry would put the key over the lintel when he wanted to lock me out."

"Lock you out? Why would he do such a thing?"

"As a warning. If the key was above the door, I was not to come inside. I was to wait until Harry passed a light before a first-floor window, like a smuggler signaling a ship at sea."

Marcus, thankfully, did not press her for details. They made a swift inspection of the premises, which struck Matilda as neglected rather than humble, and were soon back out in the frigid air.

"You are quiet," Marcus said as they walked along arm in arm. "Do you fear the men are using your home as a gambling den?"

"No. The place was appropriately dusty, and I saw no signs of recent habitation. The hearths are clean, the andirons as polished as I left them. The dustbin empty."

"You did say the men are keeping secrets of some sort." Marcus drew her back from the street when a passing coach would have splashed her skirts. "You are upset. That business with the key upset you."

"Frightened me," Matilda said. "You see before you a woman who wants desperately to believe in a happy future with a wonderful man, but who lacks confidence in her dreams. I did not move that key, you did not move that key, and Tommie did not. The only other person who'd know where to find it was buried years ago, but what if Harry passed the secret on to some criminal friend? He had plenty of those."

The rest of that speculation was too fanciful—and dreadful—to be voiced aloud. *What if Harry Merridew isn't dead?*

"I'm being ridiculous," Matilda said, glad to see the porchlight of her new home come into view. "There is doubtless a logical explanation for the key being moved. Will you stay for dinner?"

Marcus held the door for her, then accompanied her into the foyer. "I will stay for supper, though I realize we forgot the blasted account book. I don't suppose you'd like to retrieve the ledger in person the day after tomorrow? I must meet with the solicitors in the morning, else I'd extend the invitation to call for the crack of dawn."

He peeled her cloak from her shoulders as impersonally as if they had, indeed, spent the afternoon poring over figures and tallies.

Matilda passed him bonnet and gloves, and his fingers stroked over her knuckles.

Ah, well, then. When Matilda took his cloak, she brushed the wool against her cheek and sneaked a little whiff of the lapel. Marcus smiled, winked, and offered his arm.

"To the library with us, before we commit improprieties that would shock Mrs. Winklebleck herself."

"What a delightful thought." Matilda returned Marcus's smile and greeted an ebullient Tommie upon entering the library. She was treated to a detailed description of every article of furniture that had been moved to the lumber room and interrogated regarding the precise offerings on Aunt Portia's tea tray.

Marcus engaged himself in conversation with Biggs and Bentley, and all the while Matilda was admiring the line of Marcus's shoulders and listening intently to Tommie's recitation, she was also plagued with worry.

The key had been moved. Who had moved the key and why? Nothing in the house had been missing, and a thief would have replaced the key where he'd found it. Perhaps Marcus could get an explanation from the men, because Matilda needed that explanation.

Badly.

CHAPTER ELEVEN

"When Tilly walks out with her earl," Harry said, tossing half a scoop of coal onto the hearth before Sparky could waste a whole scoop, "she hangs on his arm. Doesn't just put a hand on his sleeve and mince along next to him." As she had with her lawfully wedded husband. "She's running that soldiers' home for him, if the talk in the pub can be believed. Has the boy with her."

"This time of year, the walkways are messy in the Old Smoke," Sparky rejoined. "She's yer *widda*, 'Arry. Ye can't begrudge her her freedom."

The fire was slow to catch—did nobody clean the flues in this place?—and Sparky's comment sat ill.

"I married her when she badly needed marrying. She ought to have a care for my memory."

Sparky sat forward and held his hands toward the desultory flames. "She probably thanks God nightly for yer demise. Pass a fellow a flask, why don't ye?"

Harry obliged. Sparky had ceased maundering on about returning to Ireland, and the situation with Tilly still wanted some extra eyes and ears.

"God, 'Arry. This stuff'll kill ye for sure." Sparky passed the flask back. "Had a letter from me Mary. She misses me."

Oh, for pity's perishing sake. "She's taken any other handsome lad to her bed she pleases in your absence, and she misses having you to fetch and carry for her."

The fire ate at the fresh coal, though a reprise of the Great Fire itself wouldn't warm up Harry's lodgings.

"Being dead disagrees with ye. Ye never used to be so 'ard-hearted." Sparky pulled his chair closer to the fire. "So yer missus has caught the fancy of an earl. She'd probably be happy to let ye have the house and all the memories in it if ye just stay dead. Love has a way of making people daft."

"You would know." A daft idea—a daring idea—was germinating in Harry's brain as he watched the feeble flames. All the best rigs had an element of daring. An element of art. Harry would have the house and the proceeds it fetched at sale.

What if he could have more? A good rig had a touch of daring, but the best rigs bore a hint of brilliance.

"Tilly will get money," Harry said slowly. "If Tremont makes her his fancy piece. If she can get him to marry her, she will have pots of pin money." That was the bolder prize—to coax not only the house but also a steady stream of coin from Matilda. She needed Harry to stay dead rather desperately, after all.

"And if ye try to bilk her out of her coin," Sparky said, "her fella will have the means to put ye on a transport ship or worse, 'Arry. Tremont served in Spain."

"Half the younger sons and titled wastrels in London served in Spain, and for the most part, they rode around in fancy uniforms and harassed the real soldiers into taking all the risks."

Sparky had served, though he didn't say much about his war years. He rose and went to the window, and of all the daft notions, he raised the sash a scant inch.

"Tremont was a puzzle," Sparky said. "The men thought him one of yer wastrel dandies at first, or a fool. He was an earl even then, barely shaving, no sons of his own, and yet, he bought his colors."

"Then he's a patriot, and we know what Dr. Johnson said about that lot." Harry had no use for sentimental drivel aimed at a flag or a particular patch of ground. A man should look after himself first and his mates thereafter. To blazes with Fat George and his art collection.

"If Tremont's a patriot, then the same can be said of me. Boney had been rebuilding his Navy since Trafalgar, and I didn't fancy learning to speak Frog."

"Then you are a fool, Sparky, me lad. Take it from Harry Merriman." Harry would love to know French—Matilda's command of the language had been impressive—but his upbringing had favored Greek and Latin rather than useful subjects.

Matilda had tried to teach him some vocabulary in the first few months of their marriage, to no avail and much hilarity. She'd grown quieter after that. Not as fanciful. And once the boy had come along...

"What else do you know about Tremont?" Harry asked.

"I never served under him, but we had some transfers from his regiment, and I was occasionally swapped around between the artillery and the quartermasters. Tremont's commanding officer was a devil. Liked to watch as a man was flogged within an inch of life. A fellow did what he could to get free of such a monster."

Something in Sparky's tone caught Harry's ear. "If you say he was a monster, he must have been a bad lot indeed."

"He were the son of a lord, but even the other officers eventually got wise to him. Dunacre couldn't touch Tremont because Tremont were a peer, but Dunacre could make his young lordship's life 'ell."

"Tremont's life isn't hell now. His cloak alone would keep me in fine lodgings for the rest of the winter." And he had Matilda trundling along beside him, probably hoping to become his countess, poor thing.

Tilly was fated to harbor doomed ambitions. The dear woman thought life was about fairy tales and moonbeams. Men like Tremont could look much higher than a vinegarish widow when they sought a mother for their heirs.

"Tremont's life were 'ell in Spain," Sparky said. "The stories made the rounds. Dunacre would demand the use of Tremont's horse and then ride the beast to death. Every officer set store by his cattle, and Tremont were no different."

"Nasty," Harry said, "and proof that my decision to stay the hell out of the war was the sensible choice."

"Dunacre was like ye, 'Arry," Sparky said mildly. "He had a talent for knowing how to get to people. Yer missus, for example, did not care a fig for her own good name, but to preserve her baby from scandal, she'd throw in with the likes of ye. Dunacre was like that. If he couldn't catch Tremont up in insubordination or dereliction of duty, he'd go after Tremont's men."

The fire had caught properly and finally begun to throw out some heat. Harry's feet were warm for the first time that day, but his belly plagued him. Chophouse fare washed down with blue ruin sat ill with a man of refined tastes.

"Why are you haranguing me with this ancient history?" Harry said. "Shouldn't you be off composing poetry to your Mary?"

"Ye will underestimate Tremont," Sparky said, "and I don't want to be around to see that happen. Everybody underestimated him, but he was nobody's fool. Amos Tucker tried to desert—half of us did—but stupider'n that, he tried to steal Tremont's horse in hopes of getting to the coast."

"Was he planning to ride it to death in the grand tradition?"

"He was planning to get to the seaside, sell the horse for passage home, and join the family that 'ad up and decided to emigrate without him."

"Did anybody actually fight the French in this war, or was the whole business a lot of drama and public school foolishness?" Harry was honest enough to admit some guilt regarding the war. Not because he should have laid his life on the line for Fat George's art collection, but because he'd refused to dally in war profiteering.

Fortunes had been made thanks to Boney's ambitions, but the notion of swindling soldiers out of decent rations or warm blankets had turned Harry liverish.

A smart man knew which rigs to run and which rigs to run *from*.

"Ye are contemplating foolishness," Sparky said. "Ye think 'Aarry Whoever is smarter than everybody else. You're so smart, ye had to fashion yer own death in Oxford, ye had to leave Bristol hotfoot, and ye've been run out of Dublin. Manchester won't have ye, and the other port towns will arrest ye on sight."

"Costs of doing business." Harry tried for a cheerful tone and failed. Ireland had been lucrative for a time, and the port towns were a real loss. Strangers were part of the landscape in any busy port, and opportunities for the enterprising abounded.

"Costs of committing crimes, 'Arry. I will finish me parable where Tremont is concerned and leave ye to contemplate yer sins. Tucker took off with the earl's horse. Hanging felony even in peacetime. Dunacre's spies got wind of this, and Tremont was called to account for his man. If Tremont had said the horse was merely being taken out of camp for some decent grazing, Dunacre would have had Tucker dead to rights—no groom grazes a horse in saddle and bridle. Worse, Dunacre would have court-martialed Tremont for lying to his superior officer."

"The army sounds worse than the church when it comes to rules, regulations, and stupid games."

"Pay attention, 'Arry," Sparky said tiredly. "If Tremont offered the predictable explanation—that Tucker were taking the horse to graze—then Dunacre woulda won. Tremont instead said he'd been trying to saddle his own mount, and the beast had got away from him. In that version, Tucker was risking his neck outside camp to save the horse. Dunacre's hands were tied, and that story found wings."

The swindler in Harry grudgingly admired Tremont's quick thinking. "And this Tucker person probably turned around and deserted the next day anyway. Who's the fool then, Sparky?"

"Tremont's men didn't desert in the numbers they ought, given Dunacre's mischief. They looked after Tremont, and he looked after them. His lordship took to riding mules after Dunacre killed his horse. Tremont looked the fool to some of his fellow officers; the men knew different. Dunacre's vanity kept him from trying to kill the mules, and his 'orsemanship wasn't up to riding a Spanish mule into the ground anyway. Old Scratch hisself couldn't outlast a Spanish mule."

Harry, who had reason to respect the hardiness of mules, also admitted to himself the wisdom of Tremont's strategy. He who controlled the appearances, controlled the game, usually. Tremont had figured out a way to appear foolish while, in fact, making a fool of a superior officer.

Then too, Tremont was apparently sweet on Tilly. Her finer qualities—loyalty, patience, low expectations of the men in her life— were easy to overlook, though Tremont hadn't.

And that, too, would work to Harry's advantage.

"I'm Matilda's husband. His lordship can saddle up all the mules in England, and he won't change that fact. Matilda will sign the house over to me, and she and I will come to some mutually agreeable arrangements. Tremont needn't know anything about it, provided Matilda shares her pin money with me. If she wants to be difficult—and I sincerely hope she does not—then I will make her life hell."

Sparky rose. "Ye already done that once."

"I preserved her good name."

"Such a saint, ye are, 'Arry Help Yerself. Ye should leave her in peace and thank the good Lord ye ain't dancing on a gibbet."

"Go write your poems," Harry said, saluting with his flask and drawing his chair nearer the fire. "You can move the key back under the boot scrape on your way to the pub."

"Why?" Sparky said, settling his hat on his head. "Why torment a woman who never done ye wrong?"

"I'm not tormenting her. I'm firing warning shots so she knows there's a parley in the offing. Matilda will see reason, and I will be set up quite nicely. Dying on her was the best rig I've ever run."

Sparky let Harry have the last word—unusual for old Sparky—and Harry settled in to refine plans that were already shaping up sweetly.

"If we might adjourn to the library?" Tremont asked. The entire table went silent, and a few knowing winks were passed up and down the ranks. He went on as if he were blind to the smiles and smirks. "The fires are lit in there, and the night grows chilly. We'll want Mrs. Winklebleck and the rest of the staff to join us."

Tucker stood. "The library it is. I'll fetch the womenfolk. C'mon, lad." He held out a hand to Tommie, who scampered out the door with him.

The men doubtless expected an announcement of forthcoming nuptials, but Tremont hadn't Matilda's leave to share that good news. The discussion with Tommie had yet to be handled, a special license to be procured, and some sewing to be done.

And more ledgers to review. A simple, happy list. Tremont offered Matilda his arm, and they followed the men down the corridor.

"I do believe Cook's menus have improved," Tremont said. "I know table manners are held in much higher regard than they were several weeks ago."

"'Please pass the salt' isn't complicated," Matilda replied. "I'm also making progress with those who can't read. Your men are quick-witted and determined—like you."

Never in his entire existence had Tremont considered himself quick-witted, though the determination part rang true enough.

"When I'm in Shropshire, I miss them," Tremont said as they waited for the queue to file into the library. "When I'm in London..."

"You don't miss Shropshire?"

"Not as I once did. It's home, and I will delight in showing it to you, but Mama has the place quite in hand. I feel more useful here in London, haranguing Parliament, wheedling the parsons to spruce up their churchyards, and teaching Tommie to skip rocks. I will be content to dwell wherever you please to make our home, but London does have its attractions."

Matilda gave his hand a surreptitious squeeze.

The rest of the company had shuffled into the library. Tremont remained in the corridor with his intended.

"I did not say this before..." Matilda still had him by the hand, and she had lowered her voice.

"Matilda?" Tremont steeled himself for any announcement—conditions of the betrothal, a change of heart, a request for more time. Matilda had been gracious but distracted all through supper, and Tremont hoped it was his lovemaking on her mind.

She was doubtless fretting over that damned key and that narrow house on the tired lane.

"I am all ears," he said, taking her free hand. "Though in about one minute, the staff will thunder up the steps, and we will have no privacy whatsoever."

Matilda leaned near. "I love you."

Tremont waited, for the *but*... For the *nonetheless*... For the *however*. Delivering good news or compliments first was a rhetorical strategy for ensuring the hearer was paying attention to the subsequent bad news. Good news first also ensured the hearer regarded the speaker benignly when the inevitable reservations or criticisms came along. No fellow tasked with managing subordinates ignored the tactic of delivering the good news first.

"And...?"

"And I cannot wait to be your wife. I love you. I want you to know that. I think, 'Now, I will tell him. Now when I am overcome with his tenderness or his consideration for others,' and then you say something brisk and self-possessed, and the moment passes. But I love you, Marcus. You value my son, you value these men. You know your mother enjoys running the family seat, and you give her the latitude to do that even if you're homesick. I wanted you to know. I say the words to Tommie, but I haven't given them to anybody else."

Tremont could not have surrendered his hold on Matilda's hands for all the rhetorical devices in antiquity, and thus when Mrs. Winklebleck and her maids trundled past along with Cook—the maids bearing tea trays—he remained right where he was.

Which occasioned more smirking.

"The men will want their tea," Tremont said to the housekeeper.

"We'll be along in a moment. I take it Charles is entertaining Tommie?"

"Teaching him card tricks," Cook said. "And doubtless pinching biscuits from the jar."

The corridor was again deserted, though the library door remained open. Tremont led Matilda a few steps away, though for all he cared, the whole world could overhear what he had to say.

"What provoked you to share your sentiments now, Matilda?" He wanted to understand this, because inspiring similar declarations had become his second-fondest aspiration after frequent shared reviews of the ledgers.

"You could sit upon your lordly fundament in Shropshire," Matilda said, "the ranking title, the ranking bachelor, literally lord of all you surveyed. You could spend your days as your father apparently did, socializing, terrifying the game, and riding his acres. That's a blameless existence."

Papa had also loved his family and his homeland.

"If you'd rather...?"

Matilda plastered herself to his chest. "You have more regard for your fellow beings, more decency, more generosity of soul in your smallest finger than my ordained father had in his whole life. Get that special license, Marcus, please. I don't care where we live, or how we live, as long as Tommie is with us and well cared for. You are my home, and I love you."

Tremont held his intended—his *beloved*—and despite the gloom in the corridor and the chilly wind soughing through the eaves, warmth and light suffused him. He knew what to say—a veritable commonplace for some—but it was the truth, and the truth was sufficient for any moment.

"I love you too, Matilda Merridew, and you are my heart."

They held each other, and thoughts of luscious kisses, skipping rocks in the park, and a carefully drafted letter to Mama all drifted through Tremont's mind. His body hummed with pleasure—Matilda was a delight to hold—and his imagination began to embroider on all manner of happily ever afters.

"Tea's served!" somebody called out.

Tremont bussed Matilda's cheek. "For courage and joy."

They joined the smiling, winking, nudging crowd in the library, and while people found places to sit and Matilda poured herself a cup of tea, Tremont mentally shook himself. This was a briefing, not a round of family charades.

"Mrs. Merridew," Tremont said when Matilda was seated at the head of the reading table, "you have the floor."

The smiles subsided, and the library grew quiet.

"Thank you, my lord." She let a moment of silence stretch—rhetorical devices were not the exclusive province of parliamentarians, apparently. When she took up her narrative, she spoke quietly.

"I have reason to believe that somebody has intruded into my house." She explained about her late husband's peculiar habits where door keys were concerned and went on to allude to his dodgy circle of acquaintances.

"I am worried that some ne'er-do-well acquaintance of Mr. Merridew's has decided to make free with the premises. He might not have taken anything yet, but by dark of night, he could load up a whole wagonload of parlor furniture in the alley, and nobody would be the wiser. Harry was not very discerning in his choice of friends."

"Harry Merridew?" Mrs. Winklebleck asked. "That was yer man's name?"

"Yes," Matilda replied. "He's been gone for several years, but he traveled around a fair bit and had connections in odd places, both in London and elsewhere. After all this time, I suspect one of those connections has decided to see if Harry's widow has anything worth stealing. For myself, I don't much mind, but that house is Tommie's birthright and the only part of my trousseau that Harry couldn't take to the pawnshop."

From the looks on the faces of the men, Harry Merridew was fortunate to be dead.

"Women set store by their bridal finery," Biggs said. "My sisters was sewing tablecloths and whatnot for years."

"My mother's china," Bentley said, "come to her from her great-grandmother. This Merridew fella pawned your china, missus?"

"He did, and what silver I had, but then, Tommie had to eat. I could hardly object."

"If the weans need to eat, then the papa ought to find work," Cook observed. "This husband of yours had no trade?"

Tremont resisted the urge to leap in and steer the conversation back to the business of securing the house itself. That topic needed airing, but Matilda also needed to know that nobody judged her for the sins of her late spouse—or for marrying him in the first place.

"Harry was a confidence trickster," Matilda said. "He told me he was a man of business—and he certainly looked the part. I thought that meant he was credentialed as a solicitor. He was making his way to London where all the opportunities were. Within a fortnight of speaking my vows, I realized that I'd made a mistake, but some mistakes can't be unmade."

"Ye learn from 'em," Cook said. "No use crying over spilled milk."

"If you dropped one of your cream pies," Amos Tucker said, "I'd cry."

MacIvey cuffed him on the back of the head. "What are our orders, missus?"

Matilda looked to Tremont, who wasn't about to relieve her of command, though he would offer suggestions.

"Surveillance?" he said. "Regular patrols? We replaced the key where we found it, and our inspection tour took place at sunset, meaning we probably weren't observed."

"Surveillance," Matilda said, "but also... be on the alert. Listen a little more carefully on darts night. Tell the crossing sweepers to keep an eye out for strangers who don't sound like they're from London, but who ask after me or my house. For God's sake, keep a close eye on Tommie and, for that matter, a close eye on me."

"Could there be a house-stealing swindle afoot?" Mrs. Winklebleck asked. "The cheats present themselves as the owner of the premises and accept coin for its sale. You are left with a lawsuit on yer hands and squatters in yer house. T'other house-stealing rig sees you snatched off the street. You aren't set free until you sign the papers giving up the house."

"Bad business, that," Cook said, "but London is the place to try such a scheme. Houses come dear here, and there aren't enough of them for all who need shelter."

Matilda, clearly, was not shocked by Mrs. Winklebleck's suggestion. "Harry attempted something like that once. I wasn't supposed to know about it, but I overheard him berating a... a colleague for bungling some bit of deception. Nobody is to risk injury or worse over this situation, but something is afoot, something unsavory, and I would appreciate your assistance getting to the bottom of it."

"MacPherson used to make up the assignment schedule for picket duty," MacIvey said. "We know how to take a gander without drawing notice."

"In twos, then," MacPherson said. "Every ninety minutes? That's once a night for each of us if we start at half past ten in the evening and work in pairs. The crossing sweepers generally work until ten-ish, and Charles will know who minds the corner nearest the house."

Bentley sketched a rough map of the neighborhood, and the whole household was soon crowded around the reading table, discussing approaches, places to hide, vantage points, and paths of ingress and egress to the property.

Something of a soldier's focus on a mission took over the meeting, while half cups of tea grew cold, and the hour advanced. A plan emerged, of surveillance on the house and neighborhood, supervision for Tommie, and intelligence gathering. Tremont hadn't contributed much beyond a few questions, and he knew the discussion would continue after he and Matilda left the library.

"I must see that Tommie gets to bed," Matilda said, rising from her place at the reading table. "I thank you all for your concern. This is not a problem I could handle without reinforcements."

"Won't be any problem a'tall," MacIvey said. "The lads will keep a sharp eye out and have a few quiet words in the right ears, and whoever thinks to help himself to your house will make other plans in a hurry."

If that was the scheme. Tremont thought simple theft might be at the bottom of the matter, though why move the damned key and make those intentions obvious?

"While Mrs. Winklebleck pours the nightcaps," Tremont said, "I will light Mrs. Merridew and Tommie up to their apartment and then rejoin you."

A round of good-nights followed, and Tremont tarried in Matilda's apartment long enough to read Tommie the fable about the tortoise and the hare, while Matilda got ready for bed. Bowing a proper good-night to her took considerable self-discipline, but then, Tommie was on hand to aid the cause of decorum.

Tremont did the pretty, comforted by the knowledge that for Tommie's sake, Matilda was doing the pretty, too, and someday soon, such strictures could be cast off.

He returned to the library and went straight to the sideboard. "A top-up, anyone?"

Mrs. Winklebleck spoke up first. "I'll have another nip to ward off the chill."

"A wee dram for me," Cook said, brandishing a flask, "and keep yer fancy brandy."

Tremont served, and the conversation had soon broken up into groups. MacIvey got out his fiddle, and somebody began to sing.

"Nanny," Tremont said, coming down beside the housekeeper. "What about Mrs. Merridew's situation made you think about house-stealing schemes?"

She took a dainty sip of her brandy. "I knew a fella who ran rigs like that, but his name were Harry Merryfield, not Merridew. Odd coincidence, but then, London is the sort of place that happens. He were a right handsome corker, were Harry, and didn't limit hisself to stealing houses."

She paused for another taste of her brandy. "He were a card sharp, a professional compromiser of innocents—he didn't ruin 'em in truth, but he did compromise 'em for coin, then he'd blackmail the fellow what wanted the lady ruined in the first place. He could do a lovely thimble rig... Very enterprisin' was Harry, and charming. Not much of a lover, if you take my meaning. A nibbler and always in a hurry. I cannot abide a man who's always in a hurry. From time to time, a quick poke has its appeal, but that Harry wouldn't know how—"

Tremont nearly clapped his hands over his ears. "Could you sketch him?"

Mrs. Winklebleck took another placid sip of her nightcap. "I'm not a Cruikshank, but I can wield a pencil as good as I ever did. Can get you tossed in jail, though, drawing cartoons and such. Being on the stroll is legal."

"Being a housekeeper is safer and pays just as well."

She saluted with her glass. "Pays better, and you know it, milord. Some housekeepers is even married." Her gaze had narrowed on MacIvey, who had shifted into a lilting ballad. He caught Mrs. Winklebleck's eye and winked.

"Indeed, they are," Tremont said. "The sketch is a matter of some urgency."

"And you don't want Missus to know you asked for it?" She rose and went to the desk, taking out pencil and paper.

Tremont followed. "I do not want to alarm her, but neither do I believe in coincidences. House-stealing is an audacious, dangerous crime. To pull it off takes nerve and cunning and isn't the province of the average street thief."

Mrs. Winklebleck's sturdy hand moved over the paper in swift, graceful strokes. She created an attractively masculine face, all lean angles, tousled dark hair, a sweet smile, and eyes that conveyed humor and trustworthiness.

"Told you he were handsome, but..." She bent closer and added a few lines around the eyes. "He'd be older now. I knew him in my misspent youth. Mostly."

"Your misspent youth was all of several years ago, Nanny." The face on the page changed subtly, the trustworthy eyes taking on a hint of calculation. "When was the last time you saw this fellow?"

She considered her handiwork, then passed it over. "Just before I give up the game and turned respectable. I was enjoying a pint at the Drunken Goose, and in he walks, looking quite the dandy. The Goose was always too humble for old Harry, not one of his regular haunts. I calls a greeting to him, and he turns right around and walks out. Never seen him since that day, but good riddance, I says. Harry had a temper—angry at life, he was—and he fancied himself cleverer than anybody else."

"You are quite the artist, Nanny."

"Couldn't make me living at it," she said, finishing her drink, "but it's a fine thing to be able to take a likeness. Helps keep a memory alive, if nothing else."

Sadness lay in that observation.

"Sketch MacIvey playing his fiddle. That's a happy memory for all of us."

Nanny smiled and took out another sheet of paper. "Believe I will, sir. And maybe MacIvey and I will take the first patrol around the neighborhood tonight."

That had certainly not been the plan twenty minutes ago. "Nanny, be careful. You are every bit as much a retired soldier as these fellows are, and we can lose our edge when we leave the battle-field behind."

She snorted as MacIvey's craggy, serious features came to life on the page, softened by a hint of sentiment in the eyes.

"You be careful, sir. If the Harry Merryfield I know has taken a notion to steal Mrs. Merridew's house, you be very, very careful."

"When did you say you last saw him?"

"Maybe two years ago. Certainly not more than that."

"Thank you." Tremont offered the company a polite farewell and made the frigid journey to his own quarters without much noticing the bitter cold. He was lost in thought, and dreadful thoughts they were too.

CHAPTER TWELVE

"Shall we postpone our outing?" Tremont, looking handsome and windblown, stood in the doorway to Matilda's parlor. She hadn't seen him since he'd kissed her good night two days ago, though he'd sent her a note yesterday afternoon:

Solicitors drawing up settlements. Special license applied for. Te tam desidero. Donec cras. Tremont

No parson's daughter was daunted by a little Latin—*I miss you so much. Until tomorrow*—but the sentiments were secondary to the simple consideration of the communication.

"Harry would disappear for days without a word," she said. "I was expected to carry on in his absence and celebrate the prodigal's return when he reappeared. Your note was much appreciated."

And usually when Harry had done a bunk, there'd been no food in the house.

No coin to be had.

Creditors circling.

Tommie fretful over a new tooth.

Then Harry would show up, all smiles at some success he'd allude to mysteriously, or morose and the worse for drink.

"I wanted to send flowers and romantic effusions by the hour," Tremont replied, advancing into the room and closing the door. "That note was a work of monumental self-restraint. What are you reading?"

Matilda passed him a paper yellowing with age. "Harry's death notice, more or less. This is the letter from the proprietor of the Hungry Hound, the inn along the Oxford Road where Harry died. I hadn't read it in quite some time, and I felt the need. The business with the house unnerves me."

Tremont studied the single page that had set Matilda free, at the same time it had obliterated what little security Harry had provided.

"An odd blend of courtesy and avarice. This sounds more like a solicitor wrote it than an innkeeper." He handed the missive back, and Matilda folded it into the pages of her diary.

"An innkeeper who somehow knew the exact direction of Harry's London dwelling," she said, "which Harry was usually careful not to disclose."

Tremont took the seat next to Matilda on the sofa. "Your late spouse oppresses your spirit from the grave. Would you rather stay in, Matilda?"

She leaned into her suitor—her fiancé—and Tremont's arm came around her shoulders. The sight of him was enough to settle her nerves, and being close to him took some of the chill off her heart.

"I agree with the men that an appearance of normality makes sense. That means I spend time with you."

Tremont kissed her knuckles. "But you don't want to leave Tommie here. Shall we take him to the tea shop? It's a bit brisk for a walk in the park, but some fresh air would agree with him, I'm sure."

"What do we know of Jessup and Jensen, Marcus?"

Matilda found herself hefted into Tremont's lap.

"You are like a general at the start of the campaign season," he said. "You've come off winter quarters, unsettled by inactivity, and not yet comfortable with life on the march. Every dispatch rider is suspect, every subaltern a potential spy, and the weather itself plots against you. Jessup and Jensen are known to me from my days in the stews, and I vouch for their loyalty. Is there something you aren't telling me?"

How gently he opened the trapdoor that led to so many bad memories. "There's much I haven't told you, all of it pathetic. After Harry died, I used to think I'd caught a glimpse of him, lurking beneath an awning, disappearing around a corner. Dorcas MacKay claims she had the same experiences when her mother died. She'd smell her mother's perfume without explanation, or think she heard her mama humming a favorite hymn across the corridor."

Marcus had the knack of holding a lady in his lap so she didn't feel ridiculous. She felt safe and sleepy and cherished.

"I encountered my father's ghost once," he said, "or I believe I did."

"Tell me."

"After his death, I became very... contrary, I suppose you'd call it. I was forever eluding my tutors and larking off about the estate. The staff, my sister, Lydia, and tenants kept an eye on me and occasionally had to cart me home when my ambitions exceeded my energies, but for the most part, I was allowed to ramble at will. I was in the orchard, the place where Papa proposed to Mama, and I fell asleep against a venerable apple tree."

"You've never told this to anybody else, have you?"

"Of course not. They would think me daft. When I woke up, Papa was leaning against the next tree, looking as handsome and wonderful as always. He smiled at me—I will never forget that smile —and he said, 'I am so proud of you, Tremont. Never forget that. I will always be proud of you.' I blinked and tried to speak, but then he wasn't there."

"And you've told yourself it was a dream, wishful thinking, or the product of a child's tired, fanciful mind, but you hope it was real."

"At the time, I knew it was real. He called me Tremont, and I wasn't Tremont until Papa died. Ergo, I was looking at an angel, not a memory or a dream. Or so I reasoned in my boyhood. I also knew I could not lose my wits—the Earl of Tremont did not see ghosts in his orchard—and I became passionately devoted to logic and philosophy from that point forward."

"The men say you used to quote old Greeks and Romans by the quatrain, but I haven't heard much of that."

Tremont was silent for a time, his thumb rubbing gently across Matilda's nape. His was a peaceful presence—a paradox, given how active his mind was—and she'd had too little of peace.

"I wanted safety," he said. "As a boy who'd suffered the worst blow, as a peer too young for his responsibilities, as a youth who'd thrown himself into the moral cauldron of war, I wanted a system of infallible answers. Philosophers appeared to provide that refuge, but ancient aphorisms aren't the bulwark I'd thought them to be."

"I wanted safety too," Matilda said slowly. "To me, that meant the respectability of marriage, relief from my father's constant judgment, and distance from that chilly, grim parsonage."

"We lived," Tremont said, "and we learned, and now we love. May I show you something, Matilda?"

She was learning to read the subtle signs with Tremont. His question was almost casual, meaning whatever he had to show her was likely to be upsetting.

"You may." She resumed her place beside him, and he took a folded piece of foolscap from his breast pocket.

"Nan Winklebleck drew that from memory."

Matilda unfolded the paper, and as if some part of her mind knew what she'd see, she beheld a portrait of Harry and was not surprised.

"The eyebrows aren't quite right," Matilda said. "Harry parted his hair down the center, not to the side. He usually wore a mustache, and this fellow is clean-shaven. This looks like him, and yet, it might not be him." She passed the sketch back, despite a temptation to study it further.

"What do we know of Harry's family?" Tremont asked.

A logical question, and bless Tremont for asking it. "Nothing. I assumed they disowned him, or he them. For all I know, Harry's uncle is a preacher and his aunt married to some venerable alderman. Of his immediate family, I know only that he was born in Bristol and had few privileges growing up. He spoke fondly of his mother, but fondness was one of many disguises he could put on or take off at will. He was doubtless fond of me in his way, until I refused to do as he wished."

"Then this could be a cousin or brother of your late husband. Nan knew him as Harry Merryfield, and he ran a house-stealing rig while she was acquainted with him. That would have been perhaps two years ago. She described him as charming, self-interested, and arrogant."

"That hardly narrows down the field, my lord." Even as Matilda spoke, she had the sense of hope being snatched away—again.

"For so long, I lived on dreams," she went on. "Dreams of leaving my father's house, of being special to somebody, of finding a man who would think me clever and pretty and wonderful. Joseph was the answer to my foolish prayers, and then he was my worst nightmare. Harry was the answer to a less romantic set of prayers, until he became another nightmare. Widowhood was the answer to a very practical set of prayers... I should not say that. I did not want Harry dead, but I wanted him gone."

And now Marcus was the answer to her wildest dreams, deepest longings, and her prayers, and he had handed her a sketch of Harry's twin, who'd been alive and committing crimes not two years past.

"I wanted Dunacre dead," Marcus said. "The whole regiment did, and the generals were none too fond of him either. If I thought he once again walked the earth, Matilda, I would not be half as calm as you are now."

"I am not calm. I am overwhelmed and that is a condition with which I am far too familiar. Please hold me."

Tremont obliged, and gradually, Matilda sorted through her emotions. She was afraid—the man in the portrait might be Harry—

and she was hopeful. He might not be Harry, or Harry might have died—for real—since Nan had seen him.

"If Harry is alive..." Matilda could hardly stand to finish the thought.

"I have given the matter some thought. If Harry is alive, I can inspire him to divorce you for adultery, which you have committed with my obliging self. You and I can then be married without legal impediment."

Matilda sat up to peer at Tremont. "*Divorce?* Divorce means expense and scandal and a blight upon the family escutcheon and months and months of waiting... Divorce?"

And yet, divorce was the logical, effective, legal solution.

"If Harry Merridew attempts to come back from the dead, I will make it worth his while to divorce you. He is a creature of endless self-interest, and he and I will come to terms, provided this plan has your approval."

Tremont might well have been asking Matilda if she'd like to pop 'round to the tea shop for luncheon. She, by contrast, was shocked at the simplicity and audacity of Tremont's solution.

"The plan has my grudging approval," Matilda said, snuggling against Tremont's side. "I would never have thought of divorce. I once regarded scandal as the worst fate that could befall me, and now scandal will be my salvation."

"You sound pleased with this state of affairs."

Matilda rummaged around in her emotions once more. She found both vast relief that there *was* a solution to the problem of a living Harry and vast admiration for the mind that could solve the riddle.

"I will be pleased to become your wife, Tremont. I appreciate very much what taking vows with me will cost you. Few people will close their doors to you, but I will gladly live in quiet obscurity."

More irony, that, because the quiet obscurity of a village parsonage had driven her to make witless choices as a younger woman.

Tremont squeezed her in a half hug. "I will suffer the loss of loneliness gladly. The loss of attention from the matchmakers will pain me not at all. The loss of bachelor pleasures does not signify. Need I go on?"

He could doubtless discourse at length regarding the blessings that marriage to Matilda would afford him, while she could only marvel at his devotion.

"I wish there was another way," she said. "Divorce is ruinously expensive, and the press turns the whole thing into a farce."

"The press, the public, and the peerage can all go to blazes, Matilda, as long as you and I can be married. A little patience and some coin will see matters resolved."

Tremont was so very sensible, and so kissable. Matilda indulged herself, though she realized that Tremont was holding back.

"If I am to escort you from the premises," he said, "I must be *composed*, Matilda. Bodily and otherwise."

"Composed?"

He put her hand over his falls. "Composed. On my dignity. Lord Tremont, not a randy swain panting at your heels."

Matilda gave him a squeeze and withdrew her hand. "Marriage to you will try my dignity sorely, Marcus. I'm looking forward to it."

"As am I." His smile was mischievous, but as he escorted her to the tea shop, he was every inch the proper gentleman. Matilda was his decorously devoted damsel, and she enjoyed the meal very much.

Even so, she worried, just a little. Harry—if he was alive—was indeed a creature of endless self-interest, and divorce would be impossible unless Harry agreed to the scheme.

Which, given the coin Marcus could wave before him, he'd have *every* reason to do.

"The time has come to put the cat among the pigeons, Harry Merri... dew."

The hesitation was understandable, but must not be repeated. Harry hadn't used the Merridew name for several years, and he hadn't missed it, but that's who he was at the moment, or most of who he was. Harry Merridew, with Harry Merriman lurking at his elbow. As he strolled along the walkway opposite the tea shop Tilly and her earl had patronized several days past, he admitted that he'd been a poor sort of husband to Matilda.

If dear Tilly took the time to reflect on the matter, she'd admit that he'd done her a great favor by setting her free.

She thus owed him a great favor, and that necessitated acquainting her with a few particulars—such as the fact that she was not a widow in truth. Tilly had not liked surprises, poor thing, and a warning shot across her figurative bow was only courteous. Let her contemplate the joy of wedded bliss with the lordling for a bit, and she'd likely be more amenable to parting with the house—and some coin.

The job at the soldiers' home allowed her to indulge in hot chocolate and fresh buns. She was doing well for herself, despite the dowdy weeds, and that eased the twinges that Harry called his conscience these days.

He moved along with foot traffic, adopting the walk of a gent in contemplation of good news. He was cheery, tipping his hat to the dowagers and shopgirls, but not too quick. Good news took the worry off a fellow's shoulders and put a little swagger in his step.

He had made his third pass across from the tea shop when Matilda and young Tommie entered the shop at precisely ten o'clock, the same as they had the past two Tuesday mornings. The lad had grown, as all lads must, but still... Tommie was a child now, not a baby, and that realization made Harry sad.

Tempus fugit and all that.

Matilda, for her part, had matured from girl-just-out-of-the-schoolroom dewiness into the more substantial appeal of a grown woman.

"You chose well, Harry Merri... dew," he muttered. From Matilda's walk, from the way she gripped Tommie's hand, from the businesslike swish of her pale skirts, Harry perceived that his wife had landed on her feet. Widowhood agreed with her as marriage never had.

But then, she'd been carrying the baby early in the marriage and contending with new motherhood thereafter. Perhaps now...

"None of that, Harry-me-lad." He consulted his broken watch and appeared to await some friend or acquaintance while he loitered outside the corner pub. The neighborhood was on the way up, a nice blend of shops and well-maintained town houses, with a crossing sweeper minding the intersection and the walkways free of mud and snow.

Put him in mind of the Bristol of his halcyon youth, though sea breezes had given the port cleaner air than London would ever boast.

After forty-five minutes, Matilda and Tommie emerged, a little bundle clutched in Tommie's mittened paw. He'd wheedled a bun or two from his mama and probably hadn't realized that days of good behavior was the price he'd pay for his prize.

Ah, the innocence of the very young. Harry gauged distance and speed with a pickpocket's expert eye, then started in Matilda's direction. He kept his gaze on the street's wheeled traffic, turning his head only at the last minute as he brushed against Tommie's package of buns. Tommie, unprepared for the collision, lost his grip on the parcel.

"Oh, I do beg your pardon, ma'am, young sir." Harry crouched down, handed Tommie his package, patted the boy on the head, and gave Matilda the barest instant to take in the features of the husband she'd thought dead.

He touched the brim of his hat with a single finger, winked at his wife, and sauntered on his way.

"Come along, Tommie," she said, sounding admirably calm. "Charlie is waiting to share those buns with you, and the breeze is picking up."

Well done, Tilly. She marched off, no glance over her shoulder, no hastening away in fright. She'd never been easily intimidated, much to her old pater's frustration. Harry had admired Tilly's spirit—Miss Dauntless, indeed—even as he'd dreaded the fights she'd picked. She was a gifted verbal brawler, was Tilly, and didn't believe in kissing and making up.

That was all behind them now. Tilly was apparently well set up these days, and with some judicious horse trading and a little common sense, Harry could land on his feet right beside her. She'd eventually learned to see reason, and Harry had nothing but sweet reason to offer her now.

Well, reason and a Banbury tale or two.

"Mama, who was that man?" Tommie asked. "He wasn't watching where he was going."

Matilda wanted to snatch Tommie up and run, but that would only alarm her son. Besides, Harry—who was alive and in the very pink of health—might well be watching from some shadowed doorway.

"He was a fellow who needs to be more careful." Harry's life in a nutshell, but ye gods, what of the woman who had married him—*and was still married to him?*

Though, of course, Harry would say he was always careful. He'd been carefully watching Matilda's comings and goings, he'd carefully plotted how to confront her, and he'd carefully chosen somewhere she could not make a scene and he could make an easy escape.

"He smiled at you," Tommie said. "I think he liked you and was trying to make friends. MacIvey likes Mrs. Winklebleck, so he plays his fiddle for her. He should ask her, 'Do you want to be friends?' But Tuck says MacIvey's shy. Mrs. Winklebleck isn't shy. She could ask him first."

Matilda wanted to clap her hand over Tommie's mouth and silence his chattering.

I must think. All the moments of her marriage when she'd spoken without thinking, acted without thinking, reacted without thinking kept her marching along the walkway. The only thought she could form was to get to safety and away from… *him.*

"We must leave them to sort that out for themselves, Tommie. Mrs. Winklebleck might be shy about making friends, even though she's merry by nature."

How admirably calm she sounded. A mother's gift, to dissemble for the sake of her child.

"This isn't the way home," Tommie said, glancing around.

"We are paying a call on Lord Tremont." And, please God, let him be home.

"I like his lordship. He is teaching me to whistle, but so far, I can only whistle when I draw in my breath. I want to learn to whistle when I let my breath out. Biggs whistles like that. He can sound like a bird when he wants to, and he can whistle much louder than me."

"Than I. Much louder than I can whistle."

How easily Tommie had made new friends among the soldiers and staff. And how cunning of Harry to choose one of few moments when none of them was on hand.

Harry, who was damnably, unapologetically, robustly alive.

"Lord Tremont is a good whistler," Tommie said as the town house came into view, "but Biggs is better. When I grow up, I will be as good a whistler as Biggs. Will there be berry tarts on his lordship's tea tray, Mama?"

"We just had hot chocolate with whipped cream, Tommie. I do not plan to put his lordship to the inconvenience of a tea tray."

I simply plan to tell him that we cannot marry, that my scoundrel of a husband is alive, and the dearest man in the whole world can never be mine unless we do, indeed, face the scandal and expense of a divorce.

"You don't need to hold my hand so tightly, Mama."

"Sorry." Matilda eased her grip, barely, and led Tommie up the steps. *Please let him be home, please let him be home.* Her heart was racing, and the rich hot chocolate she'd enjoyed had turned traitor in her belly.

Matilda knocked, and after an eternity of less than ten seconds, Tremont opened his own door.

"Mrs. Merridew, good day. Tommie, greetings. Won't you come in? It's half day, and the house is as quiet as a cathedral. I can well use some company."

The measured sound of Marcus's voice, his air of calm, and his graciousness were a tonic to Matilda's nerves. She handed off her bonnet and gloves and dealt with Tommie's jacket—his new jacket. Rather than surrender his booty, Tommie passed the parcel of buns from one hand to the other.

"The breakfast parlor is across from the library and still warm," Tremont said. "That side of the house gets the morning sun. Shall we allow Tommie half a bun while we partake of half a brandy in the library?"

He knew. Despite the good cheer in his voice, despite the hospitality he exuded, Tremont somehow knew that Matilda was in difficulties.

"Please, Mama?"

"Half a bun, Tommie, and you mustn't let it spoil your luncheon."

"I promise, Mama."

Tremont made a fuss out of setting Tommie up with a little plate and table napkin, though an atlas retrieved from the library was needed to boost the boy's seat at the breakfast table.

"I won't spill a single crumb on the table," Tommie said, picking up his half a bun. "Or on the floor, Mama. I promise."

"I'll be back to inspect in a moment," Matilda said. "Call out if you need anything. We'll be right across the corridor. Please remember that it's polite to knock before you come in." *Lest you find your mother in a sobbing heap on the floor.*

Tommie nodded vigorously, his mouth being too full to reply.

Tremont accompanied Matilda to the library. "You've seen a ghost, haven't you?"

"I wish." She took up pacing before the blazing hearth. "Harry bumped into us on the street, tipped his hat, and sashayed on his way. He is alive and well, to appearances, and it *was* him, Marcus. The perishing bounder *winked* at me. That was his warning, and if you don't hold me right this minute, I will fly into a thousand pieces and never put myself back together again."

Tremont obliged with a secure hug. "He frightened you."

"He terrified me. He has been terrifying me since the moment I realized that he's not who and what I thought him to be. Harry *smiled* at me, Marcus. He wanted me to recognize him and wanted me to know he's been watching me. That's what he does when he's setting up a scheme. He watches, like a cat at a mousehole, and then along comes the poor mouse..."

She shuddered at the memory of that friendly wink. "He was always two steps ahead of me, and now I feel as if I'm leagues behind him."

"You are not," Tremont said, rubbing a hand over Matilda's back. "We are not. We've flushed the fox from his covert, and now the chase is on."

Matilda stepped back. "*That's* why you set patrols on the house? To provoke Harry into showing himself?"

"A confrontation was only one of his options, but I'm glad he chose it. We suspected he might be underfoot, and now we know the truth. That's a stronger position, tactically, and he handed it to us without anybody firing any figurative shots."

Matilda felt some wonderment that Marcus could think logically. Also, horror that Harry was alive. Dread, because whatever lay ahead would mean suffering for somebody—very probably her—and anger. Old frustration, new rage, and everything wrathful and frustrated that lay between those two poles.

"This is a war game to you?"

"This is no sort of game at all, Matilda. Harry's appearance means you are married, and as you can have only one legal husband at a time, Harry becomes a problem. The best tool I have for solving problems is logic. Therefore, I apply it when I'd instead like to apply my fists. Would you care for a brandy? You've had a shock, after all."

Papa had always said ladies did not take strong spirits. *To blazes with you, Papa.* "Please, and you will join me, because you've had a shock as well."

"Half a shock. A fellow like Harry Merridew will come to a bad end sooner or later, but under the circumstances... Later was the more likely possibility."

Matilda sipped some very good brandy that warmed her insides and let the fire in the hearth warm her from the outside. Another thought warmed her heart: Tremont had not fled in dismay when he'd learned that Matilda was married. He had not despaired. He had not even been much surprised.

And thus, relief joined the other feelings racketing about in Matilda's soul. Harry was back, and that was bad, though as Marcus had said, better to know now before she'd innocently committed bigamy, better to deal with the truth.

Harry would want money, and then he'd go away. She finished her brandy, and when Tommie scampered into the library, Matilda was discussing the terms upon which she would sell the house and doing so with every appearance of calm.

~

"Merridew is probably running out of coin," Tremont said, warming his hands before MacKay's roaring fire. "Two weeks ago, he or his minions were snooping about the house. Last week, he accosted Matilda on the street. This week, he's purporting to be a buyer interested in relieving Matilda of her only tangible asset."

Matilda had received Harry's letter yesterday, delivered by a street lad to the soldiers' home and purported to be from a Mr. Harrell Merri*man.* The note had been cordially businesslike, a pitch-perfect overture to a widow regarding a financial matter.

Matilda had recognized the handwriting, and for some reason, that fact had bothered Tremont far into the night. She should, of course, recognize her husband's hand. Harry had probably been counting on her ability to do so.

"Brandy?" Alasdhair MacKay asked. "Whisky? Don't tell me to ring for the damned tea tray. Dorcas's brother is supposed to call later. Michael's visit will necessitate swilling an hour's worth of scandal broth while he drones on about the archbishop must this and the Bishop of London demands that."

When MacKay's burr thickened, he was in the grip of strong emotion. "You don't care for your brother-in-law?"

"I like the man well enough, but he's not cut out for the clergy, and... I know what it is to be stuck in a bad situation. Dorcas worries about him."

And thus, MacKay worried as well. "Whisky, then."

MacKay poured two generous servings and passed one to Tremont. "*Slàinte.*"

"*Slàinte mhath.*" Tremont nosed his drink, then took a sip. MacKay, by contrast, had bolted his at one go, then poured himself another half serving. The chill of approaching winter—or of the brother-in-law's duty visit—would be stoutly warded off.

"Without meeting Merridew," MacKay said, "how do you know this buyer is him?"

"I am not absolutely certain, of course, but one plans for the worst possibilities. Matilda reports that Harry changes his alias as often as you change your socks, though he tends to use the first name Harry or its variants. The men have seen a fellow walking past the house—on the street and in the alley—more than once. This man limps, and Bentley claims the limp is familiar."

"Former Private Benjamin Bentley?"

"Is that his first name?"

"He's a good man," MacKay said, gesturing to the wing chairs before the fire. "Never lost his head in the heat of battle, knew how to handle a team. If he tells you a fellow's limp looks familiar, then believe him."

"I do." Tremont sank into a comfortable chair whose back had been warmed by the fire. A green and white plaid pillow provided just the right support to make the chair's embrace a bit of heaven. "If the men see the limping fellow again, they will approach him with a few questions. Matilda says Merridew did not have a limp, though he might have acquired one on the occasion of his supposed death."

MacKay took the second chair with the sigh of a man whose backside was greeting an old and dear friend.

"What do you know of that death?" he asked.

"Very little. Matilda has a letter from the proprietor of the Hungry Hound, an inn just south of Oxford on the Oxford Road. The innkeeper expresses his condolences on her loss, alludes to a sudden illness, and begs that she remit a sum certain for the departed's expenses, which he elucidates to the penny. He further informs her that Harry's bill has been paid by the same good, Christian folk who arranged for the deceased's remains to be carted to London and that she can make repayment to them at a specific address."

"What about that strikes you as odd?"

Oh, everything. "I can understand an old friend paying the shot for a man felled by lung fever or food poisoning, but to pay as well to have his remains crated up in a coffin and carted all the way back to his widow in London? Burying him in Oxford would have been costly enough by the time they'd paid for the coffin, the service, the gravedigging, the bell ringing, and so forth."

"Shipping bodies is expensive," MacKay said. "You are right about that, and Merridew's impoverished widow was expected to pay for the lot of it."

"Even if you were a generous soul seized with a spontaneous charitable impulse toward a stranger, would you rely on the stranger's widow to cover those costs? And if the innkeeper was also paid—as the letter implies—then why was the innkeeper corresponding with Matilda at all? Why wasn't she contacted by these Good Samaritans directly and condoled on her terribly sudden loss?"

MacKay wrinkled his nose. "Because somebody wanted Matilda

sending that money not to the innkeeper, but to that other address, where the Good Samaritans supposedly dwelled. This all begins to smell of a scheme. Is there even a Hungry Hound on the Oxford Road?"

Tremont took a sip of his whisky, which did, indeed, have the effect of settling the nerves. "I asked Sycamore Dorning about the inns around Oxford. He did not finish his university education, but he claims to have acquainted himself thoroughly with every watering hole between London and Oxford."

"That's a lot of watering holes."

"You will be shocked to learn that the youngest Dorning brother was not academically inclined in his youth."

"Nothing about Dorning has the power to shock me." MacKay waved a hand in circles. "Get on wi' your tale."

"Dorning claims there is no such establishment as the Hungry Hound, or there wasn't when he matriculated."

MacKay swore eloquently in his native tongue. "Inns change hands."

"They do, but they rarely change their names, lest the mail go astray. Coaching inns are landmarks. People use them to give directions, to calculate distances and fares. The age of the inn is a point of pride. The Dog and Dam, serving fine ale since Adam first kissed Eve, and so forth. One does not change the name of an inn if one can avoid it."

MacKay asked the inevitable next question. "And the address to which the grieving Mrs. Merridew was to remit a small fortune?"

"I've sent two of the men to make inquiries. I was not Oxford-educated, else I might know the direction myself."

"I did my penance at St. Andrews," MacKay replied. "Michael Delancey was an Oxford man. Ordained and all that. He should descend upon us from the celestial realm any moment, trailing streams of sober piety. Before St. Michael the Arch-bore blesses us with his presence, you will explain to me why you don't simply kill Merridew before he can cause any more bother."

The Scots were so enviably pragmatic. "I already have enough to explain to Saint Peter without adding that sin to my impressively long list." Tremont hesitated, though MacKay well knew the history with Dunacre. "Matilda would not approve."

"You considered it."

"I admit to attempting some research on the legal question of whether a man officially dead and buried can be murdered, but the law offered no comforting insights. To fake one's death is not a crime, though. Deception is a sin, but that particular deception is not an actionable crime."

"I find that hard to believe." MacKay paused while a murmur of voices came from the direction of the foyer. "To put family and friends through such an ordeal ought to be a crime."

"The cases I found related to people wiggling out of debts, betrothals, and contractual obligations such as articles of indenture. To the extent fraud resulted from the faked death, the fraud is a crime. I'd have to prove, after all these years, that Merridew was attempting to defraud somebody other than his wife. She, having become his legal chattel upon speaking her vows, cannot sue him for anything. The judges opine that a cow cannot sue its owner, hence a wife cannot take her spouse to court."

"And Merridew, as a professional swindler, would think nothing of defrauding that good lady out of her meager savings or what she could borrow from Mrs. Oldbach. Harry Merridew makes up in cunning what he lacks in honor."

"And he is Matilda's lawfully wedded spouse." A fact that would not budge, no matter how long Tremont pondered it. "I'm hoping he'll divorce her, for a sum certain."

MacKay rose to set his glass on the sideboard. "You propose to bargain with the devil."

"Whether Matilda marries me or not, she and Tommie deserve to be free of that man. He might allow her a separation from bed and board, but my objective for her is a divorce."

"The penny press will have a field day." MacKay said this as kindly as it was possible to pronounce a capital sentence on a woman's good name. "Not fair, but there it is. She'll be the merry widow, and her cuckolded husband the victim of the rapacious lord."

"I usually play a convincing buffoon," Tremont said, finishing his drink and getting to his feet. "Playing the villain will be a refreshing change, however ironic, given Merridew's behavior toward his wife. I will understand if you cease to be at home when I call."

"The day I am not at home to you, Tremont, is the day Dorcas disowns me for hypocrisy. What's your next move?"

Tremont had been prepared to do without MacKay's support, without anybody's support, but the major's loyalty meant worlds. Not only for Tremont, but for Matilda, who'd had so few allies.

"My next move is to accompany Matilda tomorrow to this meeting with the prospective buyer. I will create the impression that I am her man of business and form my own opinion of the buyer, if he has the courage to show up in person. The men will follow Merridew from the meeting, or watch the solicitors' office until Merridew is sent a message."

"You've sent men to Oxford, you're regularly patrolling Matilda's house, and now you have the solicitors' office under surveillance."

"Almost as if I anticipate a battle, isn't it?"

A tap on the door effected an amazing transformation in MacKay's features. A convincing scowl was replaced by beaming benevolence.

"Come in, darling wife."

Dorcas MacKay opened the door and returned besotted fire with a dazzling smile. "Husband, our Michael has come to call. I've sent for the tea tray. My lord, are you acquainted with my brother?"

Tremont bowed as the most strikingly handsome fellow he'd ever beheld was introduced to him. Michael Delancey's features were masculine perfection, from clean jaw, to patrician nose, to dark hair curling just so over a noble brow. He was a good-sized specimen, but one did not notice that at first, given the splendor of his physiognomy.

"Lord Tremont, a pleasure." Delancey bowed in return. "I hope I'm not interrupting?"

He had the plummy vowels of the Oxonian and the cultivated deference of the young churchman-with-great-potential. Something about his eyes nonetheless conveyed restlessness.

"I was just leaving," Tremont replied. "Might I put a question to you in parting, Mr. Delancey?"

"Of course."

"You attended Oxford. Are you familiar with the surrounds of Worthy Street?"

"I am," he said, his gracious smile turning quizzical. "Among the students, the name was something of a joke. The activities common to the neighborhood were anything but worthy in the opinion of the faculty. Dicing, drink, and other dubious diversions. One learned to avoid Worthy Street unless one wanted to be relieved of all of his coin and half of his wits, not in that order."

No judgment clouded that disclosure. If anything, Delancey sounded wistful.

"And do you recall an inn just south of Oxford doing business as the Hungry Hound?"

"I recall no such establishment, my lord, and I traveled the Oxford Road frequently, because I took all my breaks with my family here in London."

"Thank you," Tremont said. "You have appeased my curiosity. A pleasure to make your acquaintance. Mrs. MacKay, Major, good day."

MacKay scooted past his wife and brother-in-law and around a footman bearing an enormous tea tray. "I'll see ye out."

In the foyer, Tremont donned his cloak and hat and prepared to walk half the length of London in increasingly wintry weather. Another conference with the solicitors was in order.

MacKay hesitated before opening the door. "Good Samaritans with the kind of coin needed to send a body from Oxford to London

don't generally dwell in the neighborhoods where drunken college boys are cheated of their quarterly funds."

"Though a professional swindler would have ample connections in such a location, if not temporary lodgings. Harry Merridew is alive and well, though he's grown so short of coin that he's willing to rise from the dead. Fortunately, I have coin to spare."

"And if he wants something other than coin?"

"You mean if he wants to resume his status as Matilda's husband?" Tremont pulled on his gloves. "Then I am prepared to use every privilege and advantage I have—and they are legion—to thwart him. Good day, MacKay."

Tremont welcomed the chilly wind on his face and welcomed the distance to march. Both would aid him to focus on strategies most likely to achieve victory in the looming conflict with Merridew.

Though defeat was always a possibility.

English law took marriage seriously. From all accounts, Matilda's wedding had been a proper affair, with her father present and offering no objection. If Harry Merridew chose to be difficult, then the coming battle was likely to end in all-out war.

CHAPTER THIRTEEN

"You are early," Matilda said as Tremont offered her his arm, "and you brought your fancy coach." The vehicle, crests hidden, four matching bays in harness, sat at the bottom of the steps, looking sober and splendid, much like its owner.

Tremont handed her up and climbed in after her. "I thought we'd fortify ourselves with a noon meal at the tea shop before we meet with your prospective buyer."

Clearly, Tremont had been thinking of much more than that. He was again the punctiliously mannered, slightly distracted gentleman whom she'd met in St. Mildred's parish hall. He took the place beside Matilda on the forward-facing bench, though he did not reach for her hand.

"I'm nervous, Marcus. I thank you for the invitation, but might we take the extra hour at your house instead?"

He rapped on the roof with the head of his walking stick, and the coach rolled smoothly forward.

"You want to swill tea in my parlor and debate tactics? This is merely a reconnaissance mission, my dear. We go to listen and collect information. Any documents you sign will be genuine enough, so exercise extreme caution if you're inclined to wield a pen during this meeting."

"I won't sign anything. I will invoke a lady's right to dither and demand time to consider the offer and discuss it with you privately. I wish you'd let me go alone."

Tremont wrapped her gloved fingers in a light grasp. "You have fought every battle on your own, Matilda. Why take this on as solo combat too? Do you doubt my thespian capabilities? Fear not. I impersonated a peer of the realm for years, when all I really wanted to do was think, putter, and ponder. In the army, my role was regimental whipping boy for my superior officer. In the stews, I took on the part of neighborhood scribe. Harry will never take me for a besotted earl. I am not a swindler, but I can play a part."

The coach came to a halt at one of London's inevitable traffic tangles.

"Harry is something beyond a swindler," Matilda said. "He is like a fox that regards a decimated henhouse as a good night's work. He doesn't hate the chickens he kills. It's just that he's hungry, and they do taste ever so lovely, and somebody went to all that trouble to pen them up for him. Other people, with few exceptions, are so many chickens to him, and he doesn't really grasp that his fine night's work destroys lives. He has his funny little rules—he abhors violence, considers it the tool of fools and drunks—but he lacks what you or I would recognize as morality."

"And nothing," Tremont said, scowling out the window, "nothing in your upbringing, your education, or your wildest nightmares prepared you to be under the authority of such a one as he. Let's walk."

Before Matilda could reply, Tremont had popped down from the coach and was holding the door for her. She followed and was soon on the walkway, being escorted in the direction of Tremont's town house.

"Listen to me, Matilda," he said, after giving the coachman instructions. "You must put from your mind any thought of sparing my sensibilities. If you want to set me aside, I will accede to your decision. I will hate that you made that choice, but I will understand."

"Why am I doomed to take to my bed men with either too little honor or too much? The last thing I want to do is set you aside." They turned the corner, and even Tremont's house brought the man to Matilda's mind. Elegant and spruce without putting on airs.

"No, that is not the last thing you want to do. The last thing you want to do is be parted from your son."

"*What?*" Matilda came to a halt and disentangled her arm from Tremont. "You aren't making any sense." Even as she said the words, she knew that Tremont always, without fail, made sense.

"Harry Merridew ensured that your father was present at the wedding, so even though you were not yet one-and-twenty, the marriage was unassailably valid. Harry was not the paragon you thought he was, but that hardly constitutes grounds for an annulment. He put a roof over your head and bread on the table, despite his many, many failings."

And of course, now the sky had decided to send down not snow, but an icy drizzle miserably blended of rain, snow, and something in between.

Matilda resumed walking. "What has the wedding to do with Tommie?"

"Merridew is legally the boy's father."

"Harry's name is not on the birth registry. He told me that later, in the midst of an argument, when he thought I'd be cowed by the notion that my son dwelled under a cloud of potential scandal."

"Merridew is still legally the boy's father." Tremont took her arm to accompany her up the steps of his town house. "What did he hope...? Ah, he wanted to blackmail Joseph's family. If they sought any connection with their fallen soldier's progeny, Harry's failure to appear on a birth record would aid that scheme."

Matilda paused beneath the porch awning to survey the dreary street. The coach lumbered into view around the corner, and Tremont waved it on to the mews.

"That scheme apparently came to nothing," Matilda said. "Joseph's family knew a confidence trickster when one showed up on their doorstep. I take your point regarding Tommie. Harry could kidnap him, and I'd have nothing—legally—to say to it. I had not focused on that scenario, having been more concerned with the damage Harry can do to me personally. I doubt he will consider Tommie's role in the whole business. Tommie was... a pet, to Harry. Amusing, until it was time to hand a squalling, malodorous baby back to me."

"That baby is how Harry inveigled you into speaking your vows. You are a devoted mother, Matilda, hence my reminder that you must set me aside if that is the best course for you and Tommie."

She let herself into the house. "That is your honor talking. What does your heart say?"

Tremont followed her into the foyer and closed the door. "My heart is ready to die for you, but not to kill for you. I wish it were otherwise, but I cannot justify a selfish, murderous impulse in this case."

"I won't ask that you die or kill for me." She let him untie the damp ribbons of her bonnet and tucked her gloves into the pocket of her cloak. "Do you recall asking me once upon a time what I wanted?"

Tremont removed his hat and ran his fingers through his hair. "The memory will delight me until the day I am summoned for celestial judgment."

"I will cheerfully be your mistress, you know." Matilda undid the frogs of his cloak and hung the garment at hook. "I'd also marry you, assuming Harry is happy to slink away with the deed to my house in his hand."

Tremont settled his hands on her shoulders, as if he knew she wanted to discuss anything—anything at all—other than the havoc Harry could wreak in their lives.

"Marriage to me will make a bigamist of you, my love, and that would give Harry even more leverage over us both. Our children would be illegitimate, and thus the shadow he casts looms over them as well. I will not put the woman I esteem above all others at risk for a felony arrest. As for becoming my mistress, that would send the respectability you fought so hard to preserve for Tommie straight down the jakes."

Matilda leaned into him. "Sometimes, I wish your intellect wasn't so formidable."

"Not formidable, but one of few tools I can rely on. Shall I order a tray, Matilda? We certainly have time."

What do you want, Matilda. What do you want? The words echoed in her memory, as did the wondrous notion of for once *having* what she wanted.

"I want you," she said. "Forever and beyond, if possible. If not forever, then here and now would be lovely."

She expected remonstrations, lectures, philosophy—if Harry was alive, cavorting with Marcus was adultery, a sin, if not a crime.

Tremont regarded her with an odd, slight smile. "You're sure, Matilda?"

"Yes." Everything—heart, mind, and what honor a woman could claim—supported that answer. "Yes, and yes, and yes again."

"So be it." He took her hand, led her to the steps, and straight up into his sitting room. "We might be late for our appointment."

"The weather has made traffic abominable."

"I'm sure it will, but I try not to tell white lies to spare my dignity. If I'm late because I failed to keep track of the time, I would rather say so, or simply apologize for the lapse, and save the lying as a last resort. Shall I undo your hooks?"

"Please." Matilda stood by the fire and gave him her back. "Do you think your papa is looking down from heaven, knowing when you've been naughty?"

"As a boy, I did. Now, Papa holds the place of a benevolent angel, hoping I don't disappoint him. Do you ever wonder what sort of father your Harry had?"

What an odd question. "He might not know who his father is." Matilda held still a moment longer while Marcus untied her corset strings.

"Where was Harry when Tommie was conceived?" He slipped his arms around her waist and embraced her from behind.

Matilda scoured her memory for an answer, because there was one. In another of their many spats, Harry had taunted her with proof he could offer publicly that he had not fathered Tommie.

"Harry was in Bristol, looking in on an old chum. He had a lot of old chums whom he looked in on when it suited him to avail himself of their hospitality. I think Sparky Lykens was an old chum in truth, hailing from Harry's birthplace. I met Sparky a time or two. Not an elderly man, but he had elderly mannerisms. He suffered an injury while taking the king's... shilling."

She extricated herself from Tremont's embrace and faced him. "The limping man is probably Mr. Lykens. Harry turned to him when nobody else would put up with him."

"When he needed an accomplice he could trust. The name is very helpful, Matilda. We'll pass it along to the men, and if this Sparky character served in Spain, somebody will know him or know of him. The name is unusual, and that helps too."

"Spartacus," Matilda said. "That's why I recalled it. Not a moniker the common folk are likely to foist upon a child."

"Who is Tommie named for?"

"Doubting Thomas, the apostle my father approved of least."

Tremont drew her into a hug. "The apostle gifted with the most rational nature. I do love you."

Matilda hugged him back and then yielded to the temptation to cling. Marcus was handsome and fit and in every way an attractive specimen, but his physical appeal was an afterthought—literally.

The true measure of the man was in the intangibles. He had pondered whether he could commit murder on Matilda's behalf and rejected the notion. A lesser person would not have faced that question seriously and thus would have preserved an excuse to commit the crime in the heat of the moment.

Tremont had used the excuse of the heat of the moment—the explanation—at Waterloo. He would not allow himself to use it again. His moral rigor, his sense of accountability, refreshed Matilda's hopes as all of Harry's ill-gotten coin never had.

"I love you too, Marcus. Please take me to bed."

Tremont was barely acquainted with Matilda in the erotic sense, and yet, he knew precisely how the encounter she sought should go. He must give her intense pleasure, to be hoarded up against the possibility of equally intense and far more protracted pain.

He had considered refusing her request, but for what purpose? To quiet some cowardly nattering in his head about adultery and the letter of the law? The law said Harry Merriman was dead, so how could allegations of adultery be brought?

"Why is the right thing not the fair thing?" he muttered, pulling his shirt over his head. "Right by whose standards? The right thing to do is supposedly to offer one's life in the defense of the crown. The fair thing would be for Fat George to sell his art collection and at least pay for a few cannon instead of burdening John Bull with that expense."

"You are vexed," Matilda said, taking his shirt and folding it neatly over the privacy screen.

"I am hoist on my own petard. I have prided myself on enjoying logical puzzles and moral conundrums. At this moment, logic and honor are no comfort."

Matilda had emerged from the privacy screen wearing her chemise and Tremont's favorite night-robe, a quilted blue going shiny at the elbows. Her hair was in a single dark braid over her shoulder, and the sight of her, ready for bed and for bedding, was both delight and torment.

To never again behold her thus, to know that Harry Merridew had that honor... That wouldn't be fair or right or honorable, but it was all too possible.

"Love is a comfort," Matilda said. "When I was at my worst, early in my marriage to Harry, we'd be spatting about his philandering or the coalman's bill, and I'd despair. What had I done, marrying that scoundrel? Then Tommie would give me a kick,"—she put a hand on her belly—"and I would be fortified. No matter what nonsense Harry dished out to me, I was free of my father, and I had dodged ruin. For Tommie, I would make a go of the situation."

Tremont drew her into his arms. "And you did, as you always have." As she would again, if necessary. The thought made him bilious—and very determined.

"It won't come to that, Marcus. I won't let it come to that. Please kiss me."

Matilda did not give him time to comply with her order. She got hold of him by the hair and commenced kissing him witless. Her kiss tasted of desperation and courage and told Tremont that she wanted loving, not philosophy, not courtship, not gentlemanly affection.

He scooped her up and deposited her on the bed, then came down atop her.

"If you want finesse from me today," he began as Matilda drew her knees up along his flanks, "I fear I am unable to oblige."

"I want your damned breeches off."

He was naked in ten seconds flat, and Matilda used the time to slip out of his robe. She lay on the bed, cheeks flushed, knees up, the chemise about her waist.

"To hurry this moment is criminal," Tremont said, crouching over her. "To refuse it would be... incomprehensible." He settled closer so they were belly to belly and breast to chest, and still that wasn't close enough.

"I want to consume you," Matilda said, linking her hands at his nape. "To inhale you and make you part of me forever."

"You are part of me forever." That admission gave Tremont a respite from the lust and bleakness riding him. Matilda was right: Love was a comfort, and love was as real as the law or honor or scandal and more powerful than all of them put together.

He stroked Matilda's hair back from her brow, took a firm hold of his self-restraint, and began a leisurely kissing campaign. Somewhere between her jaw and her shoulder, Matilda let out a long, soft sigh and retaliated with a slow glide of her palm down Tremont's back and over his hip.

They lavished tenderness on each other until easing their bodies together became the only intimacy yet to explore. Tremont went slowly and sweetly, holding out for more of those sighs from his lover. She yielded them and arched into his caresses until give-and-take blended into a shared exultation.

Matilda surrendered to pleasure twice, the second occasion being Tremont's notion of an erotic peroration. He turned a dreamy, delicious loving passionate and then explosive, until Matilda's body grasped what her mind apparently had not: Pleasure could come in yet still greater increments than she'd imagined.

"You fiend," she whispered as Tremont levered up to give her room to breathe. "You utter, shameless... You are not what you seem, Marcus."

At that moment, he was trying to mentally recite from Caesar's Gallic letters, because even withdrawing might push him over the edge.

"What am I?"

"Not a philosopher, not a peer, not a scholar... You are a lover."

Because he did love her, he eased from her body, availed himself of the handkerchief on the night table, and spent on her belly.

"I am *your* lover, Matilda." And some fine day, he would know every joy that status could confer, but today was not that day. He tidied up and gathered her in his arms. "Nap if you like. I comported myself with unseemly dispatch. There's time."

That offer was all wrong, all courteous and considerate, when the moment wanted... sweet, sleepy nothings and quiet caresses. A restorative nap and a resumption of intimacies.

"If this loving is your idea of unseemly dispatch, Marcus, I will not survive your sieges." Matilda drifted off, while Tremont arranged himself beside her and watched the hands of the clock beside the wardrobe advance.

Matilda's whole marriage to Harry Merridew had been a siege, and now the invading army was back, ready to pillage and plunder what it hadn't carried off in the earlier battles. Matilda was mentally preparing for defeat, else she would not have asked for this interlude.

Tremont took another quarter hour to review what he knew, reconsider strategy, and look for options that did not exist. The best he could do before rousing his beloved was to remind himself that the meeting would yield more information, and with more information might come more hope.

He continued to ruminate while they dressed and donned cloaks and hats, pondered yet more while they traveled half-way across London, and waited until he'd handed Matilda down from the town coach to pose his question.

"Before we go in there, Matilda, clarify one point for me: If I'm able to wrest only you or Tommie from Merridew's grasp, but not both, I am to keep hold of Tommie, correct?"

She studied the façade of a staid establishment going a bit seedy around the gutters and walkways. In spring, the row of houses probably acquired an air of genteel repose, but winter revealed age and the beginning of neglect. Only a shiny plaque by the door—Drees and Son—confirmed that they had reached a place of business rather than a domicile.

"Don't make me choose. It won't come to that."

"When has Harry Merridew ever done what you needed him to do?"

"When he married me."

"And thereafter?"

Matilda drew down the veil on her bonnet. She'd attired herself as many widows did, in dignity and perpetual half mourning. The gray dress and bonnet suited the occasion and the weather.

"Harry is not a devil, Marcus. He's difficult but, as you say, entirely self-interested, which makes him consistent, and that works to my advantage this time."

"Then you are prepared to marry me, though it will mean both scandal and poverty?"

She peered at him through her veil. "I am, but how does poverty come into it? I cannot imagine you mishandling your funds, and you describe your holdings as prosperous."

"You tell me that the man's first motivation is money. He likes the games and schemes, but the reward is coin. If Harry agrees to divorce you, then as the peer footing the enormous cost for that undertaking, I tip my hand to him. I will be named and sued in the criminal conversation case, and the extent of my wealth will become obvious to Harry."

Matilda put a hand on the coach as if to steady herself. "It will, but Harry's not a fool. You are a peer, he's a commoner, though audacious in his greed."

"Precisely, he is audacious in his greed, though he probably considers himself blessed with the virtue of abundant ambition. He's like that fox, slaughtering every biddy in the henhouse when his belly can only hold one. He is welcome to plunder my coffers, Matilda, because my ambition is to spend the rest of my life loving you. We will have enough left to realize that goal, I've made sure of it."

"The meetings with the solicitors?"

"Putting funds in trust for Mama and Lydia and making myself and Sir Dylan the trustees. Mama and Lydia have been informed by letter, and they will understand. Sir Dylan will as well. My family did want me to marry, after all."

"Causing a scandal to rock the realm wasn't in their plans for you."

"Nor mine for you, but once the press has had its frolic, we will have what we wish, won't we?"

"If I have you and Tommie, I will be content."

She would say that, and she hadn't answered his earlier question. "And if I must choose between you and Tommie, Matilda?"

Tremont hated that the question had to be asked, but it was Matilda's choice to make. She linked arms with him and hauled him toward the steps leading to the solicitors' office.

"Save Tommie. Break whatever rules you must, thwart the law, exert your privileges, but save my son. I was afraid the sweeps would get him, or the abbesses, but the real threat turns out to be his legal father. The sweeps haven't snatched him away, but if Harry tries to take him from me, save my son, Marcus."

"So be it." That Matilda would face the question rather than offer another it-won't-come-to-that declaration was more proof that she expected to lose the battle with Merridew.

The successful confidence trickster realized coin from his schemes, but he also earned proof that he was more clever, wise, and skilled than the average person. He was rewarded rather than punished for abandoning the principles of decency, and for Harry Merridew, that sense of superiority might be the greater motivation.

A divorce would leave Harry rich, but refusing to cooperate might make him happy.

And Matilda apparently shared Tremont's fear that now, when it mattered most, Harry would decide that he was entitled to more than his share of happiness.

That Tommie would be safe gave Matilda a measure of courage. Harry could be peevish and threatening, but the whole time Matilda had dwelled with him, he'd never raised a hand to her, and she'd never gone hungry for long. Marriage to him had been purgatory, but not quite hell.

God have mercy, she was *still* married to him.

Shock warred with anger over that state of affairs as she and Tremont were greeted by a jovial, mutton-chopped old fellow whose offices were spotless, though sparsely furnished.

"Hubert Drees, at your service, Mrs. Merridew. And who is this good chap?" He turned a friendly smile on Tremont, though his gaze held speculation.

Tremont had dressed soberly and carried a leather satchel. He exuded propriety along with the same banked inquisitiveness Drees brought to the occasion. But then, Marcus communed with his lawyers frequently. He would well know how to impersonate one.

"Glover," he said, giving his family name. "I was available to accompany Mrs. Merridew on short notice, and because the asset in question is substantial, she had the great good sense to bring me along."

"Of course," Drees said, beaming at Matilda. "One can never be too sensible, can one? Mr. Merriman awaits us in the library. Shall I have the clerk bring us some tea?"

"No, thank you," Matilda said. "To business, if you please, though I must warn you, Mr. Drees, my objective today is simply to hear your terms. I will not be chivvied into any premature decisions."

"Certainly not," Drees boomed, chortling as if Matilda had made a jest. "Oh, certainly not, madam. Glover, your client has a good head on her shoulders."

If he pats my arm, I shall smite him.

"She also has a competent advisor in me," Tremont replied, smiling toothily. "Shall we get to the details, Drees?"

Yes, please. The details and the great, much-dreaded reunion.

Harry stood when Matilda entered a stuffy little chamber that smelled of old books and countless pipes. He bowed with all the graciousness of a great actor acknowledging a standing ovation.

"Mrs. Merridew, a pleasure." His smile conveyed a perfect blend of hope and hesitance, the attitude of a fellow who intended to make a good impression and a better deal. His eyes told Matilda he was enjoying himself, daring her to make a fuss and knowing full well she would not.

Harry Merridew was alive and well and very much on his game—though he did look a bit skinny.

Matilda tossed off a shallow curtsey. "Sir."

"Mr. Glover is representing the lady's interests," Drees said. "Shall we be seated?"

Tremont held Matilda's chair, and the situation took on an air of unreality. While Drees launched into a monologue that made selling one small house sound more complicated than annexing a French province, Matilda tried to study Harry discreetly, looking for some sign that he was not Harry.

Oh, but he was. The same tilt of his head when he asked a question—*the lady does have clear title to the domicile?*—the same habit of pursing his lips when he wanted to convey that he pondered a delicate point.

In the space of moments, years of widowhood evaporated, and Matilda was returned to the ordeal of marriage to the man now masquerading as Harrell Merriman. His disappearances, his moods, his philandering, his unwillingness to take on honest work, and his offhand affection toward Tommie—and occasionally toward her—had all conspired to keep Matilda perpetually off-balance and upset.

She had learned to deal with the upset by keeping busy. Their lodgings had been immaculate, the mending always done, and—when matters had grown desperate—other people's mending had been taken care of as well, and without Harry's knowledge.

Such misery, and for what? So an intelligent, healthy, reasonably good-looking, and outlandishly charming grown man could survive on schoolboy schemes and think himself clever.

"You expect Mrs. Merridew to surrender the deed to the house in exchange for a promissory note?" Tremont asked when Drees came to a pause in his droning.

"That is how the agreement reads," Drees said, "the draft agreement. Perhaps you are unfamiliar with real estate transactions here in the capital, Mr. Glover? When a provincial banking institution is involved, and with the posts being unreliable, the promissory note assures good faith and a contractual obligation. The courts are happy to enforce such obligations, provided good fellows such as ourselves write them up properly."

He offered a vicar's patient smile to a gossipy dowager.

Tremont offered the same smile, not to Drees, but to Harry, the poor sod who had the misfortune to retain such a bumbler as his attorney.

"And because," Tremont said, "the posts *are* unreliable, the courts slow and whimsical, and a widow's lot trying at best, I could not advise Mrs. Merridew to accept anything other than cash or a bank note—made out on a London account—before she executes the deed. When the funds are in her account, she will surrender that deed to me for transfer to you, Mr. Drees."

Ye gods, Marcus sounded for all the world as if he were indeed a lawyer. And yet, the legal posturing was just that, because Harry had no intention of paying for the house and probably no *ability* to pay for it either.

Drees grasped his lapels and filled his oratory sails, clearly prepared to lecture Tremont into submission, and that bootless endeavor could go on for the rest of the afternoon. Matilda was abruptly unwilling to afford Mr. Drees a captive audience.

"If you lawyerly gentlemen will absent yourselves," she said, "Mr. Merriman and I will take a moment to confer directly."

"I cannot approve," Drees said, shaking a finger at Matilda. "Rank foolishness to allow the clients to go off in corners. Never a sound idea. Glover doubtless agrees with me."

Marcus gathered up the paper and pencil he'd used for taking notes and aimed a look at Matilda over his satchel.

"I take my orders from Mrs. Merridew," he said. "If she seeks a moment to negotiate directly with the prospective buyer, then I am prepared to do as I'm told, though I will remain just beyond the door, available to my client at a moment's notice."

"I'm happy to hear what Mrs. Merridew has to say," Harry so helpfully added. "In my experience, lawyers can needlessly complicate the simplest transactions."

"I leave under protest," Drees said, heaving to his feet. "Let the record reflect my protestations. Glover, you are my witness."

He huffed and harrumphed his way from the room. Marcus followed, though he left the door open three inches. Harry—of course—rose and closed the door the rest of the way.

"You are looking splendid, Tilly, but then, I knew you'd manage. The boy appears to be thriving as well."

Five years ago, Matilda would have responded to the challenge in that opening salvo, to the latent taunt—*I knew you'd manage*—sandwiched between superficial compliments. Five years ago, she'd been perpetually exhausted, anxious, and without allies.

Now, she saw the scuff marks on Harry's polished boots, the cravat carefully folded to hide a stain. His right cuff had been mended inexpertly, and the sharpness to his face suggested he'd been on short rations.

"Sit down, Harry, and stop trying to goad me. Widowhood has been challenging, but I prefer it to resuming wifehood at your side."

He sank into the seat across from her, which put the door at his back. "You've learned some plain speaking in my absence."

Matilda had learned how it felt to be respected and cared for. Powerful lessons. "Harry, what in God's name happened to you?"

"I doubt God had anything to do with it."

"You prevaricate to give yourself time to concoct a taradiddle because you did not think I'd demand a private audience. Please tell me the truth."

He linked his hands on the table before him, as if preparing to recite grace before a meal. "I wish I knew, Tilly. One moment, I was playing a friendly hand of cards at ye old posting inn, the next I was in the ditch, my head throbbing, not a coin to my name."

"Which inn?" The door behind Harry had eased open two inches. Matilda willed herself to gaze fixedly at Harry's handsome, lying face.

"I don't know. That's the hell of it. When I roused from my injuries, I not only had no purse, I had no memory. I knew I was Harry, but I couldn't even settle on a last name. The past came back in bits and dribbles, and that took months. The whole business was humbling, and I still have gaps in my recollection."

A part of Matilda wanted to believe this outlandish tale—Harry had regularly invited life to hand him a sound thrashing—and wanted to believe the bewildered tone, the bent head. Five years ago, she might have.

"Why, then, when you recalled you had a wife waiting for you back in London, didn't you return to me?"

"I was in Ireland by then, barely scraping by, and I knew very well I hadn't been much of a husband to you. I also know I'm not Tommie's father and the rest of what brought us together. When I had the means to come home, I lacked the confidence. You deserved better, Tilly, and for all I knew, you'd remarried and had other children. When I decided that no, you'd be better off knowing the truth and might not be faring so well on your own, I lacked the means to book passage. I could not make up my mind what the right thing to do was."

Having had so little experience with that exercise. "What do you want from me, Harry?"

"The house would be a nice gesture in the direction of putting me back on my feet, Tilly. I've had a hard time, and I still get the most miserable headaches. You seem to be doing well. You don't need that house, and I do. 'For better or for worse' means you can't just turn your back on me. I don't want to make trouble, but I've run out of options, and I'm still your husband."

An ambiguous declaration, part threat, part confession. "I have not missed you," Matilda said as the door eased open another inch. "But I worried for you, Harry. Every time you vanished—and you vanished frequently—I prayed myself to sleep, hoping you had not come to a bad end."

"I nearly did, but I'd like to make a fresh start. Settling matters with you is part of that."

"Bilking me of my only security, you mean?"

"Don't be like that, Tilly." He spoke chidingly rather than angrily. "You are pretty, you can run a household without trying, you're a devoted mother, and men like that in a woman. You have a lot of good years left, while I..." He spread his hands in what was probably supposed to be a gesture of surrender. "I'm ready for a change, and I can't make that change unless you'll part with the house."

"And how can I remarry, Harry, how can I meet any man I esteem at the altar, knowing myself to be your wife? Please recall that my gifts as a swindler are paltry compared to those of present company. Recall that bigamy is a hanging felony, and the children of a bigamous union are bastards. You would steal my only security—Tommie's only security—and go on your *merry* way, until the next time you decide to come around looking for any savings I've managed to build up."

"I didn't much miss you either, Tilly." This was said mildly, almost affectionately.

"So what threat are you about to aim at me to inspire me to give you an entire house in a decent neighborhood?"

The door opened another inch.

"I'd hoped it wouldn't come to this, dearest wife."

"And I knew it would."

Harry sighed. He gazed about with an air of heroic long-suffering. He pursed his lips and frowned at the table. Matilda would have applauded this grand performance of a man deliberating over a difficult choice were she not so bored by it.

"Tommie's father came from a good family," he said. "Tommie is their only grandchild, the son of their fallen firstborn."

"And they rebuffed your efforts to extort money from them on that basis."

"They are older now. They've lost a daughter, and they don't know that you and Tommie are biding with a house full of drunks and ne'er-do-wells. They don't know that Tommie is tagging around for much of the day after streetwalkers wearing maids' caps. They don't know that the boy has no father even in name, but I can make them aware of all those details, Tilly, and there's not a judge in this country who'd leave Tommie with you if the squire decides to petition for custody."

Matilda felt a familiar fissuring in response to Harry's threat. While she was tempted by the very reaction Harry had intended —*you cannot take my son!*—she had also learned to doubt every word out of Harry's mouth.

"Harry," she said, conjuring a semblance of amusement from some latent well of thespian talent. "Give it up. The squire and his goodwife have known of my widowhood for years. They've made no overture, sent not so much as a groat to their grandson, nor asked after his wellbeing. They weren't about to fall in with your schemes years ago, and they don't give a holey sock for Tommie now. You are bobbing about in the River Tick, and I'm your last option. Why don't you simply find another bride, this time with more of a dowry?"

Harry merely shook his head, and Matilda had the sense that was the first honest response he'd given her. Bigamy was apparently not a crime he was willing to commit—one of his quaint little rules— though he'd gladly see Matilda take that step.

"Then we are at *point non plus*, Harry. You cannot threaten me into giving up that house, but fortunately, for you, there is something I want even more than that dower property. My lord, you can come in now."

By the most fleeting consternation in his eyes, Harry betrayed surprise as he shot to his feet.

Marcus walked back into the room. "Tremont, at your service, sir, family name Glover. I hardly know what to call you, though cheat, liar, and scoundrel come to mind. Sit down, and don't even think about issuing me a challenge, because I will refuse. I am a peer and a dead shot, while you are"—he wrinkled the lordly beak—"Matilda's husband. For now."

Harry sat back down.

CHAPTER FOURTEEN

Matilda had never once indicated that her husband was a strikingly handsome man. Harry was not quite in the same league with Michael Delancey, but his looks were attractive in a way Delancey's perfection was not. Harry's smile had a quality of conspiratorial charm. His air was friendly and unassuming.

Dear old Harry, come to pull off another swindle.

A young, pregnant Matilda would have thought him quite the gallant knight, though she was clearly unimpressed now.

"I am Matilda's husband," Harry said as Tremont latched the door, "and I have much to answer for in that regard, but that is between me and Matilda."

"No, Harry, it is not," Matilda said, motioning for Tremont to take the place beside her. "You never consider the repercussions of your schemes beyond how much risk or reward is involved for you, but this time you have gone too far."

"Matilda, I was left for dead on the king's highway." Harry's version of injured dignity could have rivaled the late Mr. Garrick's. "I was friendless and bleeding without a coin to my name. You know how twitchy I get without a few coppers in my pocket. I mucked stalls to put bread in my mouth, suffered terrible headaches—"

"Oh, for God's sake, Merridew, spare us your histrionics."

Harry sent a look of noble long-suffering across the table. "I go by Merriman now."

"You go by whatever name suits your current criminal scheme," Tremont retorted, "but you neglected to change your handwriting when you changed your name." Tremont withdrew two documents from his satchel. "This is the cordial invitation you penned, inviting Mrs. Merridew to this meeting."

Tremont lay a single page of foolscap faceup on the table. "This," he went on, laying a second, yellowing page next to it, "is supposedly from the Hungry Hound's innkeeper, informing Mrs. Merridew of your death and asking her to remit a sum certain for the expenses resulting from her bereavement."

Harry studied both missives and had the sense to keep his lying gob shut for a change.

"Matilda sent you the money," Tremont said, returning the letters to his briefcase. "The penmanship is the same, despite the documents having been written years apart. You even make the same flourish beneath your signature, no matter which name you choose to use."

Harry sat back, not a hint of charm in his countenance. "Coincidence, my lord. Not proof, and if Matilda is such a penmanship expert now, why didn't she recognize my handwriting when I supposedly wrote to her from the Hungry Hound?"

Matilda studied the ceiling. "Because I was too busy wondering how I'd pay for your funeral and Tommie's next meal? Because it never occurred to me that *my husband* would swindle me out of the bed and board he owes me by law until death us do part? Because I do not have a criminal mind?"

"You're still a prodigious scold, Til."

"The fine Christian woman," Tremont said, "who took care of your supposed funerary expenses—Mrs. Brent of Worthy Street—is a madam of considerable renown among Oxford's randy scholars.

There is no Hungry Hound, unless I behold him at this moment, and if you ever were in Ireland, you were driven from those shores because some scheme—some other scheme—went badly awry."

"My lord eavesdropped on the private conversation between a man and his wife?"

Matilda snorted. "Tremont, at my request, knew better than to allow you any unwitnessed discourse with me, Harry. We set you up, and you waltzed into the snare, spewing predictable lies and offering not a word of apology."

She rose, bracing her hands on the table and looming over her husband. "You left me alone, barely a coin in the house, with a small child to raise. I don't care that you stole from me. I married you, and the cost of some mistakes never ends. I care very much that you turned your back on Tommie, when I married you solely for his sake. You broke your word to me, Harry, and for that, I will not forgive you."

Harry's bravado faltered, and he had the grace to look abashed. "I do stupid things when I'm desperate, Tilly. You of all people know that. I hate to be desperate. But I just can't seem... I thought maybe I'd go to America. They have land for the asking there, opportunity, a chance to start fresh, but I can't start fresh if I'm penniless."

America was a desperate measure indeed. Harry would have no old chums in the New World to turn to in a bad moment, no familiar bolt-holes, and his assortment of British regional accents would do him little good.

"You can have that fresh start, Harry," Matilda said. "All you have to do is divorce me."

Harry looked honestly puzzled. "Folk like us don't get divorced, Till. That's for the prancing lords and..." The puzzlement faded. "I see. And if I am unwilling to divorce you for his lordship's convenience, would you rather be his fancy piece than my wife? You do so value your respectability."

Matilda patted Harry's hand. "I'd rather be Tremont's *anything* than your wife. His scullery maid, his fancy piece, his undergardener.

Tremont treats everyone with honor and respect, while you regard other people as so many marks for you to bamboozle."

Harry winced. "You never used to be so harsh, Till. I work with what's on hand, same as any man who has to earn his keep." He rubbed his chin and sent Tremont an assessing look. "His nibs could kill me in a duel. It's been done, to escape creditors, to dodge a nagging wife. Says he's a dead shot, so folks would believe he'd done away with me."

Of all the schemes Harry could have concocted... "No," Tremont said. "For reasons which Mrs. Merridew will understand, I refuse to commit murder, or its theatrical equivalent. Besides, you have a tiresome propensity to rise from the dead. The simple, legal, effective solution to your problems, sir, is to divorce Matilda. You will be awarded handsome damages in the criminal conversation case. You can start afresh, and so can she."

"How handsome?"

Tremont named a figure which was not at the limit of what he could afford, but which would set him back more than a few years.

Harry gave a low whistle. "His lordship must love you, Till, and I'm all for aiding the course of true love, but in this case, I simply can't."

Matilda crossed her arms. "You won't. I know you are ruthless, Harry, and endlessly self-interested, but I never thought you were gratuitously mean. You worship the twin gods of Mammon and your own dunderheaded cleverness, so why won't you just once—after having wronged me repeatedly—give me what I want?"

Harry shot his cuffs. He rubbed his chin again, and Tremont knew exactly why the blighter was stalling.

"He cannot, Matilda, because it's worth his *life* to keep his name out of the papers. Every person he's swindled, every debt he's run out on, every friend he's double-crossed will recognize him as the supposedly dead husband of Matilda Merridew and come for him with pitchforks and warrants. I should have seen this. A man who will cheat his blameless wife will cheat half the realm, given the opportunity."

"It weren't like that," Harry said, a note of some dialect creeping past his public school diction. "Tilly was miserable with me. Hated every minute of being my wife, and I knew the Puritans at St. Mildred's would look out for her and the boy. I left the rent paid up and the larder stocked. The Puritans lent Tilly a hand, and now you want to look out for her too. She's already said she didn't miss me, so you can sod your sanctimonious—"

Tremont did not plan to snatch Harry up by his cravat and yank him to his feet, but one minute Harry was clothing himself in a martyr's robes, and the next he was clawing at Tremont's wrists.

"Cease. Lying." Tremont shook Harry once, to emphasize the point, and let him go.

"He's not lying," Matilda said, "not entirely. That's part of Harry's arsenal. He dribbles a little bit of the truth into all of his dissembling. I was utterly miserable married to him—though the rent was coming due and the larders empty—and now I'm apparently to pay for his sins as well as my own stupidity. Pay with the rest of my life."

"Sorry, Till." Harry ran a finger around his collar. "I'd like to get my hands on that money, but more than the money, I'd like to live to keep my handsome body and tarnished soul together. I can't have my name in the papers, and that's the whole truth. You could come to America with me. I'm sure his lordship would fund your passage if you asked him to."

The man was either very foolish or very brave. Perhaps both.

"Be quiet, Harry," Matilda said wearily. "Your stupid, selfish schemes nearly turned me into a streetwalker. Your dear friends condoled me with one breath and propositioned me with the next. Tremont offers me an honorable suit, but I can't... I am so angry with you right now that those creditors and betrayed friends may not be the worst danger you face."

Harry was quiet for a moment. "You aren't violent," he said. "I spotted that right off. You disdained your pa for raising his hand to you, and... I noticed that. You won't kill me to clear your path to the altar, Till, and his lordship won't either. You could pretend to die, maybe wait a year, use some henna, and study up on a Yorkshire accent. That one's easy—"

"Hush," Tremont said, when he wanted to bellow profanities. "Matilda is in an untenable situation because of your damned schemes and lies. We won't solve the situation with more falsehoods and farce."

"Harry Merridew is dead," Harry said evenly, "and that suits me well enough. With a bit more coin, I can book passage from Bristol to Philadelphia, and then my situation will be as tenable as I need it to be. Give me the money, Tilly—sell the house, charm the blunt off his lordship—and I will leave you and the boy in peace. That's the best I can do, and you know that's more decent than I usually bother to be."

Matilda gazed at him the same way the Almighty must have looked upon Lucifer after the war in heaven.

"You will leave me in peace," she said, "until you need more coin. Then you will come back around, having escaped hanging in Pennsylvania, New York, and probably New Jersey for good measure. You will wreck my life at regular intervals, my very own remittance husband, and if I balk at your demands, you will threaten to take Tommie with you. I know you, Harry. You have better angels, but they gave up the fight years ago."

Drees chose then to rap on the door. "Are we all through conferring? Glover, are you in there? Not the done thing to leave my client without the benefit of counsel." He let himself in while a boy with a tea tray hovered behind him.

"I'll just be going," Harry said, pulling on his gloves. "The lady has heard my offer, and she's said what she has to say." He tapped his hat onto his head and nodded to Tremont.

"We are finished for now," Matilda replied. "You will hear from me, Mr. Merry... I beg your pardon. I forget the name."

"Easy to do with passing acquaintances." Harry bowed to her and moved to the door, then paused with his hand on the latch, his expression distant and dignified. "I wasn't always like this. Believe that if you believe nothing else about me, ma'am. Good day and best of luck."

Tremont escorted Matilda back to the waiting coach, then took the place beside her on the forward-facing bench. He rapped once on the roof, and the coach rolled forward at the walk.

"I do not care for reconnaissance missions," Matilda muttered, "if that one was representative. Harry has aged, but he has not changed his spots. If anything, he's grown harder over the years. What did we learn, Marcus, besides the fact that we can never marry?"

"We learned that Harry Merridew-man-whatever values his life more than he values coin. We learned that his back is to the wall, probably as a result of whatever happened in Ireland. He cheated somebody in a position to press charges, or he'd never willingly take ship for America. We learned that his enemies are legion."

They had also learned that, by his own peculiar lights, Harry had made an effort to deal fairly—if not honorably—with Matilda and Tommie.

"Oh, very well, then. We learned all manner of interesting things," Matilda said, removing her bonnet, "but, Marcus, what are we to *do*?"

He put an arm around her shoulders and scoured his memory for some fortifying wisdom courtesy of the philosophers, the Bard, or poets. A protracted search confirmed that they were as inadequate to the occasion as Tremont felt, so he simply gave Matilda the truth.

"I don't know what to do, Matilda, but I am certain that I love you."

"And I love you."

Matilda had stashed all of her first pay packet into the same bank account that held her meager savings. She retrieved the whole of her means when she ought to have been taking her final turn in the MacKay nursery.

She would miss little John and his parents.

She would miss the men, the maids, and dear Nan, who was trying hard to remember her *haitches*.

She would miss stinky, crowded, bustling London, some.

She would miss the parishioners of St. Mildred's, who in their way had been kind to her when she'd desperately needed kindness.

And she would miss Marcus for the rest of her days.

"I know that walk, Tilly, me love," Harry said, falling in step beside her. "You are in a temper."

"If I hadn't been before, I certainly am now. Do you know, Harry, I have you to thank for showing me that I even possessed a temper?"

"Happy to oblige, that's me. When will you sign over the house to me?"

They waited on a corner while a stately four-in-hand negotiated the intersection. Charles's replacement waited as well, because the delay was caused by a horse unwilling to heed nature's call at any pace faster than a plod.

"I will sign the house over to you when all the seas gang dry, and rocks melt with the sun."

"Burns," Harry said. "'My love is like a red, red rose.' Sentimental drivel, but he was apparently right popular with the ladies. I need that house, Tilly."

"The lament does not improve for repetition, Harry. If you worked half as hard at legitimate employment as you work at avoiding it, you would be a wealthy man."

Matilda knew better than to pick up the pace, because Harry, being half a foot taller than she, would keep up easily. She called on old skills, skills learned early in her marriage, to separate her mind from the rage in her heart, while she examined whether the encounter could be put to any use.

"I can make trouble, Tilly," Harry said, ever so pleasantly. "I don't like to make trouble—I like to turn a coin or two and be on my way—but I can make very bad trouble."

"Why, Harry, I do believe you are threatening your own lawfully wedded wife. This follows inevitably upon denial of your purportedly reasonable requests, which are, in truth, the demands of a whiny boy. Next will come blustering, then a silence that is also intended to be threatening, but is, in fact, tedious. When I do not relent, you will do a bunk, to use the vernacular, and I am supposed to worry about my errant husband. What your schemes lack in originality, they make up for in predictability."

Harry offered his arm as Matilda stepped off the walkway. She ignored a courtesy that was entirely for show.

"Tilly, you wound me." Something in Harry's tone suggested he'd just parted with one of his rare, judiciously dispensed truths.

"You filleted me like a mackerel, sir, financially and emotionally, and I have yet to hear an apology."

They passed the tea shop where Matilda had spent some pleasant hours. She would miss that, too, as would Tommie, no doubt.

"Would you believe me if I said I was sorry?" The odd, honest note remained, not remorse, but perhaps bewilderment.

"You are always sorry. I have wondered, if anybody has ever been proud of you, or of their association with you."

Matilda was tempted to continue spewing bile, but she'd made her point. She kept her peace, wondering if Harry had followed her to the bank. He would—he was that determined and that canny.

And some other day, some day when she and Tommie were far, far away and the ache in her heart had faded to a mere agony, she'd again indulge in tears. Since weeping on Marcus's shoulder two days ago, Matilda had clung to reason with ruthless devotion.

Marcus had been closeted with his solicitors, though Matilda well knew what the result of those conferences would be. The situation occasioned by Harry's rise from the dead had a solution. It did not have a happily ever after, not for her and Marcus. Harry was just being Harry—conscienceless and self-interested to a staggering degree—but he was Matilda's husband.

"Did you for even one moment think of leaving me and Tommie in peace, Harry?"

"Yes. I left you in peace for several years, but I am tired, Tilly. I am tired of British laws, British snobbery, and British hypocrisy. I mean to go to the New World and take my chances in a new land. If you cannot see your way clear to deed the house to me, then I will simply take Tommie and leave you to your honorable earl. You can have all the peace you please."

And there it was, Harry's heavy artillery, fired with what sounded like genuine remorse.

"Your name does not appear on the birth registry, Harry. You dealt yourself out of an honor I would have willingly granted you. You are not Tommie's father in any sense."

"Happens I am. I have consulted the lawyers, and they say it's not even a question. You were married to me when the lad was born, I have not repudiated him, and thus the honor of his paternity is entirely mine."

Harry could put on and take off accents like a trained actor. Matilda had heard him glide from Cockney to Yorkshire and over to East Anglia in the space of an hour. He sounded in this conversation as if he'd had a proper education, to the manor born, even.

"Harry, who are your people?"

His steps slowed. "You ask me that *now*? I tell you I'm about to take your only begotten son halfway around the world, and when you should be shoving the deed to that house into my hands, you want to review old business?"

"Humor me. If you do plan to impersonate Tommie's father, you will have to become accustomed to all manner of outlandish questions bearing no apparent relation to anything save a small boy's curiosity. When Tommie asks about his grandpapa, what will you say?"

Harry touched a finger to his hat brim when a pair of shopgirls passed by. They giggled, he smiled, and Matilda wanted to shout profanities.

"If you must know, my father was a sanctimonious old Quaker whose own father made a fortune manufacturing guns. Papa refused to take over the business—the Friends have grown reluctant to openly dabble in war, though their banking tells a different story. In the grand tradition, I refused to wear my own father's false piety. We had a falling out, and I decamped for Sodom on Thames, to the relief of all and sundry."

"You did a bunk," Matilda said, trying to keep the surprise from her voice. "Is this why you disdain violence, Harry? Because the ghosts of your ancestors would haunt you?"

"Those ancestors could be handy with a birch rod on a small boy's backside, Till. Some of them at least. When can I have the house?"

"That is Tommie's house. Why can you not see that a child lacking many of life's advantages needs that asset more than you do?"

"Because he doesn't." The words were snarled without any pretensions to civility. "He's had you to cosset and coddle him. He had me, for a time, to pay the rent and the coalman. He has a damned earl ready to send him to bloody public school, while all I have is a pressing need to quit the home shores. I will take the boy, Tilly. I don't want to—he's a good lad, and he loves you—but I will take him. All manner of rigs suggest themselves when I can be a grieving husband with my pale little son."

Tommie was not pale, but he was little. Small enough to be snatched from the stable, despite the vigilance of the men and his mother. Besides, Harry could appeal to the authorities to return his son and his wayward wife to him, and the authorities would gladly render assistance.

While Matilda would look a fool, if not mad, claiming her husband had died on the Oxford Road at an inn that didn't exist.

"I will take ship for Philadelphia," Matilda said as they approached another intersection. "Tommie and I will, rather. Aunt

Portia has some connections there, and it's said to be a gracious and prosperous city. When I have left London with Tommie, you will have the deed to the house."

Harry smiled at a veiled dowager mincing along on the arm of a footman. "You'll leave your fancy toff just like that?"

I will do the right thing for the man I love. "Try as he might, Tremont cannot solve the problem that you've created for me and Tommie. That fresh start you mention is the only reasonable option if I still value my reputation, which I do. I have no connections of my own, so I am reduced to trading on Aunt's girlhood friendships."

"We're good at landing on our feet, aren't we, Tilly?"

For attempting that wistful, confiding tone, Matilda would have gladly pushed Harry beneath the wheels of the next oncoming coach.

"We're cowards, Harry, who are good at running. I ran from scandal, and I ran from the vicarage. You ran from me. Now you've run from schemes gone inevitably awry, and I am running from scandal again." And running straight into a broken heart.

Harry studied the sky, which today was a bright, wintry blue. "Cowards live to run another day, Tilly. Tremont wants you to be his fancy piece?"

No, he did not, though Matilda had offered. "Is that so surprising?"

"Not surprising in the least, but less than you deserve." Harry drew Matilda away from the edge of the walkway just as a phaeton splashed past. "You will find it hard to credit, erstwhile wife of mine —I find it hard to credit—but I have missed you, contrary to previous representations. You kept a wonderfully tidy house, and you were so trusting, so earnest, and then so ferociously devoted to the boy."

"And now," Matilda said sweetly, "I am so angry. I will book passage for next Tuesday, and you will not see me off. I have arrangements to make if you are to be given the deed upon my departure."

"I knew you'd see reason. Any chance I can have the deed sooner?" Harry studied a dray lugging a steaming load of manure along the muddy street.

"Tuesday is less than a week away, Harry. Are you truly that hard up?"

"Rent's coming due." Said with casual humor.

Matilda counted to ten in French, while a crossing sweeper diligently collected a fresh pile of horse droppings.

"And you think you are fit to parent a small boy," she muttered, taking out a few coins and passing them over. "Until Tuesday, stay away from me and mine, Harry, and that means keeping your skulking minions away from Tommie too."

The coins disappeared while Harry resumed studying the sky. "Never skulk. I taught you better than that. March, saunter, stroll, take the air, bustle along, but don't ever skulk. I'll expect that deed by Monday, Tilly."

"Where shall I send it?"

He recited an unprepossessing direction in Knightsbridge, one that would, alas, never see another penny in rent from Harry Merridew.

Merri*man*. He was going by Merriman now, or so he claimed.

"Don't come near Tommie, and you will not impose your company upon us in Philadelphia."

Harry shuddered. "Too many Quakers. I'll keep to Boston or New York, if the wilderness doesn't take my fancy. Is this good-bye, Tilly?"

"I dearly hope so."

"That's the spirit." He winked, touched a finger to his hat brim, and bowed. "Do you know, of all the souls in this great metropolis, I believe you are the only one whom I'd trust to keep your word? If you say I'll have that deed, then I'll have it. Best of luck, Tilly, and give my regards to the City of Brotherly Love."

He jaunted off on that grand exit line, and Matilda let him go. She'd never understood him and still didn't, but he wasn't all bad. Not nearly. Unlike Papa, Harry hadn't lied to himself, and that alone took a sort of backhanded courage.

Though thank the heavenly intercessors, she would never see him again. "Harry!" she called.

He turned slowly.

"Best of luck to you too!"

He saluted, and Matilda went upon her way. Harry had not been bluffing about taking Tommie. He never bluffed, though he did cheat, steal, misrepresent, and lie. Matilda had learned to lie as well, and her future and Tommie's depended on Harry believing the load of falsehoods she'd just served him.

CHAPTER FIFTEEN

"I do have a plan." Matilda said, looking for all the world like a mulish schoolgirl.

"Which you refuse to share with me," Tremont rejoined from his seat one wing chair and four universes of heartache away from her perch. "Matilda, have we no trust in each other?" She had come back to the house from some outing she would not disclose, but the men reported that she'd missed her usual half day with the MacKays.

And the reticule she'd deposited on the sideboard looked suspiciously full.

She gave him an unfathomable look, and that she would guard her feelings from the man who loved her nearly unhinged him.

"I will leave England for a time," she said. "Harry's schemes will result inevitably in his true demise, and when that happens, if you have not taken a proper wife, I will marry you."

"No." Tremont had nearly shouted the word, which would not do. They were in Matilda's private parlor, and half a dozen men, two maids, Mrs. Winklebleck, and Cook wielding her rolling pin would all come running if they thought Matilda was getting the sharp edge of Tremont's tongue.

"No, you will not marry me?" The question revealed a crack in Matilda's towering dignity. "My mistake. I do apologize. I should not have presumed."

She was once again the chilly, proper widow, and Tremont suspected that this time, she was not Harry Merri-dew-man-whatever's widow, she was Tremont's widow. Her grief was trussed up in propriety and determination, the twin pillars of her composure since she'd left her girlhood home.

"No," Tremont said quietly. "No, I will not take a proper wife, if by that you mean some blushing flower whose parents covet my title. The only wife I will ever speak my vows with is you."

Something bleak passed through Matilda's eyes. "You must not say that. Any day, you could be run down by a passing coach. You could catch a lung fever or fall from your horse. A cousin you despise will inherit everything you and your father worked so hard to safeguard. Your mother will lose her home, and Marcus, it isn't in you to let that happen."

Oh, for the love of honking geese. "I survived years at *war*, Matilda. I risked an ignominious death by *firing squad*. I survived living in the damned *stews*, where I should have been a lamb to slaughter. I've turned around a sizable estate my dear relations were sailing straight into *ruin*, and I've dodged London's most determined matchmakers for *months*. I will not succumb to a cold."

Matilda offered him a slight, though genuine, smile. "Hardly the recitation of a gentrified cipher, is it, my lord?"

Well, no, which was neither here nor there. "Needs must, and you haring off to Nova Scotia won't solve anything."

Her smile faded to sadness. "We define the problem differently, my lord."

Stop my-lording me. "The *problem* is how we can legally marry, such that our offspring are legitimate and you are not committing bigamy. I agree with you that Harry's death—his actual death from natural causes—would facilitate those aims."

When debating, always concede common ground to build good will with one's opponent.

Matilda shook her head. "The *problem* is how to ensure that your honor is not compromised by devotion to a woman you haven't known all that long. Suppose you do contract that lung fever? As you lay dying, no heir save your scurrilous cousin, will you be comforted to know that you could have ensured better for your mother, your dependents, and tenants?"

"Mama has been amply provided for by trusts I've established and by her dower portion. No scurrilous cousin can imperil her welfare."

Matilda rose and went to the window, which looked out on a gray winter day. "Your mother pawned her jewelry before, Marcus. Dorcas shared that with me. Lady Tremont and Lady Lydia had to scheme and scrape to keep the estate afloat. Heirlooms that had been in the family for generations were discreetly sold on Ludgate Hill or given to your cousin to cover his debts. That estate is your mother's link with your father's memory, and you put it at risk with your loyalty to me."

"Then Mama will have to do as many widows have done and cope with her grief. My father was a living, breathing man who loved her dearly. He was not a pile of granite and some rural vistas. She is welcome to bide with Lydia and Sir Dylan, and in winter, she often does just that."

Matilda turned, and more than her expression, her physical attitude made Tremont's heart sink. Her features were nearly blank, so great was her self-possession—marriage to damned old Harry had probably imbued her with that skill—while her posture was more resolute than a newly promoted lieutenant at his first parade inspection.

"Why are you doing this, Matilda?" She had not lied to him, but neither had she trusted him.

"I told you: We have no honorable way forward, except to wait for Harry's actual death, and waiting is the one thing you must not do. Ergo, I am quitting the field. When I took up with Joseph, I was thinking of myself. When I took up with Harry, I was still mostly thinking of myself. I must think of Tommie now, and that means removing myself from the ambit of your affections. If you love me, you will marry another lady, a sweet woman who esteems you sincerely, which, God knows, is easy enough to do. You will have a half-dozen sons and live to a ripe and contented old age."

Matilda passed that sentence on him with a dispassion that would have flattered a judge, save that two spots of pink had bloomed in her cheeks, and she was staring fixedly at the untouched tea tray on the low table.

Why do this? Why make this great, stupid sacrifice? Everything Matilda said was true. Cousin Wesley was a self-absorbed spendthrift who'd stop at little to indulge his many appetites. He'd run Tremont into the ground, of that there was no question.

But the tenants would all have time to find other properties if Wesley inherited, and Marcus had equipped them with letters commending their stewardship and diligence. Mama and the pensioners were taken care of, and the property was in as good repair as Marcus could make it.

This was not about an estate, or even about Marcus's honor, or even the impact on Tommie of having a mother in an irregular association with an earl.

"Have your feelings for me changed, Matilda?"

Her chin came up, and she glowered at him. "No. Were I free to marry you, I'd do so on the instant."

He'd seen that same battle light in her eyes before, in St. Mildred's hall... when she'd thought he'd been about to take Tommie to task.

Well, of course. The issue was not Tommie's social standing, but rather, *his safety.* "I can keep Tommie from harm," Tremont said. "We'll have him educated in Finland, and Harry will never find him."

"*Finland?*"

"Britain is all but out of lumber. The Finns have seas of magnificent pine to sell and land they want cleared. I'm importing that lumber and making a tidy sum doing it. Lovely people, and a beautiful country, what little I've seen of it."

Matilda marched over to him. "I am not sending my son to perishing *Finland* when he's barely old enough to dress himself. Besides, Harry would get wind of it somehow, and he is Tommie's legal father, as he has been at pains to remind me, and..."

Her breath caught. A small sound, one easily ignored, and Matilda would doubtless prefer that Tremont did ignore it.

"*Harry threatened Tommie.*" Tremont waited for Matilda to refute that conclusion. She instead sank back into her seat.

The rotten, revolting rat had accosted Matilda when she'd been without allies and played a hand she could not beat. Sound tactics and very unsound honor.

"Harry has consulted the attorneys," Matilda said. "They tell him paternity is not remotely at issue."

Tremont took the opposite chair, feeling as if the discussion had just now reached productive ground. Difficult ground, but productive.

"Harry Merridew is dead, Matilda, if we're to resort to legalities."

She brushed her fingers over the arm of her chair. "I haven't a death certificate, and Harry does have a convincing tale of lost memory and destitute circumstances."

"Convincing? How does he explain that letter from a nonexistent innkeeper from a nonexistent inn, written in Harry's own hand? Shall we exhume the corpse and find dog bones in the coffin?"

Matilda regarded him with something like pity. "Harry will claim he was the victim of a scheme, left for dead, and all in a muddle. He makes the most outlandish tales credible. I've seen him do it. Everybody believes Harry—I believed him enough to *marry* him—and I believe him when he says he'll take Tommie with him when he sails."

"He can't sail without blunt." Tremont had made inquiries, and Harry apparently had no creditors in London—no legal creditors. That didn't mean he had enough to pay for transatlantic passage.

"He can only sail if I deed him the house, my lord, and I very much want that man out of my life."

Tremont sat back and forced his mind down logical paths. "You brought up that business with Mama and the estate because you are protecting Harry. I commend the subtly of the strategy, but we have already established that I will not physically harm your... I will not do violence to Harry."

"I might." A grudging thread of humor illuminated those words, but only a thread. "I've arranged to deed the house to him. Major MacKay connected with me an affordable solicitor. With the wages you've paid me, I can leave England."

Tremont's worst fear stated in the calmest tones. Another grief, another bereavement coming from out of nowhere.

"What you mean is, you can leave *me*," Tremont said softly, "because I must be fruitful and legitimately multiply, lest the family barbarian sack Shropshire." He was barely making sense. He knew only that Matilda, for admittedly sound reasons, was conceding the battle and the war.

"I refuse to be the reason your birthright and your good name are put at risk, Marcus, and I will not let you be the reason I lose Tommie. In my undistinguished life, I have done the easy thing, the tempting thing, the too-good-to-be-true thing. For once, I shall do the right thing, as you so often do."

Despite that unflattering characterization of her past, Matilda had reason on her side, dammit, and logic and—most powerful of all—mother-love.

"When do you sail?"

"Tuesday. Philadelphia seems like a worthy place to start over. Aunt Portia knows some people there who will look kindly upon Tommie and me. Harry says he will avoid that city owing to a surfeit of Quakers. His family were prosperous members of the Society of Friends, if you can believe that, and Harry became a prodigal after a falling-out with his father—assuming what he told me was true. I will send an executed deed to him on Monday. He's keeping rooms in Knightsbridge."

Not as fancy as Mayfair, but a more than respectable neighborhood. "Did he give you a specific direction?"

Matilda recited the name of a modest lodging house catering to bachelors enjoying a limited stay in Town. "You must leave him alone, Marcus. As unfair as it is, Harry has the law on his side, and he does not make idle threats."

"Right now," Tremont replied, rising, "I do not give a shovel full of Charlie's finest for the law, for common sense, or for reason. The woman I love is leaving me, and I haven't even the comfort of arguing with her motivations."

He kissed Matilda's forehead and lingered near her long enough to breathe in her scent, then took his leave of her.

And she, to his eternal sorrow, let him go without another word.

Matilda drove the market pony along Park Lane and barely felt the cold. Obliviousness to discomfort warned her that she'd relapsed into a mode of coping that she'd doubtless pay for.

Married to Harry, she'd learned to keep her feelings in a locked emotional linen closet. Anger sat stacked on top of worry, worry was folded atop fear. Thoughts of vengeance occupied a wide shelf, as did regret. She tucked away that most unruly impulse, hope, in a dim and dusty corner.

When Harry had "died," unpacking that linen closet had been the substance of her mourning. She had felt some genuine sorrow. Harry had in his way tried to be the best husband he could—and failed miserably—but he had tried. He'd never put Matilda at serious risk for criminal charges. He'd never taken out his frustrations on Tommie.

At the time, though, she'd been convinced his demise was the result of some scheme gone awry, the just deserts of a professional swindler.

Her sorrow for Harry had been eclipsed by her ire at him. She'd married him to secure a place of modest respect in society, but respect could not feed a baby or pay the coalman. For months, Matilda had darned Mr. Prebish's socks and mended Mrs. Oldbach's shawls, sewing both fury and fear into every stitch.

How could he do this to me? How could he do this to Tommie?

Did widows cling to their veiled bonnets and retiring ways not because grief demanded it of them, but rather, because a raging woman knew better than to wear her anger in public?

That rage was back in full spate—damn Harry to New South Wales for that—along with enough sorrow to fill the Thames. Sorrow for herself, and for Tremont, whose great crime was to be a decent, loving, lovely man.

"He will cope," she muttered, steering the pony into the less elegant surrounds of Knightsbridge. "He has coped with..." Marcus had coped with *everything*. From losing a parent at too young an age, to joining a war, to repeated betrayals by a superior officer, to that ghastly business at Waterloo, to restoring an estate on the brink of ruin...

Tears threatened, again. Matilda clucked to the pony, who gamely picked up his pace and soon had her in the quieter surrounds of Chelsea. Aunt's modest cottage had acquired some early holiday greenery, and the sight nearly undid Matilda's self-possession.

Merry Olde England did such a fine job by Christmas, and this year, Matilda had hoped the holidays would be different. Warm, well fed, jolly...

She drove the pony to the livery, tipped the groom as handsomely as she dared, and made her way to Aunt Portia's door. Her aunt received her with the same guarded warmth that always characterized their dealings, and perhaps a little relief that Tommie had not joined the outing.

Portia did set great store by her few porcelain treasures.

"I got your note," she said, taking Matilda's cloak and hanging it on a peg. "What on earth requires that you hare about London in this cold, Matilda? You must be half frozen and one-quarter daft."

"I am neither." Though she was done with allowing any and everybody to judge her for no reason. "I have made some difficult decisions, and you deserve to hear of them directly from me."

Aunt's fussing hands went still on Matilda's cloak. "Brandy, I think. To ward off lung fever."

Brandy would do, considering Matilda's mood. She held her peace until she and Portia were seated in a warm parlor, and Portia's long-haired gray cat was sniffing delicately at Matilda's skirts.

"What has you in a taking this time?" Portia asked, sipping her drink.

The vintage was excellent, which made Matilda wonder whether Portia had acquired an admirer. Good for her, if she had.

"Tommie and I are leaving London," Matilda said. "I've put it about that I am sailing to Philadelphia for a fresh start. You will please support that fiction should anybody inquire."

"Phila—Phila*delphia*? Matilda, what on earth precipitates this unseemly drama?"

Matilda would have objected to the implications, except that Portia sounded genuinely worried.

"Harry Merridew, alive and well, precipitates my decision. He is not dead, Portia. He concocted a scheme to make me, and probably his creditors and enemies, think he was dead. He's short of funds and has come around, expecting me to sign my dower house over to him. He will assert custody of Tommie if I balk. Harry is unwilling to divorce me because the press would become involved, but he doubtless knows enough crooked judges and magistrates to quietly take my son from me."

The cat climbed onto Portia's lap and stropped himself against her such that his tail waved before her face. She scratched the base of his neck, and he settled on his haunches and began a stentorian purr.

"Harry Merridew," Portia muttered. "Well, of course. I am

ashamed to say I rejoiced when he supposedly died, Matilda. He was a desperate measure indeed, and you paid dearly for throwing in with him. When your father told me he'd approved the match, I nearly did him an injury."

What on earth could motivate Portia to violence? "Papa was likely paid—by Harry—to bless the match."

The cat settled to all fours, a miniature smoky sphinx, doubtless getting hair all over Portia's gray skirts. Did she dress to accommodate her presuming cat?

"Your father was not paid to allow Merridew to wed you," Portia said, setting her drink aside without disturbing the cat. "Whilst kicking his heels in the village and courting you, Harry got to nosing about the parish registers. He happened across the record that showed when your father, while still a curate, had taken a bride. Less than seven months later, you showed up in the birth registries, and whatever else was true about your Harry, he could count."

"I came a bit early, then?" Even as Matilda spoke, another explanation was beating on the door of one of her mental linen closets.

The cat sent Matilda a sagacious squint, his expression oddly mirroring Portia's.

"From what your mother intimated, Matilda, you came precisely when you were due to arrive."

Matilda felt an odd prickling down her arms. "Mama and Papa *anticipated their vows?*" She could barely recall her mother, a quiet, pretty woman with an air of patient good humor.

"Courting couples do," Portia replied, "though I wasn't about to take that risk with your uncle. As fond as he was of his port, he might have left me widowed before I'd wed, as the saying goes. Harry would have bruited about your parents' indiscretion had your father thwarted the courtship. The good vicar was vain and hypocritical enough to be manipulated that easily."

The fire crackled softly, the cat purred, and Matilda downed half her remaining drink. "Is every adult woman forced to constantly manage and accommodate the self-indulgence and arrogance of the men around her?"

Portia nudged the brandy bottle closer to Matilda's elbow. "Tremont isn't self-indulgent or arrogant, and he's marvelously well-read. He didn't simply memorize his lines for the day and then spit them out for the headmaster. He is a learned man, Matilda. Smart enough for you, and a good man."

How smart was a woman who'd not known the circumstances of her own birth?

Matilda rose to pace, her progress around the parlor tracked visually by the cat. "My father... My father berated me constantly for laughing, for curtseying too quickly, for smiling at the butcher's boy, or not making a long enough production of grace on the few occasions he allowed me to say it. He assured me over and over again that I would come to a bad end, that I was a burden sent by the devil to try his patience."

"Your father was impatient, and he certainly tried your mother's nerves. He also lied if he claimed you were sent by the imp, Matilda. You were an ominously well-behaved girl, and your father's own precipitate wooing occasioned your conception. If you didn't realize that Harry was a born deceiver, maybe that's because your father lied to you from your birth. He told you that you weren't quiet enough, pious enough, submissive enough to God's will... The lack of virtue never lay with you. I'm sorry we didn't have this discussion years ago, but I thought Harry would have told you."

Matilda paused before a very good sketch of the cat posed beside a vase of irises. "Papa would doubtless take the oldest dodge in the Bible and blame Mama for tempting him, though she married straight out of the schoolroom. What does 'ominously well-behaved' mean?"

Portia stroked the cat and gazed at the fire. "When a girl is held to an impossible standard for too long, she eventually stumbles, and that stumbling can feel... good. Like freedom and honesty and power."

What experience did Portia speak from? "Portia, why do I feel as if it's only now, as I'm on the brink of leaving England, that I begin to know you?"

Portia set the cat in Matilda's vacated chair and rose. "Stumbling comes at a price, and we have both learned caution in a hard school. You are leaving London because you don't want your earl to stumble, aren't you? Has he offered to set you up?"

"No." A relief, because Matilda would be tempted to stumble yet again. "I thought that was his interest in me initially, but I was mistaken. Tremont is unlikely to risk illegitimacy for his offspring, and he and I cannot marry with Harry so hale and whole. Tremont is a peer, he votes his seat. He cannot abandon his homeland."

"So you will abandon him. This feels right to you?" The question was merely curious rather than judgmental.

"I took up with Joseph Yoe because he purported to offer me a way to leave the vicarage. I took up with Harry because he promised me a scintilla of safety and propriety. My motivations in both cases were selfish and desperate, and I hoped a man would solve my difficulties. My motivation in this case... Yes, the decision to leave England feels right. Miserable, but right, and my choice."

"Because you love him," Portia said, passing Matilda her unfinished drink and picking up her own glass. "To love, then, though your earl might well show up in Philadelphia, Matilda. What will you do then?"

She finished her drink. "I won't be in Philadelphia."

"I see. You will write from wherever you end up and let me know how you're getting on?"

Marcus would doubtless turn to Portia once he learned Matilda was not in America. "I will write eventually, after Tommie and I are settled."

Portia crossed the room and opened the central drawer of a delicate inlaid escritoire. "Take this," she said, passing over a velvet bag. "Consider it a loan, or an early bequest to your darling Tommie. He's such a dear boy, and you should know he will inherit this house when I die."

Matilda did not want to take the money, but Portia had brought up Tommie. Shrewd of her.

"Tommie is no blood relation to you, Portia. You need not leave him anything, but I am most grateful for the assistance."

"I am leaving the house to your son, Matilda, because I know you would not accept it for yourself. Besides, I am in roaring good health and plan to stay that way for some time. You will write?"

"I shall. You will support the fiction that I have gone to Philadelphia?"

"I will not lie, Matilda, but when it comes to prevaricating, I can be skillful. Let's leave it at that, shall we?"

And that was as close to a promise as Matilda was likely to have from Portia. "I will be on my way. Thank you for the brandy and for your kindness."

"I could not do enough for you and Tommie when your uncle was alive, but you made time to look in on me, to attend your uncle's funeral, and to bring Tommie around. He is so lively. Perseus has no idea what to make of him."

Perseus being Portia's familiar, of course. Matilda took her leave, surprised nearly to tears when Portia imposed a fierce hug on her at the door.

"Be happy, Matilda. Find a way to be happy, and if you cannot be happy, at least don't be bitter. You have Tommie, you are in good health, and for what it's worth, you have me."

Matilda could not be happy, not now and no time soon, but she knew what Portia was saying: Don't stuff your whole future into one of those linen closets, shoved between decorum and prudence, stashed next to living within one's means and never giving cause for offence.

What do you want, Matilda. What do you want?

She wanted to safeguard Tremont's good name and his hard-won self-respect. She also wanted to be the sort of mother of whom Tommie could be proud.

"You be happy too, Portia, and I will write."

Matilda slipped out the door and into the chilly wind. The drive back to the soldiers' home passed in a preoccupied blur. The pony seemed to know the way, while Matilda's thoughts wandered. When she passed Hyde Park, she was reminded of the day she'd thought Tremont was propositioning her.

She'd been mortified at the time, and so, apparently, had he. The memory was sweet now, as were most of her memories of Marcus, Earl of Tremont. That was fortunate, because those memories would have to last her a lifetime.

"Where is the boy?" Tremont asked, his gaze taking in a library filled with people trying to look as if they hadn't been having some sort of war council. "I was very clear that Tommie wasn't to be without the escort of an adult male at all times."

Alasdhair MacKay rose from a wing chair in the corner. "Tuck and Jensen took the lad for a hot chocolate, with Mrs. Merridew's prior permission. She's calling upon her aunt and made certain we knew to keep a sharp eye on Tommie."

What are you doing here? Rather than pose that rude question— MacKay was clearly a reinforcement brought in from the former officer ranks—Marcus bowed.

"MacKay, good day. Has anyone thought to offer you refreshment?"

Nanny Winklebleck, who occupied one of the chairs before the hearth, shook a finger at her employer.

"Don't you be gettin' all lordly on us now, sir. We're trying to sort out what to do for Missus, and a tea tray won't make that exercise go any better."

"A wee dram never went amiss," Cook muttered, brandishing her flask and tipping it to her lips.

Mrs. Winklebleck's chin came up. "I'm for putting that Harry Merriman on a transport ship and giving the ship's mate a false name for him. He'd stay dead for a proper long time that way, long enough that no magistrate would believe him if he showed up again fourteen years later, claimin' to be some old swindler nobody much liked to begin with."

"Her plan has merit," MacKay said, resuming his seat.

Her plan was criminal. Kidnapping was a hanging felony, bearing false witness a sin, and Tremont was tempted to commit both. He set the decanter before MacIvey, who'd parked at the reading table.

"Cook should not drink alone," Tremont said. "MacPherson, the glasses, please."

Tremont took the desk beneath the mezzanine, and while the business of passing drinks around occupied the assemblage, he mentally set aside the scheme to put Harry on a transport ship. The plan did have merit—Harry had committed many crimes—but also risk.

Matilda said everybody believed Harry, and Tremont believed Matilda. Cousin Wesley had that same ability to charm, wheedle, and deceive. Some people were given great good looks, others had beautiful singing voices.

The Harrys and Wesleys of the world had guile.

While I have... logic? Reason? Honor? Those gifts were not much comfort when a man's heart was breaking.

"My objective," Tremont said, "is to ensure that Mrs. Merridew need not leave familiar surrounds to make her way alone in the world without friends or allies. I intend to accomplish that goal by guaranteeing Harry cannot set foot on British soil without taking an enormous risk."

"You'd put him on remittance?" MacKay asked.

"Of course, if I must, which will be the carrot, but I also need a stick. Mrs. Winklebleck, what else can you tell us about the man's past?"

A few bits and bobs of information emerged from a general discussion. Harry was a confidence trickster of some renown, but had few friends. He eventually left any accomplices in awkward circumstances, and women soon realized he was more parasite than protector.

While the talk eddied and a second decanter was emptied, Tremont realized that Harry Merridew must be a profoundly lonely man. No home, no friends, no family... Harry, while telling himself London was his own personal patch, was lost in the stews of vice and deception.

"Who are his people?" Tremont asked. "He has family somewhere—cousins, an auntie, somebody. What do we know of them?"

Silence crept over the library.

"He never mentioned family," Mrs. Winklebleck said. "Never mentioned a village, never talked about going 'ome for Yuletide or to pay a call on his granny in 'igh summer, but then, who'd 'ave a grandson like 'im? I'll 'ave another tot, if you don't mind, MacIvey."

"Best give it a rest, Nanny," MacIvey said, making no move to surrender the decanter.

"She's Mrs. Winklebleck to you," Tremont muttered, though his heart wasn't in the scold. Somewhere in her words, in what Harry Merridew lacked, was a thread of gold.

"He doesn't go home," Tremont said, feeling again an unwanted kinship with Matilda's husband, "but he has a home. The situation wants more information, and as it happens, I know how to come by it. Who here recalls a man named Spartacus Lykens?"

The discussion went on for another quarter hour before a quartet of former infantrymen was detailed to patrol—to harmlessly wander about, rather—a certain neighborhood in Knightsbridge. Five minutes later, Tremont was escorting MacKay to the door.

"Do you know what you're about?" MacKay asked, whipping a green and white plaid scarf about his neck.

"Part of me knows what I'm about. I am securing for Matilda and Tommie the freedom to remain in England. If she leaves, that should be a choice rather than her only option."

"And the rest of you?"

"I want to kill Harry Merridew, MacKay. I want to slowly

strangle him and watch his eyes as he realizes that he cannot swindle, rig, lie, cheat, or bamboozle his way out of the fate he deserves. What that man has done to Matilda... Except that, for a time, I wanted my mother and sister to think I was dead, didn't I? I hid in the slums and hoped the sins of my past would never reach the ears of my family. Having made egregious wrong turns myself, I can judge no man for his faults."

MacKay, who had served under Dunacre, looked thunderous. "You had your reasons."

"And Harry Merridew must have his. My job is to ferret them out and use them to Matilda's advantage. She said he comes from good Quaker stock and had a falling-out with his father. If any people on the entire face of the earth go about their disputes with deliberation, it's the Friends. Somebody somewhere will recall the details of this family scandal. Failing that, Lykens might impart some names and dates that I can use to persuade Merridew to stay more or less dead."

MacKay settled a high-crowned beaver on his head at a jaunty angle. "So you can keep Matilda as your mistress?"

That question was a kindly attempt to turn despair into anger. "Of course not, but neither will I see her banished from her home-land with a child to support while it's in my power to make her circumstances easier. I will not allow her to get on that ship bound for Philadelphia unless and until I've done all in my power to see her disentangled from her scapegrace husband."

"Because," MacKay said with a lopsided smile, "you love her. Dorcas saw this coming, damned if she didn't. 'For aught that I could ever hear by tale or history, the course of true love never did run smooth.' Let me know what you get out of Lykens. He was a tough old boot at too young an age."

"My regards to your lady, MacKay."

"And mine to yours."

Tremont offered a polite bow in parting, but he wanted to apply *his* boot to MacKay's backside. Matilda was not Tremont's lady, and she might well never be.

Also, MacKay had bungled the quote. "It's 'for aught that I could *ever read*,'" Tremont muttered as he watched MacKay stride along the walkway, "'could ever hear by tale or history, the course of true love never did run smooth.'"

In that much at least, the Bard had hit upon the sorry, stinking truth.

CHAPTER SIXTEEN

"Are we in trouble, Mama?" Tommie asked, snuggling down beneath his blankets.

Matilda had waited until Sunday evening to explain to Tommie that a journey was in the offing. She'd read to him about the tortoise and hare—the story had become his favorite—and then explained that on Tuesday, he'd go sailing with her to start a new life in a distant land.

"We are not in trouble," she said, sitting on the edge of his bed and brushing his hair back from his brow. "We are soon to be off on an adventure."

"Because if we were in trouble, Tremont would help us, and so would the men and the ladies."

"They have helped us, tremendously, and we have helped them. It's simply time to go." Parental license rather than a lie, surely.

"Tremont fancies you," Tommie said, sounding older than his years. "MacIvey says so, and he fancies Mrs. Wink, so he knows the look."

"MacPherson told you that?"

Tommie grinned. "He bet Bentley we'd hear wedding bells. I

don't want to leave, Mama. I like my bed, and all my storybooks, and old Arthur, even though he isn't keen on being carried about. I've learned how to groom Tidbit and to milk the goats and knead Cook's bread dough. MacIvey is teaching me how to play the fiddle, and Charlie says I can help him with the boots too."

More than that astonishingly long list of accomplishments, Tommie had learned what it meant to be part of a household, a family of sorts.

"Everybody has been very kind to us, and we will miss them, but we will also make new friends where we're going."

"If we don't like it far away, can we come back?"

Matilda heard the sound of misery beating desperately on a locked mental door. "Eventually. Travel is expensive, though, so we won't be larking back to England anytime soon."

Tommie yawned hugely. "Can Tremont come with us?"

"His place is here. The men need him, and his family needs him." England needed him, needed his integrity and acumen, his voice of reason and compassion in the Lords.

"I still don't want to go."

Neither do I. "We will pack tomorrow, and Tremont will take us to an inn by the docks. We'll depart Tuesday at midday when the tide begins to ebb." Tremont would think them bound by boat to Portsmouth, the first leg of a transatlantic journey. Matilda would try very hard not to disabuse him of that assumption.

"Where we're going is beautiful," she went on, "and they put chocolate into not only warm milk, but also little cakes and cream puffs. They don't speak quite as we do, but the people are reported to be friendly."

By some.

"I would rather stay here, Mama. Maybe you should go ahead without me, and when you are sure we will like it, I can follow you."

"Not a chance I will leave my best boy behind, Thomas Merridew. All too soon, you will grow up and take your place in the world. I am still your mama, and I will not embark on an adventure without you."

"Will they have ponies where we're going?"

"Yes, and cats and goats and dogs and sweet buns." If God was merciful, Matilda could find a job as a companion or governess in a household that didn't mind that she had a small child. She might even eke out an independent existence teaching deportment, music, and drawing.

Harry had taught her resilience, if he'd done nothing else.

Tommie curled onto his side and closed his eyes. "If you don't like living here, Mama, why don't we just go back to the stinky house?"

"I'm selling the stinky house." Giving it away, to a man who'd done nothing to earn it.

"Doesn't Tremont like us?"

Where on earth...? But Matilda, raised to have no faith in herself whatsoever, knew where such a question came from. "Tremont likes us quite well, and we like him—very much. I never promised I'd take this position for anything other than the short term, Tommie, and I am determined to leave London now that the chance has arisen."

"I don't want to go," Tommie mumbled. "Where's Cope?"

Matilda tucked the stuffed horse into Tommie's embrace. "Right here. Go to sleep, and we'll enjoy a farewell cup of chocolate tomorrow if you can manage to behave yourself. Sweet dreams, Tommie. I love you."

"Love you too, Mama."

Matilda blew out the bedside candle and stayed for a moment, watching her son drift into dreams by firelight.

We have been so happy here at the house without a name. When Tommie's breathing eased into the soft rhythm of slumber, she tucked the covers up around him and his beloved horse and crossed the corridor to her sitting room.

Tremont sat by the fire with a book, or possibly he dozed. He was in one-quarter profile to the door, and the sight of him, long legs crossed at the ankle, coat hung over the back of the sofa, imprinted itself on Matilda's heart.

I want decades of this, decades to come upon him at the end of the day, lost in thought or communing with the latest pamphlet on the Irish question.

"I did not want to intrude," he said, rising and remaining by the fire. "Tommie's asleep?"

"Exhausted for the nonce. I've told him we're leaving."

"Going out with the tide on Tuesday afternoon," Tremont said.

"Well, it's not Tuesday yet. Come have a seat, and I'll tell you what I learned from an interesting interview with Mr. Spartacus Lykens."

Matilda stayed by the door. "Whatever you learned, it's not enough, is it?"

"Nothing, short of your hand secured in mine by legally binding holy matrimony, will be enough, but the news is interesting. It might make forgiving Harry easier."

And to Tremont, that would matter. Matilda longed to climb into Tremont's lap and give way to sobs. She instead took the wing chair at a right angle to his lordship's end of the sofa.

"What did Mr. Lykens have to tell you?"

"Harry has a sister," Tremont said, resuming his seat. "And an auntie, and he hails from Bristol, just as he claimed. Growing up in a port town, he heard all the accents and learned to mimic them as a sort of hobby. He also told the truth about being from Quaker stock, and yet, he wanted to become an actor."

Matilda did not give two rotten tomatoes for Harry's youthful ambitions, but she loved even the sound of Tremont's voice, and so she mustered the effort to turn his recitation into a conversation.

"I can't imagine Harry's ambitions went over well with his family, but he has become quite the thespian nonetheless."

Tremont had more to say, about an unbending father, unyielding discipline, and piety used to smother joy. About a young man's high spirits turning to rebellion and his gifts into weapons. When Tremont fell silent, Matilda found that her eyes had grown nearly as heavy as her heart.

"I will," she said, "on some fine and distant day, feel some compassion for that Bristol boy imprisoned in his father's dogma—one feels grudging sympathy for such a one—but right now... I wish I'd never met Harry Merridew. I wish I'd had the patience to wait for my father's death, for some other man to come along, for somebody to hear of a governess's or companion's post. But for Tommie, I'd wish I never met Joseph Yoe, and I do wish I'd never met Harry."

"But you did," Tremont said, smiling slightly. "Do you wish you'd never met me?" He managed to make the inquiry merely one of curiosity, though Matilda knew her answer mattered to him.

"I will never, ever regret knowing you, Marcus. I hope you can say the same about me." She shifted out of her wing chair to tuck herself against his side, and his arm came around her shoulders.

"You are the delight my heart has longed for," he said, "and the day I met you, every wrong thing in my life came right. I won't stop loving you just because you sail off to Philadelphia on Tuesday."

Matilda fell asleep to the sound of Tremont's steady heartbeat, and when she woke the next morning, she was tucked beneath her covers, fully clothed save for her boots, and quite, quite alone.

"Matilda is packing to leave as I speak," Alasdhair MacKay said. "I have been tasked with delivering the executed deed to you. Alasdhair MacKay, at your service."

Harry Merridew appeared to have already gathered up his worldly goods. A battered valise sat by the door, along with a traveling desk and a leather knapsack of ancient provenance. A half-empty glass of libation suggested Harry had been sitting before the fire, perhaps contemplating his sins.

"And I wish my wife fair winds and following seas," Merridew replied, smiling genially. "I'm sure she wishes me the same, provided I sail in the opposite direction."

MacKay did not want to like Harry Merridew or feel any sympathy for him—Dorcas assuredly did not—but the fellow had charm.

"Where will you go?" MacKay asked.

"Why do you want to know?" Merridew countered, making no move to take MacKay's hat or cloak.

"So I can be sure to avoid the place and keep my family well away from it too."

Merridew's smile dimmed. "I deserved that. I've the dregs of a decent bottle of brandy to share, if you'd like to warm up while you sermonize at me."

"I would not waste the breath, but I will accept the hospitality." Tremont was too honorable to spy outright on his enemy, while MacKay's conscience wasn't half so delicate. Besides, the day was brutally cold, and the quality of a man's brandy said a lot about his prospects.

"You might want to keep your cloak on," Merridew said. "My landlady is parsimonious with the coal, though with any luck, she won't be my landlady beyond the end of this week."

"You think you can sell Matilda's house in a week flat?" MacKay unbuttoned his cloak and left it about his shoulders. The room was chilly, though not quite see-your-breath cold.

Merridew gestured to a musty wing chair, took a seat in its equally disreputable twin, and pulled a shawl over his knees.

"I could sell that house by sundown," he said, "but desperation seldom wins the best price. You truly have brought the deed?"

How casually he inquired. MacKay withdrew a rolled-up document tied with a red ribbon. "A quitclaim, executed before witnesses in favor of one Harrell Merriman, and I can vouch for the solicitor who drew it up."

"Merri*man*?"

"Is that a problem?" MacKay dearly hoped it was, though in

another hour or two, Matilda and Tommie would be on their way to a dockside inn. There'd be no revising the deed to suit Harry's swindle of the moment.

"Harrell Merriman will do," Harry said. "I've always liked him. He's a personable chap, but nobody's fool." He poured a tot of brandy into a second glass and passed it over to MacKay. "To your health and Matilda's safe journey."

"And the boy's."

Merridew winked and drank up, something he likely did differently depending on whether he was Merriman, Merridew, or any one of his other names.

"Where will you go?" MacKay asked again. Dorcas had wanted to know this fact in particular, and MacKay was loath to disappoint his commanding officer.

"Someplace Matilda will never have to see me again," Harry replied. "She never should have married me. I know that."

Matilda doubtless knew it better. "You told her you were bound for New York, I believe."

"Or Boston, but not Philadelphia. She can have that patch."

The smile playing about Harry's lips stirred MacKay's instincts. "You told her you were going to the New World, and she knew that was a lie. She's banishing herself to the one place you all but promised her you would not be. Why not simply tell her you'd leave her in peace?"

"I will leave her in peace. I wanted to leave her in peace, but Matilda knows better than to expect the truth from me. I do tell the truth when it's advantageous, but with a wife... Marriage is the most complicated rig I've ever worked. I don't care for it, and I daresay Matilda would agree with me."

More lies. Something about marriage to Matilda had appealed to Harry strongly, and that had likely scared him witless.

"You are a coward," MacKay said, rising without tasting his drink. "She cared for you, and in some misbegotten corner of her heart, she would still rather see you thrive than struggle. My wife would love to see you gelded—she has no patience with parasites strutting around in the guise of grown men—but you deserve her pity. You certainly have mine."

"Spare me," Harry said, all pretense of cordiality gone. He tossed back his drink and rose. "My thanks for delivering the deed. You can see yourself out."

MacKay sketched a bow. "You never did tell me where you're going."

"Straight to the devil, of course."

Oh, very well, then. MacKay made as if to button his cloak, but instead snatched Harry hard by his lapels and hauled him up to his tiptoes.

"For myself, I hope you and Old Scratch are soon personally acquainted. He has much to learn from you. Tremont is planning to put you on remittance such that wherever you go, you are inspired to stay there. My wife, however, wants to know where you are so that when you do expire, and let us hope your passing is humiliating and agonizing and *soon*, news of your actual death can be conveyed to your widow. Your continued existence is a blight on her happiness, so now would be a good time to dredge up a bit of that advantageous honesty."

He gave Merridew an admonitory shake and let him go. To assault a man in his own dwelling was a bitter insult, and yet, Merridew hadn't offered the least resistance. MacKay entertained the notion that his host was flirting with inebriation and hiding it well.

Why get drunk? Why sit here swilling cheap brandy when victory was at hand?

"Why would Tilly care…?" Merridew paused, mid-brush at his lapels. "She loves that damned prig, doesn't she? Has fallen for him, really fallen, not simply talked herself into him because he'll look out for the boy."

"Answer the question or prepare to part with a few teeth." Dorcas would have advised him to relieve Merridew of what passed for his testicles. Mrs. MacKay wasn't one to muck about when direct action was called for.

Harry took up the shawl and wrapped it around his shoulders. "Cheap, sunny Rome. Enough Latin was banged into my youthful head that I'll be able to manage the language. Tell your wife I've gone to Rome, and the British Embassy will know my whereabouts. They're fussy about that sort of thing in the Italian states. The French aren't as bad, but I'd have a harder time with the language in France, and too many Englishmen find their way there."

"How do I know you're telling the truth?"

Harry smirked, though the expression came across more tired than flippant. "You don't. Good day, MacKay. Regards to your lady wife, and may God have mercy upon her soul."

The insult was a distraction from the fact that Harry Merridew had for once in his life been honest, and not because the truth had served him any advantages.

"Start over," MacKay said. "Clean slate, take yet another name if that helps. Get a legitimate job as a secretary, teach English, or offer your services to the embassy as a professional listener at keyholes, but make your peace with the past or be strangled by it."

"You speak from experience?"

"I'm not quoting from The Rubbishing Book of Common Prayer. Of course I speak from experience." MacKay let himself out and left Harry standing before the meager fire looking both dignified and ridiculous in his tattered shawl.

The encounter had been distasteful and somewhat informative, also sobering.

"There but for the grace of God and Dorcas MacKay, laddie..."

The major wrapped his scarf more snugly about his ears and turned his steps in the direction of the park. Tremont would expect a report by nightfall, and then MacKay, as was the duty of a true friend, would do his best to get his brokenhearted lordship roaring drunk.

Parting was not sweet sorrow, it was bitter hell.

Matilda came to this conclusion as Tremont handed her down from his coach and four and then assisted Tommie to alight. Had the stink of the Thames not been so intense, the earl might have been dropping them off at some elegant seaside resort.

The inn was an oasis of grandeur and decorum amid the otherwise indifferent offerings along the riverfront.

"London exerts itself to make a good first and last impression on certain travelers," Tremont said, eyeing the wide veranda. Liveried footmen and porters bustled about with luggage, and swags of holiday greenery adorned the first-floor balcony. "They serve meals on that balcony in fine weather, but the best views are from the back. You can watch all the river traffic and pretend you are the harbormaster."

That was said for Tommie's benefit, and Matilda's heart broke all over again. "Will you spend the Yuletide holidays in Shropshire, my lord?" she asked.

"I hardly know." Tremont offered his arm, and Matilda took it, all too aware that the moment of separation loomed ever closer.

"Tommie, come along." Tommie latched on to Matilda's free hand. Copenhagen peeked out from the top of his coat, a measure suggested by the earl when Tommie would not stop fretting over the possibility of his stuffed friend going missing.

Tremont dealt with the business of room keys and fare for the accommodations. "Your meals will be brought up to you," he said, "and your rooms are reserved until you board the packet for Portsmouth tomorrow. Shall I see you up?"

He'd been the proper, punctilious earl since retrieving them from the soldiers' home. Matilda grasped that Tremont's demeanor was intended to shore up her flagging composure, but she also resented that he was able to maintain such effective command of himself.

Did his mental linen closets and pantries never spill open? Never spew their contents forth at inopportune moments?

"I would rather not say good-bye in public," she muttered. "Upstairs with us." Tommie came along, though he dragged at her hand, gawking over his shoulder at every step.

The stairs seemed to go on forever, one pretty, quintessentially British landscape after another, every step muted by the spotless carpets underfoot. Condemned felons probably climbed to the gallows with only slightly more foreboding than Matilda felt. They at least faced an end to their troubles, while she...

Don't be pathetic, Matilda. That voice, oddly enough, belonged to Papa, and for once, his admonition was appropriate. She gained the first floor and let go of Tommie's hand.

"This way," Tremont said, striding past more landscapes. "You have the corner, where the light is best, and you have a superlative view of the river. I allowed myself to stay in that suite for one night when I returned to England. I watched the sun come up over the Thames and knew I was finally home—except I wasn't, not truly."

He fell silent and fitted a key into the lock of the last door at the end of the corridor.

When will I finally know I am home? "It's lovely," Matilda said, stepping into a parlor that would have been of a piece with the earl's own dwelling. "Tommie, take a peek out the window."

Tommie ran to the window and simply stared at the vista of the river below. Even on a winter afternoon, the light sparkled off the water, and the distant shore—an unremarkable collection of shops, warehouses, and tenements—had the aspect of a magical land.

"We're sailing away on the river?" he asked, nose pressed to the glass.

"With tomorrow afternoon's outgoing tide," Tremont said, which spared Matilda having to prevaricate with her son. "You will travel to a new world and have many fine adventures."

Tommie turned away from the window, his features set in an obstinate cast Matilda knew all too well.

"I don't want to have adventures in a new world, Mama. I want to have them here. With Tuck and Jensen and Cook and MacIvey. I want to learn to polish boots like Charlie and speak the Erse like the major and MacIvey and MacPherson. I miss Tidbit, and Arthur, and—"

The earl scooped Tommie up and perched him on his hip. "My boy, this will not do. Do you recall that in my youth, I had to imagine sailing away in my longboat? I had to make believe some old tree or ruined cottage was my ship? I was an earl, a peer of the realm, and I'd never seen the sea. I'd never heard the sails luffing in the breeze, never felt the deck shifting as my ship got underway. By this time tomorrow, you will know firsthand all the things I could barely imagine."

"I don't want to be a Viking." A note of true despair undergirded Tommie's petulance. "I want to go back to the happy house and learn to play the fiddle. I hate the stupid ocean."

Tommie had reason on his side. From his perspective, this journey was purely one of loss.

"The Atlantic Ocean is merely a lot of salt water," Tremont said. "Do you know some ships cross the whole thing in little more than a fortnight? Those ships carry letters, and I am hoping you will write to me."

"My lord..." Matilda began. Correspondence was not in her plans. Correspondence could ruin everything.

"Will you write to me?" Tommie asked, knuckling an eye. "I can write my name and spell Arthur and Tidbit and Mama."

"Matilda?"

"I have told Portia I will write to her. I'm sure any correspondence for Tommie that she receives from you, my lord, she will be happy to forward to us. If Tommie is inclined to write to you, Portia will doubtless send his letters on to you as well."

Even that compromise left Matilda uneasy, and Tremont clearly hated it.

"You see?" he said, setting Tommie on his feet. "We will become loyal correspondents, and you will tell me all about your travels and the new friends you make. You must practice your penmanship so I can make out your words easily. Shall we shake hands in parting?"

He extended a hand to Tommie, and Tommie shook, then wrapped his arms around Tremont's waist. "Please look after Arthur and Tidbit and the goats and Tuck and Jensen and all the rest, sir. I will write to them too."

The lump in Matilda's throat eclipsed Gibraltar by an order of magnitude. "The bedroom is through there," she said, pointing to an open door. "Decide which side of the bed you want, Tommie, and get Copenhagen acquainted with his new paddock."

Tommie cantered off, waving his horse, and Tremont watched him go.

"Do you truly object to letters, Matilda?"

"If you are merely being considerate of a small boy's homesickness, no, I do not object, but you must not try to follow us."

Tremont ran a hand through his hair. "I have no great wish to see Philadelphia, but if dear Harry should be run down by a dray Wednesday next, I would most assuredly want to convey that development to you. I can guarantee I will hear that news before Portia does."

"Harry would never be so obliging as to step out in front of a heavy vehicle."

Tremont smiled crookedly. "Suppose not. I've sent for his sister, though. She might knock him flat for us."

"You did *what*?"

"That long talk I had with Spartacus Lykens—who is on his way back to Ireland with funds in his pocket as we speak—included a few more details regarding Harry's origins that I meant to pass along to you, except that you drifted away on the arms of Morpheus before I got around to it. Harry is of the Merchant family of Bristol, a fine lineage and well-heeled. Cousins in banking, uncles in shipping. I sent an express to the sister, who yet resides in the family's Bristol home. I suspect Harry owns that property, does he but know it."

Oh, the irony. "Why do this? Why give his family a chance to reclaim him?"

Tremont's smile faded. "I suspect many a boy runs away from home just to make sure he'll be missed at supper. He ends up hungry and humiliated, whether or not his family misses him. I can't begin to know what passes for motivation in your husband's head, but he's more muddled than even he knows, and sisters have a way of sorting a fellow out."

"I do not care whether Harry is ever sorted out. If he grasps what's good for him, he will stay far, far away from me and Tommie."

"Depend upon it. Contrary to his prevarications with you, he's off to Rome, according to MacKay. Harry apparently considered France, but chose Rome as the cheaper and sunnier alternative, also one where he's less likely to encounter familiar faces. The French should consider that they've had a narrow escape."

"He doesn't speak the language," Matilda said. "As facile as Harry is as a mimic, he could never quite get the knack of French, while I had French drummed into me, along with Proverbs and Fordyce's Sermons."

Words, coherent words, were coming out of her mouth, but Matilda's heart ached with the knowledge that when Tremont walked out the door, her path and his would never cross again.

"You won't need much French in Philadelphia," Tremont said, "though Proverbs might come in handy." He shifted his gaze to the river. "Matilda, I don't want to leave you, but if I stay another five minutes, I will succumb to strong hysterics."

"As will I." She would whether he remained or departed. "My stores of fortitude are ebbing by the moment, so let's say farewell and wish each other the best, shall we?"

Tremont held open his arms, and Matilda lacked the ability to resist.

"I will miss you for the rest of my life," she said, burrowing close. "If I were a different woman, if you were a different man, we'd not need to part."

"But we are who we are," Tremont replied, "and I would not have you any other way. I will miss you, too, Matilda, but I will also love you and thank the benevolent powers that you have been a part of my life."

"Tell me you'll take a wife, Tremont. Please. You need to take a wife."

He kissed her cheek and stepped back. "I will write to Tommie, through Portia if you insist, and I will wish you a safe journey. I promise not to follow you to Philadelphia, and I will keep some eyes on Harry in Rome for the good of all concerned. Be well, Matilda."

He bowed and withdrew, closing the door softly before she could disgrace herself by begging him to stay. He'd given his word not to follow her, and Marcus, Earl of Tremont, would not break that word.

She should have been relieved. Instead, Matilda sank into a chair and commenced silently weeping.

CHAPTER SEVENTEEN

"The MacKays mean well," Michael Delancey said, "and Dorcas sets a fine table. Shall we walk together for a bit?"

Tremont would rather have walked alone, but left to his own devices, he'd find himself standing outside a certain genteel riverfront inn, baying at the inky winter sky.

"Thank you, Delancey," he said. "I'd be happy for the company. Do you ever refuse your sister's invitations?"

"I don't feel I have the right." Delancey set a relaxed pace along the deserted street. "I was off in the north for years, while Dorcas was all but running St. Mildred's and contending with other challenges. I should have been here for her and for my father. She still keeps a hand in at St. Mildred's, while I..."

Delancey's voice trailed off, and his gaze narrowed on a heap of shivering blankets tucked against the door of a grocer's shop.

"You are to rise swiftly through the ranks at Lambeth," Tremont said, "and make your father proud of you?" The reminder that other men had burdens was timely. Matilda and Tommie would sail out of Tremont's life tomorrow, and some comparable sorrow had apparently sailed into Mr. Delancey's pious and worthy existence.

"Oh, something like that. MacKay pulled me aside and said I was not to mention Mrs. Merridew's name. I gather she's left her post?" Delancey approached the heap of blankets and knelt. "You'll catch your death out here, my friend. Do you know where St. Mildred's is?"

The heap scrabbled back against the wall, revealing the crossing sweeper Patrick. "Don't touch me, mate. I've got a knife aimed at yer..." The boy leaped to his feet. "Milord. Evenin'."

"Mr. Delancey means you no harm, Patrick. It's too cold to weather the elements tonight. Take yourself off to share the kitchen fire with Charlie and tell him you've missed your supper."

Patrick shoved unkempt dark hair from his eyes. "I dint mean to fall asleep."

Delancey unwound a green and white plaid scarf from about his neck. "Do as the earl says, lad. As cold as it is, you might have awakened without the use of a few fingers and toes, if you awoke at all." He wrapped the scarf around the boy's ears. "Away with you. My sister knits me a different scarf every week. You'd do me a kindness if you kept that one. The colors do not suit me."

"Smells good," Patrick said, taking an audible sniff. "Like the bakery on biscuit day. I can keep it?"

"Please do."

The boy trotted off before Tremont could toss him a coin. "If you're crossing the river, Delancey, you have a long walk ahead of you. You're welcome to spend the night with me and take my coach to Southwark in the morning."

"No, thank you. The walk will do me good. About Mrs. Merridew. She's quit her post?"

"She's quitting England. Ready for a fresh start."

Delancey muttered something that sounded like, *Aren't we all?* "Dorcas left me with the impression that you and Mrs. Merridew might suit."

What was this interrogation in aid of? "The lady decided otherwise, for reasons I cannot question. What's it like, working for the archbishop?"

Tremont turned down his street, and Delancey accompanied him. "I do not work for the archbishop. I work for the Almighty, or so I'm to believe. Who would have thought that the Creator had need of so many glorified clerks?"

"Perhaps you should take ship for Philadelphia."

Delancey shook his head. "I'm needed here." An automatic and somewhat bleak reply.

"As am I. Sure you won't join me for a nightcap? Allow me to loan you a scarf? Mine are all in the best of subdued good taste."

"I will decline your kind offers and bid you good night." He bowed at the foot of Tremont's front steps. "You'll keep an eye on Patrick? He's set himself up for lung fever, at best."

"I will keep a roof over his head if he'll allow it. One must deal gently with puerile pride."

Delancey smiled. "And its adult equivalent. You are welcome to spend the night roaming the metropolis with me, my lord. I promise not to pry, and I won't lead you into any gaming hells or dens of vice."

How would a bishop-in-training know to find his way to such entertainments? "Most kind of you. I'll page through a few scenes from one of the Bard's plays, and I should be ready for slumber. Wander carefully, Delancey. The MacKays would take it amiss if you should run into foul luck."

"I am ever cautious, thank you. If you want the best soporific known to man, may I recommend ecclesiastical law? I defy any sentient creature to remain awake for more than one page of the bishops' maunderings. Thanks to the arcane proceedings of the church courts, I have become a sleepwalker of no little skill, but you must not tell that to my superiors. Adieu, Tremont, and pleasant dreams."

He saluted with his walking stick and strolled off into the night.

Tremont paused outside his home, watching Delancey disappear into the gloom. *He doesn't feel the cold.* Saints were that detached from bodily concerns, but so was a particularly miserable class of sinner. Tremont had been among their number when he'd first returned to London.

Melancholia was too simple a label for such a complicated problem. As Tremont made his way up to his apartment, he offered a prayer for Delancey's eventual waking. Sleepwalking took a toll, though as to that, waking could be nearly as painful.

Memories took a toll as well, and because Tremont did not want to toss and turn in the very bed where he and Matilda had become lovers, he opened a volume of Shakespeare and found himself staring at *Romeo and Juliet*, act 2, scene 2.

Two lovers caterwauling into the night, about family feuds, birthrights, and names, and Romeo offering to cast his name aside for Juliet's love. *A rose by any other name...*

Utter tripe.

He turned some pages and let his mind wander over the entire situation with Matilda. She was married to Harry Merridew. No getting 'round that. She'd married of her own free will to ensure her child had legitimacy, and her vicar father had been present and unobjecting at the ceremony. No hint of coercion, nobody committing bigamy, nobody operating under a mental deficit such that consent was in question.

Logic, reason, and common sense all united to dash hope, not for the first time. The sonnets were no greater comfort. *This thou perceivest, which makes thy love more strong, To love that well which thou must leave ere long...*

Only the thought that Matilda would chide him for disrespecting great literature stopped Tremont from tossing the book onto the flames. Rather than yield to that impulse, he stretched out on the sofa and woke several hours later, cold and stiff. His mind was cobwebbed with images of Matilda on the balcony of the coaching inn, her arms full of roses.

Not until he'd shaved and dressed did Tremont realize what Shakespeare's doomed lovers had been trying to tell him.

"Send the coach around," he said to his first footman. "I'm off to Southwark, and time is of the essence."

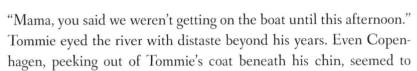

"Mama, you said we weren't getting on the boat until this afternoon." Tommie eyed the river with distaste beyond his years. Even Copenhagen, peeking out of Tommie's coat beneath his chin, seemed to regard the water with contempt.

"I misspoke," Matilda said. "We are actually taking two ships, one to Dover and then another that departs from Dover."

Tommie's brows knit. "I thought we were going to Ports... Portssomething and to America."

"America is very, very far away. Sailing there can take weeks and costs a lot of money. Do you recall my telling you that England and France are only twenty miles apart?" Matilda injected the question with a brightness at odds with her mood.

"We are going to France? The French are our enemies. The Corsican Monster fought for France."

I am not arguing international politics with a five-year-old. "We are at peace now, and the French are our friends. Let's explore the ship, shall we?"

Tommie wrinkled his nose. "It's not a longboat. I don't see any dragons."

Matilda took his hand, picked up her traveling valise, and gave their names to the steward several yards down the pier from the gangplank. Exhaustion dragged at her, because she'd slept barely two winks.

"We will have to imagine the dragon on the prow and a square sail on the mainmast. The inn packed us a nooning, and we'll be at Dover before nightfall. Do you know, I've never set foot on a sailboat before."

"Tremont said we're having an adventure. I don't want to go to France, and I don't like this adventure very much so far."

I perishing hate it. "Adventures can be like that. A bit tedious when you're in the middle of them, but fondly recalled. Shall I teach you how to say something in French?"

"Teach me how to say 'I miss Tremont, and Arthur, and Tidbit, and the goats, and Charlie, and MacIvey.'"

Matilda paused at the foot of the gangplank and summoned every ounce of courage and determination she possessed. This journey was for the best. The only way to preserve dignity and honor. A remove to Paris was...

Awful.

She started up the incline, keeping a very firm grip on Tommie's hand. "In French, you would say, '*Mes amis me manquent.*' I miss my friends." *My friends are lacking to me, literally and more poignantly.*

The ship rose and fell at its mooring, and a bitter wind whipped along the river. Tommie clambered onto the deck, where another steward greeted them and took Matilda's valise.

"This ship stinks worse than our house did." Tommie had spoken too clearly for the steward not to have heard him.

"The river has an odor," Matilda said. "The sea is far more fresh. Let's get out of this wind, shall we?"

They were shown to a tiny stateroom, with two bunks folded up against the wall and two chairs set on either side of a table no larger than a chessboard.

"We cast off in a quarter hour," the steward said. "Should make good time to Dover, though the wind can be fickle this time of year if you're bound for Calais. The Dover inns are cozy, though, and they are used to waiting on the weather."

He bowed and withdrew as Tommie dragged a chair over to the porthole and stood on the seat.

"I can't see anything, Mama. The glass is too dirty."

"The sea air leaves brine on everything," Matilda said, "but the ship isn't going anywhere for another fifteen minutes. We'll go back up on deck then. Shall we play some cards?"

"Tell me again how to say 'I miss everybody.'"

Matilda did not miss everybody, not yet. She was too consumed with missing Tremont. "*Mes amis me manquent.* Can you say that?"

Tommie parroted the French exactly, and then Matilda translated each word for him. She wrote the words out and pointed to them as she spoke. Tommie asked how to say *France is stupid* and *Vikings are brilliant* and a dozen other phrases while the minutes dragged by.

Please come, Matilda thought, sending that silent plea to Tremont. *Please tell me that your great, busy mind has found a way for us to be married, despite Harry, despite everything. Please, please...*

But by the time she was explaining to Tommie how to say *I call myself Thomas*, the motion of the boat had changed, becoming less gentle.

"We're moving," Tommie said, his head coming up like a horse who heard the groom pouring oats into a bucket. "We're sailing on the sea!"

Not quite, but they were underway. Matilda took Tommie up on deck, where other passengers were assembled along the rail, waving farewell to friends onshore and doffing hats in a general gesture of parting.

"Mama, we're sailing away! The ship is moving!"

"I know, Tommie. I know."

She searched the crowd on the pier for a particular tall, quietly elegant gentleman and found no one answering to that description, which was to be expected. She'd led Tremont to believe they were sailing later and from a different pier.

"We are sailing away!" Tommie called again, waving to nobody in particular. "I'm a Viking on my longship, and I'm sailing away to France!"

His exclamation provoked a few smiles, and Matilda tried to return them, but she was not a Viking, and she was not on her longship, and Tremont was not going to save her from the wretched burden of living her life as a loving mother and an honorable, decent adult female.

And that hurt, brutally, but the pain was gilded with a little pride. *You were wrong, Papa. I have not come to a bad end, nor will I. So there and to blazes with you and your hypocritical judgments of me.*

The boat caught the current of the outgoing tide, and the shore receded. Tommie's teeth were chattering by the time he agreed to return to their stateroom, and Matilda was chilled to the bone. The steward came around to ask if they'd like tea, coffee, brandy, or hot chocolate.

Tommie asked for hot chocolate, while Matilda declined any refreshment. The motion of the ship did not agree with her, and they would not see Dover for hours.

~

"What in blazing perdition do you mean she's already departed?" Tremont kept his voice down, though it was a very near thing.

"She and the boy left not an hour ago," the desk clerk said. "With all their luggage." He was an older fellow, balding, and skinny. His coat was shiny with age and his gloves less than pristine. "Be you her husband, sir?"

"I am." Harry spoke up from Tremont's elbow. "And I am very curious to know where my wife has got off to. Curious enough to summon the authorities if she's bolted with my son."

"Shut your lying mouth," Tremont growled.

"You won't get anywhere with the likes of him," Harry said, jerking his chin in the clerk's direction. "He can't be bribed, but he can be bullied. I know the type."

The clerk drew himself up. "If you was a proper husband to the lady, she'd have no reason to bolt, would she?"

"Precisely," Tremont said, "but I am not her husband, and I am most concerned for her and the child. This fellow"—he jerked a thumb toward Harry—"has no idea where she's gone. She is not on the manifest for the Portsmouth packet, and her only relative—an auntie—gave us reason to doubt the Portsmouth itinerary in the first place."

The morning had been busy, starting with a raid on Lambeth Palace and progressing to an invasion of Aunt Portia's breakfast parlor. Tremont had press-ganged Harry into joining the affray, because he hadn't time to tarry in Knightsbridge playing skittles with a swindler.

Moreover, Harry deserved to know the result of Tremont's consultation with Mr. Delancey regarding the niceties of ecclesiastical law pertaining to voidable marriages.

Portia had been unforthcoming in every regard, except that when Tremont asked for an address in Philadelphia where he could send any correspondence for Matilda, Portia had replied that she had no acquaintances in Philadelphia who might be prevailed upon to hold Matilda's mail.

Philadelphia had been a ruse, which left only the entire rest of the world for Tremont to search.

"What other packets depart from the nearby piers?" he asked.

The clerk sent a dubious glace toward Harry.

"I mean the woman no harm," Harry muttered. "But she's leaving England under a serious misapprehension."

The clerk addressed Tremont. "All manner of packets tie up on this part of the river, from Aberdeen on south and around west to Bristol. Many of them also call at Dover, though some passengers prefer to take the stage overland to Dover."

Would Matilda subject Tommie to more than seventy miles of stage travel? "And from Dover?"

"Oh, my gracious," the clerk said. "She could sail to Calais, of course, but also to Le Havre, Cherbourg, Amsterdam, Dieppe, the Channel Islands... If she sails from Dover..."

"She's gone for good," Harry said. "*If* she's gone to Dover. She might well be headed for Yorkshire. Just when you think a woman's become predictable, she surprises you."

"Where is the porter who took her luggage?" Tremont asked as a well-fed elderly woman in weeds and black bonnet stepped up to the reception desk. She'd pinned back the veil of her bonnet, probably the better to glower at all and sundry.

"The porters assemble at the far end of the veranda, sir, and come when summoned by the doorman. No telling which one took any particular guest's luggage."

"I'll have a word," Harry said, tipping his hat to the older woman and sauntering out the door.

"Pity the lady if she is married to that one," the clerk muttered, "but I'm afraid I cannot help you, sir."

"She is married to him," Tremont said, "but there's hope." He bowed to the glowering woman and stepped out into the malodorous cold of the winter day. The sense of activity was relentless, on the walkways, the veranda, and the street. Somewhere in this morass of bustling humanity was somebody who'd caught a glimpse of Matilda and Tommie, somebody who'd watched them climb into a stage coach or...

"No luck," Harry said, sending a scowl in the direction of the loitering porters. "The fellow who took Matilda's bags was subsequently tasked with taking a load of trunks to some Mayfair hotel. He might not return to his post until tomorrow."

"Then Matilda and Tommie did not go far," Tremont said. "If they left only an hour ago, and the porter had time to see them to their destination and then return for another assignment, they did not go far."

One of the porters watched them, though clearly neither Tremont nor Harry had any bags to be carried. Something about the man looked familiar, as if—

"The porter coming back quickly doesn't tell you anything," Harry said. "Tilly could have gone a quarter mile down the wharves or two streets over to a coaching inn. She's gone, and she learned from me how to hide her tracks. She'll speak with an accent—Dorset or Yorkshire, one distinctive enough to leave an impression, but not an impression of the Matilda you're searching for. She'll walk differently and maybe use an alias."

"You and your damned aliases. Matilda is not trying to hide from me. She will travel as herself."

The same porter had sidled closer, a tidy fellow with the wiry strength of a yeoman and the wheat-blond hair of a Saxon.

Harry droned on, about all the theatrical tricks he'd used to disguise himself, while Tremont focused on Matilda and *what Matilda wanted.* Safety, of course. Security. Peace and quiet. She'd go someplace affordable—most of the Continent was affordable compared to England. Someplace where nobody knew her. Someplace where she could find honest employment, which meant no tiny villages.

What else did she want? If granted three wishes, what would they be?

"Beg pardon, sir," the towheaded porter said. "You'd be Lord Tremont?"

"I have that honor."

The fellow stood straighter. "Thought that was you. Wanted to wish you a fine day."

While Tremont wanted to toss the fellow into the river. Manners and something more—a niggling at the back of Tremont's mind—stopped him.

"Thank you, and the same to you. I have the sense we've met."

Harry glowered at the fellow, who was grinning as if he'd just been given the Freedom of the City and all its pubs.

"I knew you'd remember me. Shores, sir. Corporal Dennis Shores, which is a joke now that I'm working on the riverbank, innit? I served under Dunacre along with you, and I heard what you done for some of the men now Boney's been trounced."

Vague recollections, of a skinny fellow who'd advanced to corporal thanks to excellent aim with a rifle and a well-timed jest.

Every moment spent passing the time of day was a moment Matilda and Tommie were farther away. And yet, one did not snub a former comrade-in-arms.

"Shores, how good of you to introduce yourself. I hope you are thriving."

"Keepin' body and soul together. And it's thanks to you I'm alive to do that. My brother was with us at Waterloo, too, and he's got a fine job as a footman. I heard this' un"—Shores jerked his chin at Harry—"asking after a young lady and a lad. Did the lad have a stuffed horse stickin' out of his coat?"

Thank the angels of mercy and a small boy's attachment to his friends. "He surely did."

"They took ship for Dover not an hour past. Martin hauled their luggage for 'em, though 'tweren't much. Long gone, given the tide, but she were Dover-bound, sir."

"Shores, I could kiss you."

"A handshake will do, sir."

"No, it will not," Tremont said, extending a hand. "If you or your brother are ever in need, you come by the soldiers' home two streets from St. Mildred's. Come by for a drink even when you're not in need. The men will be glad to see an old friend, and Cook always makes enough for a guest or two."

"I'll tell me brother. You're for Dover, sir?"

"On the fastest horses I can find."

"You'll want to go to the Jolly Bullock, sir. They handle a lot of expresses for the captains and crew. Fastest nags this side of the Thames, and the grooms will tell you where to make the next change. You tie a red kerchief to the horse's right rein, and the tollkeepers will wave you through if you toss 'em a few pence for their trouble."

Harry looked fascinated by this recitation.

"Shores, you have been a godsend. Thank you for keeping a sharp eye, and I meant what I said about looking up the old crew. Bring your brother and anybody else you happen across who served with us."

"You were the godsend, sir. Took us a while to realize that, but Waterloo isn't a day we'll ever forget. The Jolly Bullock is two streets up that lane, and you tell 'em Shores sent ya."

"I'll do that."

An ornate coach pulled up to the foot of the inn's steps. Shores tugged his cap and jaunted down the steps. "Best of luck, sir."

Harry watched as the coach disgorged two women, clearly mother and daughter, both dressed in the first stare of fashion. "What was that all about?"

"That was about Waterloo and doing the right thing. You are going to do the right thing now too, Merchant."

"Don't call me that."

"That is who you are. I must away to Dover, but you must stay put until I can retrieve Matilda and get her free of you."

Harry shifted so his back was to anybody coming up the steps. "Staying put is not my forte, Tremont."

"How well we know that, but you're about to turn over a new and better leaf."

The ladies swept past, and Harry turned again so his back was to the door of the inn. "I've tried turning over new leaves. Matilda was supposed to be a new leaf. Oxford, Dublin... I've littered my path with new leaves, and they always wilt."

"Do you know where Matilda has gone, Harry?"

Harry's expression turned bleak. "Dover, and from thence... God knows, so you'd best be on that fast horse and leave me to be about my business."

"Matilda is going someplace *you* can never plague her," Tremont said. "Someplace she can turn over a new leaf and go about it properly. She is going to Paris."

The elegant coach rolled around to the side of the inn, where the porters and footmen would deal with the luggage out of sight of the inn's guests.

"I did not plague her," Harry bit out. "I *rescued* her from scandal and ruin."

"The two are not mutually exclusive. You would never set foot in Paris, because it's nearly overrun with Englishmen of all stripes. Merchants, nabobs, peers, debtors, and thus *creditors*. As ripe as the pickings might be for one of your ilk, you cannot risk trolling in those waters."

Harry ran a finger around the inside of his collar. "I also can't speak Frog. I've tried. Tilly used to laugh at my attempts. I can read it some, thanks to her and a few years of Latin, but attempting to ply my trade when I can't understand the language is asking for disaster."

"You have no trade," Tremont said, "but you would make a first-rate actor."

The longing that flashed in Harry's eyes was astonishing. "Maybe once upon a time. Hadn't you best be on your way, Tremont?"

"I have one small task to see to, and then I'll gallop for the coast."

"I'll wish you Godspeed." Harry swept off his hat and made an elegant bow. "And give my regards to Tilly."

"You may offer them yourself upon her return to London, because any plans you had to quit the metropolis are now postponed. Ah, here come my reinforcements. Major Alasdhair MacKay, may I make known to you one Harry Merchant, late of Bristol and various unlucky locales. MacKay is assisted by MacIvey and MacPherson, and I suspect Bentley and Biggs are canvassing the surrounds. MacKay, your charge. If he tries to do another bunk, carve up his handsome face. Distinguishing scars would all but put him out of business as a swindler—and as an actor."

MacKay nodded. "I'd let Mrs. MacKay have a go at him. She's not as softhearted as I am. MacKay, at your service, Merchant. We've met."

Harry was frankly staring at Tremont. "You never did tell me how you learned that name."

"I asked a few honest questions of a mostly honest man. Now behave for the major and his missus until I return."

CHAPTER EIGHTEEN

"I don't want to get on another ship," Tommie said. "All we did was watch the shore go by, and pass other boats, and listen to that pale lady moan, and watch more of the shore go by. Sailing on the sea is boring. *On-wee-ooze.*"

He said this loudly enough that the lady at the inn's reception desk smiled.

Boring, stupid, foolish... Tommie had asked for all manner of pejorative French vocabulary as the journey—and Tommie himself—had grown tedious. He was a prodigious mimic, which would serve him well learning a new language.

"The lad's tired," the lady at the desk said, evidencing a slight French accent. "*Le garçon est fatigué.* The mama is tired as well, I suspect."

"Exhausted," Matilda said, "but determined to press on. We need a decent meal, and then we'll be on the evening packet for Calais."

"I don't want to go to Calais," Tommie bellowed. "Copenhagen doesn't want to go to Calais. Calais is stupid and boring and stinky."

"*Le ville est puant,*" the lady said mildly. She was dark-haired, dark-eyed, and trim. "Is Copenhagen your horse?"

Tommie touched Copenhagen's yarn forelock. "He's my friend. I won't ever lose him."

"Did you know there's a whole city that shares a name with your horse? Copenhagen is beautiful, right on the sea. They speak Danish there, a language of the Vikings."

Tommie looked askance at Matilda.

"Madame is right," she said, "though I don't know even a word of Danish. We can eat in the common, and I'm told our luggage can be stored here while we wait for the tide to go out."

"Of course, ma'am. And under what name shall we keep your trunks?"

Harry would have used an alias, of course. Damn him and his schemes. "Matilda Merridew."

The lady made a note on some ledger. "Mrs. Merridew, might I suggest a private dining room? We are not full, and I believe the young man could use some peace and quiet. I do not charge you for this. Even Vikings can tire of travel."

"I'm not a Viking," Tommie muttered.

No, but you are impersonating a barbarian quite well. "Peace and quiet sound marvelous."

The fare was simple but hearty—bread and butter, beef and barley stew, served with steaming mulled cider. Tommie tore into his portions while Matilda lectured herself about the need to eat.

Thanks to Tremont and Aunt Portia, funds were not an immediate issue, but an upset tummy and a breaking heart were. While Tommie pretended to offer a spoonful of soup to his stuffed horse and managed to dribble a mess onto the table, Matilda nibbled bread and butter and missed Tremont.

What was he doing while she prepared for yet more hours of bobbing on the waves? Was he reading the Stoics? Tending to the account books? Staring off into space and wishing life could be different?

Was he missing her or resigning himself to that which could not be changed? A tap on the door interrupted her musings.

"Evening, ma'am. I've come to take the dishes, and Missus sent along some apple cobbler for your sweet. The wind has picked up, and that's a good thing if you're catching the evening tide."

"I don't want to catch the evening tide," Tommie said. "Tides are stupid."

"Somebody's tired," the serving maid said, putting Tommie's empty soup bowl on a tray. "Travel can be wearying, but it's ever so lovely to finally reach home."

"We aren't going home," Tommie began. "We are going to stupid Paris in stinky old France, and I don't want to go, and nobody will listen to m-me."

He hugged his horse and buried his face against Copenhagen's velvet neck as loud, hooting sobs filled the small parlor.

"The crossing should be swift," the maid said, collecting Matilda's soup bowl. "Winter weather can make for choppy currents, but you do get to Calais in good time. You'll be in France before dawn, young fellow."

This assurance inspired Tommie to greater volumes of misery.

And for Matilda, to be free, to be away, to be on French soil and know the parting was complete... She longed to close the door on her hopes with that much finality. To lose herself in the simple business of survival as she had when Harry had abandoned her.

Thomas the Vexatious would likely fall asleep before they'd been underway for an hour, though he hadn't slept for the entire journey down from London. Matilda put a hand on his shoulder, prepared to reason and wheedle and bargain, but he jerked away from her hand.

"Don't touch me! I hate you!"

"He doesn't mean it," the maid said, setting an apple cobbler before Matilda. "Overly tired, he is. The little ones don't always travel so well, do they?"

Matilda was half tempted to deal with Tommie severely. A day of patience and placating him had resulted only in this spectacular tantrum, and they had quite a distance yet to travel.

"Thomas, look at me." *Or so help me, you will wish you had.* Papa's voice again, as he slapped a birch rod slowly against his palm.

Matilda was assailed by an old, old memory, of being squashed beside her father on a stage coach journey to London. She'd been about Tommie's age, and she'd had to use the necessary, but hadn't known how to communicate that need to her father.

She'd wet herself and got a smack and a protracted scolding for her stupidity. All the while Papa had been berating her, and the stink of her incontinence had risen from her clothes, she'd thought, *I hate you. I hate you, you stupid, selfish, angry old man. I will always hate you.*

And if she hadn't quite loathed Papa from that day forward, neither had she respected him.

"France can wait," she said to the maid as Tommie's wailing subsided into brokenhearted whimpers. "You are right. My son is exhausted." The proprietress had also reminded Matilda of the same obvious fact. "Might we have a room for the night?"

"The wind could die in the morning, missus. You could be stuck here for days."

"Then the wind dies, but my child will be well rested. I have asked too much of an otherwise very good little boy, and the last thing I need or want is for him to take sick because he's been overtaxed."

"It's cold on the water," the maid said. "No mistake about that. We have rooms to spare this time of year. Eat your cobbler, and we'll get a fire going for you upstairs."

She bustled out, and Matilda was left with an overwrought child who was clinging to his stuffed horse as if Copenhagen were the last spar floating on a storm-tossed sea.

"Thomas, you owe me an apology."

"S-sorry." He sounded not the least bit remorseful, for which Matilda was proud of him.

"I owe you an apology as well. I'm not an experienced traveler, and I was so anxious to get us away from England that I did not plan our itinerary very sensibly. We'll rest tonight and catch the morning packet. The ship leaves at low tide, weather permitting, and there will always be another low tide."

Tommie sighed. "I m-miss Tidbit."

"So do I. He is a wonderful pony. Would you like a bite of cobbler? It has apples in it, and I'm sure Copenhagen would enjoy a taste."

Tommie sent her an annoyed look. "Cope isn't real, Mama."

"And you don't hate me." *Yet.*

Tommie picked up his spoon. "I was mad. I should not have said that. This has cinnamon on it, like the hot chocolate from the tea shop. Do they have cinnamon in France?"

"Yes, and hot chocolate." *But they do not have Marcus, Earl of Tremont, and for that, I hate France a little bit too.*

Tommie had finished his cobbler and was sending longing glances at the remaining three-quarters of Matilda's when the serving maid reappeared.

"Your room is ready, though the packet is just now boarding, ma'am. You could sail tonight and have the crossing behind you."

"Mama..."

"I know, Tommie. We'll take the room." Matilda would far rather have boarded the packet, but removing to France could not be her excuse for turning into her father. "We are in no hurry, and we are both quite tired."

She carried Tommie up the steps—he'd grown more substantial in recent weeks—and left the maid to bring up the traveling valise. The room was cozy and smelled faintly of lavender, and the bed was a fluffy four-poster liberally covered in quilts. Beyond the latticed window, moonlight glinted off dark, undulating waves, and the occasional running light marked the progress of a vessel out at sea.

"The coals are in the warmer," the maid said. "And we can send up breakfast at first light if you prefer that to a meal in the common."

"I do, thank you. Shoes off, Tommie."

He blinked at her from the depths of a wing chair before the hearth.

Matilda knew what it was to be that tired and chided herself for pushing Tommie too hard. He wasn't yet six years old, and if she was exhausted, he had to be at the very limit of his resources. She got him undressed and into the trundle bed, where he subsided into sleep, Copenhagen clutched in his arms.

Matilda washed, changed into nightclothes, and took down her hair, though the brush had somehow acquired the weight of a cannonball. She managed a braid and nearly fell asleep on the vanity stool.

"To bed with you," she muttered, though now that no food was on hand, she was almost as hungry as she was tired. She climbed under the covers, closed her eyes, and said one prayer for Tremont's wellbeing and another for an uneventful journey to Paris.

She surrendered to welcome oblivion only to be awakened what felt like moments later by an insistent pounding on her door.

~

Matilda, looking rumpled and grumpy, peered at Tremont as he stood in the doorway to her room.

"Am I dreaming this, my lord, or are you truly here?" Her eyes were underscored by dark half circles, her braid was half undone, and on her feet was a pair of heavy wool socks. She was covered from neck to ankles in a brown quilted dressing gown going frayed at the collar and cuffs, and the color accentuated her uncharacteristic pallor.

Matilda had never looked more dear to him or more thoroughly vexed, and while Tremont longed to take her in his arms, he had come to her in all his considerable dirt. More significantly, the proprietress—Madame Howard—hovered at his elbow, doubtless ready to pitch him down the stairs if Matilda took umbrage at his arrival.

"I am truly here," he said, quietly because Tommie slumbered in a trundle bed not eight feet away. "And you, thank the guardian angels of my fondest dreams, are here. You are not, however, legally married to Harry Merridew."

Matilda put a hand on the bedpost. "Is this a nightmare?"

She sounded genuinely bewildered and looked as if she was about to collapse. Tremont advanced into the room and led her to the sole chair before the banked hearth.

"Perhaps we could light a candle or two?" he said, rather than presume to order Madame Howard about.

"*Non*," she replied. "You and Mrs. Merridew may use my parlor at the end of the corridor. I will stay with the boy. I believe the lady could benefit from some brandy, *my lord*."

She reproached him by using his title, which he'd forgotten to mention when he'd been babbling about perilous journeys and utmost concern and whatever else had come out of his exhausted, desperate mouth.

"Thank you," Matilda said, rising with Tremont's assistance. "Some explanations are in order, and the privacy is appreciated."

"I have very good hearing," Madame Howard said. "Madame need only call out, and I will wield an iron poker on his lordship's handsome head and throw his body into the sea for the sharks." She made a shooing motion toward the door.

Those threats—or promises—inspired a faint smile from Matilda. "No need for dire measures, Madame. His lordship is the quintessential gentleman under all circumstances."

Tremont processed with Matilda down the corridor before Madame took a swipe at him for practice.

"I like her," Matilda said. "She's fierce and kind, and I like her. Tommie does not want to go to France, and for that matter, neither do I, but what are you doing here, and how did you find me? If Harry is dead, I will try to mourn his passing, but that will be uphill work."

He ushered her into a toasty parlor done up in red, white, and blue. A bow window overlooked the sea, and the setting moon spread streamers of gold over the dark water.

Matilda had planned to sail across that expanse, never to be seen again by the man who loved her to distraction.

"Let's sit, shall we?" he said. "My guess is that Madame Howard will have very good brandy, if you'd like some."

"Will you join me?"

"I'd best not. I've ridden seventy miles through winter weather on horses whose sole redeeming qualities were speed and stamina. Some of them were carnivores, all of them had miserable gaits, and two were prepared to commit homicide, so fiercely did they hold to the conviction that they must return to London. A nightcap might lay me low."

Matilda subsided onto the blue sofa and took up a matching blue pillow embroidered with gold fleur-de-lis. "And yet, despite the perils of the journey, you are here."

He poured her a generous portion from a decanter on the side-board and brought it to her. "May I sit beside you?"

She accepted the drink. She did not pat the place next to her on the sofa. "Tell me about Harry. He's mixed up in this somehow, isn't he?"

Tremont shifted a wing chair such that it faced the sofa rather than the sea. "He's not Harry Merridew. He's Harrell Merchant, scion of a respected Quaker trading family from Bristol. He's prob-ably quite wealthy, if—in a singular irony—he hasn't been declared dead."

Matilda sipped her brandy. "Then I am Mrs. Matilda Merchant?"

"You need not be Mrs. Anybody. I consulted in some detail with Mr. Michael Delancey, who has a thorough grasp of ecclesiastical law. You and Harry were married by special license, and that license was sorely defective. Harry lied about his name, he lied about belonging to a Church of England congregation, and through marriage to you, he got his hands on much of your dower property."

Matilda stared at her drink. "Perhaps the lateness of the hour and a day spent in Tommie's disgruntled company has addled my wits. What is the significance of Harry's prevarications?"

"The marriage is *voidable*, Matilda. Harry deceived you and the Church when he stood up with you. He's not who he said he was, he's not of the faith he claimed to be, and the only property you are entitled to control are your dower goods. The case can be made that Harry defrauded you of valuable goods, and if necessary, that case shall be made."

Now that Tremont was sitting, his body reminded him of every mile he'd spent wrestling fractious horses, while his ears, nose, and toes stung, and his mind filled with thoughts of packets lost at sea with no survivors.

"What does 'voidable' mean?"

"With a stroke of the pen, the bishops can render your marriage a nullity. If they do, Tommie will become illegitimate in the eyes of the law. I will understand if you choose not to visit that fate upon him."

Tremont would have to understand, because Tommie was a blameless child and Matilda his only champion.

"Tommie *is* illegitimate." Matilda set her drink aside and rose. "My unwillingness to take responsibility for that fact is why I ended up marrying Harry in the first place." She faced out to sea, staring at the black and gold water as if she could read wisdom in the waves.

Tremont got to his feet as well, though his every muscle and joint protested. "You took that young fellow Yoe at his lying word, Matilda. When you married Harry, you were trying to protect a child abandoned by his father and his father's family. Your scheme worked to the extent that Tommie is regarded as Harry's son."

"Was I thinking of Tommie, or was I trying to get free of the mess I made and the father I abhorred?"

Tremont could not answer that for her, nor could he decide Tommie's fate, so he waited and hoped and held his peace.

"You'd marry me," she said, turning her back on the sea, "knowing all of society will question Tommie's antecedents?"

"I'd marry you if you had ten illegitimate children, Matilda. I did more than curse my mounts on the way here. I did some thinking."

"At which you excel." Some hint of humor colored her observation.

"At which I bumble convincingly." He took a step toward her. "Who is your family, Matilda?"

"Tommie," she said, "Portia. Dorcas MacKay has been a good friend. You are more than a friend. Major MacKay is something like a protective older brother, though he knows better than to overstep. I was growing quite fond of Mrs. Winklebleck and MacIvey and... the lot of them."

"Precisely. My family includes a lot of former soldiers, one of whom happened to hear that you and Tommie were taking the Dover packet. I did not know Corporal Shores numbered among my relatives, but there he was, wishing me well and aiding my cause as any brother would have. My family includes Nanny Winklebleck, who never let me get too familiar, and Cook, who never allowed me to go hungry.

"MacKay is a self-appointed Scottish cousin," he went on, "and even Michael Delancey offered to listen to my brokenhearted maundering for the length of a midnight stroll. These people are my family. Their opinions of me matter. Your opinion of me matters. They will not judge Tommie for his origins, and they will not judge us either should we decide to marry. Those who do judge us are of no moment."

"You *have* been doing some thinking." Still, she did not come any closer. "So have I, mostly along the same lines. Madame Howard, who never saw me before tonight, is more protective of me than either my father or my so-called husband ever was. Dorcas MacKay, MacIvey, *you*... You all wished me well and aided my cause, as you put it. I set my sights on France because that much distance was intended to guarantee I would not beg you to keep me as your mistress. I did not want Tommie to be ashamed of me, or so I told myself."

"And now?"

"Tommie—a grown-up Tommie, or even half-grown—will be more upset with me for turning my back on those who care for us than he will be for turning my back on blasted *propriety*. I'm not saying I should have become your leman, but I behaved precipitously, again, and I fear some stubborn element of evading my father's judgment once again drove my actions."

She took a step closer. "I was evading Harry, too, make no mistake about that. I wasn't evading you. Am I making sense?"

"Some, though I can't pretend to grasp the nuances in my present state. Are we to be married, Matilda? There will be talk and scandal, and Tommie's path won't be easy. Harry Merridew-Merriman-Merri-whatever will not face pillorying in the press if the marriage is quietly declared void. Harrell Merchant can walk away from his past relatively unscathed."

"I do not care that,"—she snapped her fingers under Tremont's nose—"for the fate that befalls Harry. Can he stop this voiding of the marriage?"

That was the best part, of which Michael Delancey had been very certain. "No, he cannot. Harry lied, Matilda, and for once, he lied to an organization in a position to hold him accountable. You make your petition and put your proof before the bishops, and Harry can argue the case if he wants to, but the facts tell the tale. You need not mention faked death, swindles, or the fact that Harry tried to extort a house from you. The marriage license and some testimony will be enough to make the case."

Matilda paced back to the sofa and picked up her drink. "I signed that house over to him. Executed a legally binding quitclaim."

"You executed a quitclaim to Harry Merriman, who does not exist. I had occasion to remind Harry of the legalities, and he conceded my point." Grudgingly, of course. He apparently truly thought himself in need of the funds.

Matilda held her brandy up to the firelight. "Then Harry has neither house nor wife nor son. He's in trouble with the bishops, and his family in Bristol might have had him declared legally dead. Maybe there is some justice in this life. Shall we sit down? You have to be exhausted."

He remained on his feet. "Are we to be married?"

She set her drink aside without tasting it and took to studying the flames crackling on the hearth. "I am afraid..."

Oh God. No. "Don't be afraid. We can face anything if we face it together." Brave words, though Tremont was at that moment terrified. If Matilda rejected him, if she chose legitimacy for Tommie rather than happiness for herself... Tremont would cope, eventually.

He hoped, but it would a bitter, empty coping, and lonelier than he could sanely contemplate.

Matilda wrapped her arms about her middle. "I am afraid," she said again, "that if we embrace, I will never let you go. I will make a complete cake of myself, turn into a watering pot, and abandon dignity entirely..."

"And," Tremont said, holding his arms wide, "I will yield all my pretensions to self-possession without caring a whit for the loss."

She hurled herself against him, and they clung to each other in silent rejoicing. When Madame Howard tapped gently on the door half an hour later, she found Tremont and his beloved lady entwined, fast asleep on the sofa.

She draped two blankets over them, banked the fire, and left them to their dreams, which were sweet indeed.

"Harry stayed put," Alasdhair MacKay said, taking a tea tray from the footman. "What honor could not accomplish, Dorcas's fine table, clean sheets, and a roaring fire did. I believe our Harry is tired of being without funds, cold, and haunted."

"He is not 'our Harry,'" Matilda snapped as MacKay set the tray before his wife. "He is nobody's Harry, and that is entirely his fault. What are we to do with him?"

A week of decent sleep and good meals had put Matilda very much on her mettle. That Tremont took her driving and for outings to the tea shop had also served to raise her spirits—and her frustrations.

"Tremont has a few ideas for Harry's next steps," Dorcas MacKay said. "Michael tells me the bishop should have your marriage dissolved within a fortnight, if you're sure that's what you want?"

"I have never been more sure of anything in my life."

And where was Tremont? Tommie bided with the soldiers, as Matilda had been doing since returning to London. They were a well-behaved lot compared to when she'd first met them, but then, her definition of good behavior had shifted.

The men cursed fluently. They forgot to scrape their boots when they came through the front door. They occasionally neglected to say grace before a meal and descended into fisticuffs with ungenteel frequency, but they were hardworking, loyal to their friends, and honest.

They had had a few pointed suggestions for what to do with Harry, while Matilda increasingly favored Madame Howard's solution—toss him into the sea to take his chances with the sharks.

"You are angry," Dorcas MacKay said, passing Matilda a cup of tea. "I like that you are finally angry. Harry has been dreading this meeting, and you aren't to let him off too easily, Matilda."

Whatever that meant. "Harry was never violent," she said. "He cheated, he stole, he extorted, and lied. If we're to revert to Old Testament guidance, then he should make remuneration in proportion to his sins."

"You don't want to see him hanged or transported," Dorcas observed, passing the major his tea. "Would you like to see him on remittance?"

"Tremont claims Harry has family. If we send my erstwhile spouse to India or Argentina, they will never see him again." And yet, Matilda wouldn't mind if Harry went halfway around the world, provided he stayed on his side of the globe and left her in peace.

"Ah, but does his family want to see him again?" Major MacKay said, setting down his tea untasted.

"*I* don't want to see him again," Matilda muttered, "but I suppose I must."

"You need not," Dorcas said, glancing at the mantel clock.

Matilda considered bolting, except that she was through with bolting.

Harry joined the gathering in the parlor before Matilda had taken the first sip of her tea. He looked... attired for running one of his Mayfair rigs. Togged out as a gent, right down to a cravat pin in the shape of a four-leaf clover.

And yet, his eyes lacked the watchful edge of the swindler, and he'd abandoned his charming smile.

"Matilda." He bowed. "You are looking well."

"I am in quite good health." She did not append a thank-you. "I am also furious with you."

"You have every reason to be."

How she itched to slap him. "Is that genuine remorse, Harry, the manipulative show of humble contrition, or something in between?"

He glanced at MacKay, whose expression was one of supreme indifference. "It's a statement of fact. Tremont destroyed the quit-claim deed."

"And you nearly destroyed me."

"I never meant..."

Matilda glowered at him, and Harry took to studying the green and white plaid pillows on the sofa.

"You, sir, meant to bilk me and my son out of our only security. Then you would doubtless have set about blackmailing me to keep word of your resurrection from becoming known. I married you—more's the pity—but you willingly took on responsibility for Tommie, and you betrayed that trust. One day, you will have to explain to

Tommie how you could contemplate wronging a small boy so grievously."

The parlor door clicked open, and somebody cleared his throat.

Tremont, and thank heavens he'd arrived, because Matilda, for the first time in her adult life, was on the verge of flying into a rage.

"You're free of me," Harry said in a voice without inflection. "I cannot imagine anything I could say or do would improve upon that result in your eyes, Tilly."

"Matilda. My name is Matilda, and unlike you, I do not duck behind aliases at the first sign of difficulty."

"I apologize," Harry said, with some force. "I abjectly, endlessly apologize, Matilda, but I was raised to be a gentleman, which is the same as saying I was raised to be useless. I can spout Shakespeare and Etherege and Sheridan by the scene because my sole rebellion was an interest in the theater. I can do sums in my head correctly to the penny because my father was an abacus. That is the totality of my accomplishments. My esteemed father did not allow me into the family business, and my mother would never have gainsaid her husband. If I have descended into vice, I am merely living down to Octavian Merchant's prophecies for me."

I will not feel sorry for him. I will not feel sorry for him. I will not... "Your apology is rejected. Words are too easy for you, Harry. The question becomes, how do you intend to show me—and Tommie —that your words mean something?"

"I will leave you alone, Matilda. I promise that. I vow that. Send me to New South Wales, to darkest Peru. I will stay the he—the blazes away from you and the boy."

"Not good enough," Matilda said, rising. "Not nearly good enough. You ran from us before and hadn't the courtesy to stay dead. Running away is your third skill, Harry—after sums and a taste for the theatrical—and I can tell you from experience, running creates as many problems as it solves. I want you to put right what you have put wrong."

Harry ran a hand through immaculately styled hair. "Till—

Matilda, they'll kill me. The law won't come into it. In Dublin, Manchester, York... There's a price on my head even if the reward isn't offered by the crown. If I try to pay back what I've earned through my confidence games, I won't live out the month."

"What you mean," Tremont said, from his place by the door, "is that Harry Merridew *et alia* has a price on *his* head. Harrel Merchant, long-lost scion of a respected Bristol family, carries no such burden."

For the first time, Harry looked afraid. "You cannot expect me to go back to Bristol, Tremont. Anything but that. The piety alone will strangle me as effectively as any noose. I'll choose Newgate over Bristol, gladly."

A tallish, dark-haired woman swept past Tremont, who closed the parlor door behind her. She looked to be shy of thirty and was attired in subdued azure fashion that brought out the blue in her eyes. She advanced on Harry and delivered a sharp crack to his left cheek.

"I've been read out of meeting," she said as Harry's cheek turned crimson. "The stated reason was my unseemly lack of humility in the face of guidance from my elders—meaning I would not allow our uncles to steal you or me blind—and apparently, I have a propensity for violence as well. I've missed you, Harry."

Tears glistened in her eyes, and yet, she stared at Harry without flinching.

"Esther?" Harry touched his cheek. "*Esther?*"

She nodded. "I am worldly now. All tarted up and fallen into wickedness, to hear the aunties tell it. I understand why you left, Harry, but I cannot understand why you never wrote to me. You disappeared in a cloud of righteous fury, and for years, Papa refused to speak your name."

Harry blinked at the curtains. "If I'd written to you, you might have tried to find me. You were safe in Bristol, and I wasn't managing all that well. I've gone some better than you in the wickedness department, Esther."

"Lord Tremont has implied as much, but, Harry, that's all behind you."

Matilda's heart hurt to hear the hope and determination in Esther's voice. "Tell your sister she's right, Harry. You are turning over a new leaf on a new branch on a whole new tree, aren't you?"

Harry met her gaze for the first time since he'd entered the room. "This is my penance? To go back to Bristol?"

Matilda's hands bunched into fists. "This is your salvation, you dolt." As Harry's wife, she would never have addressed her husband so disrespectfully. As his not-quite-widow, she barely refrained from profanity. "Esther never gave up on you, Harry. She would not allow your uncles to declare you dead and divide up your share of your father's estate. You are a wealthy man by most people's standards, and you have at least a sibling willing to claim you."

Harry, glib under all circumstances, was quiet for a moment. "Papa mentioned me in the will?"

Esther Merchant shifted to stand before her brother. The resemblance was strong, though Esther radiated hope, while Harry seemed genuinely bewildered.

"Papa eventually regretted the rift between you. He put notices in the paper, Harry, and I have a letter he wrote to you on his deathbed. He blamed himself, and rightly so, in my estimation. You were little more than a boy, and he was all stubbornness and pride dressed up as moral conviction. I've managed your share of the estate, and you are indeed quite prosperous."

Tremont took the place at Matilda's side. "Prosperous enough to buy yourself a theater, Merchant, if that's what you please to do, and to produce all the bawdy farces and comedies you please."

"The tragedies have the better speeches," Harry murmured.

"Harry," Matilda said, wanting to shake him until his teeth rattled, "you can write whatever blasted speeches you please. You can hire London's finest thespians to give benefit performances. You can do as Mr. Sheridan did at Drury Lane and pay urchins and pickpockets to be your extras. You have a prodigious imagination, and now you have an equally impressive opportunity to use that imagination for worthy purposes."

"Come home," Esther said, taking her brother's hand. "Please, Harry, come home. I've missed you and prayed for you and cursed you, but I need you to c-come home."

"Don't you dare cry, Esther," Harry said, eyeing the door. "Don't you dare, don't you even think... Blasted hell." He wrapped Esther in his arms and buried his face against her hair. "I'll come, just don't cry. You'll hate me for it, but I'll come back to Bristol."

MacKay picked up a decanter from the sideboard. "We'll be in the formal parlor, celebrating—or fortifying ourselves for the next act, or some damned thing or other." He offered his arm to Dorcas, and Matilda and Tremont followed him out the door.

EPILOGUE

Tommie was riding atop the box with John Coachman, and Copenhagen lay forgotten on the opposite bench.

"Our son is growing up," Tremont said, and even those simple words filled him with a quiet wonder. "Poor Cope can't hold a candle to the prospect of taking the actual ribbons."

"Tommie won't last two miles out in the elements," Matilda said. "The cold will drive him to rejoin us, despite the lack of excitement to be had in our company."

"I like that," Tremont said, wrapping an arm around his wife. "I like the lack of excitement. The placid joy of seeing you and Tommie at breakfast, the pleasure of hearing you at the pianoforte, the way Tommie squirms sitting between us in church, as small children have squirmed at divine services from time immemorial. I love all the mundane sweetness and even the tedium of travel."

"Going to bed with you is anything but mundane, Marcus."

He liked even more when his countess, wife, lover, and best friend addressed him by name in that particular tone.

"But that's the thing," he said, taking her hand. "The mundane is marvelous with you. We've been married less than a month, and our first Christmas was special. Our first Boxing Day. Our first New Year."

Matilda nudged the curtain aside. "Our first journey to Shropshire. I hope your mother approves of me."

"She will adore you, and she will be smitten with Tommie, and the staff will spoil him rotten, and we will have our hands full."

"I adore you," Matilda said, letting the curtain drop and snuggling closer. "I've missed the countryside, the fresh air, the trees, and cows and sheep. I'd lost sight of how busy and noisy London is, and I'm glad to be away from it."

"We'll go back in the spring to see how the men are faring at Elysium House. MacKay will keep them in line until then. I do believe we're slowing down."

"Either Tommie has tired of having his nose frozen, or you have highwaymen in Shropshire."

Tommie rejoined them, his teeth chattering as he regaled them with the unparalleled thrill of taking the ribbons *all by himself.* Tremont listened, though he also spared a thought for his late father, who'd missed so much of his son's upbringing.

Papa, I'm happy. I'm bringing my bride and our son home with me, and I am so happy. This is what you had with Mama, and now I have it too. I wish I could tell you how happy I am.

When Tommie had gushed at length about his career as an under-coachman and done justice for the third time to the comestibles in the hamper, he raised the same curtain Matilda had.

"You have good clouds here in Shropshire, my lord. Better than the clouds in London. We have smoke in London, but these are truly white clouds."

"They are your clouds now too, young man."

"That one looks like a longship," Tommie said, squinting at the sky. "Look, Mama. It's a longship cloud."

Matilda dutifully looked, and Tremont did as well, the sight making him even happier than usual, and also—comforted?

"By Jove, boy, that is a longship to the life, complete with square sail and dragon prow. By night, it sails the stars, and by day..."

"The longship is sailing home with us," Matilda said, smiling at her husband as if she could divine his wistful thoughts and slipping her hand back into his.

They had removed their gloves to aid Tommie's plundering of the hamper, and Tremont was glad to have the contact. The longship was still sailing off the coach's starboard prow when Tommie again took to pointing and waving.

"That is a castle! Look, Mama! A real, true castle! They have a castle in Shropshire and Viking clouds and sheep and everything!"

Tremont shared some of Tommie's excitement and all of his joy. He'd come back to Shropshire from time to time in recent years, but this trip was different.

This was a homecoming, not a flying pass to keep an eye on rural duties.

"That is a castle," Tremont said, "and also a family seat, and a stately manor, and a historical building, but mostly, Tommie, that is *our home.* My mama is there on the steps, you see? She can't wait to meet you, and you must point out the Viking cloud to her too. My sister, Lydia, and her husband, Sir Dylan, are coming for a visit next week, and they are looking forward to meeting you too."

Tommie sent Matilda a questioning look. "You didn't say we would live in a castle, Mama."

"We shall live in our castle," Matilda said, handing Tommie his stuffed horse, "happily ever after. Now put on your gloves and prepare to make a proper bow to her ladyship. You can tell her all about driving the coach and introduce her to Cope and ask her impertinent questions about when Tremont was a boy."

Tommie bounded out of the coach the instant the steps were let down and pelted up the staircase to the front terrace, waving his horse and yelling about longships in the sky.

Tremont handed Matilda down with slightly more decorum. "We will, you know," he said, offering his arm.

"We will what?"

"Dwell in our castle, happily ever after."

"We shall," Matilda said, kissing his cheek. "With you, I'm sure of it."

Tremont handled the introductions, and the hugs, and the kisses, and Tommie trying to slide down the terrace's stone banister, and more hugs and kisses.

Before he escorted his wife and mama into the castle, he spared a smile and a wave for the longship soaring peacefully aloft in the beautiful Shropshire sky.